THE KNIGHT SCHOOL

JOURNAL

Gretchen L. Winkler

Disclaimer

All characters in this book are fictitious. Any resemblance to actual people, living or dead, is purely coincidental.

Copyright 2025 Gretchen L. Winkler

An original story by Gretchen Winkler.

No generative artificial intelligence (AI) was used in the creation of this book

Library of Congress Control Number: 2025927151

Visit our website at www.cyberhawkheros.com

Original cover art by *Gretchen Winkler*
Graphic Design by *Andrew McCall*

Published By User Friendly Media Group, Inc.
UserFriendlyNation.com

DEDICATION

For those with Knight Templar hearts…

This is dedicated to Peter Mayhew – thank you for believing in me. The Wookiee should win! I know if I had been able to give this story an ending, you would have succeeded in getting it published. You opened my eyes and helped me realize that I could pursue my dream of being a writer. Thank you for introducing me to your Star Wars friend, so that the process could continue after you departed this world. Your kindness will forever be in my heart.

And thanks to Jeremy, Bill Sikkens, Farren Robinson, and Bill Connolly for your input and support while I worked on this project.

Foreword

Please note that the writing and research for The Knight School Journal began in 2012 and reflects the culture and technology of the years closely associated with 2012-2014.

CHAPTER 1: THE INTERVIEW

"Why do we need to take him in for an interview? He's just a kid, and this is a school, not some job interview," she complained as the car zoomed along the rainy streets.

"I don't know. It's bad enough we both have to be there. Let's not make this any worse," he replied, as he remained somewhat focused on driving his SUV.

The wipers flipped back and forth, removing the rain from the windshield. Kyle remained silent to make sure that nothing he did would make the situation any worse. Neither of them wanted to be there, and at times it seemed like neither of them wanted him around. Their solution to their problem was to have him attend a private school, so that they would not argue about custody as much. Kyle's only say in the matter was that he got to choose what school he attended, which was only after his parents had spent months arguing about which school he should attend. His mother, half Mexican and half white Texan, grew up on a modest cattle ranch. She was a born-again Christian and wanted him to go to a Christian school. His father, the son of a Swedish immigrant and a Canadian socialite, was a doctor of theoretical and applied physics. As a self-proclaimed agnostic, he wanted him to go to a non-religious school. It seemed as if they had nothing in common.

"I don't think it was such a good idea to allow him to pick a military school. They'll only teach him to kill, and that's against God's will," she remarked. "And there is nothing in their brochure about religious training. It says they respect and accept a variety of religious backgrounds. What's that supposed to mean? Will Kyle have to celebrate some weird, blue-armed heathen ritual where he has to light a bunch of candles and burn incense?"

"No, that sounds more like the crap that your witchcraft-loving sister is doing," he replied bitterly.

"I don't want to talk about her. We pray for her every day, and sooner or later she'll hear the call of Jesus," she angrily retorted.

"Yeah, perhaps if she were really stoned out of her mind on those antidepressants that she's been taking for years with no results," commented Kyle's father.

"And just what's... *that* supposed to mean?"

Kyle was watching the numbers on the buildings, looking for the correct one, when the SUV raced past the entrance to the parking lot.

"Uh, Dad, the...," said Kyle.

"Hush, honey. Mommy and Daddy are talking," said his mom.

"But we just passed the entrance to the place where the interview is located."

"Damn!" said his father as he looked around and at the GPS device, which showed that they had just driven past their destination. "Damn it, Marie. You're so hot-tempered about everything, and you made me miss the building."

"Is this another slight against my heritage? My father was not hot-tempered."

"Yeah, then why did he always get mad when I wanted him to speak English to me? Considering my father learned English, I don't think that's too much for me to ask for."

"Oh, it's always back to how high and mighty your family is and how backward we are. I am so sick of it," replied Kyle's mother, folding her arms and facing out her passenger car window. "I wish we had taken my car. I would drop you off to take a bus home."

"If we had taken your car, we'd be over an hour late since you are so busy talking on the cell phone while driving," snapped Kyle's father.

"I don't think you ever loved me," she sobbed.

"Oh great, now cry in front of Kyle and make me look like the bad guy. I am so sick of that."

Finally, Kyle's father pulled the SUV into the parking lot of the office complex where the school interview was scheduled to take place. Kyle was looking forward to being in a place where his parents would not feel so free to argue and snap at each other.

As Kyle walked up to the glossy, dark glass doors, he saw his reflection and realized how much he looked like his father. He had golden blonde hair, bright blue eyes, an average height and build for his age, and skin that was somewhere between his mom's and dad's coloring. Other than that, and the ability to get a nice tan during the summer months, he was an exact younger version of his dad. Kyle stepped into the building, leaving the rain and dreary attitudes of his parents behind him. The lady at the reception desk eyed him as he looked around at the office building's very clean and nicely designed reception hall. His Canadian grandmother owned a building similar to this one, and probably several more, in Toronto.

"Can I help you?" asked the lady at the reception desk. Kyle smiled at the thin young woman with pale skin, light-colored hair, and deep-set eyes. Her unusual accent reminded him of Chekov in the old Star Trek movies. He was about to reply when his mother and father entered the building.

"Kyle, don't disturb that lady, she's busy," said his mother in an authoritative tone.

"Oh, no worry. He is not bothering me," said the receptionist with the strange accent. "Can I help you find where you are going?"

"We have an appointment with an... S.K.C. Pembroke. We want to enroll our son into a private school, and they require an interview," said Kyle's father before his mother could speak up.

4

"Oh, I see. Let me look up the schedule," replied the receptionist, who started typing and eyeballing the flat-screen computer monitor. I see you have a ten o'clock appointment... You are Mr. and Mrs. Bergendahl..."

"No. We are no longer married. I am *Ms.* Marie Gomez," his mother emphasized the Ms. part of her name.

"Yes, but I am Dr. Bergendahl, and this is my son Kyle. And the three of us have an appointment with Mr. Pembroke."

"I see," said the receptionist. I will note the name correction in our database so that the mistake will not happen again. Please take the elevator up to the tenth floor and go to office 1015."

Kyle eagerly went over to where the elevators stood, waiting, and pushed the up button. The elevator light turned on in response to the request.

"Kyle, don't touch," scolded his mother.

"Why are you bitching at him? He just pushed the elevator button. I want him to think for himself and be self-reliant," said his dad.

"Oh, I am bitching? He has no self-control. I don't want him going off and just pushing buttons whenever he pleases. At least I care about what he does," replied his mom.

Kyle sighed and wondered when the arguing would stop. He felt embarrassed and ashamed that his parents could not be civil to each other, not even for a few minutes, let alone for him. The ride up in the elevator was not much better, but at least there was no one else to hear what was being said. At least that is what Kyle thought at the time.

When they reached the tenth floor, Kyle exited immediately and started looking for number 1015. Kyle's father was the first to figure out which way to go and requested that Marie and Kyle follow him. Kyle hoped that his parents would be nice during the interview. He was excited about going to school and being in the same place to make new friends. For the last couple of years, he was sent back and forth to different places since his parents moved away from their old home in New Mexico. His father moved to Seattle, Washington, and his mother moved to Reno, Nevada.

His mom was dressed sharply, in dark high-heeled shoes, like she always wore, form-fitting trousers, a colorful blouse, and a smart, tailored leather jacket. Her jet-black hair was neatly styled up, allowing the pretty earrings to dangle fashionably. Meanwhile, his father was wearing nice blue jeans, casual loafers, a neatly pressed button-up shirt, and a blazer. They all looked a little damp from the rain, but that was to be expected in Portland, Oregon. Kyle hoped they would make a good impression so the school would accept him.

When they found the office, the door was wide open, and a short, smiling man with brown hair dressed in a sharp suit greeted them at the door.

"I have been expecting you," he said in a cheery voice.

"You must be Mr. Pembroke. I am Jon Bergendahl, this is Kyle, and this is his mother, Marie Gomez," said Kyle's father in a congenial manner.

Kyle watched Mr. Pembroke smile and shake hands with both of his parents, then finally turned his attention to Kyle. He extended his hand to shake Kyle's and said, "Very pleased to meet you, Kyle."

Kyle beamed back, "Thank you. I'm pleased to meet you." It was so nice to be acknowledged as important enough to be greeted by Mr. Pembroke. Often, adults disregard kids when they are involved in such matters.

"Please sit down. Would anyone like any coffee or water?"

"Coffee would be great," his dad replied.

"No coffee for Kyle. He is a little boy. He can have water if he wants, and I am fine. I don't need anything," Kyle's mom responded.

"Very well," the man said, turning to his assistant. "Could you please bring Mr. Bergendahl a coffee and Kyle … a bottle of water?" Mr. Pembroke said as Kyle nodded and smiled at him.

"So, let's get down to business," said Mr. Pembroke, sitting back down behind a desk with a name placard that said S.K.C. Pembroke. He was shorter than average with neatly trimmed brown hair, clean-shaven, and hazel eyes that sometimes seemed to twinkle. "Just what made you interested in attending our school?"

"Well, to be honest, we did not select your school. Our son did. My ex-wife and I could not come to terms on where we should send him, and the therapist suggested that we should allow him to make the choice. I told him that he needed to be sure that the place he selected was the kind of school he wanted to attend," said Jon Bergendahl.

"I see," said Mr. Pembroke.

"Hopefully, that will not reflect negatively on your evaluation of Kyle. He's a good boy, and he used to get good grades while he was up in Seattle with me... so I am sure he'll meet up to your standards as soon as he gets settled in."

"And you, Ms. Gomez, do you have any thoughts about your son's choice?" asked Mr. Pembroke.

"Well, I can't afford all the tutors down in Reno," grumbled Marie, and paused momentarily. "We just need to give Kyle a place where he can be happy and learn, and neither of those places is in Seattle or Reno."

"Okay, well then, I think it would be best to interview Kyle first to ensure he fully understands what kind of school we are. Do you mind if I interview him alone?" Mr. Pembroke asked.

"Yes, why do you need to talk to him?" asked Marie. "He is a child and should do as his parents tell him." Kyle looked away and down at the ground, feeling embarrassed.

"Well, I don't have a problem. You're just going to be in the next room, right?" said Jon.

"Oh... that's right, just say the opposite," complained Marie.

Jon raised his eyebrows and rolled his eyes as he turned away from her direction and twisted his mouth a little in irritation.

"Well, come in here and inspect the room if you like," said Mr. Pembroke as his sunny disposition wore thin. "We have a table with chairs set up, and I must have Kyle take a few tests and answer a few questions before I can formally submit his request for entrance into the Academy. He will be on his own at the school and living many miles away from either of you. During the interview, he'll be just behind this door. It doesn't even have a lock."

Marie got up and inspected the room, which looked rather plain. A square wooden table with a glossy finish and four comfortable office chairs positioned around its perimeter was in the center of the room. Next to the wall was a computer station set up with a keyboard and monitor. Two posters were displayed: one showed a knight on horseback from times long ago in a beautiful landscape, and another depicted an airplane flying above some farmland below, with the sun rising in the distance. There was nothing strange or significant about the room. Marie turned about and said, "Okay, you can interview him alone."

Mr. Pembroke watched as Marie Gomez sat back in the chair and pulled her cell phone out of her purse. Jon had gotten up, looked into the room, and remarked, "Cool posters. Reminds me of some that I had in high school. Do you have any brochures about the school that I can browse through while you're doing the interview?"

"Certainly, but they are online. I can give you a tablet to browse our website," offered Mr. Pembroke.

The young male assistant returned with Starbucks coffee for Jon and eyeballed Marie as she was texting back and forth with some unknown person. As Mr. Pembroke searched through his desk for a tablet for Jon to use, the assistant whispered something to Mr. Pembroke, and Mr. Pembroke replied quietly. Kyle watched this and thought he heard the words 'Sir Knight' spoken, but he was unsure. The younger man went to a cabinet and immediately pulled out a tablet for Kyle's dad.

"Thank you," responded Jon.

"Just open the browser and you will find our website listed as the opening home page," said the young male assistant wearing a small red and white lapel pin on his suit jacket.

"Kyle, would you come with me into the interview room?" requested Mr. Pembroke.

Kyle got up and went into the room. Mr. Pembroke closed the door, and suddenly, it became very peaceful. There was no more bickering between his parents or the sound of his mom texting with her friends. Mr. Pembroke offered him a seat and took the chair directly across from him. He set down a modern, slim-looking laptop and turned it on.

"I'm going to use this to make notes concerning our interview," he said reassuringly, showing Kyle the data entry software. I don't want you to think I am playing games on Facebook."

Kyle laughed and said, "Yeah, my mom spends lots of time on Facebook when she isn't at work."

Mr. Pembroke just smiled.

"Kyle, how old are you?"

"I am ten years old. I just had my birthday in May."

"So why did you pick our school?"

Kyle shifted uncomfortably in his chair, unsure how to answer this question.

"I didn't want to go to the All Christ Saves Private School, which my mom wanted me to attend. All they do there is read the Bible and make you recite scripture, and... I don't find that very interesting. Then my dad wanted me to attend the Nobel Academy of Science School in Washington, which was cool since it was near where he lives, but it looks like a place filled with nerds, and I don't think I would like a school that only focuses on math and science. I like outdoor stuff."

"Okay, but why did you select our school? We expect our students to learn math, science, literature, history, foreign languages, writing, and art. We also offer a range of excellent outdoor activities. So... what made you think you would like to attend the Academy?"

Kyle shifted a little in the office chair, rubbed his open palms on his blue jeans, and wiggled his feet inside his tennis shoes while thinking about what Mr. Pembroke had asked.

"This is gonna sound dumb, and I hope you won't think I'm stupid for saying so, but I saw this cool picture of the castle on an island on the website... and another picture showed a knight sitting on horseback. I suppose that's the school mascot or something, but I always liked stories with knights in them. There was a forest around the building, and pictures of students using canoes. It just looked like a really nice place to go, and it seemed like the best place to go when... no one really wants you around," Kyle finally answered.

"I see," paused Mr. Pembroke as if he were in deep thought. "We expect our students to work hard on their studies, and we offer outdoor activities, and you would be far away from your parents and friends. Don't you think that you will miss them?"

"Yeah, I guess so, ... but I have already moved several times, and when I come back, sometimes my friends have moved away, or they are hanging out with different kids. I used to enjoy hanging out with Dark Cloud in Reno, but his parents have decided to take him out of regular school and enroll him in the new tribal school, and I am not allowed there. Plus, it is far away from where I live with my mom. We used to have fun, but Mom thinks he's a bad influence on me. She says his parents are godless heathens," replied Kyle, looking up at Mr. Pembroke, who was looking at him intently. "Soo... I really don't have that many friends to miss."

"Okay," said the man in the neat suit, turning to his laptop and clicking the mouse button several times. This brings me to another topic. Kyle, our school accepts a variety of religious backgrounds, and to best place you for your family's cultural and spiritual background, we do need to know what faith you belong to, if any," said Mr. Pembroke as he continued to make notes into the database.

"Don't tell my mom this, but I'm not really sure what I believe in. My mom is part of God's First Choice Baptist Ministries, while my dad is an agnostic, or something like that. While I think they both have good points in their opinions on various things, I really have no idea what to believe. Each of them wants me to believe in what they believe, but honestly, I just have not found any real answers," replied Kyle, squirming in his chair. He did not like questions about religion since it was so often the source of his parents' arguments.

"Well, I can understand that, Kyle. We all do our own soul searching from time to time, and that's just a normal part of life. I need you to do one more thing for me. We need to get an idea of your level of skills, so if you could come over to this computer console and have a seat," said Mr. Pembroke as he got up and turned on the computer setup next to the wall. "There's no rush. You take all the time you need to answer those questions and do your best. I'll be outside with your parents, and you can come out when you are done."

Mr. Pembroke left the room and closed the door behind him. Kyle made himself comfortable in the chair in front of the computer. He looked at the screen and began to read through the questions, which started with simple math problems. Those were ridiculously easy, thought Kyle, and then after many more, the test became very difficult. And then, much to Kyle's relief, the test changed to a different topic. Kyle enjoyed taking the test even though Mr. Pembroke did not call it a test; Kyle knew that's what it really was. He was also relieved that whenever the test became unpleasantly difficult, the topic would change and restart with simple questions. This continued through math, science, spelling, reading, U.S. History, World History, Art, and a section that seemed like a problem-solving exercise, asking odd questions about cooking, shopping, traveling, and outdoor topics like camping. When Kyle finished the test, he got up and slowly opened the door to the main office. He peeked out and, much to his relief, his parents were both quiet with his dad reading a book and his mom texting on her phone.

"I'm finished with the test," Kyle announced to no one and everyone in the room.

"Excellent, Kyle! Now that wasn't too bad, was it?" replied Mr. Pembroke.

"No," replied Kyle somewhat bashfully.

"Glad to hear that. Now, Dr. Bergendahl and Ms. Gomez, the school, will contact you in about a week to inform you of their decision regarding Kyle's entrance eligibility. I'm sure Kyle did excellent on his questionnaire," said Mr. Pembroke as he shook both parents' hands.

"Well, thank you for meeting with us. Do you have a business card in case I have any questions?" asked Jon Bergendahl.

The man looked slightly surprised, shuffled through his suit coat pocket, and pulled out some business cards. "This is not my normal office, and I only have my personal cards with me, but you are welcome to call or email me with any questions," he said, handing a card to Kyle's dad.

"Well, I would like one too," said Kyle's mom as if Mr. Pembroke was offering small gifts and she did not want to be left out.

Jon eyed Marie, and she sneered back at him as she placed the card into her designer purse, where it would never be looked at again. This little scene was not missed by Mr. Pembroke, who smiled and acted as if nothing was amiss and offered a card to Kyle, who accepted the item as if it meant that he had achieved manhood. Kyle ran his fingers over the black glossy raised text that said, 'Sir Knight Chester T. Pembroke, Prior Master – Las Vegas, NV.' Next to the name and all the contact information was a logo with a bright red equilateral cross.

Chapter 2: Waiting

Kyle looked up at the calendar, and it had been exactly seven days since they met with Mr. Pembroke in Portland, Oregon, about the Academy school. He wondered if they would call or send a letter by mail. He opened a red Sharpie marker and drew a red X across the day square to show that the seventh day had arrived. Would they call in the morning or perhaps in the afternoon? What if the school people did not know he was at his mom's house in Reno? This thought disturbed Kyle, so he went into the family room to log on to the computer and email his dad. He didn't want his dad to ignore the mail when he came home from work today, since the letter might have arrived with today's delivery.

Sitting at the small desk, Kyle waited for the Windows startup music to play and then for the operating system software to display the desktop picture with icons. Rojo barked nervously at him as he waited, while tons of icons populated the desktop picture that used to show a landscape scene from his home state of New Mexico so clearly. He liked the picture but hated all the icons his mother insisted on putting on the desktop. She said it made finding things on the computer easier, but Kyle thought it just looked messy.

Rojo barked again at Kyle. He looked down at his mother's nervous-looking little Chihuahua and reached to pick up the strange little dog. Rojo seemed happy that Kyle scooped him up into his lap. Kyle thought that Rojo looked continuously cold as he shivered, but Kyle knew that could not be the case since it was the middle of summer and the air was unusually warm this morning. The whole summer had been unusually hot, and Kyle longed for the more moderate climate of his dad's home in Seattle. Too bad Mom didn't have air conditioning, thought Kyle, but then again, maybe that would make Rojo quiver even more.

"Don't play on the computer all day," said his mother as she came in from her bedroom. She was all dressed for work. She was employed as a medical assistant and had to be away for most of the day.

"I won't," replied Kyle. "It's been seven days since we met the Academy school people in Portland, so if they call you, Mom, make sure you let me know what they said."

"Don't worry about that. They probably won't call for a few days, so don't get too worked up about all this. They may not accept you, okay? You understand? Your studies have not been so good lately. You should read more," replied his mom.

"But Mom, this is important. Please let me know if they call you," requested Kyle.

"Don't worry, sweetie, I will let you know," she replied, picking up her purse, coming over to Kyle, and kissing him on the forehead. "Don't forget to do your chores. Rojo needs his water bowl cleaned and fresh water put in it. Don't spill water all over the floor. And don't stay on the computer all day. Go watch some TV or read."

"Yes, Mom. I will remember," replied Kyle somewhat sullenly.

"And don't open the door for any strangers and keep it locked," said Marie as she stepped out the front door of the house.

"I never have opened the door for strangers…" Kyle murmured under his breath to Rojo, who looked up expectantly at Kyle.

He listened to the sound of his mom turning the deadbolt latch on the front door.

"Well, Rojo, we're alone again for another fabulous day of sitting and waiting," said Kyle. "I'm already bored. Let's find some breakfast."

Kyle opened the refrigerator and peered in to see if anything in particular captured his fancy. There were leftovers from last night's meal, including some cold pizza from his favorite pizza place that they had visited two days ago, as well as milk, orange juice, and a variety of other items that did not look particularly appealing. He thought about making toast with jam and peanut butter, but eventually, he decided that cold pizza and orange juice would make a great breakfast. Rojo seemed to agree, as he gratefully accepted a few cheese-covered pieces of pizza crust.

Kyle returned to his spot in front of the computer and carefully placed his glass of orange juice and pizza slices nearby. He was extra careful since his mom hated it when he had food near the computer. While stuffing his mouth full of cold pizza, he logged into his own email account, which his dad set up for him, and composed a message to his dad.

Dear Dad,

Don't forget that today is the seventh day. The Academy is supposed to let you know if I have been accepted. Please check your mail and phone regularly, just in case they sent the message. Please let me know right away if you find out.

I miss you very much, and so does Rojo. He still shivers a lot. I think he misses Pickles. I miss Pickles, too. Does she still like to play tug-of-war?

Love,

Kyle

Kyle hit the "Send Message" button and waited for the software to confirm that the message had been sent. Kyle looked at Rojo and remembered how he and Pickles used to play together. Pickles was his dad's Basset Hound, who was at least four times bigger than Rojo. Just one of her ears could be a blanket for Rojo to sleep under.

The day pressed on in an agonizingly slow fashion, and Kyle tried to make time go by while playing video games and talking to his friend Dark Cloud, who had just returned from a camping trip with his older brothers and uncle. It sounded like they had a lot of fun camping out in the desert and hearing old stories told by their uncle. Kyle was somewhat envious. Dark Cloud was deeply ingrained in his family's traditions and was allowed to participate in activities with the other people in the tribe. Sometimes Kyle wished he were part Paiute, Washoe, or Shoshone, and then he could be a part of a group, too. His mom's relatives didn't like Kyle. They would not speak to him and acted like they didn't speak English, so he often had to sit alone and be ignored. And she would not believe him when he told her. It was always his fault for not being friendly enough. She could not accept the idea that they didn't want him around.

It was five o'clock, and it was hot outside and inside. Kyle sat beside a whirring fan and watched TV since he felt like doing nothing else. There was no mail at all today, and no telephone calls. How could this be? Perhaps his mom was right, and he didn't get into the school. The day had dragged on so slowly, and the heat was miserable, and poor Rojo was too exhausted and hot to shiver anymore. Then an abrupt knock on the door woke Kyle and Rojo from their drowsy TV-watching. Rojo barked frantically and leaped about as Kyle got up to look out the front window. He heard a delivery truck rev up its engine and then drive off. It had been FedEx delivering, and they left something on the front porch. Kyle looked both ways out the front window to see if anyone was around. Only Mt Rose loomed across the valley with no hints of any winter snow left to support the water needs of the Truckee Meadows. Just the promise of dry heat and no afternoon thunderstorms of the past. Perhaps it would be all right to open the door now that the deliveryman was gone, and then he could quickly relock the door once he got the package.

Kyle gingerly unlocked and slowly opened the front door, peering outside to see the package lying about four feet away from the door. Rojo was bouncing about happily and barking.

"Rojo! Shhhh! You stay back there," ordered Kyle as he tried to open the door more so that he could get a better look outside and then pick up the flat package.

No one was around, so he wasn't breaking his mom's rules. He opened the door more and stepped out to retrieve the package when Rojo zoomed past him onto the front lawn. Kyle nearly lost it.

"Rojo, come back here! Rojo! Come! Come on, you, silly dog," Kyle started to plead, worrying that he would have to chase the tiny Chihuahua all over the neighborhood. The little dog barked gleefully in the green grass and scampered about. Kyle dashed off the porch and onto the grass in pursuit of the tiny dog.

"Come on. Rojo!" said Kyle. He chased him around the yard a few more times, and finally, the little dog stopped to sniff at some bushes. By then, Kyle was able to pick Rojo up quickly, but by that time, his mom had pulled her car into the driveway and was looking very furious at him. Kyle's stomach turned. He was in trouble now. Before his mom could say anything, Kyle walked up to the car and told her that Rojo ran out the front door and that he needed to catch him.

"And just why was the front door open? Did Rojo open the door himself?" she retorted to Kyle.

"He snuck past me when I opened the door to pick up the package the delivery guy left. I waited until he was gone," replied Kyle.

"That's no excuse. You know the rules. You are not to step out the front door unless the house is on fire, and I don't see any signs of fire. And Rojo could have gotten lost because of your carelessness," she replied sternly. "Get back inside right now!"

Kyle walked back to the front porch and stooped down to pick up the package when his mom told him to leave it and she would tend to it. When Kyle got inside, he put Rojo back down on the floor and watched as his mom walked in with the package, took it into her bedroom, and then came back out again.

"What was the package? Was it from the school?" asked Kyle.

"That is not the concern of little boys who do not follow the rules. It is dinner time now. Go clean off the table and then set the table."

"Yes, ma'am," replied Kyle.

"Don't take that tone of voice with me, or else there will be no video games for a week."

Kyle kept his mouth shut, not wanting to get into further trouble. Dinner was eaten in silence as his mother watched her favorite TV programs and talked to Rojo, feeding him small table scraps. When dinner was over, Kyle collected the dishes, put them near the sink, and then wiped off the table. He hoped that if he did all these things without being told, she would look at the flat package that had arrived.

"So, Mom, can you now look at the package?" asked Kyle.

"Later, dear, Mommy is tired from working all day and is watching her favorite TV show. I will look at it tomorrow," she replied.

Kyle knew that if he pressed the matter any further, she would only prolong the agony of not knowing what was in the flat package. He went off to his bedroom to read some of his favorite books. He had his Ranger's Apprentice books, his dad's old Hardy Boys novels, and another about Templar Knights, but he decided he was more in the mood for reading his Thor comic books. He selected one from his collection that he hadn't read in a while and made himself comfortable on his bed. On his wall was a large comic book poster of Thor, holding his mighty hammer and wearing a winged helmet. Kyle often wished he could have a cool winged helmet, too.

The next morning, Kyle was woken by his mother, who told him he needed to wake up because she was leaving for work. But before Kyle could get out of bed and feel steady enough to walk, he heard the lock on the front door deadbolt click into place, followed by the sound of his mother's car engine turning on. He looked at the clock. She left half an hour earlier than normal. He was surprised and somewhat disappointed that he hadn't had the chance to ask her what was in the flat package left by the delivery man. Then he had an idea that perhaps she had left it on the kitchen table for him. He quickly rushed out to the kitchen and looked around; no package was in sight. Then he looked in the family room, thinking that perhaps she had opened it while watching TV. No package. He looked everywhere in the house except his mother's room. That was the only place left. He stood at her closed bedroom door. There was a standing order that he was not allowed in her room, and he was never to enter it unless in the case of an absolute emergency. This was not an emergency.

He stood at the door for what seemed like a long time. Why did she not tell him what was in the flat package? Maybe she forgot about it. He opened her door and peered into the room. The bedroom smelled like her perfume and was very girly with flowers and artwork that was not to his liking. She had her bed nicely made, and nothing was out of order. The closet door and her bathroom door were closed. There was no sign of the flat package. Kyle closed the door without setting foot into her room. He had already broken the rule about opening the front door and nearly lost Rojo. He would have to wait until she came home tonight and ask if she received anything from the school. Then he thought that perhaps the flat package had nothing to do with him, and he was acting foolishly about the whole thing.

This made him feel better, and he closed the door firmly before walking down the hall into the kitchen to get some orange juice and cereal. He turned on the TV and rubbed Rojo's little head affectionately. The noise of the TV made him feel less lonely. He wished he could go out and play, but Chris, who had lived just down the street, had moved away last year, leaving him only one friend, Dark Cloud, and now he was no longer going to be at the regular school and would spend more time out at the Pyramid Lake Reservation. All his friends in Reno were either gone or unavailable. He suddenly wished he could be with his dad. At least his dad had a college student who rented the downstairs room and worked as his dad's lab assistant. And his dad would take him to Day Summer Camp, where he could learn new things and do all sorts of things. There was nothing to do in Reno.

Then a happy thought hit Kyle's mind. Perhaps his dad had received the letter or phone call and forgotten to call him, so Kyle went to the computer, where he found a sticky note from his mother stating that he was not to spend too much time on the computer. He pulled the note off the monitor and turned the machine on. He eagerly waited for the machine to accept his passwords and for the email software to come up. There were no messages from his father. This was disappointing. However, there was one from his grandmother in Canada. He clicked on the message and read it.

Hello Kyle,

I talked with your father, who said you could visit us for a few weeks this summer. I will purchase your plane ticket after I speak with your mother. I look forward to seeing you soon. Grandpa and I have missed you. I'll have Jasper set up the archery range before you come.

Love,

Grandma

This was good news, but when would he be able to find out if he was accepted into the Academy? And would his mother let him go to see his grandparents in Canada? She often got grumpy about his staying with them.

Dear Grandma,

I can't wait to see you and Grandpa. Did you know I will be going to a special school this fall? First, I have to be accepted. I am waiting to hear from them. The school is called the Academy and is kind of like a military school, but without the army stuff. I will tell you all about it when I come to see you. I hope Mom lets me visit.

I love you,

Kyle

Kyle clicked the send button for the email letter to his grandma and watched the software go through its processes. The whole day was ahead of him, and he had nothing interesting to do. He could not go out and play, so watching TV was the only option. The next three days seemed to repeat themselves, and Kyle was growing increasingly frustrated. His mom was getting up early and coming home very tired, but her next day off was tomorrow, and she had to be able to answer his question about the flat package. Kyle set his alarm clock that night to ensure he was awake before his mom, so she couldn't rush off without him being able to ask any questions. He was worried that she would go shopping or do something else.

The next morning, his mom woke him up early and told him to take a shower right away and that she had to talk to him about something important. When Kyle came to the breakfast table, he was all showered and dressed. His mom had made a splendid breakfast of scrambled eggs, bacon, and what she called Texas-style hash browns that Kyle loved. It was his favorite breakfast.

"So, Mom, did you ever look at the flat package that arrived the other day?" asked Kyle.

"Yes, dear. It was nothing important," she replied, pouring herself some coffee.

"Oh," replied Kyle, feeling somewhat disappointed. "Did you ever get a call from the school?"

"No, dear, but I did get a call from your grandmother in Canada, and she wants you to visit," she replied.

"Oh, really?" Kyle said, trying to act surprised. "Can I go?"

"Yes, dear. You may go. She purchased your tickets for today, so I will be taking you to the airport in about an hour. I have already gotten the suitcases out of the closet, so you will need to help me pack what you want to take. You may want to take most of your stuff since afterward you will be visiting your father," she said, and then burst into tears. "I'm going to miss you so much."

Kyle got up and hugged his mother. "It will be okay, Mom. I will miss you too, and I won't be gone forever. And you'll have Rojo to keep you company and your friends Anita and Carol," Kyle said, hoping to make her feel better.

She picked up her table napkin and wiped her eyes. "Yes, that's right, I will have Rojo. Now eat your breakfast before it gets cold."

The ride to the airport was not as emotional, and Kyle was excited about visiting his grandparents in Canada. He rarely got to see them since they did not like coming to the United States. It was something about nosy airport authorities that upset them and made them feel like criminals. Kyle did not understand what they were talking about, but it was bad enough to make them avoid flying. Kyle always found flying to be exciting and had often thought it would be cool to be a pilot.

All arrangements had been made to ensure the flight attendants would assist him in boarding the plane and escort him through the Portland International Airport (PDX) to catch his flight to Toronto's Pearson International Airport. There were no direct flights from Reno to Toronto. If something went wrong with the flight, then Jon Bergendahl would make the five-hour drive to Portland to take care of Kyle. It was all neatly planned, and Kyle was loaded down with all kinds of papers that his mom stuffed into his carry-on backpack. She also gave him a cell phone, which surprised Kyle.

"You can call me whenever you want, and it will work from Canada as well," she said as she tucked it into the front pocket of his backpack. However, you must not turn it on until you arrive at the airport. You will get into trouble if you have your phone on while the plane is in flight. I want you to call me and let me know that you arrived safely at each destination."

"I will. Thanks, Mom. This is really cool!" said Kyle.

"And remember that it is not a toy. And be good and don't cause your grandparents a lot of trouble," she said as they stood in line for the security checkpoint.

When they reached the security checkpoint, Kyle had to remove his shoes, empty his pockets, and take off his wristwatch, then place everything in gray plastic bins that slowly moved along a conveyor belt system. His mom put his backpack into a plastic bin.

"You have two large, checked bags. Don't forget to collect all this stuff once you are through security. You have two bins… and hold onto your passport and airplane tickets. I put some cash into the front pocket of your backpack, so if you need something, you can buy a soda or water. Be respectful of the flight attendants," she coached as he started to walk through the metal detector.

"I will, Mom. Don't worry," he replied to her. She stood back because she was not allowed to go through without a ticket. Some of the other passengers gave her irritated looks, as she seemed to be making the line move more slowly with her motherly coaching.

Kyle looked at the man in the uniform, who was watching a computer monitor as he walked through the device, and then nodded to him to proceed and pick up his belongings. Kyle felt nervous. He had flown once before with his parents, but did not remember it being so scary. He waited for his stuff to come through the X-ray machine. His plastic container with his shoes and the contents of his pockets came through, so he immediately took the container and started putting his shoes back on.

Then, a rather grumpy-looking woman in a uniform said aloud, "Whose backpack is this?"

Kyle looked up as he put his wristwatch back on and stuffed the junk from his pockets back into his pants. The woman in uniform was holding his backpack aloft.

"It's mine," he said uncomfortably.

"We have to check it," she said sternly. "Where are your parents?"

"My mom is on the other side of security. She said she could not come through because she did not have a ticket," replied Kyle.

"Okay, well, please stand here while I check the contents of the backpack," she ordered him.

Kyle stood there feeling frightened that he had done something wrong, and wondered if he would be arrested. The thought scared him. The security officer opened his bag, pulled out a water bottle, and then searched through the rest of the bag. She closed the bag and then turned toward him.

"You can't take this," she said, holding the water bottle aloft.

"I'm sorry. Am I going to be arrested?" asked Kyle.

The security agent looked at Kyle's frightened and perplexed face and replied, "No, not this time. I will have to confiscate the water bottle, though. And next time, you need to remember no liquids."

"I'll remember," Kyle replied, wide-eyed.

The security officer handed Kyle his backpack, and he gratefully took it from her, feeling relieved that she did not find anything else that broke the rules. Kyle was beginning to understand why his Canadian grandparents no longer wished to fly. And once Kyle had regained his self-composure, he walked down the hallway and turned left around the corner to find his airline gate number. The bathroom was another good stop after all that excitement as well.

His first flight would be with Southwest Airlines to Portland, Oregon, from where he would catch an Air Canada flight to Toronto. After the incident with the security checkpoint, Kyle felt completely unsure and scared about the whole trip. His confidence completely evaporated, and now he just felt frightened. He found his gate and walked up to the desk where the Southwest people stood.

"Is this my flight?" Kyle asked the woman at the counter who took the paper from him and read it.

She smiled at him and said, "Yes, Kyle Bergendahl, your plane will board on the right side over there. And since you are young and by yourself, you can be a part of the early boarding parties. Your plane will be ten minutes late due to some bad weather in Phoenix, but after that, it will be all smooth flying. If anything changes, you keep looking up here, or if you need to ask any questions, just come back up and ask me."

"Thanks," replied Kyle. "You're a lot nicer than the woman in the security checkpoint area."

The Southwest agent smiled and replied, "I have heard that several times."

Kyle looked around for a good place to sit and thought about the cell phone. He was not on the plane. He could call his mom and tell her about the mean security agent, which would... just upset her. Perhaps he could call his dad. He switched on the phone and entered his father's number to call him. He struggled to listen to the phone ring as the noise from the slot machines kept beeping and dinging loudly since someone had just won something. Then he heard his dad answer.

"Hello?"

"Hi, Dad, it's me, Kyle."

"Kyle! Where are you calling from? That is not your mom's number."

"I know. Mom gave me a cell phone so I could call her and let her know I arrived okay. But I'm scared now."

"Why? Where are you?" asked his dad.

"I'm at the Reno Airport waiting for a plane to go to Portland so that I can take a plane to Toronto to see Grandma and Grandpa. But the woman at the security

32

checkpoint was mean and now... I... feel kind of scared. I wish Mom could wait with me."

"Yeah, I wish she could, too. You say you are going to switch planes in Portland?"

"Yep. I'm supposed to take Air Canada to Toronto," replied Kyle.

"Which flight from Portland?" asked Kyle's dad.

"The one at three o'clock, so I have to wait for a couple of hours in the Portland Airport."

"Well, if I pack a quick bag, I might be able to join you... Hold on while I check the flight availability."

Kyle could hear his dad clicking and typing on the computer over the phone. As Kyle waited for him, he watched strange-looking people walk around with rolling bags, looking tired, as they disembarked from various flights across the concourse. Some looked happy while others looked irritable or busy.

"Kyle, I can get a ticket to fly with you to Toronto. I don't think you should fly alone, and I'm not even sure you're allowed to fly internationally alone, so I will pack my stuff and get on the next flight down to Portland. Okay. Buddy, are you alright with that?"

"That would be awesome, Dad. Thanks! Don't tell Mom that I was afraid to fly alone. I don't want her to think I'm a big baby. She already treats me like a baby now," replied Kyle.

"Don't worry. It will be our secret," his dad replied. "Talk to you later, and I'll see you in Portland."

"Bye, Dad," Kyle said as he ended the phone call, and then wondered if he should turn his cell phone off. He decided that if his dad needed to call back, he should leave the phone on and then turn it off when he got on the plane. This change of events made the trip much more fun, and he would also get to see his dad.

The Southwest Airlines staff made Kyle feel at ease, and he was able to select a seat next to a window near the front of the plane, allowing the flight attendants to keep an eye on him. He remembered to turn his cell phone off. Then he enjoyed every moment of the aircraft taxing on the runway, the engines roaring up, and then suddenly speeding across the landing strip and taking off into the bright blue, cloudless sky above Reno. The view was fantastic, and he could see Lake Tahoe as the plane banked around the south end of the valley and then turned north toward Portland, Oregon. As they gained altitude, the trees, cars, and buildings grew smaller, and the terrain shifted from a high desert city landscape to the forested mountains of the Sierra Nevada Mountain range. Kyle enjoyed watching the landscape slowly change and noticed how bright it was. It made his eyes sore to look out, so he decided to pull a book out of his backpack. He was glad that his Ranger's Apprentice books weren't illegal to take on a plane, and when the flight attendant came and asked him if he wanted something to drink, he gratefully accepted a cup filled with orange juice and some roasted peanuts. His mom never allowed him to have a morning snack, so this was fun.

The flight was an hour and fifteen minutes long, and as they flew closer to Portland, more and more clouds were in the sky until Kyle could no longer see the land below. It was a sea of puffy white clouds. They looked so solid, as if one could step out onto them. It was strange to think that he was seeing the other side of the clouds. Normally, one only saw the bottom side of the clouds. He would have to tell Dark Cloud that he saw the top side of the clouds, and then he remembered that his mom had packed his digital camera, which his grandparents had given him for Christmas. Reaching down for his backpack, he sorted through things until he found his camera. He took several pictures that he could send to Dark Cloud. Then he heard the announcement that all electronic devices had to be turned off and that preparations for descent into Portland PDX Airport would begin soon. The plane lowered into the clouds, and soon there was nothing but white stuff outside, and water droplets appeared upon his window.

The stewards and stewardesses walked up and down the aisle, collecting cups, napkins, and any other trash, and began making sure that everyone had returned their tray tables to their upright position. Then the plane made a strange whirring noise as the flaps were extended, which initially made Kyle nervous until he realized that everyone else ignored the sound.

Kyle was excited to see Portland again and wished he knew if he had made it into the Academy or not. He wondered why they had not contacted him. Mr. Pembroke said they would let them know, and he didn't seem like the kind of man who would be telling lies. Kyle wondered if he had done poorly on the test that he had taken. He hoped that his dad had heard. He hated not knowing whether he would get in or not.

The plane's windows suddenly revealed the wet, green landscape of the greater Portland Metro Area and the vast Columbia River, located right next to the airport. Kyle marveled at how large it looked. The Truckee River in Reno looked like an irrigation ditch compared to the Columbia. But the river wasn't the only thing that was bigger… so was the airport. Kyle wondered when his dad would arrive and what he would do while he waited for him. The plane stopped, and it was time to disembark, so he gathered his backpack and followed the others out the jet bridge and into the airport building. He felt excited and a bit scared. The airport was attractive and well-lit. There were no bells or dings from slot machines, and the people seemed different. He wasn't sure what made them different; they just looked different. Then he saw a middle-aged woman holding a sign with his name on it. The woman was wearing a green airport courtesy staff vest with a badge that read "Betty" on it.

Betty looked straight at him, and Kyle said, "I'm Kyle Bergendahl."

"Oh, great, we were worried that I might miss you. Your father sent word that you would be getting off the plane unattended, and that he would be in flight and could not contact you about his plans. He said that you are to meet him at Gustav's restaurant. He has already contacted the restaurant manager, and he knows to expect you. Your father said that you could order anything you like as long as it is not just dessert," Betty said with a big smile.

"Great. Where is Gustav's? And what about my luggage? My mom said that I was to collect it and bring it to the Air Canada counter," replied Kyle.

"We'll collect your bags now, and I'll escort you to the Air Canada counter so that you can check into your flight," replied Betty as she adjusted her glasses and gestured for Kyle to follow her.

Together they walked down a long concourse with all kinds of shops and passed Gustav's restaurant, which Betty pointed out to Kyle. She told him that she would escort him back when they had taken care of the luggage. Downstairs, they located the luggage carousels and waited for Kyle's two bags to appear. He knew right away which ones were his, since his mom had tied big blue ribbons on each bag to make them stand out easily for him. When they had finished checking in with Air Canada and handed his bags over to the airline's security service, they went back upstairs to Gustav's. It was nearly noon when Kyle sat down in the restaurant and was greeted by the manager, Peter, who was a close friend of his father. Peter told Kyle what his favorite items were on the menu, making Kyle's lunch decision very easy. While Kyle waited for his food, he called his mom to let her know that he was alright and that the airport staff in Portland were very kind.

Just after Kyle's plate of schnitzel strips, red cabbage, and spätzle arrived, his dad joined him. Jon Bergendahl warmly hugged his son. The whole trip was turning out to be an incredible adventure.

Chapter 3: Caledon House

Kyle had a terrific lunch with his father, and the restaurant manager, Peter, commented on how much they looked alike, which Kyle enjoyed hearing. He missed being with his dad. He often wished that his parents had stayed together, but then again, the arguments were rather painful to sit through. He often wondered why things could not have gone better, but today was turning out to be fantastic. He chatted with his dad nonstop until they were on the Air Canada plane, where exhaustion from a busy day caught up with him, and he soon fell fast asleep.

Kyle woke up the next morning in a strange but vaguely familiar place. The bed was large, and the sheets were soft. There was a window to the right side of the bed, and the glow from the morning sunlight poured through the window, and he could hear birds chirping outside. The walls of the room were a pale-yellow color, and the ceiling featured white crown molding. A closet was to his left, and the closed bedroom door was also to his left and farthest away. Another smaller window was on the wall where the bed was placed against. This was a corner bedroom in his grandparents' country house, a few miles outside of Toronto, Canada. It felt so peaceful and grand. The room was huge compared to his old bedroom at his mom's home in Reno.

Kyle stared at the two huge suitcases that he and his mother had packed along with his backpack. They were sitting on the floor just in front of the closet. He felt like his mom had packed most of his belongings into the two suitcases. Anything that she thought he would need or might need was packed along with some of his favorite toys and books. It seemed odd for a vacation at his grandparents' home.

Suddenly, Kyle heard his stomach gurgle. He realized that he was hungry. He didn't have dinner last night. He didn't even recall arriving.

So, he hopped out of bed and peeked out of the open window to smell the fresh, clean air and see if anything exciting was going on outside. The room was on the second story of the house, and he could see most of the surrounding area from this vantage point. It was so lush and green in comparison to Nevada. It looked like it was about eight or nine o'clock in the morning. He looked around for an alarm clock in the room and spotted one sitting on one of the nightstands. Two nightstands in one bedroom, and the bed was so nice and big, marveled Kyle. This was what it was like to have a grown-up's bedroom. He could get used to being in a place like this. His stomach grumbled again, reminding him that breakfast was a priority on his list of things to do this morning, so he walked over to the bedroom door and peeked out just in time to be spotted by his father, who was just about to go downstairs.

"Oh, hey Sport! How are you doing this morning?" Kyle's father greeted him. "I bet you are super hungry this morning."

Kyle nodded, somewhat still sleepy, and replied, "I'm famished. I don't even recall getting here last night." Then Kyle suddenly remembered he had not called his mother to tell her he had arrived safely in Toronto. "Oh no! I didn't call Mom!"

"Don't worry. Your grandmother called her last night to let her know that you had arrived safely and that you were so exhausted that you had fallen asleep in the car. We could barely get you awake enough to put on your PJs and brush your teeth before bed," replied Jon Bergendahl with a big grin. "So don't worry, she knows that you arrived safely."

"Thanks, Dad."

"Don't thank me, thank your grandmother."

"Okay. I will."

They walked together down the big stairway that curved grandly into the main foyer of the house, where the floor tiles were made of white marble with delicate gray swirls embedded in the stone. When Kyle stepped down upon the marble with his bare foot, it sent a surprising cold sensation up his body. He had been so accustomed to the heat of Nevada that he was not expecting the cold floor during the summer, which was a shock. He eagerly made his way toward one of the many area rugs that were placed in the hallways throughout the downstairs. He and his father walked toward the large kitchen and breakfast room, which had a splendid view of the vast garden and swimming pool area behind the house. The water looked bright blue and inviting, thought Kyle.

"Good morning!" his grandmother cheerfully said. "I hope you both slept well last night."

"Mom, I always sleep well in the Caledon House," Jon replied, smiling. "So, I see we are not eating in the dining room anymore."

"Well, some of the staff are on vacation this week, and I thought it would be easier for Jasper to have breakfast set in here. And besides, when we don't have company, we eat breakfast in here, anyway. I love the view of the swimming pool and gardens," replied the elderly Lily Bergendahl.

"Where's Dad?" asked Jon.

"He had to get up early this morning and tend to some business. He'll be back before lunch. You are staying for lunch?"

"Yes, and then I have to get to the airport," replied Jon.

"Dad, you're not staying?" asked Kyle.

"Sorry. My trip here was unexpected, as you know, and I had to drop everything and leave my lab assistant with all the work duties as well as looking after Pickles," replied Jon as he sat down at the breakfast table.

Kyle took the seat next to his father and looked down at his empty place setting with a sense of disappointment. He did not want his father to leave. He had not seen much of him in the past months, and it did not seem fair.

"Hey… cheer up. I plan to make some time in the next few weeks to visit you before your school starts," replied Jon.

"So, you heard from the school?!" exclaimed Kyle.

"Uh, well, they left a message on my phone yesterday that they had sent you the information about your acceptance and wondered when you would complete the information forms they sent. I assumed that you received the package or envelope," replied Jon.

"No, I didn't, but there was this package that arrived at the house, and I got into trouble by going outside, and Mom was mad at me. I almost lost Rojo," replied Kyle.

"You almost lost Rojo?!" remarked Jon as he poured some creamer into his piping hot coffee that Jasper, the butler, had just poured. "Jasper, do you have orange juice?"

"Certainly, Sir," replied Jasper.

"Oh, I love orange juice. Can I have a big glass?" asked Kyle eagerly, looking at the gray-haired gentleman, who wore neatly pressed black slacks, dress shoes, and a white button-up dress shirt.

"I think that can be arranged," Jasper replied with a smile and air of efficiency. The butler left the breakfast room and went into the kitchen to obtain a larger glass and a container of orange juice for Dr. Jon Bergendahl and his son, Kyle.

"So did you get any information from the school or not?" asked Kyle's father.

"I don't know. I could never get Mom to tell me what was in the package. She was pretty angry at me for breaking the 'don't open the door while she is away' rule," replied Kyle. "So did they say that I got into the school?"

"Well, I got the impression that it was important for you to fill out the forms to make it official," replied Jon, starting to look somewhat annoyed.

"Perhaps we should call the school and see what they say," said Kyle's grandmother. She could tell that her son was starting to look upset, and she knew just where that was going. She wanted to avoid another angry conversation about Marie, especially one that would take place in front of Kyle. Lily Bergendahl loved her son dearly and knew it must be tough for Marie to be separated from her only child. Divorce was always such an unpleasant situation that created so many problems, not only logistically but emotionally as well.

Lily skillfully steered the conversation away from an angry one about Marie and toward a solution of simply contacting the school, then getting Kyle to unpack for his visit, and Jon's possible visit in two weeks. And during this more pleasant discussion, Jasper worked to bring a delicious breakfast of freshly baked croissants, Canadian bacon, and eggs, which served to aid the Lady of the House's goal to keep her son in a more positive mood. Jasper had been the Bergendahls' butler for over thirty years and had proven to be an excellent house servant and a reliable family ally. They often thought of him as a member of the family. And both Clara and Jon missed him bitterly when he left for two weeks to attend to the death of his father. The two Bergendahl children saw Jasper as an essential member of their family.

After breakfast, Kyle went upstairs and took a shower, while Jasper unpacked his luggage for him. Kyle thought this was odd, but he knew that his Canadian grandparents had a different approach to things, so he didn't argue with them. When Kyle had finished his shower and came back into the bedroom to finish getting dressed, he discovered that Jasper had put away all his clothing into the closet and dresser. A large assortment of personal belongings was left upon the bed for Kyle to decide where they were to go.

Kyle looked at all the stuff on the bed and then up at Jasper.

"I thought you might like to decide where you would like these items placed within the room unless you wish me to pack them away," said Jasper.

Most of the items on the bed were toys, books, Kyle's favorite candy bars, some American money, the cell phone, and the camera.

"Oh no, I don't want it packed away," said Kyle. "You mean I can put this stuff out like this *is* my room?"

"Certainly, this is your room to use while you are here, young Master Kyle," replied Jasper.

"Wow, that's cool," replied Kyle as he pulled on a T-shirt that Jasper had left out for him to wear for the day. Then Kyle's eyes landed upon the flat package that the special delivery man had left on the front porch in Reno. Kyle's eyes grew big as he picked up the package, read his name on the address label, and then read that it came from the Academy.

"This is the package from the school!!" exclaimed Kyle. "Oh my gosh, this is exciting. I gotta tell Dad and Grandma right away!"

"Well, put your socks and shoes on first before you go running downstairs to tell them," Jasper suggested, holding out a pair of white sports socks and tennis shoes to Kyle, whose eyes had grown large with joyful excitement.

Kyle sat down on the floor, pulled on his socks, and spoke excitedly to Jasper, "Do you think they have accepted me into the school?!?"

"We will only know once you are dressed and take the package downstairs to share with your father and grandmother," replied Jasper, watching the boy struggle to get on his shoes as fast as possible.

"I really want to go. It looks so exciting, and there are other kids there that you get to live with all the time," remarked Kyle.

"Indeed, there are. That is the nature of a boarding school, you know," replied Jasper, holding the package for Kyle until he was ready to go downstairs.

Kyle got up, accepted the flat package from Jasper, and immediately raced downstairs to look for his father.

"Dad, Dad! I have the envelope from the school!"

Kyle heard no reply and rushed downstairs to the kitchen, where he found his dad outside on the patio, standing near the pool, talking on his cell phone. Kyle opened the fancy glass French doors and stepped out into the fresh, fragrant air of the garden and pool area of the

Bergendahl Caledon estate house. He wanted to tell his dad right away, but his dad gave him a signal that he was on an important phone call and not to be bothered. Kyle felt impatient and hoped the phone call would not take too long, then he noticed his grandmother sitting on a lounge chair not far away. His grandmother motioned for him to come over, so Kyle walked over with the package in hand.

"What have you got there, sweetheart?" she asked her green eyes twinkling as she lifted her sunglasses.

"It's the package from the school," replied Kyle.

"Well, isn't that fortuitous? Shall we open it to see what they have to say?" she asked Kyle.

"Yeah," said Kyle, sitting down next to her as she moved her legs off the lounge chair and gestured for him to sit beside her. "What is fort-to-it-tus?"

Lily looked at her grandson for a moment and then responded, "It basically means something happening by chance, and in this particular situation, a lucky event. Now we don't have to call the school." Lily Bergendahl looked at her grandson and started to open the flat package that he had handed her. "Well... what made you decide to pick this school? And are you sure you want to live for months away from your parents?"

"I don't really want to live away from them, but I am tired of being unable to stay in the same place and make friends. They live so far away from each other, too. I don't understand that," replied Kyle.

46

"Hmm. I think they were both angry with each other and decided to live as far away as they could from one another, and they did not think about how that would affect you," replied Lily. "Sometimes, grown-ups can be thoughtless and selfish. And that is the trick of life… to learn how to grow up and not be thoughtless or selfish. Now let's see what kind of paperwork they put in here for you."

Kyle watched as his grandmother pulled out a bunch of papers from the envelope and began sorting through them. She began reading the letter on top of the pile of documents.

Attention to: Mr. Kyle Bergendahl, Dr. Jon Bergendahl, and Miss Marie Gomez

Please accept the Academy's congratulations on being accepted for this school year. To complete this process, the Academy requires additional information so that we can place Kyle in an environment that best suits his learning needs. Complete all the necessary forms and return them by 15 August to ensure proper placement within the Academy.

If you need any assistance or have questions, please don't hesitate to contact me. If I am unavailable, one of my staff members will be happy to assist you with your concerns or questions.

Kind Regards,

S.K. Chester T. Pembroke

Lily Bergendahl quickly looked at her watch, which sparkled in the morning sunlight. She frowned and looked at Kyle.

"We need to fill out all these forms right away. These are due at school tomorrow. I wish we had more time. When did you get this package?"

"It arrived about a week ago," replied Kyle. "Is this going to be a problem?"

"I am sure we can figure this all out. I can always call Sir Knight Chester if I have any concerns," remarked Lily as she started to look through the various documents that needed to be read and filled out.

Jon Bergendahl walked over now that his phone call was over.

"So, what have we got there?" he asked.

"It's the paperwork from the school, and it needs to be completed and sent to them by the fifteenth of August," replied Lily, looking a little frustrated with her son. "You should have taken care of this. You know that school has a waiting list, and you can't afford to mess up and lose Kyle his spot in the rolls."

Jon's facial expression changed.

"Look, this is the first time I have seen any of this stuff. I am assuming that it was sent to Marie's place, right?" Jon said, looking very annoyed. "She can never be trusted to understand what is important."

48

"Well, you can't get too mad. She did send it along with Kyle for us to take care of," replied Lily, putting her sunglasses back. "She could have thrown it away and never said anything about it."

"Yes, but I don't have time to get all this done. I have a flight this afternoon," complained Jon.

"Don't worry about that. We shall sit down and start working on it right now, and I will finish what you can't," said Lily. She then looked at Kyle. "Well, are you ready to start some important paperwork regarding your future?"

"Sure, Grandma," replied Kyle, looking at her and then up at his dad, who appeared as if he were deciding whether he was going to be grumpy or just drop it. "Dad?"

Jon looked at his son's hopeful blue eyes and realized that getting mad at Marie wasn't going to solve anything. "Sure, Sport, I'll sit down with you and your grandma and get this stuff done, but next time I see you, we get to do something fun like archery."

"It's a deal," said Kyle, beaming.

The three of them spent the next three hours filling out forms, and then Kyle had to answer a questionnaire that only he could answer. By the time they had completed all the forms, it was lunchtime, and Karl Bergendahl had come home to join them for a nice lunch outside on the veranda, overlooking the swimming pool and gardens. After lunch, Jon Bergendahl left for the airport, promising to come back for a visit with Kyle before he started school. Kyle was sad to see him go, but seeing his father was never part of the original plan, so he was lucky to have had the opportunity to see him at all.

His grandmother made sure that the forms were sent back in time to meet the school's deadline, so all Kyle had to do was wait for the final letter announcing the Academy location where he would be attending. The Academy had locations worldwide, so Kyle did not even know where he would be going.

It was evening, and Kyle had already been tucked into bed by his grandparents, but he was restless, and it was a lovely summer night. He pulled the curtain sheers back, stood, and looked out the open window, smelling the fresh air, and listened to the crickets. He liked listening to the crickets at night in Reno, too. He looked at the nearly full moon in the sky and how it lit the ground below. There was something restless stirring deep down in his soul that he could sense but not truly understand. It was like a longing. Perhaps it was a longing for adventure. He wished his friend Dark Cloud could be here with him and they could sneak outside, play in the gardens, or swim in the pool. His grandparents also had horses to ride, and his grandfather had promised to take him riding in the next couple of days. He always wanted to ride a horse but had never done so. Dark Cloud also wanted to ride a horse, and they often talked about how it would be fun to capture a wild Mustang and train it to be their horse.

Kyle realized that he had not talked to Dark Cloud in two weeks. Tomorrow, he would ask his grandmother if he could use the computer to send an email to his friend. Kyle looked at the cell phone, which sat in its charger with a red glowing light, and figured he could give the phone number to Dark Cloud, and then they could talk once in a while. Perhaps Dark Cloud would have exciting news about the new tribal school that he would go to this fall, out at Pyramid Lake. Kyle wanted to go out to Pyramid Lake, but his mom had said it was too far out in the middle of nowhere, and she did not want him to be out there. It was as if she thought he was delicate or something, which was annoying, and it made him cringe and feel somewhat embarrassed.

Kyle thought about the day's events and remembered something his grandmother had said that caught his attention, but he had forgotten to ask her about it. She had referred to Mr. Pembroke as Sir Knight Chester. It was curious, as he thought he had heard someone mention knights during the interview visit in Portland, Oregon. Kyle sat at the open window for another hour, enjoying the view and dreaming about what it would be like to live in this new place with other kids. He wondered if he would make any friends. He wished Dark Cloud could come with him. He could see the lights in the distance from Toronto, far off, reflecting in the sky. Kyle yawned and suddenly felt very tired. He crawled up onto the large light-colored bedspread, found the opening for the sheets, and crawled in. The moonlight shone through the curtain sheers onto the bed, and he drowsily stared up at the sheers before drifting off to sleep.

Chapter 4: The Bergendahls

The next couple of days, Kyle enjoyed playing in the pool and lounging about the gardens while Lily Bergendahl had instructed Jasper to set up a laptop computer for Kyle to use in his room. Kyle was ecstatic about this because he could use it anytime he wanted to. He could contact his mom or dad and use Skype or Google Hangouts to talk with them and see them simultaneously. Kyle emailed Dark Cloud about his new adventures and that he now had access to a computer with a webcam. He wondered if Dark Cloud would have access to one as well. It was worth a try to ask. In the meantime, Kyle enjoyed the much more comfortable, moderately warm August days in Caledon than the hot ones in Reno, which were often unbearable.

His grandfather, Karl Bergendahl, woke Kyle up early one morning, had him get dressed in a pair of long pants, and told him they would go for a horseback ride. This was incredibly exciting for Kyle until he fully realized how big a horse really was. He had never been around large animals before and felt very apprehensive at first glance. His grandfather proceeded to explain what needed to be done with the horse for riding and care, but in this situation, the grooms and stable hands would take care of everything.

"So, if the stable hands and grooms take care of all of this stuff, then why do I need to know this?" asked Kyle, wrinkling his nose, not liking the smell of the stables.

"Because you never know when you might find yourself alone and needing to know how to do things for yourself," replied his grandfather with a broad smile and a twinkle in his eye.

"Oh. That makes sense," agreed Kyle, looking up at his grandfather with admiration. It was as if his grandfather believed he could take care of himself if he knew all the right things to do. Kyle liked that feeling.

Karl Bergendahl proceeded with an elementary lesson about the different parts of the saddle and how it was attached to the horse. Kyle thought the saddle looked very strange. These were not like the ones he saw in the Nevada Day Parade or up in Virginia City. These saddles were smaller and seemed more streamlined. His grandfather explained that the saddles Kyle was used to seeing were Western ranch-style saddles, designed for working on cattle ranches, whereas the saddles at the Caledon House were more suited for military and dressage riding, like what was done in the Olympics.

Once up on the horse, Kyle felt like he was very high up. It was a great view from up so high, but a little scary. He had never ridden a horse before. The horse was a mare named Pearl because she was a creamy white color and had a sweet personality that was perfect for a beginner rider. She was patient, and Karl told his grandson that Pearl was used to carrying novice riders, unlike the horse that he was riding. Kyle eyed the large, impressive-looking black stallion that his grandfather was riding. The animal tossed his head about in an arrogant fashion and seemed to be showing off for Pearl. The stallion's name was Clyde.

Together, Kyle and his grandfather rode in an enclosed grassy pasture for about forty-five minutes, during which Kyle learned how to instruct Pearl to move forward, stop, turn left, or turn right. It was a wonderful experience, and when Karl decided it was time for breakfast, he asked Kyle if he wanted to continue learning how to ride.

"Grandpa, I would love to continue to learn how to ride! Can I ride every day? Can I ride Pearl?" asked Kyle as he reached up and stroked her soft nose.

Kyle's grandfather smiled and replied, "I think we can arrange that. I think Pearl likes you."

"I like her too," replied Kyle.

"I am glad to hear that," replied his grandfather as he offered up Clyde's reins to the groom who patiently waited for his employer to be ready. "Young Kyle here will learn how to ride a little each morning. I want Pearl to be available for him since they seem to get along fine."

"Certainly, Mr. Bergendahl. Sir, do you want Clyde to be ready as well? Or do you wish one of us to show Kyle how to ride?" asked the groom.

"I would like to show Kyle how to ride, so please have Clyde ready as well."

Kyle gave Pearl's reins to the groom, and the man walked off with a horse on each side of him. From this vantage point, Kyle could see how much bigger Clyde was than Pearl, not to mention how small a human looked in comparison.

"Clyde is huge," commented Kyle.

"Yes, he is. And he is a fine animal. Very smart," replied Karl Bergendahl with a tone of great admiration for the horse. "Pearl's a gem and is also very smart. She's the type of horse that would bring her rider home regardless of the situation."

They walked together toward the house as the morning sun rose to mid-morning.

"I'm hungry. Are you?" Karl asked his grandson.

"Yes, I am famished. I could eat... a lot," he replied jovially. They walked on, and then a more serious question popped into his head: "Are you going to train me how to be a better rider?"

"Certainly, why wouldn't I make the time for my grandson?" responded Karl without thinking much about the topic.

"I'm just really surprised and pleased, Grandpa," Kyle replied.

Karl looked down at the ten-year-old blonde boy who strode alongside him. He looked so much like Jon when he was a boy.

"Kyle, I am thrilled that you are here, and I can and will show you how to ride."

Kyle beamed at his grandfather, feeling the warmth of the morning sun upon his face and the wonderful feeling inside of being wanted and somehow belonging.

Later that afternoon, the good news arrived that Kyle had been accepted into the Academy and would attend the location just outside Toronto, Canada. Kyle was so excited that he didn't know who to call first, his mom or dad. When he called his mother, she was only vaguely happy for him. Then, she proceeded to tell him all about events concerning herself and her two friends, Anita and Carol. Kyle had hoped his mother would be more excited for him, but she seemed uninterested and wanted to talk about what was happening in Reno. She also told him that her job hours would change and that she may need to move out of the house and into a smaller place. Kyle didn't like this idea. It made him feel like he would have nowhere to return to when he was out of school. His home would be gone once again. Then Kyle called his father, who seemed much more excited than his mother, but was so busy that he couldn't talk for long. By the time Kyle had gotten off the phone with both of his parents, he no longer felt the joy and enthusiasm he had initially felt after getting the news. He thought about calling Dark Cloud, but he hadn't yet emailed him back with a phone number to call, as he was staying out of town at the Pyramid Lake Reservation with his uncle. There was no one to call. No one to share the good news with.

He left his bedroom and went downstairs to find something to amuse him. He didn't feel like swimming in the pool and had already had his riding lesson with his grandfather. He wandered aimlessly throughout the hallways of the large house that was still somewhat unfamiliar to him. He came across a wing of the house that seemed seldom used, with all the doors closed. He slowly

56

opened one of the doors and peeked in. It was a guest room. It was nicely decorated with a queen-sized bed. He closed that door and found another similar guest room, and so on until he came across a locked door. This surprised him. He knelt down to peer under the door, but no light came pouring from underneath like the other closed doors down this hallway. Kyle scratched his head in bewilderment and then turned to the last door in the hallway that he had not tried. It was at the very end of the hallway. Not much light poured in from under this door, but there was some. He reached for the doorknob and wondered if it would open. Much to his delight, it did. It opened into a huge room that was a library.

Kyle was shocked and amazed by the number of books and shelves in the room. The ceiling went up at least two floors, and there were ladders and walkways along the edges of the room. It was the most fantastic kind of room in a house that he had ever seen before. He felt as if he were part of a movie, and this place was a great, mysterious discovery that he, alone, had found. The floor was hardwood with large area rugs, and there were two huge wooden tables with sturdy, ornately carved legs. Several kinds of chairs were in the room. Some were high-wing back chairs with plush fabric just waiting to be sat in, while others were hard and wooden, more like antique dining chairs. He figured these were used with the big tables. Kyle marveled at the paintings and statues displayed and wondered where all this stuff came from. There was even a suit of armor that stood against the wall. Kyle approached it and immediately wondered if someone could be in it. It was the right size to hold a person. He reached out, gingerly tapped on the suit, and listened to the hollow response from his knuckle rapping. This eased his mind.

Located near the suit of armor was a display cabinet with protective glass for a variety of weapons, including several swords. Kyle looked at the old-looking weapons, lifted the display glass carefully, and gently touched the sharp edge of one of the swords, and gingerly ran his fingertip to the very pointed tip.

"Wow, that's sharp," he said aloud to himself. "I wouldn't want to get stabbed with that."

The room was terrific, with a wonderful ambiance. It felt like history. Kyle sat on the floor next to one of the huge bookcases and browsed through numerous books. He pulled a few books out and read their titles. Some had strange names that didn't make sense, while others were completely unreadable, as if they were written in a foreign language. He found books with soft, old leather covers that had an interesting smell; some had hard cloth covers, and the pages within had turned an odd, yellowish color. He had never seen so many of such a variety before. Most of the ones in this area had only text and appeared to be old. Despite sitting on the floor, he spotted another shelf with larger books, like encyclopedias or picture reference books. He got up to inspect this shelf.

These books were heavy and stood twelve inches or more in height. One was called the Compendium of Autumn and had a greenish cover. He pulled this heavy tome out, carried it to one of the heavy wooden tables, laid it down, and opened it. The paper was heavy and smooth.

It was filled with descriptions and drawings of trees and leaves. The book described the life cycle of each tree in detail. There were drawings of leaves, flowers, buds, bark, seeds, and moss that would sometimes grow on the trees. It wasn't exactly a topic he was interested in, but the pictures were very nice and sharp. He rarely saw images like these in his schoolbooks, nor did he see pictures like these on the Internet. He flipped to the front of the book, as his teachers had taught him, and looked for the publication date. The book was published in 1927. The year 1927 seemed like a long time ago to Kyle, and upon thinking about it, he realized that they must not have had the Internet then and would have had to use a book like this to get information and pictures. He tried to imagine what life would have been like without the Internet, and it seemed strange and unfathomable to him.

Kyle suddenly realized that time had gone by, and he was hungry. He looked at his watch and realized he had wasted two hours exploring the house. He didn't want his grandparents to get worried, so he decided to put the book back on the shelf and come back down another time to see if he could find anything interesting to read. With this many books, there had to be a couple of good adventure stories lurking somewhere on the shelves. Making sure that he left nothing out of place, Kyle carefully closed the library door behind him and went to the kitchen to see if Jasper had started anything yet.

He could hear noises in the kitchen and found the butler busy chopping vegetables and preparing a fresh garden salad to accompany dinner.

"Hello, Jasper."

"Hello, Master Kyle," replied Jasper.

Kyle wrinkled his brow and asked, "Why do you call me Master Kyle?"

"It is a term of respect for the people of the house that I serve and take care of," replied Jasper. "Some house servants think it is old-fashioned, but I come from an old-fashioned family that likes to do things with style. Just because one is a house servant doesn't mean one can't have a sense of style."

"Oh, okay," replied Kyle, not completely understanding but not wanting to offend the man who made such great dinners. He liked Jasper very much. Living with a butler was akin to having an extra motherly figure in the house. Except it was a guy. He did so many things for his grandparents and lived with them. It was certainly something that he was not used to. He knew no one back home who had a butler.

"Is that what we are having for dinner?" asked Kyle.

"Yes, it is," replied Jasper.

"I'm hungry."

"Would you like a slice of cucumber or red onion?" asked Jasper with a playful grin.

Kyle wrinkled his brow and replied, "An onion! Ugh, I don't think so, but the cucumber slice would be fine."

Jasper picked up a couple of cucumber slices from the cutting board and handed them to Kyle, who accepted them.

"Thank you," responded Kyle. "So, what else are we having besides salad?"

"Pork tenderloin and potatoes," responded Jasper.

"Oh, I love potatoes and pork tenderloin. That sounds great," replied Kyle. Kyle watched Jasper in silence as he intently studied how the elderly man prepared the food with such precision and grace.

"So, do you like being a butler?" asked Kyle.

Jasper looked up from the lettuce that he was carefully breaking apart with his hands and replied, "Yes, I do very much."

"Why?"

"Because I enjoy taking care of people and the Bergendahls are like family to me."

Kyle smiled. "I like my grandma and grandpa too. I often wish my parents were more like them."

Later that evening, Kyle was able to get onto Google Hangouts and talk with Dark Cloud. He told him all about the school and that his grandfather was teaching him how to ride a horse named Pearl. She was incredibly fun to ride. Then Dark Cloud told Kyle all about the fact that he was going to live with his uncle so that he could attend the new Three Tribes School, and that his uncle had taken him camping. His uncle was teaching Dark Cloud all the old traditions of their people. He told Kyle that his uncle was learning to be a shaman and would teach Dark Cloud how to communicate with the land spirits.

"It's a good thing you weren't telling me that while we were at my mom's house, she would have thrown you out!" laughed Kyle. "She's so weird about that kind of stuff."

Dark Cloud just shook his head and took no offense. He'd also seen enough of his own people take that religious route, and it seemed odd to him. He was proud of his heritage, and no one would tell him otherwise. He told Kyle to be proud of his heritage and not let his mom's relatives make him feel bad. Dark Cloud was a year older than Kyle because his parents had been late enrolling him in school, so he often felt like a big brother to Kyle. They even tried to make themselves become blood brothers after watching a movie in which the two main characters cut themselves to mingle their blood. Kyle's mom had walked in on the beginning of this process and stopped it right away. She nearly took Dark Cloud home, but Kyle managed to sweet-talk his mom into not doing so.

They talked for an hour, until Kyle realized it was long after he promised his grandmother that he would go to bed.

"I gotta go. It's long past my bedtime," said Kyle.

"What does that matter? You are in a room by yourself, and you have nowhere you need to be in the morning," remarked Dark Cloud.

"Yes, but I gave my grandmother my word of honor that I would go to bed by a certain time," responded Kyle.

"I see," said Dark Cloud, nodding appreciatively. "Then I will talk to you after I return from the next camping trip."

"Okay. Sounds good. Bye," said Kyle.

"Good-bye," replied Dark Cloud with a grin.

The screen went blank as Kyle clicked the buttons on the software and logged off so that he could turn off the laptop computer. He still marveled at how cool the laptop was and that it was all his to use. The room went dark as the computer screen turned off. Kyle easily found his way to bed, removed his street clothes, and slipped on his pajamas. Putting his head upon the cool pillow and listening to the crickets from outside, he suddenly realized that even though he missed his parents, he felt very content. It was a nice feeling.

The month of August disappeared very quickly, and soon it was September and time for Kyle to travel to the Academy location for the very first time. His grandmother made sure Kyle had his required Academy clothing, which was less formal for the younger children. The first five grade levels did not wear dress blazers and ties except for special occasions. She bought him several sets of gray and black trousers, white button-up shirts with both long and short sleeves, several blue sweaters, and several hooded sweatshirts featuring the school crest. The female students wore the same thing, except they had an additional choice of two types of skirts.

When the school sent a detailed list of required items, Lily Bergendahl took care of it personally and brought Kyle with her to make the selections according to the school's required list. This all made Kyle very happy, except that his dad never found the time to come back and visit, and his mom was never interested in what was happening. He found his parents' lack of interaction very frustrating, and Lily noticed that her grandson's mood would fluctuate curiously.

After an especially frustrating conversation with his mother about her plans to move out of the house and to a new location, and her packing up all his belongings, Kyle decided to go into the library to take his mind off everything. The room seemed so fantastic that he hoped it would soothe his hurt feelings. He didn't like the idea that she would move. She even hinted that she was thinking about returning to Texas, where her family was.

Kyle glumly walked through the library and started pulling books out to see if anything looked exciting. He pulled out a leather-bound book that was part of a set of similar-looking books and read the title. It was called The Knight School Journal, and it was completely handwritten. The handwriting was very fluid and neat. It looked somewhat familiar, but he could not remember where. He opened it to the middle and started to read.

The archery competition went very well for me, and I think all my classmates were very impressed with how well I did. I think I even earned the respect of the Archery Master, which has made me especially pleased since I don't think he believed that I had it in me to do so well, nor had the concentration. I truly wanted to prove that I was worthy. I told my best friend...

Then Kyle heard the library door start to open. Kyle quickly put the book back on the shelf next to the others. His grandmother entered the room, looked around, and spotted him standing by the bookshelf.

"Oh, there you are," said Lily Bergendahl.

"Hi, Grandma," replied Kyle, unsure if he was supposed to be in the room.

"Kyle, come sit with me on the sofa," requested Lily Bergendahl as she sat down on the dark burgundy red leather sofa and patted a space beside her.

Kyle slowly walked over. His grandmother did not look like a grandma. Her hair was blondish white and curled gently. She was elegant and still very beautiful. She was of medium height and slender, with a youthful twinkle in her eyes. She was fashionable and always looked very nice, even if she wore something plain and simple. Kyle sat down next to her.

"What's up, Grandma?" he asked her.

"I want to make sure you are alright," she replied. "I have noticed your mood changes from time to time. Are you sure you want to go away to school?"

Kyle pondered a moment before he answered.

"Yes, and no. At times, I feel like I don't know what I want," replied Kyle. His grandmother remained quiet, patiently looking at him with concern. "What I *really* want... is for my parents to get along, live together, and pay attention to me."

"I can understand that," replied Lily. "But you must understand that they decided to divorce because they could no longer get along and be civil with each other. It had become unhealthy for both of them."

They sat in silence for a moment, and then Lily asked her grandson, "Do you want to go to school? If you don't, I could arrange for you to stay here and go to another school."

Kyle looked up at his grandmother and replied, "I'd like to try it. I am nervous that the other kids will not like me, and I miss having Dark Cloud around."

"He's your friend who is of the First Nations people, right?"

"First Nations? He's half Paiute and Washoe," replied Kyle, correcting his grandmother. He did not know that the Canadians referred to the Native Americans as First Nations.

"Well, regardless of what tribe he belongs to, perhaps he can visit you when you are home from school," replied Lily Bergendahl.

"It won't happen. Mom is thinking about moving away from Reno," replied Kyle.

This surprised Lily Bergendahl since this was the first time she had heard of Marie wanting to move to a new location. She hid her surprise and said, "I meant that he could come here and visit. We have plenty of room for one of your friends to visit occasionally."

"Really?" Kyle said, looking up at her with delight and surprise.

"Yes. Really."

"That would be wonderful, Grandma," Kyle responded, throwing his arms around his grandmother and hugging her. She hugged him back warmly and wondered how her son, Jon, and Marie could have become so strange to their son. She noticed Jon had not kept his promise to return to Caledon for a few days before Kyle's school began. He had also left everything regarding the school in her hands, and she heard nothing from Marie. Lily wondered what was wrong with them. They had a wonderful son who was so bright, intelligent, and good-natured.

They sat for a while longer in the library, and Lily assured Kyle that he was welcome to read the books, but he must be careful because some of the books were very old, delicate, and somewhat rare and valuable. Kyle promised to be careful. He hugged his grandmother again.

"Thank you for letting me stay here with you and Grandpa," said Kyle.

Chapter 5: The Academy

In two days, Kyle was expected to travel to the Academy location, just north of Toronto and Caledon, which would make it very easy for him to visit his grandparents during the holiday season. This was just one of nine locations around the world where the Academy had schools. Kyle was nervous and excited at the same time, and unsure what to bring with him. He kept thinking he needed to bring a pillow and sleeping bag, but Lily Bergendahl kept reassuring him that the school provided those items, including an actual bed with linens and blankets. Jasper took care that all of Kyle's garments and school items were labeled correctly, as well as his luggage. Jasper also made sure that other non-essential items, such as the cell phone, charger, and digital camera, were labeled correctly. The school was very particular about listing all non-essential items and submitting them to the administrative staff for security to avoid any possible disputes that could arise among children. Kyle thought this was rather curious, but then again, he had never been to a private school where he would stay for months. His ownership of the cell phone was permitted only on the condition that he never used it in the classroom and did not violate any school rules regarding cell phone usage. Kyle had to read through the code of conduct book and sign that he had read the rules and understood them.

As the days and then hours ticked away, getting closer and closer to his departure time, Kyle grew more nervous and excited all at once. He was scared and thrilled all at the same time, and he wasn't too sure what to think of his new state of mind. His grandparents did their best to reassure him that everything would be fine, and if he absolutely hated being at the school, he could return to Caledon House and stay until his parents decided what to do next. They promised him that he would not get into trouble if he decided that a private boarding school was not for him.

Kyle had crawled into his bed with his grandmother standing by, making sure that all was well.

"Just try to go to sleep. We have a big day tomorrow," said Lily Bergendahl.

"I don't know if I can sleep," replied Kyle. "What if the teachers don't like me because I am American?"

Kyle's grandfather had just walked into the room and replied, "The school has children from all over the world. Boys, girls, rich, poor, elementary school age to teenagers, and they don't mind Americans." Karl Bergendahl was smiling at his grandson.

"Just mind your manners and follow the Golden Rule, and you will be fine. It's a very nice place with good teachers. We would not allow you to go unless the school had a good history of excellence and professionalism. We love you, and your parents love you. So, close your eyes," suggested Lily Bergendahl as she watched her grandson close his eyes and smile a big grin, "And go to sleep."

"I will. Good night, Grandma, good night, Grandpa," replied Kyle.

"Good night," said the elderly Bergendahls as they turned the lights off and gently closed the bedroom door.

Kyle lay still in his bed listening to his grandparents' slowly disappearing footsteps. He wished all the waiting was over with and that he could get dressed and go. He wondered if the pictures of the school were as good as the real thing. He thought back to when his parents were still together, and they all went on a vacation trip to the beach. When they arrived at the motel near the beach, it didn't look as good as it had on the website. Kyle remembered the look on his mom's face. She looked like someone had handed her a bag of dirty laundry and asked her to wash it, and his dad was mad. Luckily, they were able to find another place to stay, and Kyle's dad had told him that advertisers were often good at making things look better than they truly were. Kyle thought about that for a moment and then thought of the nice Mr. Pembroke. Kyle didn't believe that Mr. Pembroke would lie to him. Kyle wondered if he would see Mr. Pembroke at the school, and then remembered that there were many school locations worldwide. His thoughts seemed to lose focus, and before he knew it, he was awoken by Jasper pulling aside the bedroom curtains and letting in the morning sunlight.

"It's morning, young Master Kyle, and the day you journey to the Academy," said Jasper.

The morning was a flurry of packing bags, attending to last-minute details, consulting lists, and rechecking them to make sure nothing was forgotten. Jasper had the BMW sedan all packed and fueled up for the hour-and-twenty-minute drive to Lake Simcoe. After eating a special breakfast to celebrate Kyle's achievement of being accepted into the school and the great new adventure that lay before him, Kyle's grandparents accompanied him in the sedan to drive northeast up to Lake Simcoe, where the Canadian school was located. Kyle looked out the window of the luxury sedan across tree-covered farmland with the morning light spreading across the fields in the process of harvest. His grandparents chatted lovingly with each other and pointed out various places of interest to Kyle. A golf course here and there that they enjoyed playing at, and a family friend's home that was along the way. He never heard a bitter word exchanged between the two, and they also chatted cheerfully with Jasper, who drove the car. He wondered what his parents were doing at this very moment. His mom and his father would both be at work. He would call them after he was settled into his dorm room.

The drive seemed very short, and before he knew it, he was glimpsing the homes along the edges of Lake Simcoe with their tree-filled yards and small boats stored in the side yards for summertime fun. After staying with his grandparents and riding through the areas around Caledon, Kyle understood why his father decided to move to Seattle. The landscape in this part of Canada resembled that of areas in Washington State. It must have looked like home to his dad. Kyle kept looking out the window of the comfortable BMW. The areas around Lake Simcoe appeared to be ideal places to live, with parks, basketball hoops set up in yards, and soccer fields for teams to play on. The houses looked nice, and the trees were slowly turning golden as autumn approached. The lake looked huge to Kyle. When looking out across it, he did not see

71

hills or another shore like he would at Lake Tahoe. Lake Tahoe was not far from Reno, where his mother was living, and sometimes, when she had time, she would take him up to the beach for a day trip. They would sit on the beach at his favorite spot at Sand Harbor and have a picnic. He would play in the icy, cold mountain waters that were very clear and deep, but he could see the mountains across the lake. But Lake Simcoe seemed different. It had to be bigger than Lake Tahoe, he realized. If he squinted and watched very carefully, he could spot land in the distance, and some of those spots of land were islands within the lake. Lake Tahoe had only one island, located in Emerald Bay.

"So that's an island in the lake?" asked Kyle, making sure that he was seeing things correctly.

"Yes, and you will be staying on an island in Lake Simcoe," his grandmother replied.

"The school is on an island?!" exclaimed Kyle.

"Yes, didn't you realize that from the description and all the rules concerning going into the lake?" asked his grandfather.

"No, I just thought that the school was next to the lake, not in the lake," replied Kyle. "How do we get out to the island?"

"There are several ferries that go out there, and the school owns a boat as well. They also built a helicopter pad about twenty years ago. They use the helicopter for emergencies and on days like today, when many people travel back and forth to the island. You must realize that the school is not the only thing on the island. There are quite a few homes there as well," remarked Lily.

"I wonder if they ever fixed the small airfield?" Karl wondered aloud to no one in particular.

"I would hope so," replied Lily as the car slowed down.

Kyle's mind was now buzzing with wonderment. The idea of living on an island was exciting.

"This really is like going on a Hogwarts adventure! I get to live on an island on a beautiful lake where there are boats and helicopters. There may not be any magic or griffins, but helicopters and an island on a lake are cool. Is there anything else that I didn't realize?!" exclaimed Kyle.

"Oh, I am sure there are many things for you to discover about the school and its location, but if you were to know about it all now, then where would be the fun of discovering it for yourself?" replied Kyle's grandfather with a smile.

"Are we taking the boat or the helicopter?" asked Kyle.

"I believe we are taking the helicopter while the luggage is taken on the boat," replied Lily with a smile. Her eyes twinkled as she glanced over at her husband, who was also looking very amused about Kyle's excitement. They were both relieved that Kyle was finally allowing himself to enjoy the experience and have fun with the prospect of attending the prestigious school that could open up his future to many possibilities. They knew full well that his education and well-being had been put on the back burner while his parents argued.

"The helicopter! Oh awesome!! I can't wait to tell Dark Cloud!! This is going to be so cool!" remarked Kyle as he eagerly looked out the car window, some more, hoping to get a glimpse of the island that the school was located on.

Jasper slowed down and pulled into an area where parking was available along the shore of the lake, with many floating pathways jutting out, and personal boats of all kinds, sizes, colors, and shapes were docked. The parking lot was full, and Kyle could see other children with their parents unloading suitcases and making their way across the lot, while others walked down to the piers to load their luggage into small speedboats docked there. Further down the parking lot was another rampway for vehicles to drive onto the ferry boat, which was preparing to take people out to the island.

Jasper halted the car and turned to address the Bergendahls, "Do you wish me to bring the car onto the island or simply have the luggage taken aboard?"

"It's awfully crowded this time of the year, and I am sure the local residents are hard pressed for spots on the ferry boat, so let's just leave the car on the mainland. Jasper, do you want to come along?" asked Karl.

"No, Sir, I spotted a Timmies back in Georgina, so I think I will simply wait and have a coffee down the road after I get the luggage safely on board with the school's stewards," replied Jasper.

"Okay then. I will call on the cell phone when we are about to depart from the island," replied Karl.

"Very good, Sir. I will await your call," replied Jasper as he put the car into park and then got out to open the door for Lily Bergendahl.

Karl opened his own door and spoke a few words privately with Jasper while Kyle kept close to his grandmother, who was pointing out various types of sailboats to Kyle. Jasper then took the BMW to the area where people could board the ferry boat without a car or have items shipped to the island, while Kyle walked with his grandparents to the helicopter pad. This area was restricted, and only those with specific identification were permitted to enter beyond the chain-link fence. The helicopter was in the air, returning to the mainland landing pad.

"That's a Bell 525 copter," commented Karl Bergendahl as he shaded his eyes from the sun, peering up into the sky to see the approaching helicopter. "They must have purchased a new one, or the Order loaned it out to the school today."

"I have no idea, dear," replied Lily, looking up into the sky. "As long as it flies well and the pilot is good, then I am happy."

Kyle contentedly watched as the flying machine grew larger and larger as it drew closer, and the sound of the blades chopping through the air became clearer and clearer. A rush of air swept over everyone who stood nearby. Karl Bergendahl walked up to one of the people standing near the entrance way. They all wore white short-sleeved polo shirts with red collars and cuff accents, paired with plain black slacks. A woman who appeared to be about twenty years old turned to Mr. Bergendahl. She had long brown hair neatly pulled back into a single ponytail.

"How many can fit into this new helicopter?" Mr. Bergendahl asked, his Swedish accent still slightly noticeable.

"It seats sixteen passengers," she replied with a smile. "This is the first time we have made serious use of it. It's completely used for the school, but in the event of any medical emergencies on the island, we can easily assist the residents. That's part of the agreement we made with the island's permanent residents, allowing us to maintain a helicopter and the old airfield. I think it was a good arrangement for everyone."

"I would say so," replied Karl as he continued to watch the helicopter. It slowed its speed and then started to descend for landing on the helipad. "My grandson is incredibly excited about going for a ride."

"I think everyone is excited," the brown-haired woman replied loudly with a big smile. The copter noise was getting loud. "I know I was impressed with how nice it was inside. It features all the latest radar capabilities and onboard computer systems for navigation and weather tracking. It's amazing."

The ride in the new helicopter was terrific, as Kyle had never been in a helicopter before and got a seat next to the window so that he could look out across the lake's surface and at the surrounding landscape. Kyle could hear and feel the intensity of the copter blades gaining speed. When it was finally ready, it gently lifted a few feet off the ground and then acted as if it were gaining its balance, then it started moving upward and forward, which was nothing like the forward dash that the jetliner would take across the airfield with its jets roaring and the tires rumbling across the pavement. It was another fantastic experience to add to the list of events that had happened in the past two months. Kyle wondered if the school would be as exciting. How could it not? He had never lived at a school before or in Canada.

He looked out at the island that wasn't very far away from the shore. It was big enough to have at least thirty houses spread apart along the shoreline, with the school's property located in the center. The island was covered in a dense forest of trees and shrubs, with small trails crisscrossing the terrain. Kyle could see the small airfield where the helipad was located and a modest hangar that probably housed up to three small aircraft. Fairly close by was a large barn with stables, a pasture, and an equestrian training arena. Many areas resembled old-fashioned estate structures and gardens, but what stood out the most was the main building of the school, which had an old European fortress-like appearance. It was a strange and amazing building with four impressive wings that came from the center point of the building's structure. Kyle was thrilled to discover that this was the main building of the school where he would stay and have classes. He had seen that cross shape before in paintings and schoolbooks.

As the chopper lowered toward the ground, Kyle could see how the shrubs and grass wavered violently as the intense blade wash hit the ground. People dressed in white polo shirts and black slacks stood waiting in attendance to greet the newcomers to the island property. Kyle finally looked around the helicopter's interior and at the other passengers. His eyes settled upon a thin, red-haired girl who sat with her parents near the helicopter's hatch door. She turned in Kyle's direction, and their eyes met. She gave him a smile, and then her attention was drawn away by the sound of the helicopter door latch being opened. Kyle continued to look in her direction. She appeared to be about the same age as him. He wondered if they would be in the same classes.

New students, accompanied by their parents or guardians, assembled in an auditorium where they received their schedules and room assignments. Maps and names of academic advisers were given to students. The luggage had already been placed into the assigned rooms. This was to be Kyle's fifth year of education, but since he had not started at an Academy school, he was scheduled to attend an orientation class for students who had never been enrolled in an Academy school. This was done to help children adjust to and learn any new procedures with which they may not be familiar. Kyle looked at his academic schedule and realized it was nothing like what he was used to in the United States at the regular public schools. Among the traditional fifth-grade requirements were Math, Reading, Composition, Geography, History, Science, Art, and Music, as well as more specialized classes such as Primary Languages,

Secondary Language, Paraphysics, Religion, Martial Arts, and Computer Technology. Some of these classes looked exciting, while others looked a bit foreboding. Religion did not sound like much fun, and he had no idea what Paraphysics was.

As his grandparents gave him loving kisses and hugs goodbye and left with all the other parents and guardians, Kyle finally looked around the auditorium and noticed that most of the students were high school students, a few who looked close to his age, and a few who looked like they were early elementary school students. Once all the guardians and parents said their goodbyes, the new student Academy coordinator came out on the stage and addressed them.

"Greetings to all of you and welcome to the Canadian location of the Academy of Knights," said a cheerful, round-faced man who was a bit plump around the midsection. He was balding on the top and had a thick, bristly walrus-style mustache. "We like to think that the island school is one of the best. I am Sir Knight Wolfram, and I'm the new student coordinator. I will be the person that you turn to when things don't go right or if you find yourself having difficulties. Now, I would like all the Senior Level Squire students to gather over here to the left, the Junior Level Squire students to gather in the midsection, and all the Page Level students to my right."

There was a sudden upheaval among the older students, who immediately got up to sit where Sir Knight Wolfram had requested. Kyle picked up the folder containing his class schedules, maps, and other important papers and found a seat in the area Sir Knight Wolfram had requested. Kyle was in the Page Level student section. He appeared to be one of the oldest students in this group. Ten younger children were sitting with him, all looking scared or nervous. On the other hand, the students at the Squire Level did not appear nervous at all, especially the oldest ones. They looked confident and pleased. There were about twenty of them, and many of them spoke with accents or appeared to be from faraway places.

"Do you mind if I sit next to you?"

Kyle looked up to see a skinny, dark-haired boy with a pale complexion, thick glasses, and soft, dark brown eyes.

"Sure, it's okay with me," replied Kyle.

The boy sat down next to him. He appeared to be the same age as Kyle.

"This is really something, isn't it?" said the boy to Kyle.

"Yah," replied Kyle with a smile. The boy looked like a nerd to Kyle.

Two more adults came into the auditorium and stood with Sir Knight Wolfram.

"Sir Knight Anthony will be working with the Senior Squire Level students, and Lady Knight Andrea will be overseeing the Junior Squire Level students," said Sir Knight Wolfram as he introduced the two other adults, who immediately went to their groups of students while Sir Knight Wolfram approached the youngest.

"Hello, children! How are you all doing? Your parents have left, but if you have any concerns, you are welcome to ask me for help. That's my job," said Sir Knight Wolfram with a twinkle in his eye and a big smile. He was doing his best to reassure the dozen young students who sat before him.

One of the small girls raised her hand.

"What might you need, dear?" asked Sir Knight Wolfram.

"Where's the bathroom?" she asked meekly, and a few others giggled.

"That's an excellent question. One should always know the location of important facilities, such as the bathroom. If you would like to inspect one personally, just go up there and go to the right," Sir Knight Wolfram directed.

The girl smiled, immediately got up, and started to go up the walkway. Another little girl stood up as well, but then stopped and turned to look at the knight who was in charge of their group.

"You can go with her. We would not want her to be lonely," said the knight with a chuckle, and the other little girl dashed off after the other one.

"Well, while they are getting to know where things are, I would like everyone to write their name on a sticky tag, so I can get to know everyone's name. I am terrible with names, so it's going to take me a bit to learn them, and this will help me."

Sir Knight Wolfram handed out pieces of paper with sticky backs and marker pens so everyone could write their name. One little boy made a face and handed the name tag and pen back to the knight. Wolfram looked down at the child.

"You don't know how to write your name?"

The little boy shook his head and tried to mouth the words that he had forgotten.

"Can you tell me your name?" asked the knight gently.

"Timothy," the boy barely replied.

"Good name," said the knight as he wrote the name down on the piece of paper for Timothy. The boy smiled and then peeled the sticky paper off the back of the name tag, placing it on his shirt just like the other children had done.

The girls returned looking much happier and got their name tags done as well. Of the twelve Page Level students, only two were Fifth-year students, and the rest were first-year students, which put Kyle in the company of the skinny, dark-haired boy with glasses, whose name was Geoffrey. Geoffrey generally went by Geoff for short and was a good-natured sort of lad that Kyle found to be favorable company. This was Geoff's first time at the Academy, but he had attended a small charter school in Vancouver, Washington, where he was from. They walked together as Sir Knight Wolfram led the group on a tour of the school grounds, which eventually led to the school dining hall. Today's lunch menu was a choice of sandwiches served with chips, fruit, and juices. Sir Knight Wolfram sat with the group of youngsters, ate lunch with them, and answered any questions or concerns the children might have. The younger children seemed to be bonding with each other as their fears of being away from home seemed to melt away. The hefty knight was good at making everyone feel at ease, and he laughed with them and made sure that no one left the dining room hungry. The rest of the day was spent touring the grounds, showing them the classrooms, and finally, in the late afternoon, where they would be sleeping. There was a boys' wing and a girls' wing of the Page Level students' dormitory, and those areas were divided into five different age groups. The group of children would remain in the same room for their years at the school, but the age designation of their room would change with each year as they matured. This allowed students to feel a sense of familiarity, as they remained in the same location each year until they advanced to the next educational level.

When Kyle and Geoff arrived, there were already twelve boys assigned to the room for fifteen students, so Kyle and Geoff had to choose from the three remaining bed chambers. They were almost like low-walled office cubicles, with an IKEA-style bedroom setup that utilized the space as effectively as possible. This allowed each student to have a bed, nightstand, small desk, chair, and furniture to store clothing and other gear, as well as a lockable footlocker. The space was utilized amazingly well and presented opportunities for personalization by each child, such as displaying photos or posters. This arrangement allowed for some privacy, yet was still part of a large mass bedroom. In the center was a coffee table surrounded by two long couches and two heavily stuffed armchairs for students to relax on. Kyle walked toward an empty space which was along the wall with windows.

"You may not want that one," remarked a curly red-haired boy.

"Why?" asked Kyle.

"It's really drafty. I used to sleep there and was always cold," replied the curly red-haired boy.

Kyle frowned and looked at the space. There was another one in a corner and another across the room, along the wall with no windows.

"But I like having a window near my bed. Is it *really* that bad?" asked Kyle.

"I didn't like it," replied the boy.

Kyle watched Geoff put his stuff in the corner, which would have been his second choice.

"Well, I'll sleep with an extra blanket if it bothers me. Thanks for the warning," replied Kyle. "My name is…"

"Kyle. You're still wearing the name tag," said the curly red-haired boy. "My name is Lothar."

Kyle looked down at the name tag, somewhat embarrassed, and removed it. "Pleased to meet you, Lothar."

Lothar leaned closer to Kyle and said in a whisper, "Some of the others will try to tell you it's a ghost that makes that spot cold, but don't listen to them. They are just trying to have fun with you."

Kyle's eyes widened with surprise, and then he nodded, "Okay, I'll keep that in mind."

Another boy, who was unusually tall and dark skinned, walked up to them and said, "You'd better get yourself unpacked. Dinner will be in about thirty minutes, and on the first night, they don't give us much time after dinner to do our own stuff. You'll be tired and will want to go to bed if you can sleep at all. And that's because DuBois snores like a freight train."

Kyle nodded, walked into his new bedroom for the school year, looked around at his new space, and realized that his luggage was missing.

Lothar, who had been watching him this whole time, said, "Luggage is over there." Lothar pointed to the space by the entrance of their room.

Kyle spotted his bags and hauled them over to his bedroom cubicle, where he started to unpack and organize his belongings. It didn't take him long to get ready for the night. He paused momentarily and looked out the large window that looked out over the airfield, hangars, and the forested area beyond. It was a nice view. He did not feel cold in the bedroom cubicle. He wondered if maybe it was only cold at night or when the wind blew. He remembered that his mom's house in Reno would collect dust on the windowsill when they had super-strong windstorms. He gazed out the window for a few more minutes, lost in his thoughts, and then turned around to see Geoff standing in the doorway of his space, waiting.

"Nice spot, but the others say it's haunted," said Geoff.

"I know," replied Kyle. "I'm not going to worry about it. I like looking out the window."

It was time for the students to go downstairs to the dining hall for the first meal of the year, which often celebrated the return of students and welcomed new arrivals. A special meal was prepared, and later, movies were shown in the auditorium. This welcoming dinner was served like a feast from a Henry VIII movie or something along those lines. Between the meal courses, announcements were made regarding basic school rules and conduct, which were reviewed as a gentle reminder.

"...Students not involved in the aviation courses are to stay off the airfield and out of the hangars unless escorted by an authorized student or instructor," Sir Knight Wolfram read aloud. "And that goes for the helipad as well. We are now offering emergency flights to the residents on a moment's notice as a part of our community outreach program."

Kyle and the other students listened to the announcements, most of which they had already read about in the code of conduct book. The announcement about the emergency helicopter flights was a new thing that got a lot of attention.

Kyle sat with Geoff, Lothar, Tyrrel, the tall black kid, and the boy whom Tyrrel referred to as the loud snoring machine, René Francois DuBois. He spoke with a French accent and was from Paris. He spoke excellent English, and Kyle found the accent not as hard to understand as he expected. René had a large, prominent nose, shoulder-length brown hair, and claimed to come from an old family of knights that could be traced back to the twelfth century. This was one of his favorite topics.

Dinner was excellent, and Kyle found himself enjoying the chance to meet his new classmates and roommates. So far, everyone seemed to be good company. He sat at one of the long tables assigned to the Page Level students and recognized some of the younger children he had met during the new student orientation. He also spotted the thin red-haired girl he had seen on the helicopter in the morning. She was busy chatting with several girls, and then one of her friends noticed that Kyle was looking at her. The other girl pointed in Kyle's direction, and the thin red-haired girl turned to look at Kyle.

Kyle felt his throat tighten. He smiled shyly back at the thin red-haired girl and then acted like he needed to say something to Geoff.

"Where do you know her from?" asked Geoff with appreciation.

"I don't. I just saw her on the helicopter this morning, and she smiled at me then, and well, I recognized her," he replied.

"Well, I think she's pretty. Hey, you got to ride on the helicopter?!" said Geoff.

"Yes, it was cool. Didn't you?" replied Kyle.

"No. My parents had to take me on the ferry boat, and it made me feel sick."

"I see you two are talking about my cousin, Freya," remarked Lothar.

"She's your cousin?" asked Geoff.

"Yes, can't yah tell?" replied Lothar, pointing to his red curly hair and facial structure.

"Well, that could be a coincidence," remarked Geoff. "So did you get to ride in the helicopter?"

"Yes, of course," replied Lothar.

Geoff frowned a bit. Kyle turned to Geoff and said, "My grandfather had to show some special card to the people at the gate. Perhaps your parents will get one next time."

"Not likely. The helicopter is reserved for children whose parents are part of the Order," replied Lothar.

Kyle was about to ask Lothar what order he was referring to when Sir Knight Wolfram announced that those who had finished dinner and wanted to watch the first movie could go to the auditorium, get popcorn and drinks, and watch The Lorax. There was a sudden surge of noise in the dining hall as the younger children rushed to get up and secure a good spot in the auditorium to watch the movie with their friends. The first movie was geared toward the Page Level students, and when it concluded, they exited for bedtime, while the older Squire Level students got to stay up later and watch another movie suitable for older kids.

"Let's go. I liked that movie. The animation was awesome," said Geoff, forgetting about his disappointment about not getting to ride in the helicopter.

"Okay. Are you guys coming too?" Kyle asked Lothar, Tyrrel, and René.

"Why not? But I often find American films to be so obvious," said René as he tossed his hair back.

Tyrrel grimaced at René and said, "Just keep your snooty opinions to yourself, and we shall enjoy the movie."

René shrugged off Tyrrel's rebuff to his comment, and the five boys got up and walked to the auditorium to watch the movie with the other younger students.

It was nine o'clock when Kyle had crawled into bed for the first time, when the main dorm room lights had been turned off. The boys talked to each other in the dark for another fifteen minutes, until one of the older students assigned to be a Dorm Room Assistant came by to tell them to be quiet and go to sleep. Kyle could still hear a few whispers in the dark until no more, and then the sound of someone breathing heavily. Kyle thought it was probably René. All in all, it had been a good day. He wondered what the next ten months would bring.

CHAPTER 6: FIRST WEEK

Kyle heard his personal alarm clock go off. He wanted to wake up a few minutes before the standard school alarm. A few other boys had the same idea and were already moving about in the room. A trip to the bathroom was in order, so he hopped out of bed and grabbed his morning wash-up gear. After getting a quick shower and finishing his morning preparations, he went back to the dorm room and got dressed. Kyle selected a pair of gray trousers and a white, short-sleeved button-up shirt and put on the black shoes that his grandmother had helped him choose. He looked around the Fifth-year boys' dorm room and saw a sea of other boys dressed much like him, with only a few slight variations. It seemed strange to see so many others dressed just like him. School back in Reno was not like that until middle school, nor was it that way in Seattle either. Everyone wore whatever they wanted. But here, Kyle stepped out into the common area for the Page Level students and found himself in a sea of blue, gray, white, and black.

Kyle stood still outside the doorway, looked down into the large common area for the younger children, and watched a group of girls who had gathered together downstairs. They were all chatting merrily and greeted each other as they arrived. The girls had plaid skirts in addition to their wardrobe choices.

"Checking out the wildlife?" a voice said from behind. Kyle turned around to see Lothar. He was smiling broadly, his green eyes twinkling, and the freckles on his face more noticeable in the bright, cheery morning light that poured in from the large downstairs windows.

"I've just never seen so many people dressed alike that were not part of a marching band," replied Kyle.

"Don't you have school uniforms where you are from?" asked Lothar.

"No. I mean, yes, in the private schools like the Catholic ones, but the regular schools for my age group... we all just wear whatever," replied Kyle, still eyeballing everyone. "There are some rules about wearing stuff with rude comments or skirts that are too short. Stuff like that isn't allowed."

"Hmmm. Must be interesting," commented Lothar as Geoff spotted them and came over.

"I'm famished. Where's breakfast? Do we go to the same big room? Can we have it now?" asked Geoff as he stuffed his hands into his black trousers' pockets and stood stiffly with his skinny arms and elbows jutting out.

"Yeah, it's time for breakfast. You look like you need food. Don't your parents feed you?" Lothar asked Geoff.

"Well, yes, but they say I am a bottomless pit where the food disappears into," replied Geoff nervously, adjusting his glasses on his nose. "So, can we go?"

"I was waiting for Tyrrel and René," replied Lothar. "They are my best mates here and we always eat together. You are welcome to join us, or you can go on to get breakfast now."

91

Geoff looked as if he was considering leaving for breakfast, but Kyle spoke up quickly and said, "I think Geoff and I will wait here and eat with you guys. Is that okay with you, Geoff?"

"Uh, ...sure, sounds fine." Geoff really wanted to go and eat, but realized that having friends at a new school might be beneficial, and Lothar certainly seemed like the guy to be friends with.

It wasn't too long before Tyrrel and René came out of the Fifth-year boys' dorm room, bickering at each other.

"I don't care if I'm supposed to like rap music because I'm black. I don't. And I won't be stereotyped like that," Tyrrel said to René as they stopped to join Kyle, Geoff, and their buddy, Lothar.

Kyle, Geoff, and Lothar looked at René and Tyrrel without saying anything.

"I am assuming you three are waiting for us?" asked Tyrrel. "We'd better hurry or else we won't get good seats, and the bacon will all be gone!"

"Then let's go now! I love bacon," remarked Geoff. "Someone, lead the way. I'm still not sure where everything is."

Lothar grinned and led his group of friends down to the great dining hall. Kyle spent his breakfast listening to his new companions discuss various topics concerning music choices this morning, while Geoff wolfed down enough breakfast for two people. Kyle's big concern this morning was figuring out his class schedule. Moving from one classroom to another was not a common practice for the elementary schools that he had attended. He was accustomed to being assigned to a desk where he stored all his belongings, and that was where he spent most of the day, except for lunch, recess, and music class, which only occurred once every other week. Now he had a schedule to follow, rooms to find, and materials to carry. He hoped he would not look like a fool and get lost.

Tyrrel spotted Kyle going over his class schedule.

"Don't worry. You'll get used to it. I came here from Las Vegas in my third-grade year and had to learn this system immediately. Some classes are in the same room, so not all the classes require a room change. Your first class should be Primary Languages: Reading and Composition. Am I right?" asked Tyrrel.

"Yah, how did you guess?" said Kyle.

"Because everyone goes to those classes, even René," replied Tyrrel with a grin revealing his bright white teeth.

"The English language is a mess of other languages and is therefore an abomination," said René, rolling his eyes in disgust as his accent became a bit more pronounced. "Now, French is a proper language. The Canadians are wise in making sure that everyone learns French."

"Don't get me started this morning," retorted Tyrrel to René.

"Come on, guys, let's get upstairs and grab our stuff for class. We'll show you where the first classes are," said Lothar, getting up from the table. "More than likely, we shall have most of our classes together."

Geoff looked up as he finished putting some butter on another muffin. "Are we done already?"

"Yes, and we had better leave before you turn into a great blob," said René.

"It's not going to happen. Everyone in my family eats a lot, and we are all skinny," said Geoff with a smile, taking his buttered muffin along with him.

Kyle discovered that finding the classes was easy, and most classes did not meet daily, so the school week was enjoyable and gave him time to catch up on more challenging assignments. It also seemed to allow the teachers to instruct more involved projects for the lessons. Saturdays and Sundays were reserved for completing homework projects or assignments. This free time also provided an opportunity for the children to play games and socialize with one another. Organized games and activities were often planned for Saturday afternoons, and students had a choice whether to join in or not. This allowed the students to contact family and friends back home if they wished. Kyle planned to call his mother and father on Saturday to tell them about his experiences.

The first class was Primary Languages, which included English and French, since the school was in Canada. He would only attend twice a week, which was quite different from back home, but the class was four hours long.

"I would like to welcome you all to Fifth-Year Page Level Primary Languages. Most of you will remember me from last year's Fourth-year class. I am Sir Knight Mary Sorenson. You may address me as Sir Knight Mary or Lady Mary for short. I am married, so if you call me Mrs. Sorenson, I will not be offended. I see we have a few new faces this year," said the tall, thin elderly woman with steely gray hair. She looked about the room, and Kyle felt her intense, dark brown eyes, framed behind wire-rimmed glasses, fall upon him.

"I would like all the new students to stand up and introduce themselves. Say your name, where you are from, and something about yourself," requested Sir Knight Mary.

Three children stood up: Kyle, Geoff, and a girl with jet-black hair that he had not seen before. Sir Knight Mary requested that the girl start first.

"My name is Hanako Takahashi. I am from Tokyo, Japan. My parents just moved to Toronto for my father's work. He is an expert in banking and financial matters," said the Japanese girl with a heavy accent. Kyle was impressed with how pretty she looked. She looked just like one of the pretty anime heroes from some of his comic books. Her hair was sleek and jet-black, neatly pulled back into a ponytail with a blue ribbon that matched perfectly with the Academy's blue-gray plaid skirt she was wearing.

Geoff was next.

"My name is Geoffrey Powell, no relation to the big bookstore in Portland. I am from Vancouver, Washington, not Vancouver in B.C., and I love computer gadgets and comic books," said Geoff with a smile as he finished and re-adjusted his thick glasses.

It was Kyle's turn. He had no idea what to say. Everyone in the classroom turned to look at him.

"Uh, my name is Kyle Bergendahl. My parents are split apart, so I am from Reno, Nevada, and Seattle, Washington, both in the United States, and I... like comic books too, and archery," said Kyle.

"Very good. Now you may all take a seat. It's good to get to know everyone, since we'll be spending about ten months together, and that can seem like a very long time. I don't plan to assign seats, but if I find too many people chatting instead of working, then I will do that. Please keep that in mind. There are always consequences for our actions in the universe, regardless of good or bad," said Sir Knight Mary.

Kyle hoped he did not sound too stupid when he introduced himself. He felt keenly aware that all the children around him seemed to be very well off or very smart and self-assured. He didn't feel that way at all. He could see Lothar's cousin, Freya, sitting with several girls across the room. She looked like a model of virtue and beauty, and he wondered why he kept noticing her wherever she went. Lothar and Tyrrel had already given Kyle a grin after he had sat down, so his introduction could not have been too bad.

The Primary Languages class went well, except when they started the French refresher lessons. Kyle did not know any French. The Computer Technology class went well, and he knew he would enjoy that one, but the Secondary Language class caused him great concern. While Lothar, René, and Tyrrel went off to their Secondary Language class, Kyle and Geoff found themselves sitting down with Sir Knight Wolfram, who explained to them that the school needed to place them in a classroom with younger children.

"So have either of you ever had any foreign language classes?" Sir Knight Wolfram asked the boys as they sat across a table from the balding knight in an empty classroom.

"One of my aunts is Russian, and she was teaching me some basic phrases, but the Cyrillic alphabet was too hard to learn with the strange vocabulary," Geoffrey offered.

"Hmmm. Well, it's good to know you were exposed to a different language, but unfortunately, we do not have any instructors teaching Russian here anymore," said Sir Knight Wolfram. "Kyle? Any languages studied back home?"

"I heard a lot of Spanish, but I had no idea what was being said," replied Kyle with a less-than-enthusiastic tone. He remembered some of the visits with his mother's relatives in Texas, most especially his cousins. Kyle was pretty sure that the words spoken were not friendly.

"But no actual language studies?" asked Sir Knight Wolfram.

"No, Sir Wolfram," replied Kyle.

"Well, boys, that leaves us with really... only one option. All our students are required to study a second language, and since this location is in Canada, we have to offer two primary languages. Therefore, our standard requirement is for students to learn two languages, which essentially becomes three here in Canada. However, since you have no prior experience with additional languages, we will need to take special measures regarding your situation. With permission and special scheduling with Miss Nadeau, we will place you with the beginning students, who will be the First-year students."

"Oh my god, we will be... social outcasts," sighed Geoff.

Sir Knight Wolfram kindly glanced at Geoff and continued his explanation. Kyle felt a lump sink into his stomach. He felt so embarrassed. What would the others think, he wondered.

"Now, if you can progress rapidly, we can move you up grade levels until you are no longer in need of the extra training," said Sir Knight Wolfram, eyeing both boys to make sure they were fully paying attention to what he was saying. "Perhaps if you both... work together, you can speed up your progress. Teamwork. Well... what do you boys say?"

"I would like that," commented Geoff. "I'm gonna feel kind of stupid sitting in a class with a bunch of first graders."

Kyle wasn't thrilled about the prospect of learning French, and no one seemed to realize that it was a requirement for attending school in Canada. The only positive aspect of this situation was that he was not alone, and Geoff had to take the class as well. And the truth of the matter was that he was somewhat disturbed when Lady Mary, the Primary Languages class teacher, started talking about what she expected them to learn in their French studies. Learning the basics first would be very helpful.

"Yes, I'll work with Geoff. Perhaps we can make a bad situation fun?" agreed Kyle, as he glanced over at Geoff hopefully.

"Then you two shall be a team," said Sir Knight Wolfram with a smile. "I will introduce you both to Miss Nadeau. She is a very kind and patient person and has specially organized the First-year class to have their French lessons starting at two o'clock, when you two would have taken another language class. She will probably have you work in the Rosetta Stone software to help you develop your vocabulary and ear for the language."

"I like computer stuff, so that should not be too bad, right?" Kyle said to Geoff, who nodded in agreement.

Sir Knight Wolfram escorted the boys to Miss Nadeau's large classroom, where she instructed the first, second, and third-year students. She also had two teachers' assistants who helped manage the classroom as she moved around getting projects started. By having all three grades present at the same time, she could move the more gifted students to a higher grade level and keep them challenged. The gifted third-year students were often given extra reading and writing assignments to keep them progressing upward.

By the time Kyle and Geoff had completed their first day of learning basic French with first-year students, they were both looking forward to their first martial arts class. They were both expecting to see their dorm mates, Lothar, René, and Tyrrel, but instead they found themselves in a gymnasium with all the Page Level students. The martial arts classes were focused on skill level rather than age, allowing less skilled children to continue perfecting their training until they were ready to advance. Kyle and Geoff were ushered into the beginning group to start, with the promise that they could advance later. Beginning students were given a wide variety of activities to help them get an idea of what they enjoyed and what they were talented in.

"I am Mrs. Jones, and yes, I am married to the German teacher," she said with a big, broad smile. "And I will be your instructor for the first levels of your martial arts training."

Alison Jones was a petite woman with short, spiky brown hair and bright blue eyes. She was dressed in comfortable clothing that allowed her to move with flexibility.

"So, who here knows what martial arts are?" she asked, watching a sea of little hands go up in the air. She noticed the two unfamiliar, bigger boys who remained motionless in the class of mostly younger children. She called upon a little girl with curly blonde hair.

"Kung Fu," said the little girl.

"That's correct. That is a martial art. Can anyone name another?"

"Karate," answered another child.

"Good. However, karate and kung fu are similar types of martial arts. Can anyone name a different type of martial art?" asked Mrs. Jones.

Kyle remembered that some of his books had referred to archery and sword fighting as martial arts, so he raised his hand, hoping he was correct. Mrs. Jones smiled and called upon him.

"Would archery and sword fighting be martial arts?" suggested Kyle.

"Yes, they are. Archery and sword fighting are excellent examples. Sword fighting is referred to as fencing. Here, at the Canadian location, we offer nine types of martial arts for students to learn: archery, fencing, sword and shield, tai chi, kung fu, wrestling, shooting, stick fighting, and javelin. In this class, we will try each of these for a few weeks, allowing you to experience them all. We will start with archery, then proceed to javelin, wrestling, tai chi, kung fu, fencing, sword and shield, stick fighting, and conclude with target shooting. I hope you all will enjoy trying out these different martial arts. Maybe you will find a favorite."

Kyle was excited to hear that archery would be first. He had never had an actual class in archery, and he knew that Dark Cloud would be terribly jealous of his good fortune. None of the schools back home ever did anything as exciting as having martial arts classes. It was always dodgeball or some sissy version of baseball with a big rubber ball. This was going to be exciting. His mind was racing with numerous hopes and dreams of being the most amazing athlete in his class. He then looked around and realized that his competition looked pretty meager, and there would be no glory in being the best amongst a bunch of little kids. He tried not to let that realization bring him down. He'd still get to do things that he had never done before.

The rest of the class time was spent playing a game that allowed the kids to learn each other's names. They divided into teams, and Mrs. Jones had Kyle and Geoff act as the opposing team captains, who then selected their teammates. By the time they were done playing, everyone knew each other's names and had an idea of who had good balance and could run fast or not.

When class was over, Kyle and Geoff walked back to their dorm room, getting lost a few times along the way.

"You know that was the first time I was ever made captain of a team," said Geoff. "I'm used to being the kid who is always selected last."

"Really?" Kyle said politely, knowing that Geoff's appearance did not exactly inspire thoughts of athletic prowess.

"Yeah, I was always picked last. It was pretty darn disappointing," said Geoff.

"Well, who knows? Maybe your luck is changing," said Kyle with a grin.

Together, they made it back to the dorms in time to drop off their gear and immediately leave for dinner with Lothar, Tyrrel, and René, which made Geoff very happy. He was already complaining that his stomach was rumbling from hunger pains. By the time Kyle found himself back in the dorm room, he felt exhausted. His first day at the Academy had been nothing like he had experienced before, and he felt relieved as he pulled the covers over his shoulder that he had not changed his mind about going to the school. He had a feeling it would be worth all the changes, even learning a new language like French.

The rest of the week went fine and was filled with traditional courses expected of a normal fifth-grade student: math, science, geography, and history. However, Friday was an unusual day that included classes Kyle was unaccustomed to having at all. Friday morning was Art & Paraphysics, and after lunch, there was Religion and Mythology. None of these classes sounded much like fun, except for the art part, which was mixed in with something called paraphysics. What the heck was paraphysics, he mused to himself. Kyle sat down at his computer, which was in his IKEA Bedroom Cubicle, and found an online dictionary website, where he typed in the word "paraphysics."

"The study of the evidence for phenomena such as telepathy, past life recall, remote viewing, psychokinesis that are currently inexplicable by science," Kyle read aloud.

Lothar popped up to look over into Kyle's space, "What are you reading?"

"I'm trying to understand what on Earth … paraphysics is…" replied Kyle as he read through more of the page and read another section aloud. "*Paraphysics is the companion science to parapsychology and psionics. Paraphysics explores the dynamics behind such paranormal aspects as psychic abilities like telepathy, telekinesis, clairvoyance, remote viewing, etc., as well as ghosts and such broad areas as the mind, the soul, and even life itself.*"

Kyle spun around with his brow furrowed and looked over at Lothar.

"What the heck is that supposed to mean?"

Lothar continued to be partially hidden by the wall that separated their bedroom spaces and appeared to be thinking and finally replied, "I think it means the study of stuff we don't easily understand. You know things we can't actually… touch or easily measure."

"Like ideas, concepts, or souls," said Tyrrel, who was eavesdropping as he walked by. "We can't touch them, but we know the stuff exists, or at least we, as human beings, like to argue about them."

"Oh. Okay," said Kyle, nodding his head slowly, mulling over what his new friends said. "So, a friend being taught about being a shaman and talking with nature spirits would be paraphysics, right?"

"Yes, that's my understanding of the word," replied Tyrrel. "So... who do you know is learning to become a shaman?"

"My friend, Dark Cloud, back home in Nevada, said his uncle was going to teach him a bunch of stuff because his uncle was training to be a shaman," replied Kyle.

"Incredible. I wonder what his uncle will have to do to learn shaman work," Tyrrel wondered aloud. "I wonder how he quantifies his results."

"I don't know. I could ask Dark Cloud. I haven't talked with him or emailed him for a week. I should check my email," said Kyle, thinking about the email and realizing that he had been avoiding it since he did not want to find that there were no messages from his parents.

"So, why were you looking up paraphysics anyway?" asked Lothar.

"This weird art class that I have to go to tomorrow," Kyle responded, holding up his schedule and pointing to the class listed there.

Tyrrel took the piece of paper, looked at it, handed it back to Kyle, and said, "This is nothing to worry about. It will be fine. The art teacher explains weird stuff to us because it is the basics or foundations necessary for upper-level Knight Studies."

"Night studies? We have classes at night in the dark?" questioned Kyle.

"No, you incredibly naive fool," said René's voice from another part of the room, his French accent bursting forth more than usual. "It is Chevalier training. You know, like times of old when men rode on horseback and carried swords."

"Knights?!" Kyle exclaimed, "Like real knights?!"

"Yes, didn't you realize that you were enrolled in a school basically for knights?" asked Lothar.

"No. I didn't. I thought the picture of the guy on horseback was just a mascot," replied Kyle. "You mean I could learn how to become a real knight? For real? You guys aren't pulling a practical joke on me or something."

By this time, René and Geoff joined in on the conversation, and they were all huddled around Kyle's space. Xavier Nunez and Trevor Allen Smith also stopped watching TV to listen in on the conversation.

"No, they aren't playing a joke on you. This is truly a school for knights," said Xavier.

"But there are girls here?!" said Kyle.

A couple of the boys opened their eyes wide and rolled them.

"Oh, no dates for him!" Lothar laughed.

"Yes, I would not say that too loud. The girls can be… not so forgiving to the guys who take that… only guys can be knights attitude," said Tyrrel in his normal, official, informative tone of voice. "It would be prudent to keep quiet about that opinion."

"It's not an opinion. I didn't know girls could be knights too," replied Kyle. "This is all new to me."

"How on earth did you manage to come to the Academy?" asked Trevor with a somewhat disdainful tone of voice.

Everyone looked at Trevor and then at Kyle for the answer.

"I picked the Academy after my parents could not agree on a private school for me to go to, so their counselor suggested that I be allowed to select the school," replied Kyle.

"Wow, that's intense," commented Geoff.

"And… I am supposing everyone else here knew exactly what kind of school they were going to," said Kyle.

"Yes, I think that would be a correct assessment of the situation," replied Tyrrel.

"I feel so stupid for not knowing," commented Kyle.

"Well, yes, obviously," retorted Trevor. "This is a prestigious school that only accepts the best students and will make some leeway for the children of knights. How did you get in?"

"They accepted me after I applied," replied Kyle.

"You'll be fine. Don't listen to Trevor, he can be a pretentious ass," said Lothar.

Trevor eyed Lothar.

Trevor gave his usual snooty expression and smoothed back his thick, brown hair, which was always neatly cut and groomed. Lothar mimicked him, running his hand over his wavy red hair. Trevor said nothing but turned away and went back to watching TV with Xavier, who had already jumped back onto one of the soft, cushy couches.

"It's getting late. We should all be getting ready for lights out in fifteen minutes," remarked Tyrrel, looking at his smart watch.

Kyle logged off his computer and shut it down for the night. He turned off his desk lamp and turned around to see Lothar still peering over at him.

"What?" exclaimed Kyle with surprise.

Lothar moved so his forearms rested on the top of the dividing wall and said, "So your parents are not knights."

"No. My dad is a doctor of theoretical and applied physics, and my mom is a medical assistant," replied Kyle.

"Have they ever acted like they were part of something secretive and did not share it with you?" asked Lothar.

Kyle thought for a moment as he went to his bedside and pulled open the covers. The room began to quiet down as the other boys started turning off the equipment and the television. Kyle recalled his father having work projects that required a security clearance, but his father was never secretive about it. He never felt like his father was hiding anything. His mother was not that way either.

"I can't think of anything," Kyle replied in the darkening room.

"Perhaps something will come to you," said Lothar as he started to back away from the wall to get ready for bed.

"Why is it important? Will I have to leave if they are not? Because I don't think my mom is a knight. She didn't want me to go to this school, and my dad seems too busy with his work to do other stuff, but I could be wrong."

"Really. Your mom didn't want you to go? Why?"

"She said it was a military school and all they would do is teach me how to kill, but I thought she was being silly because there are girls here. I didn't think girls were allowed in military schools."

The room grew very quiet, and the sound of René snoring from across the room slowly started. Kyle was now wide awake with hundreds of thoughts passing through his mind.

"Lothar," Kyle said quietly.

"What?"

"I don't want to leave. I like this school even if it means that I must learn French."

Lothar chuckled.

"Don't worry, Kyle. They don't let just anyone ride in the helicopter," replied Lothar. "Go to sleep before René starts to snore loudly."

Kyle tried to relax and let the warmth of his body heat up the bed sheets as he tried to get comfortable. René was not snoring that badly. Rojo was worse if he slept on the bed and would start having dog nightmares right next to Kyle's head, so the light snoring sound wasn't going to bother him. His mind was racing with thoughts about real knights and the fact that he was enrolled in a school where he could become one. He also wondered what Lothar had meant by saying that they don't just let anyone ride in the helicopter. Geoff did not get to ride in the helicopter. And there were teachers here who were real knights. Lothar and his cousin, Freya, got to ride in the fancy high-tech aircraft. He needed to call or email his parents tomorrow. Maybe he could get them to tell him something. He had so many thoughts racing through his mind, taking him in many different directions, that he did not even take much notice of the cool breeze that seemed to float across his face.

Kyle yawned and snuggled his face into the soft pillow, and within moments, he no longer heard René's snoring or took notice of the continuing cold draft that seemed to be moving across his bed.

Kyle woke up the next morning feeling refreshed and realized he was awake almost forty-five minutes earlier than necessary. He decided it would be a good time to gather his belongings for his morning shower and check his email. He had not sent any messages all week because he had been so busy, and he was starting to feel a little guilty for not doing so. He quickly logged into his email account to see if anything had arrived. There were four new emails, and two of them were spam messages that he immediately deleted. The other two remaining were not from either of his parents. He had a message from Dark Cloud and one from his grandmother.

He clicked on the message from his friend.

Hi Kyle,

You wanted to know what the new school was like. It feels very different. Your mom would hate it. It's entirely of our ways, along with another group that is of the old ways of Europe.

I did not know there were other old ways of your ancestral people. I have talked with some of those kids, and for the most part, they seem okay.

I will let you know more later. Perhaps this is something you can do since your dad is half Swedish. I will learn more about these kids and their ways after we go on some field trips and work on projects together.

Dark Cloud

     Kyle wondered what Dark Cloud was referring to. He never knew that Europeans had old ways, like those of Dark Cloud's people. His mind was racing, and he wanted to know more. Without more information, it would be difficult to research, so Kyle sent Dark Cloud an email in response.

Hey Dark Cloud,

Can you find out more? Let me know what this old European stuff is. It would be cool if it were like your people's stuff. Then maybe we could do vision quests together or something like that.

The school here is great. I could be trained to be a real knight. I didn't realize that this was a school for knights. I did not even realize that real knights still existed, except for the ones made by Queen Elizabeth in England. I am really excited about this. And the girls can be knights too. I had no idea. One of my new friends, Lothar, has a pretty cousin, named Freya, who is going here. I saw her on the helicopter ride, which was awesome! And the school is out on an island in a lake! We must take a boat, a helicopter, or a plane to get off the island.

I wish you could be here too, but it sounds like your new school is great. Can't wait to hear more. I don't know if we get to go on field trips.

Kyle

Kyle hit the send button and then clicked on his grandmother's email message. He quickly glanced at the computer clock and knew he still had time to answer another email. He felt somewhat annoyed that neither of his parents had sent him a message.

Hello Kyle,

The house seems too empty without your smiling face. Your grandfather misses the daily horseback riding lessons with you, and Jasper even said he misses the conversations you two would have while he was preparing the food for dinner.

I hope you are having a wonderful time at your new school. Please remember that if, for any reason, you wish to return to the Caledon House, you are more than welcome.

We all look forward to hearing about your progress and seeing you during the next holiday break.

Love,

Grandma

Kyle grinned as he read the message. They missed him. Even the butler. This made the lack of a letter from his mom and dad not so bad. At least someone was thinking about him. He decided he would send messages to both of his parents later, regardless of whether they wrote to him or not.

The whole morning was scheduled for art class, which he was still unsure about. The art room was enormous and had numerous windows that let in the morning sunlight. It was a vibrant, bright space with all the drafting tables and easels that any artist could want in a studio. Kyle had never seen an art room this big. There were small desks for the younger students and spaces on the carpeted floor where bean-bag chairs and handheld drawing boards could be used. He could also hear music faintly playing in one area of the studio. There were cabinets for art supplies and numerous sinks for washing up.

The room had an unusual circular shape, allowing the instructor to remain at the center of six areas, each serving a different purpose. Kyle gazed at the enormous room that was nothing like he had ever seen before. There was a section for relaxing and drawing with markers and crayons. This was the section with the carpet, bean bag chairs, and portable drawing boards. The next art area featured traditional drafting tables that could be adjusted to an angle or laid flat. It was equipped with stools and appeared to be for more serious drawing efforts. The third section had easels arranged in a circle with a central area designated for a still life to be displayed. Then, the area next to that had sturdy, low tables that could be scrubbed and cleaned, and were ideal for basic crafting work. This section was located next to the clay work area, where a few pottery wheels were placed, as well as basic sculpting tables and a rack for storing projects to dry. The final area appeared to be designed for multiple purposes and featured simple drafting tables that could be used for almost any activity. Most of the students sat in this area, waiting for the instructor to address them. It was at this point that Kyle noticed that all Page Level students were present for this class.

The instructor was a woman of average height, appearing to be middle-aged, with long, white hair and large, bright blue-green eyes. She had an intense look about her that made Kyle think he didn't want to get on her bad side. She appeared to be very serious, yet was quick to smile when someone greeted her. She had a drawing tablet connected to a projector that showed an image on a view screen high up on the wall. She wrote her name clearly in drafting-style handwriting. She was Sir Knight Greta Tyrson.

"For those of you new to the Academy," she said in a commanding voice. "Art studies are not divided by age groups but by skill level. Not everyone is a Rembrandt, but everyone needs to learn how to use their imagination and express ideas. Art is the foundation for opening the doors to the mind, where creativity in many forms can emerge. You may wish to become an engineer, mathematician, writer, or medical doctor when you mature, so why should you draw pictures, paint on canvas, model clay, or glue colored paper and other materials together? Because ideas and concepts often need to be expressed in a concrete manner so that we can share them with others. Art also allows us to experiment with ideas as well."

She strolled around the room, clasping her hands behind her back, and surveyed the faces before her. She seemed to note Kyle, Geoff, and the Japanese girl, Hanako.

"I am so pleased to see you all again this year and would like to welcome our new additions, the first-year students, as well as a few new students in the upper years," Sir Knight Greta continued as she walked about the area. "I would greatly appreciate it if the older students, in the tradition of the Academy, would be helpful to our younger and new students. Help them find the materials cabinets and clean-up stations. Everyone is assigned a cabinet for their supplies and projects. Before the class concludes, all materials must be put away so that the area is clean for the next set of students."

Suddenly, a hand flew into the air and caught Sir Knight Greta's attention. She turned to the little girl, whom Kyle recognized as being the one who had asked Sir Knight Wolfram about the bathrooms.

"Yes, do you have a question?"

"Yes. I have never had an art class before. Do we get to paint? My mom would not let me paint because she said it was too messy for children my age," the girl responded in a fashion that mimicked what her mom may have sounded like.

The serious look on Sir Knight Greta's face turned to a bit of a smirk, and she replied, "Yes, you will get a chance to paint. And if you make a mess, the floor in the painting area is washable. We have smocks for the messy projects to keep our clothing clean. Does that answer your question?"

The little girl nodded with a self-satisfied smile.

"Do we have any more questions?"

Kyle watched the instructor eyeball the room of students once more, and no more hands popped into the air.

"Okay, today we have a simple assignment. I want everyone to do their best, as this will help me determine the level of instruction you will need. I want everyone to take a box of crayons and a drawing tablet, which will become yours. Please make sure to put them into your storage locker afterward. And I want everyone to draw a picture for me. It can be anything you want. Something from your imagination. The person sitting next to you. An object in the room that appeals to you. Take your time and don't rush. You have two whole hours to do this. Find a comfortable place to sit and make friends with the other students. You can talk as long as you keep working. If talking is distracting, I will have music playing in the bean bag chair area for those of you who like music instead."

The older students had started to get up and gather drawing materials, so Kyle followed their example and did the same. Lothar, Tyrrel, and René urged Kyle and Geoff to join them at the drafting table, where they joined several other groups of students formed into little groups. Kyle spotted Freya with her friends sitting at the crafting area, where they sat around the table and made themselves comfortable.

"I have no idea what I should draw," stated Geoff in a nervous manner.

"You should draw food, since that seems to be what you think about most," commented René.

"Oh, hey, that's a great idea!" replied Geoff, not realizing that René was trying to be obnoxious.

René frowned as his attempts were foiled by Geoff's good nature and naivety.

Lothar gave Tyrrel and Kyle a sideways glance and smirk.

"What are you going to draw, René?" asked Lothar, expecting to hear an interesting answer.

"I have no idea. These unsophisticated tools that are for children," René eyed the crayons with distaste, "are an affront to my natural artistic nature."

"Yes, but the great masters were willing to draw with burnt pieces of wood and sticks, so if I were you, I would get over being affronted and get to work," came an unexpected remark from behind the group of boys.

Kyle turned to see the instructor, standing behind them, looking quite imperious.

"Yes, Sir Knight Greta," replied René quickly as he opened the box of crayons.

And when Sir Knight Greta disappeared to see the progress of other groups of students, René turned to Lothar. He said something in French that Kyle did not understand, but it did not sound good.

Tyrrel and Lothar laughed while Geoff looked up momentarily, utterly oblivious to the events around him, and then happily went back to work on his composition.

"So, what exactly are we expected to do?" asked Kyle.

"You heard her, did you not?" said René.

"Yes, I heard her," replied Kyle. "I'm just not sure what to draw."

"Anything you want," said Tyrrel. "As long as it falls within the parameters of what Professor Tyrson asked for."

Kyle looked around the room and struggled to find something that he found inspiring. He even looked out the windows, wondering if he could find something that he would want to draw. As he scanned the room for inspiration, his companions started on their drawings. Then his eyes landed upon Lothar's red-haired cousin, Freya, who sat with her friends. The desire to draw her came to him, and then the idea was suddenly pushed aside by fears that he did not understand. He looked around again, but nothing inspired him. He looked back at Freya and her friends. If drawing just Freya made him nervous, then what about all the girls sitting around the table, he wondered. Kyle peered at the table of girls and the sunlight from the window behind them. He glanced at what Geoff was drawing. If Geoff could draw pictures of food, then he could draw a group of girls sitting at a table.

They spent the first hour fairly intent on their drawings, with only a few mishaps by Geoff, breaking three crayons and having to re-sharpen them before he lost his great inspiration. René seemed to ignore everyone as he drew something that made no sense to Kyle. Tyrrel proceeded with a very nice, detailed drawing of a fancy office complex that could have been in Seattle or Toronto, and Lothar was making a picture of a dragon with fire bursting from its open mouth.

"What are you drawing?" asked Lothar as he peered up from the arduous task of putting in hundreds of loops for the scales on his dragon.

"Uh, just some students sitting at a table," replied Kyle.

"Why?"

"I couldn't think of anything else to draw," replied Kyle, not wishing to share his curious desire to draw a picture of Freya. For some reason, he just really liked looking at her, which he found rather odd since he never thought any of the girls back home were all that interesting to look at.

"Geez, my cousin is at that table. You'd better not make her look goofy," replied Lothar after he looked at what Kyle was drawing.

"Well, I'm trying not to make anyone look goofy," Kyle said with a scowl, "Stick to your own drawing."

"That is the reason why I do not draw people. Buildings are straight lines and angles, and buildings do not get upset if they are not pretty enough or too fat," remarked Tyrrel.

"Oh, be quiet, you uncultured peasants. Now this is art," said René as he held up his drawing.

"What is that?!?" exclaimed Geoff. "It doesn't look like anything?"

"This, you guileless buffoon, is abstract expressionistic art. I am using color, shape, texture, pattern, and design to express my feelings of dissatisfaction with these crayons," replied René, sticking his nose in the air and looking down at Geoff and anyone else who would make negative comments regarding his drawing.

Kyle stopped working on his drawing of the girls sitting at the table to look at René's picture. René's picture was a series of shapes and colors arranged artistically, but other than that, Kyle was not sure what it was about.

"Well, I think this is art," said Geoff, lifting up his composition of a plate with a cheeseburger, French fries with ketchup, and a glass of milk.

All the boys turned to look. René rolled his eyes with a sigh of indignation.

"That… is… actually pretty good," commented Tyrrel.

"Yes, I would have to agree," said Lothar appreciatively.

"That could be an advertisement," said Kyle.

"Yes, it appeals to the *common* masses," commented René with folded arms.

"You guys like it?" asked Geoff. "Really?"

"Yah, really," replied Kyle. "That's pretty good."

The boys, except for René, continued to view Geoff's drawing to the point that it caught the attention of Sir Knight Greta.

"What is going on here?" she asked as she came over.

Lothar turned to the art instructor and replied, "We are admiring Geoff's drawing. It looks pretty good."

"Yes, it does capture the food concept," commented Tyrrel. "In a pleasing fashion."

Sir Knight Greta walked over to see Geoff's drawing.

"This is an excellent start, Geoff," she said. She looked intently at his artwork. "Do you feel like you are finished with it?"

Geoff looked at his picture critically and then replied, "Well, I'm not really sure. There is something about it that I would like to be better, but I'm not sure what."

"Come with me and bring your drawing and your crayons. I want you to look at some photos that may help you get some ideas," said Sir Knight Greta.

Geoff picked up his stuff and followed the instructor. Tyrrel, Kyle, Lothar, and René watched Geoff disappear into the computer room with the teacher. They were all quiet for a few minutes.

"I didn't know he could draw that well," remarked Kyle.

"I still don't know," grumbled René.

"I wonder what she wants him to look at," said Lothar.

"She'll probably show him some way to improve his picture. She did that for me. I'm still working on learning perspective, and I am getting better," commented Tyrrel.

"Maybe I should have drawn a landscape instead," mumbled Kyle as he looked at his picture and then at Tyrrel's. "My drawing looks like a cartoon."

"I thought that's what you were going for," remarked Lothar. "You said in class that you liked reading comic books."

Kyle examined what he had done and then realized that if he continued with a comic book style, it might look pretty good. "You know, you're right. That's a good idea."

There was more grumbling from René's direction, but nobody paid attention.

"My cousin's hair is longer than that," remarked Lothar. "And the girl next to her has a rounder face."

"Thaaank you. You tend to your dragon, and I will work on my girls at the table," said Kyle as he got back to work on his drawing with new inspiration.

The rest of the art class went well, and Geoff came back with his cheeseburger picture, which looked even better than before. Everyone turned in their drawings for evaluations, creating a huge pile of artwork for the art instructor to review.

Kyle approached Geoff after he had turned in his assignment and asked, "Hey, how did you improve your drawing?"

"Oh, Sir Knight Greta showed me still life photos of food, and that if I added shadows in the right places, it would make the burger, fries, and glass of milk look more realistic. I had never noticed or thought about the shadows on things. They are everywhere!" remarked Geoff.

Kyle looked about the room and realized that Geoff was right. It seemed like every object and person in the room had a shadow on or under them. He looked down at his hands and clothes. The creases in the fabric of his clothes had shadows, and so did his hands as he held them up. Why hadn't he noticed them before, he wondered. And now he wished he had seen them and would have added shadows to his picture of the girls sitting at the table. It would have made his drawing look better. It certainly improved Geoff's, and it already looked good.

"Geoff, I'm gonna look for the shadows next time I draw a picture. Your picture turned out great," said Kyle.

"Where did you two go to school before?" asked René, looking at Kyle and Geoff with great scrutiny and shaking his head a bit. "Those are basic concepts taught when we learn to draw shapes."

"I've never had an art class that taught us how to draw shapes. We just colored in Thanksgiving Day turkeys, holiday trees, autumn leaves, and sometimes would get to draw and color our own stuff," replied Kyle.

René stared at Kyle. "Then your education was seriously lacking," he remarked, his French accent coming through thickly again.

"Hey, René," said Tyrrel as he joined them. "Calm down, Kyle was attending regular school, and they don't have the funds for the great teachers and cool supplies like we do here. I know, I used to attend one before my parents

124

realized that I would do better in a more advanced environment. Now, when I go home to visit, I can easily do my brother Joey's homework, and he is two years older than I." Tyrrel shrugged his shoulders and said, "I'm just smart, and this school is making me smarter by giving me opportunities to grow and advance in my knowledge base."

René frowned at Kyle, not knowing what to say.

Kyle didn't know what to say either. This made him feel stupid, but Tyrrel, who was probably the smartest of them all, understood that regular schools were different. Kyle hoped that he would do better soon, too. He knew he used to get good grades when he was going to school in Seattle, but Reno was just different, and he didn't feel challenged. And his mom did not have time to spend with him on his homework or anything related to school. Dark Cloud was the best part about going to school down there.

"Hey guys, it's lunch time. Let's get going before all the good food is gone," said Geoff.

"That will not happen until after you have been through the line twice," René grumbled under his breath, not loud enough to be heard by Geoff.

The five boys made their way to the lunchroom, satisfying Geoff's concerns and giving the boys something else to talk about other than previous school experiences, which made Kyle happy. René could be a real jerk at times, but Kyle knew he was right about some of the observations he made. They may not have sounded nice, but they were true. He had not learned much about real art in his old school.

Once again, Kyle found himself purposely sitting on the side of the table, which allowed him a good view of Lothar's cousin, Freya. He started to realize that something was happening with him and her. It wasn't how she dressed, because the other girls wore the same clothes. Nor was it anything else that seemed logical. It was starting to bother him, so he decided to stop noticing where she was.

Lothar noticed the strange expression Kyle was making.

"Are you alright? You look ill or angry?"

"Naw, I'm fine. I… have to call my parents tonight and let them know I am okay," responded Kyle, thinking up something quick. "They can be tough to get a hold of, and I have to call them separately."

"Oh," nodded Lothar appreciatively. "You just had that look on your face like…"

"…like there was a bad tomato in his sandwich," said Geoff with an inarticulate mouthful.

Kyle just smiled and went back to eating his lunch. It was true. He did have to call his parents tonight, and they could be difficult to contact, especially his mom on Friday night. She enjoyed going out with Anita and Carol. Kyle recalled spending many Friday evenings alone with Rojo, and if he had been lucky, Dark Cloud had been allowed to spend the night. Now, Rojo would have to spend the evening by himself.

Even though the rest of the afternoon was filled with more classes, he found his thoughts centering around Rojo and his parents. He wondered if Pickles was ever lonely, too. Perhaps being away from his parents would be just a little harder than he realized. That evening, Kyle called his mother shortly before Carol and Anita showed up to take her out dancing. Kyle asked her how Rojo was doing, and she said that the little dog was fine but seemed to miss him. She told him that she missed him too, and before the conversation could get too complex or involved in what he was doing at school, Carol and Anita showed up, and his mom had to end the phone call.

Then Kyle called his dad to see what he was up to and let him know how school was going. His dad had more time to listen to what his son had to tell him, but he was also somewhat preoccupied. Finally, Kyle asked his dad what he had been doing, and his dad explained that a quantum physicist consultant was coming to his workplace on Monday to work on a project. His father wanted to read all the papers written by this man before he arrived. This was the first time he would meet Dr. William Sikkens, and he wanted to make sure he was familiar with the guy's work. Kyle's father proceeded to discuss Hamiltonian equations, explaining that they worked well for classical mechanics but not so well for quantum mechanics. Kyle was utterly lost for the next ten minutes of conversation until his dad said he had a lot to review before Dr. Sikkens arrived on Monday.

"I miss you and love you, Sport. I'll drop you an email soon. Good-bye," said Jon Bergendahl before Kyle fully realized the conversation was over.

127

He was left with the silence of the empty dorm room and wondered if Rojo felt the same starkness in the air when he was left alone all day. Then his ears caught the sound of laughter coming from down the hallway. It sounded like some of the guys. Kyle got up and decided he wanted to be with people more than ever, right now.

CHAPTER 7: THE FABULOUS FIVE

Kyle had survived and enjoyed his first month of school and had been lucky enough to find four new friends. This was more friends than he had ever had before, and it was a wonderful feeling. He would finally get to hang out with them for a whole school year without the fear of them moving to another school or his parents deciding that he should live at a different location. The idea appealed greatly to him. He had already finished his homework for the evening and quickly wrote to his grandmother, letting her know that things were going well and that he missed them. He told her about his new friends and about his new classes. At times, he felt somewhat behind the others, especially in the foreign languages, but he had Geoff to hang out with, and together they progressed well as a team. He told his grandmother about the embarrassing fact that he and Geoff had to be with the little kids in the French class. However, according to Miss Claire Nadeau, he and Geoff were progressing well and should be allowed to study with the second-year children in a few months.

Kyle also wrote that he was looking forward to winter break and hoped his dad would find the time to visit during the school vacation. He already knew better than to ask his mom since she had told him she might be going down to Texas for Christmas. She had also hinted that she might look for other jobs while she was there, and he was not to be surprised if she decided to leave Nevada and return to Texas.

Kyle had finished his email letter to his grandma and pulled open the notebook he was supposed to write in every day. It was called a journal. But it seemed more like a diary to him, which he did not like the idea of doing. It seemed so... girly. He did not want to write about his feelings or the boring events of the day. But events and feelings kept coming to him while he sat there with a pen in his hand. It also had to be handwritten and not done on an electronic device. He tried to ignore the angry feelings that his mom might move away from Reno. But these thoughts wanted to be spilled upon the blank pages for this day's entry.

Finally, he could think of nothing he wanted to write about and resolved to document the weather instead. That got boring as time went on. He was required to write at least three complete sentences, and if Sir Knight Mary discovered that he was only doing three basic sentences, his grade would go down. So, with a bit of reluctance, he began to express how he did not want his mom to move from Reno, as it would make it hard for him to see Dark Cloud again. He described how Nevada could be lovely and lonely all at the same time. How could it be beautiful and ugly all at the same time? It was a strange high-desert climate. It was nothing like the beautiful area where Lake Simcoe was located, or like where his dad lived in Seattle. Those places were easily and obviously beautiful, with tall trees, numerous rivers, and lakes. He did not like Texas for some reason. Perhaps it reminded him of the aspects of Nevada that he disliked.

Kyle set down his pen after he had written two paragraphs in his journal. That was enough of that, he thought. He could not imagine why anyone would, of their own free will, write in a journal or diary. He sat still for a moment and listened to the sounds of the dormitory room for the Fifth-year boys. He could hear others typing and rustling through papers. He wondered if anyone else had finished their homework for the night. He wanted to escape his cubicle bedroom and do something fun. He got up and found Lothar sitting in the center area, wearing headphones and playing one of the video games.

Lothar momentarily looked up at him and then paused the game.

"Do you want to play 88Day Race Cars with me? I am currently driving through the Swiss Alps. It's crazy with avalanches, giant snowballs thrown at you by Snow Trolls, and the Swiss Police stopping you for driving too fast through a village. It's great fun," said Lothar with a smile as he pushed back his red hair away from his face.

"Okay, I've never played, but I am willing to learn," replied Kyle.

"Terrific. It's more fun with several players. We can work together against the guys in the black and gold cars. They are the bad guys for this game," replied Lothar as he grabbed a set of headphones and handed them to Kyle. "We have to use these, so we don't bother the others while doing their homework."

Kyle placed the headphones on his head and adjusted them for comfort. He could hear the music and instructions for the game. He watched Lothar reach to the side of the headset and pull down a mic that made him look like a pilot. Kyle did the same, and he could hear Lothar.

"Talk quietly, if you must. The mics allow us to hear each other easily, but try not to talk too loudly, or else we'll get yelled at."

"I take it you have done this before," replied Kyle as quietly as he could without lifting the headphones off his ears.

Lothar smiled at him, pointed to the screen, and explained the game to Kyle. It was easy to learn, as Kyle controlled the make-believe car. The setup was similar to his old Wii, which he had loved playing. He had never seen this game setup before and asked Lothar about it.

"It's a prototype done by the Knights of the Order. We get to play with it and test it out for them," replied Lothar. "The rumor is that they will make a VR version of the game."

"Sounds like fun," said Kyle.

Kyle suddenly felt a surge of pride go through him. The knights could do a lot of things, and they weren't just restricted to guarding old castles or fighting battles. They had many professions and did a wide range of things, which appealed to him. The idea that he could train to be a knight when he was older seemed almost like a dream or a fictional story.

He sat with Lothar for about ten minutes, and they started the game over when René came by, pushing his long brown hair back away from his face, revealing his very prominent nose and soft brown eyes.

"I want to play, too," he announced as he picked up a set of headphones, turned them on, and talked into the mic before putting them on.

Lothar, who was in control of the game, hit the pause button again while René secured the headphones and used them to hold back his shoulder-length hair.

"Which team are we on?" asked René.

"We are the red and white team," replied Lothar.

"Uh, as it should be," remarked René, getting comfortable in an armchair next to the couch that Lothar and Kyle sat upon.

Together, the three of them zoomed their digital cars through the Swiss Alps at record speeds, avoiding avalanches and giant snowballs thrown at them by frosty-looking snow trolls that seemed to hate anyone driving near their mountain lairs. What more could a boy of ten ask for?

It was Friday morning, and it was time for Art & Paraphysics. The group of five boys walked down to the enormous studio space for art instruction, and Kyle still felt like he did not understand what paraphysics had to do with art. Sir Knight Greta accepted the homework from the previous class session. She then assigned the next drawing assignment for the three levels of art instruction within the Page Level student session.

"Anyone with questions?" she asked.

Kyle raised his hand in the air with vigor. The elderly female knight noticed him immediately.

"Where does paraphysics come in? What is paraphysics?" asked Kyle.

"Good question," replied Sir Knight Greta. She appeared to be collecting her thoughts, pausing for a few minutes, as if she were collecting data in her mind.

"Let me start this out with a short story, if you will, in another direction," she started. The class was quiet and transfixed. Unknown to Kyle, Sir Knight Greta rarely told stories or spoke much.

"As a Tyrsman, a follower, a student, or companion to Tyr, for those of you who are younger and have not gotten very far in your religious studies... I wanted to define what it meant to be a person who related best to Tyr. I wanted to understand what it meant to want to follow in his footsteps. People who are Thorsmen, Odinsmen, Buddhists, or even followers of Christ all appear to have well-defined practices of what it means to be mentored by that entity. Some individuals are better at it than others, while others struggle to follow their mentor's teachings. I often wondered if I seemed off target. Was I floundering, showing the world my lack of understanding? I had observed misconceptions about who Tyr really was and had to work to define my understanding and relationship with him independently. I also struggled with the fact that I appreciated and enjoyed the company of all the other entities that were a part of the traditional northern western European spirituality. Some of these beings also belonged to other pantheons, such as the First Nations teachers or gods, which left me confused by the conflicting attitudes of some Asatru or Heathen followers. Our path is not stagnant; it is dynamic. It changes as humanity evolves and grows, unlike many Middle Eastern spiritualities, which have very defined and unchanging ideas. I often wondered if Tyr would be annoyed that I also honored and learned from other entities. It seemed strange to ignore them."

Sir Knight Greta looked about at the classroom filled with students. They all seemed very interested in what she was saying, so she continued the story as she slowly moved around the room like usual, watching and observing her students.

"Eventually, I realized that Tyr, also known as Sky Father, is not a jealous entity. It's not in his nature. His true nature is shown in the unique image often associated with him – the Irminsul. The Irminsul is a stylized looking device that is a long staff or stand with a T-shape at the top," said Sir Knight Greta as she went to the drawing board that projected images so the entire class could see visually what she was explaining. She proceeded to draw a version of the Irminsul.

"I woke up one morning realizing that this strange device that looked like a ball with wings centered on a stick, balancing, was like an old set of scales. You know the ones that we see the image of Lady Justice holding in her hands." She paused to look at her students.

Kyle was listening and watching intently. Some of these images and ideas he had never heard of before. At the same time, his other Fifth-year classmates had already had several years of religious studies and understood some of what Sir Knight Greta was referring to.

"While the Irminsul is not necessarily a scale to weigh or judge things, it does balance at this center point. And one of Tyr's primary traits is balance," said the elderly knight.

A small hand shot up in the air with a question, and the art instructor acknowledged the First-year student.

"So is Tyr like a tight rope walker?" asked the First-year student.

Sir Knight Greta smiled and replied, "That activity does require balance, but what Tyr advocates is balance, which is a much broader concept. He is about the balance of nature and the universe. We need balance in our lives. If we only learn from one entity, then there is no balance. Remember what I said about Tyr – he is not a jealous god or mentor, so when I woke up that morning after wondering what it meant to be a Tyrsman, my question was answered. By working and learning from others, I was living a balanced existence."

She paused for a moment and then looked at Kyle.

"You wanted to know what paraphysics had to do with art class…" The art instructor replied as she moved her long white hair back. "Art is about making ideas, thoughts, concepts, and feelings into a visual format and making those intangible ideas more concrete and sharable with others. Architects and engineers do this all the time; they must learn how to express ideas clearly, and visual tools are essential to ensure that everyone understands precisely how the project is to be done. And, of course, images can transcend time and language barriers. I have not yet read that Tyr's Irminsul is a symbol of balance, but I have come to understand this idea through its visual representation and some paraphysical communication. Perhaps someone wrote that down somewhere, but it never arrived at my doorstep in that form; the information was delivered via imagery in a most useful dream and verified in meditation. Paraphysics seeks to define an empirical understanding of things that fall outside traditional understanding. Things we have not advanced enough as a civilization to understand scientifically. It is outside of normal physics, such as when a Jedi lifts an item into the air. What is that? How do they do that? Paraphysics is working towards giving solid explanations for these events."

Sir Knight Greta concluded her explanation and then asked, "How many of you have seen cartoons where no one speaks or there is almost no dialogue? Think about it. I think there have been several cartoons where no one speaks."

The instructor watched a few hands go up in the air, but not enough to satisfy her point.

"Tomorrow, we will watch *Paperman*, and you will see how images alone can convey a story without needing language. This is a very powerful tool," said the art instructor. "Please continue working on your assigned projects for the rest of the class period."

Kyle, Geoff, and Lothar were in the intermediate-level art class while René and Tyrrel went off to work with the advanced art students. Sir Knight Greta had decided that Lothar still needed to improve his basic skills before being allowed into the advanced group. Geoff and Kyle both required training in the basics, although both showed great promise after the first test assignment.

"So how many of these darn ellipses must we draw?" asked Geoff as he opened his sketchbook.

"She wants fifty of them," replied Kyle despondently.

"My arm is going to fall off before I finish that many ellipses," retorted Geoff as he waved a skinny white arm into the air.

"Yah, me too," replied Kyle as he continued to draw the first ellipse.

"What did you think of Sir Knight Greta's story?" Lothar asked Kyle and Geoff.

"It does sorta look like something balancing," said Geoff. "My grandma has a set of old scales that look like that."

"I'm still not sure I understood what it all meant. We never studied religions or mythologies back home. People tend to get too upset about things like that. I don't even understand what a Tyrsman is," replied Kyle. "It all sounded like stuff that my mom would get super upset about, and my dad would simply say it's nonsense."

"I see. Do you know what saints are?" Lothar asked Kyle.

"Yah, according to my mom, they are people that did good deeds, but the Catholics worship them, and that is wrong," replied Kyle.

"Wow!" said Lothar, starting to laugh. "Your mom has some very intense opinions."

"Yeah, I don't like religion. She thinks that everyone else is wrong and only her church is right," Kyle replied with a scowl, revealing some of his frustration.

"Man, what church does she go to?" asked Geoff as he broke another pencil tip onto his paper and started to search through his pencil box for another drawing pencil.

"She attends... God's First Choice Baptist Ministries Church," Kyle replied, growing somewhat uncomfortable with the topic.

"Never heard of it," replied Geoff. "We have a lot of Apostolic Lutherans in our area back home. Actually, there are a lot of different churches back home, but I have never heard of that one. My parents only go to church on holidays. I don't even know which group we belong to. I don't see why it matters."

"I'm not sure I do either," Kyle replied as he finished his first ellipse and proceeded to his second one.

"The reason why it matters is because they all argue about little details," replied Lothar. "And sometimes these little details start big wars. Look at European history for an example."

"Creepy. I don't understand why people can't just leave others alone. It seems dumb to me," said Geoff as he started his ellipse with the new drawing pencil.

"I agree," said Lothar.

"I don't want Archery to end," said Kyle, since he wanted to change the topic of discussion to something he was more comfortable with.

Lothar looked at him.

"The topic of religion really bothers you, doesn't it?" observed Lothar.

"I just don't find it… all that interesting," Kyle lied.

"You do seem pretty uptight about it," said Geoff as he finished some more ellipses.

"Well," Kyle paused as he continued to draw and did not look up. "You guys may be right. I don't mind the classes about the different ideas and stories around them, but I hate the arguing and bullying of other people to force them into believing 'what you want them to attitude'. It gets old."

Kyle had flashes of several arguments his parents had had over the years, many of which were very upsetting.

Kyle finally looked up from another finished ellipse and said, "I still don't want archery to end."

"Neither do I," said Lothar as he sketched out the crosshairs that helped him build a properly shaped ellipse.

140

"And I can see why you don't want it to stop either. I think you are probably the best in the class."

"You think so?" asked Kyle.

"Yes, you are the best in the class. Everyone knows it," said Geoff. "We'll all be struggling trying to get steady and focus on the target," Geoff explained while making wild gestures with his long, skinny arms. "And you will be all like this. Calm and composed."

The flailing arm gestures caught the instructor's attention.

"Geoff," hissed Lothar, "You caught the attention of Sir Knight Greta."

"So how are we doing over here?" she asked with her blue-green eyes flashing a bit as she quickly examined everyone's single page of ellipses.

"Geoff was just explaining how good an archer Kyle is," replied Lothar.

"I see," said Sir Knight Greta. "Judging by the wild arm gestures, I should stay inside while Kyle takes his shots."

"Oh no, it's not like that, Sir Knight Greta," said Geoff apologetically. "Kyle is actually… a wonderful archer. I was describing how everyone else was compared to him."

Geoff smiled as if that made everything okay. Lothar wrinkled his brow at the idea that he should be included with the groups of people unable to control their arms and aim properly. He did not consider himself to be that bad.

"Speak for yourself, Geoff. I don't shoot that way," retorted Lothar under his breath.

"Well, regardless of how everyone is shooting… less gesturing and more drawing… You three are well behind the group over there," replied the white-haired instructor as she gestured to a table filled mostly with girls, one of whom was Lothar's cousin.

"Yes, Sir Knight Greta," said Kyle, acknowledging her desire for them to be further along.

After she was out of earshot, Kyle commented, "This is hard to do without some fun conversation. It is so boring drawing all these ellipses."

"I agree," said Lothar as he looked past Kyle and at the instructor who wandered quietly through the large studio classroom. "Have you ever noticed how quiet she is? She barely makes a noise when walking."

"She's like a ninja," commented Geoff as he proceeded to break another pencil lead.

"More like a well-trained knight," remarked Lothar as he continued to watch her. Sir Knight Greta started to turn in their direction, and Lothar quickly turned his head down and proceeded to create the upper left curve of his ellipse. "It's like she knows when people are talking about her," continued Lothar, keeping his eyes down on the paper and making the upper right side of the ellipse.

"I need to sharpen my pencils," said Geoff, getting up with a handful of broken-tipped pencils.

Kyle watched as Geoff got up and went to the pencil sharpeners. He had a variety to choose from, including electric, old-fashioned, stationary hand cranks, as well as small handheld sharpeners for special-color pencils. Then he noticed that Lothar was watching the instructor again.

"What's up?" asked Kyle as he turned and looked at Sir Knight Greta. She instantly turned in their direction. Kyle smiled and then turned back to his drawing, as did Lothar.

"She knows when someone is talking about her," commented Lothar.

"Are you sure?" asked Kyle.

"It seems like it," said Lothar. "The rumor is… that she is a high-level knight and might even be a part of the Order's leadership."

"But she's a girl…" Kyle, realizing what he said, stopped speaking.

"There you go again," said Lothar.

"I can't help it. All the stories I have read have only men as knights, and there are seldom any female leaders," replied Kyle.

"You like the Harry Potter series, right? And Hermione is a powerful witch, often portrayed as the most talented in her class," replied Lothar.

"Yes, but she's not the main character, Harry is, and he is a boy. And she's more like those nerdy, brainy girls you have in every class, kind of like a Lisa Simpson," replied Kyle.

"Who is like Lisa Simpson?" asked Geoff as he returned with a handful of finely sharpened pencils.

"Hermione," replied Kyle.

"Hermione, who?" asked Geoff, feeling utterly confused.

"Never mind. It would take too long to explain. The point is that our instructor… is not a low-level knight," replied Lothar.

"Oh, okay," Geoff responded as he sat down. "Does that matter? I still am not sure I understand the whole knight component of the school, anyway. My parents just wanted me to get a good education."

"For those of us with parents who are knights, it is interesting," replied Lothar. "Most of the time, our parents do not share any important stuff about the Order with us. They say it would endanger us, and some of us… meaning… René, Xavier, Trevor, and Tyrrel like the idea of figuring out what they are doing. What's the big secret?!"

"I thought Tyrrel's parents were not knights," commented Kyle.

"They aren't, but Tyrrel wants to be a knight, and he's a perfect candidate for being accepted," said Lothar as he searched his page for enough space to start another ellipse.

"So, what makes him a perfect candidate? I think I want to be a knight," said Kyle.

"Tyrrel is super smart, and he's a great guy. You can count on him to be trustworthy and honorable about everything. He and René argue about stuff, but they enjoy that. They would be lost without each other. Tyrrel will do great at whatever he wants to when he grows up," said Lothar, deciding that a new drawing page was necessary to continue the assignment.

"Hmm. I may not be smart enough to be considered then. My grades at my last school were not very good, and I have noticed that I seem to be falling behind in everything. Heck, I am just learning a second language, and you all are starting a third one?" said Kyle.

Kyle let out a deep sigh.

"I'm not. I'm with you, Kyle," Geoff added to the conversation. "Speaking of languages, we have a vocabulary quiz today in French, and we did not practice last night. Do you think we'll have time after lunch?"

"Oh, I forgot about that," said Kyle, feeling a bit overwhelmed.

"Maybe if we get our ellipses done before class ends, I can quiz you both," said Lothar.

For the next couple of days, Kyle kept an eye out for Sir Knight Greta, and Lothar was right about her being super stealthy. She seemed to sneak up on people without even trying, and on top of that, Kyle was never sure which age group she belonged to. She had white hair, like that of an elderly woman, with a few lines on her face, but she was energetic, dressed in sporty school attire, and was well-versed in current trends, which made her seem younger. She did not wear old people's clothes or act like a normal senior-aged teacher. She was undoubtedly an enigma. But what was truly pressing on Kyle's mind lately was that archery lessons would end soon and be replaced by the Javelin class. He did not want archery to end. He loved the feeling of walking up to the target, lifting his bow, pulling the string taut, then shutting everything out of his mind and putting it at a comfortable distance, and simply focusing on the target. And when he felt that he had his sight on target, he gently squeezed the trigger device he had grown so comfortable using. The device would release the bow's string, and the arrow would be sent forward, zooming toward the distant target. He often had arrows grouped in sections the size of an American silver dollar, and on better days, his arrows were grouped together in the size of a quarter. He was skilled at archery, and it was a wonderful feeling to be good at something.

The fact that Geoff and Lothar both said he was the best in their class also made him feel very proud, and he did not want to lose that feeling of accomplishment. He wanted to go further and learn more, but archery was scheduled to end. Today was the last day of Archery lessons, and Kyle had very mixed feelings. The instructor, Alison Jones, planned a class competition to wrap up the year's archery lessons.

"Hey, look, it's the fabulous five," commented one of the Fifth-year girls who tended to hang out with Lothar's cousin.

146

"Hello, Ivy," said Lothar.

"Are you five now a gang?" asked Ivy, who had dark curly brown hair, a large nose, soft olive complexion, and deep dark brown eyes that exuded life.

"No, Ivy. We are not a gang. I would never belong to such a group of people," retorted Tyrrel with a bit of edge in his voice. The idea of being part of a gang was something that Tyrrel found offensive since his hometown was Las Vegas, Nevada, and from time to time, there were serious gang problems there. He hated it when people assumed that he was part of a gang because he was black.

"Are you sure? You all seem to hang out a lot together," said Ivy to no one in particular, ignoring the tone in Tyrrel's voice. "I have not been introduced to your new friends."

"Ivy, this Kyle Bergendahl," said Lothar, gesturing to Kyle.

"Oh, I know who you are. You're the boy who is always watching Freya. You'd think you had a crush on her or something," said Ivy as she took Kyle's hand and shook it. "By the way, she thinks you're cute." Then Ivy turned her attention to Geoff and said, "But it's this cutie that I wanted to meet."

"Ivy, this is Geoff Powell," said Lothar.

"Hi there, no relationship to the store," said Geoff, turning pink with a nod and a smile to Ivy.

"Oh, you are so dear, aren't you?" replied Ivy to Geoff. Then one of the girls from Freya's group of friends called out to her. "Oh, I must get back to my friends. They just can't do without me."

The five boys watched as Ivy rejoined her friends, who then erupted into more conversation and giggles.

René took a deep breath and watched the group along with the others.

"Ivy Rosenplat-Levi is the only Jewish child who has gained entrance into the Academy. She's sort of a celebrity," commented René.

"Why is she the only Jewish child in the Academy?" asked Kyle.

"The Academy does not appeal to all religious backgrounds, and there are plenty of prestigious private Hebrew schools that Jews could send their children to," replied Lothar.

"So why is she here?" asked Geoff. "Do you know?"

"They won't say where she and her family came from, but they lived in a place where you had to be Christian or Islam not to get bullied or worse. The rumor is that her family was in danger, and they had helped some of the knights, so the Order offered to allow Ivy to attend one of the Academy locations where she could get an education and be safe," replied René.

"Wow, kind of like witness protection," said Geoff, still feeling a bit flustered by the compliments he received from her. "I think she's nice."

"Well, at times she can be nice and other times a pain in the butt," remarked Lothar.

Tyrrel and René laughed.

"What's so funny?" asked Geoff and Kyle.

"Ivy helped Freya play a practical joke on Lothar one time, and he still hasn't forgotten it," replied Tyrrel as he and René continued laughing.

Lothar just pursed his lips and said nothing.

Before Kyle and Geoff could ask them to elaborate, the martial arts instructor called all the students to attention and to line up.

"Line up in your shooting groups. Everyone gets three arrows. Take your time and do not rush. All who hit one arrow within the target circle will get to go on to the next level. Remember to wait for everyone in your set to finish shooting before going down to retrieve your arrows," said the short female instructor as she scanned the students who started to fall into their shooting groups.

Kyle, Geoff, Lothar, René, and Tyrrel were all in the same shooting group, along with ten other students who were mostly younger, except for Hanako and Trevor, who had their younger brothers alongside them. Hideaki and Andrew were both second-year students and had become instant friends. Perhaps their friendship had been encouraged by the fact that both of their families were involved in the banking industry. The older students would shoot first to avoid causing the younger children to feel under pressure, while the others waited. René, Tyrrel, Kyle, and Lothar all made it past the first round, but Geoff had a hard time focusing on his target and being comfortable with his bow. He completely missed one of his three shots, while the other two hit the board but did not hit within the target circle. Geoff was disappointed, although he did not appear to be surprised.

The second round was reduced to ten students shooting in their group. The second round had to hit all arrows within the target circle to advance. This reduced their group to nine. The third round required all arrows to land within the target circle, and at least one arrow had to land within the blue target ring or better. Kyle was well within this requirement and advanced along with Lothar, René, Tyrrel, Hanako, and Trevor, which meant that only six of their shooting group would go on to the fourth round. The fourth round required that all arrows land within the red perimeter or better to advance to the fifth round. Trevor, Tyrrel, and Lothar had arrows that landed outside the red target perimeter and were left out of the fifth round of shooting. Kyle noticed that their shooting group had been reduced to three people and saw that the other ten groups had also been drastically reduced. Some groups were eliminated entirely from the competition.

Hanako seemed very pleased that she had made it to the fifth round of the competition but was very nervous about the next set of arrows. Kyle was enjoying the challenge and felt that the previous shots had been great warm-ups for the more challenging ones. Most of his arrows had landed within the red zone, and some in the gold. The sixth round required that all three arrows land somewhere within the gold zone, which was the innermost circle of the target.

Hanako was the first up for this round and let loose her first two arrows that landed within the gold zone, although very close to being in the red zone. Kyle and René could tell that she was nervous as she raised her bow with the last of her three arrows. Kyle could see Hanako's arm slightly tremble, either from fatigue or stress. She let go of the final arrow, which landed in the blue zone. She sighed and dropped her head in disgust.

"Hey Hanako, those were pretty good. Isn't that your best set of arrows so far?" asked Kyle.

Hanako, looking upset, seemed to think about what Kyle had said, then smiled. "Yes, that was the best set of arrows I have done so far."

Kyle grinned at her and nodded his head.

Then it was Kyle's turn, and all his arrows landed within the target's gold zone. Kyle smiled and then turned to René, who was up next.

"Good job. Now let's see if I can continue with you," said René.

When the range was clear, René pushed his long hair behind his ear, pulled his first arrow, and made it land safely within the center area of the gold zone of the target. The next arrow landed on the edge of the gold and red zone. René said something in French under his breath that Kyle did not understand. Then he proceeded with some effort to calm himself and place his third arrow well within the gold zone.

"That was great!" exclaimed Kyle.

"But it may not count," retorted René, angrily thrusting his shoulder-length brown hair out of his face.

"Oh, I see what you mean. It does look rather close to the red area," replied Kyle, looking back down the range.

The students who were acting as arrow retrievers called for Instructor Alison Jones to decide on René's third arrow. René walked down to see exactly where his third arrow had landed, and much to his dismay, the third arrow was more on the red side than within the gold zone, and the instructor had to decide that he had not made it to the next round of competition. The moody French boy walked back up to where Kyle was standing and shook his head.

"I did not make it. It's up to you to win honor for the Fifth-year boys in this competition," he said as he patted Kyle on the back and walked off to sit with Tyrrel, Lothar, and Geoff.

This statement made Kyle feel a bit nervous for some reason. He did not want to let his new friends down.

The final round would be based purely upon who got their arrows closest to the center of the target. Only ten remained out of one hundred and fifty students, and Kyle was one of them. All ten finalists would shoot simultaneously, with only five advancing to the final round, where they would compete for placement ribbons. Kyle glanced down at the row of competitors and was shocked to see that Freya was one of the finalists. Then he heard someone from the crowd yelling, "You'd better stop staring at Freya!"

It was that Ivy girl. Kyle thought he must have turned ten shades of red. He kept his face away from the crowd and turned his attention to the target. It was just him, the bow, the arrow, and the target. He lined up the site with its destination and tried to think about holding still and closing his fingers on the release tab without jerking. The first arrow flew, and it went to the gold area of the target. Kyle took a breath and calmly picked up his second arrow, placed it into the bowstring, and pulled back. He calmly looked down at the target and reminded himself to relax and allow all other noises and thoughts to flow past him. He let the second arrow loose, and it also landed in the gold zone of the target. One more arrow, Kyle thought to himself as he reached for the last one. A slight breeze moved across his face, and he paused to look at the trees to see how the leaves and branches were moving. They had stopped again. He needed to be mindful of any strong crosswind that could disrupt his aim. He placed the last arrow and readied his bow. He focused on the target and felt no breeze across his face, and the tree branches in the distance seemed calm as well. Gently squeezing the trigger to let the arrow release was his main thought.

The third arrow landed in the gold zone of the target. Would his three shots be good enough to take him to the final round? Kyle finally looked around at the other archers. Most of them were done. He looked at Freya. She looked lovely, holding a bow in her hands. Freya looked over at him and smiled. He returned the smile and nodded to her in appreciation of her last shot.

Waiting for the judges to calculate the results seemed to take forever as Kyle stood with the other finalists. Then, Instructor Alison Jones approached the ten finalists.

"I want you all to know how proud I am of the results you have obtained. You have all improved so much, and I hope to see all of you at the archery range in the future," said the short, spiky-haired instructor. "But since this is a competition to win ribbons, I must eliminate five of you. The five best scores were Bergendahl, Miles, Westmoore, Nunez, and O'Brien."

Kyle looked up at Freya after all the names had been listed. She looked disappointed. She came up to him and patted him on the forearm.

"Good luck. I know you can do it," she said, leaving the competition area with the other four students who did not make it.

Kyle momentarily forgot everything and absently stared after her.

"Bergendahl, go take your position at range number five," said the instructor. "This is no time to get your head in the clouds."

Kyle nodded absently and walked to range five, where he would shoot from.

"Once again, this will be based upon the highest scores. The highest score will receive the first-place blue ribbon, followed by the second-place ribbon, and so forth in descending order. Good luck to everyone!" said Jones while the eager crowd of martial arts students watched to see who the winner would be.

Kyle glanced at the Third-year girl standing next to him, who seemed to be shaking with either excitement or fear. He could not tell which, as he tried to ignore how she had trouble pulling her bowstring back. He needed to forget her problems or the fact that he kept thinking about how Freya had patted him on the forearm and wished him luck. She wanted him to do well! His heart seemed to skip a beat as he let loose his first arrow, which appeared to be in the gold zone but not as central as he would have liked. He had two more arrows to make up for the points lost from that shot. He could feel the tension building in his throat.

Kyle closed his eyes and tried to let his shoulders relax and push away all the concerns about winning, Freya, and the fact that his friends were all watching him. He took a couple of slow breaths and then opened his eyes, picked up his second arrow, and put it into place. He let it fly effortlessly, and it seemed to go straight to the center as a bull's-eye. He heard cheers in the distance but ignored them and picked up the last arrow. Remaining focused on the target and slowly squeezing the arrow release, the third arrow landed right next to the second one, creating a furor in the crowd. Kyle finally allowed himself to acknowledge the other students and saw that his friends seemed to think he had done very well, but he wasn't convinced by the first arrow's result.

"That was awesome, Kyle!" exclaimed Geoff while Tyrrel, René, and Lothar gave him words of congratulations and pats on the back.

"I think I did alright, but that first shot was not so good..." replied Kyle, a little worried.

"Yes, but we think you did at least well enough to place and get a good ribbon," replied Tyrrel. "It was hard to calculate points at such a distance."

Kyle nodded and waited nervously as the instructor returned with her panel of student judges.

"Alright, the scores have been determined," announced the instructor, holding a handful of ribbons. "Our first runner-up is Robert O'Brien," said Alison Jones as she handed him an orange honorable mention ribbon. "And our next runner-up is Sarah Miles."

Kyle watched the nervous Third-year girl standing next to him go up and receive her green honorable mention ribbon. He was going to receive a placing ribbon, and his throat tightened a little with excitement.

"So that leads to our third-place winner, Phillipe Nunez," said Jones with a smile as she handed the Fourth-year student his white third-place ribbon that was noticeably bigger than the honorable mention ribbons.

Phillipe smiled and held his ribbon high so his classmates could see it as they cheered for him.

This left Kyle standing with Julia Westmoore, another Fourth-year student, who had attended the school since her first year.

"Now we are down to the last two, and this was very close indeed," said Instructor Jones with her blue eyes flashing. "A certain young man made two amazing bull's-eyes, but his remaining shot was much lower. Then a certain young lady made three very consistent arrow placements that earned her a strong score, but once the scores were tabulated, the consistent ones had better numbers than the two bull's-eyes with a stray. Congratulations, Julia, you won first place. And Kyle, you were so close and did such a fine job."

Kyle held the big red second-place ribbon in his hands and felt pleased, regardless of his second-place finish. He had a ribbon in his hands. This was his first tournament ever, and he had beaten 149 other students to earn his ribbon. He raised his red ribbon in the air as his friends cheered for him and congratulated him. Freya and her friends also came over to congratulate him. Kyle felt like he was on a cloud. He couldn't wait to call his family about his victory.

Chapter 8: The Island Exploration

Kyle checked his email again and then his phone messages to see if either his dad or mom had gotten his message about winning second place in the archery tournament. He looked at the brilliant red ribbon that hung on his wall next to where he had his desk and laptop computer. He had taken a photo of the ribbon and sent the image with the message. He had been so excited about the whole thing, but now it had become a source of annoyance. His grandmother had responded to his message right away by calling him that evening. She told him how proud she was of him and that she had even enjoyed archery herself as a girl. However, there was no word from his parents, and it had been a week.

Why had they not responded, he wondered. Perhaps the email did not arrive, or it was accidentally erased. Perhaps they were both so busy that they hadn't had a chance to check their email messages. As he made more excuses for them, the more hurt and angrier he felt. He could not understand why his grandparents would respond but not his parents. He stared at the red ribbon and felt like grabbing it off the wall and tossing it into the trash. It seemed to mean nothing without their joy for his success.

Kyle removed the red archery prize from the wall, stared at it, and was about to chuck it into his wastebasket when Tyrrel's unexpected presence stood in his cubicle space doorway.

"Don't do it," he said in his usual way of saying things with poise, knowledge, and confidence. The whites of his eyes seemed to flash with emphasis as he stared at Kyle with his dark brown eyes. "René did the same thing with some of his trophies because his parents had not responded to him. It turned out they had gone on a family emergency trip to France and had to attend to some serious matters, and checking email messages was not at the top of their list. He thought they did not care. Luckily for him, I removed his trophies from the waste basket before they were emptied."

"How did you know?"

"I've seen that look before. And you did mention the other day that your grandmother called you, but nothing about your parents," replied Tyrrel. "Sometimes adults just don't understand what is important to us."

"Yeah, it seems like that, but they are supposed to be the smart ones who know better and all. At least that's what my mom acts like," replied Kyle.

"Put the ribbon back up. We're all proud that at least one Fifth-year student did well enough to place," said Tyrrel.

"It's embarrassing to have the Fourth-year students do better than us," commented Trevor as he walked past. "We're supposed to be the leaders of the Page Level students."

"You see, even Trevor is pleased that you got that ribbon, so don't be too hasty to dump it away. You saved the honor of the Fifth-year boys," said Lothar from the other side of the bedroom cubicle wall.

Kyle exhaled deeply and put the red second-place ribbon back up on his wall with a renewed sense of accomplishment. The guys were right. An achievement is an achievement regardless of what his parents thought. Perhaps he did not have to do things for them but for his friends and, perhaps more importantly, for himself.

As the trees burst into their autumn colors and shed the vivid greens of the summer, Kyle noticed a change in the weather and the appearance of Lake Simcoe. The Lake now had a cold, gray-blue appearance, and an almost unforgiving chill began to seep in with the wind whenever they went outside during the early or late hours. Kyle finally heard from his mother, who was still living in Reno. She told him about the drought conditions in the area and that fall had been unseasonably dry and somewhat warm. Mt Rose received no snow, so none of the ski resorts had opened yet. This, of course, was nothing new, since most of the time they opened in December. However, old-timers in the area spoke of the snow in November and massive winters, when the snowpack in Lake Tahoe would reach as high as the telephone wires. Kyle could never imagine that until someone showed him a picture. He wondered how anyone could survive in snow that deep.

Tomorrow was Saturday, and the only homework that he had was to study for a French test on Monday, which he could do with Geoff. They had planned to quiz each other several times over the weekend. They were both looking forward to studying with an older group of students, and if they performed well, they would be allowed to progress to the next level. However, they had been warned that it would not be an easy transition. Kyle and Geoff didn't care; they were embarrassed about hanging out with the First-year students. Kyle also realized he was tired of feeling stressed about his parents and wanted to do something interesting and get out of the dorm. The normal scheduled school activity for Saturday would typically be some group game with teams, but he just wasn't interested in participating.

"Hey, are any of you guys doing something fun tomorrow?" Kyle asked Geoff, Tyrrel, and others who were standing nearby. "I'm sick of being inside and don't want to play with the little kids."

"I hear you on that one," remarked Lothar from the other side of the cubicle.

"Have you permission to go into town on the ferry boat?" asked Tyrrel.

"I have no idea. I didn't even know we could go on the ferry boat to town," replied Kyle.

"If he doesn't know about it, then he's never submitted the form for permission. So, it's probably a no on that one," commented Lothar as his head popped up and his eyes twinkled. "But we can do the walk around the island without permission passes, and Kyle and Geoff have never done the walk."

"Good idea, Lothar," replied Tyrrel. "I need to take water samples for my science project this year. I am part of the Academy Lake Awareness Project, which is participating with the First Nation community and the Chippewas of Georgina Island concerning the Lake Simcoe Protection Plan, which is about the reduction of phosphorus in the lake waters."

Geoff stared at Tyrrel for a moment, unsure he understood what Tyrrel was talking about, and then asked, "What's this about going for a hike around the island?"

"We are going for a hike tomorrow," said Lothar. "Tyrrel is doing the science project stuff. We're going for fun."

"Great. Count me in," replied Geoff.

"Me too," said Kyle, nodding his head.

"Well, I should get my sample collecting kit together, camera, and tablet for taking notes," said Tyrrel.

"You need a Tricorder," said René, flaring his French accent again. René's accent always seemed stronger when he was excited about something.

"I wish I had one. Then I could download all my collected data into my computer," said Tyrrel as he left to get his sample-taking gear ready for tomorrow.

The next morning, the boys woke up, got ready for breakfast, and were already in deep discussion about their plans for the day. Trevor and Xavier planned to join the Fabulous Five, as they were beginning to be known, for the trek around the island. Since it was acceptable for students to explore the island as long as they respected private property and filed a trip plan with the administration office, they could request packed lunches to take along on their field trip.

"We need to take a packed lunch along?!" exclaimed Geoff. "How far is it around the island?"

"It's about eight miles. That's why we are leaving before lunch, and we are not going on a forced march, so it may take some time," explained Lothar. "By the way, you'd better take a windbreaker. The lake starts to get windy this time of the year."

"I had no idea," Geoff complained to himself, but Kyle heard him anyway.

"I didn't either, but I want to go. Let's grab our French notes so we can quiz each other along the way. I want to get out of the baby class," said Kyle.

Geoff nodded in agreement with this idea as the group of Fifth-year boys ascended the stairs from breakfast to get their jackets and any gear they wanted to take along. Kyle planned to make good use of his new digital camera.

"Is everyone ready?" Tyrrel asked as he stood in the middle of the Fifth-year boys' room, his windbreaker zipped up and a heavy canvas satchel over his shoulder.

A volley of affirmatives came his way as each boy had the right equipment for their field trip. Kyle was excited. He had never gotten to go exploring with a group of friends. His mother never allowed him and Dark Cloud to go anywhere alone, and his father usually took him to places of interest when he had time. Geoff walked up with his blue Academy hooded sweatshirt and a strange pair of orange plastic dark sunglasses worn over his regular glasses.

"Where did you get those?" asked Kyle, somewhat perplexed by the strange eyewear.

"Uh," Geoff paused as he pulled the sunglasses off, looked at them, and then put them back on, "I think I bought them at a gift shop at Multnomah Falls. Why? Do you like them?"

"Well," Kyle started to reply.

"Those are hideous," remarked Lothar.

"I think they will scare away the wildlife," added René as he walked past with an attitude.

"Well, I like them," said Geoff. "Besides, I need to be careful and protect my eyes from the glare off the lake water."

"That's why I am wearing a hat," announced Xavier as he adjusted the brim of his baseball cap.

"Whatever," said Trevor as he walked past and followed René out the dorm room door.

"Come on, Geoff. Let's go," said Kyle, quickly checking his pocket for his camera.

"So where do we go to get our lunch?" asked Geoff.

"Downstairs in the dining hall kitchen. They should have a set of seven ready for us," replied Lothar.

All seven of the boys trekked downstairs to the main floor, where the dining room was located, and the large professional chef's kitchen was off that. Kyle caught sight of Freya, Ivy, and several other Fifth-year girls who hung out together. Kyle still fondly recalled Freya telling him that she believed he could do well in the archery competition. This thought made him inadvertently smile at her, and much to his surprise, she smiled back at him. Even more surprisingly, she walked over to the group as they were about to enter the kitchen.

"Lothar, where are you all going?" she asked her cousin.

"We're going to do the traditional hike around the island today before it gets too cold to do so," replied Lothar.

"Oh, yeah. That was always fun to do. The girls and I were just wondering what to do today as well," she replied thoughtfully. "Perhaps you will see us out there, too," Freya said with a swift glance at Kyle before she turned to go back to her friends.

Lothar looked sideways at Kyle and then led the group into the kitchen to get their lunches. Kyle brushed back his golden blonde hair, thinking about Freya and hoping he would see her on their hike.

Kyle slung the portable insulated lunch satchel over his shoulder as he walked out of the kitchen with the guys. He looked over at Freya and the girls, who all seemed to be in deep conversation about what to do for the day.

The morning air was cool and crisp, but the sunlight hinted that the day would grow warmer. Kyle zipped up his blue Academy hoodie and pulled the hood up over his head. The air was moist, unlike Reno, but more like Seattle, where his dad lived. The trees were a fantastic explosion of color that he found himself gaping at, and the air smelled strange. It was somewhat sweet and earthy as the odor of decaying leaves and other vegetation began to emerge. Kyle was still not used to the smell of the water being so close by. Reno did not smell that way. The best smell in the high desert region was after it had rained during the summer. It was the fresh, strong scent of desert plants and soil becoming hydrated in the warm air. Kyle wondered what Dark Cloud would think of this place, which was another reason to take pictures of the island location.

Kyle and Geoff followed the others since they did not know the path down to the water's edge and were content to let the others lead their expedition. Geoff wore his ugly orange sunglasses shamelessly while Kyle pulled out his digital camera whenever he found something of interest to photograph. When they reached the beach, Kyle was amazed at the size of the lake. It was enormous. The water felt like it would never end. He wondered if going to the ocean felt that way.

"Everyone, hold on while I take water and soil samples in this area," said Tyrrel as he opened his canvas satchel filled with his science equipment.

Kyle absently watched Tyrrel pull out high-quality plastic tubes, a pencil, paper, a map, and some small

166

spoons to fill the tubes with soil. Then Tyrrel began collecting vegetation growing along the shore.

"Hey Kyle, I forgot my camera. Could you photograph some things for me?" asked Tyrrel.

"Sure, not a problem. Just tell me what," replied Kyle, feeling a sudden shudder from the cold wind that came off the lake.

"Hey, while you do that, I'm going to see what the others are looking at over there," said Geoff as he stuffed his hands deep into his jacket pockets.

Tyrrel seemed consumed entirely by his efforts to collect stuff for his science project. He reminded Kyle of his dad when he would get wrapped up in a project. Kyle recalled watching his dad write all kinds of formulas on several giant whiteboards in his study, and he would sometimes spend hours just staring at the boards. He would erase something and then write it back, but Kyle had no idea what it all meant. It could have been some type of mysterious code for all he knew. Kyle patiently watched the tall black boy deftly handle all his equipment without a drop in his determination and focus. A breeze blew off Lake Simcoe and made Kyle shudder from the chill. From time to time, he could see the white caps form on the waves. It did not look like a good time to go to the lake. The sky had a few stormy-looking cumulus clouds, but the sun grew in strength as it progressed across the sky.

By the time Tyrrel was done collecting samples and they had caught up with the other boys, Kyle realized that he had inadvertently become an intrinsic part of Tyrrel's sample-collecting process and would be expected to take part in all the other samples that Tyrrel collected. He didn't really mind helping, but he had hoped to do some exploring of his own. He found himself peering around to see if anyone else would be out walking around the island today. It was midday when the boys found themselves on the Northeastern part of the island and ready to eat their lunch. After finding a comfortable spot along the shore where the waves would not interrupt their meal, they sat down to warm themselves in the sunlight.

Kyle snapped a few photos and then proceeded to enjoy his sandwich. He figured he could share some of his pictures with his grandparents and perhaps his parents as well. As he relaxed and enjoyed his lunch, he looked off across the lake's vastness and thought he saw something in the water. He wasn't sure if it was a boat or a floating log.

"You should have worn sunglasses," remarked Geoff.

"Huh?"

"You should have worn sunglasses. You are squinting from the glare," replied Geoff.

"Actually, I thought I saw something out there," he replied as he continued to look.

"It's probably a boat," said Tyrrel.

"Or the lake monster," said Lothar with a smirk.

"A lake monster?! Oh yeah, right," said Kyle with disbelief.

168

"Where are you looking?" asked Geoff.

"Over there, where that dark lumpy spot is. It looks like it may be moving, but it's hard to tell," replied Kyle, pointing out the direction to Geoff.

"Hmm. I don't see what you are seeing," Geoff replied. "Are you going to eat your grapes?"

"Yes, I am going to eat my grapes," replied Kyle.

"Hmm. Well, if you change your mind, give them to me."

"Sure, but I want my grapes," replied Kyle, turning away from Geoff to address Lothar, who had made the lake monster comment. "So, do they have a lake monster legend here?"

"Well, I don't know if the local people do, but it seems to be a story amongst the Academy," replied Lothar.

"Do you know anyone who has seen this lake monster?" Trevor asked.

"Not any of the students, but Freya's dad tells a story about seeing something one night. It's a family joke now, and we always make references to it. I don't know if it was real or not, but from the way he tells the story, it seems like he believed he saw something."

"Well, I have never seen anything in the lake, and I've been going to school here since my first year," replied Trevor.

Kyle nodded and continued to eat his lunch. He did not want to get involved in an argument between Trevor and Lothar. Trevor could be somewhat pretentious and haughty at times. His parents had a great deal of money, and he rarely let anyone forget it; for some reason, this made him feel that his opinions were more important than those of others. Lothar, on the other hand, seemed fearless and had natural confidence. He never talked about money, but he did not look like he was in need of anything.

Kyle continued to look for the object he had seen in the lake, but it was no longer visible.

"We should get going if we are to make it back on time this afternoon," said Tyrrel as he finished his lunch and packed up his gear.

"Yes, that's a good idea," agreed Trevor as he looked at his watch and absently brushed back his perfect hair.

Kyle got up and brushed the sand and dirt from his trousers.

"Did you finish your grapes?" asked Geoff.

"Yes, I told you that I wanted them. Next time, we need to ask for an extra sandwich for you," commented Kyle as he continued to look around again. Part of him hoped to see Freya, and another part wanted to see that dark shape out on the waters to prove to the guys that he had seen something.

"Hey, that's a good idea," replied Geoff. "I've still got an empty spot in my stomach. A second sandwich would have filled that nicely."

The boys headed westward along the northern shore of the island, where there was a sloping edge, which forced them to choose either high ground or to stay along the water's edge. Tyrrel urged for a water's edge route so that he could continue to take samples for his science project, but the hazard of getting their feet wet was a consideration. Trevor and Xavier opted for the upper route while the Fabulous Five opted to stay together and help Tyrrel collect his samples. René figured it would go much faster if they helped Tyrrel with the collection. Trevor and Xavier decided to wait for the others at the northwest point of the island, past the privately owned houses, to resume their trek. It was on this side that the boys had to be careful not to disturb the island's regular residents. They would walk along the road in this area and stop only in the shore areas that did not get too close to the houses. It was two in the afternoon when the boys regrouped.

"We are not as far along as we should be for this point. We need to speed things up a bit or else we will not be back in time for dinner," commented Lothar, opening his jacket, enjoying the afternoon sunshine.

"Yes, in the past, we were much further south on the long straight road by this time," remarked René.

"Well, that's just down a couple of curves. If we hurry, we could make up some lost time," suggested Trevor.

"Okay, let's do it, but I still need to take samples in the areas where we are allowed to access the shore," said Tyrrel.

171

Kyle had no idea how long this trip would take, but by his observation, they were not even halfway around the island. He wondered if there were any shortcuts through the main section to return to the school grounds before dinner hour.

"Well, I'm glad everyone else is as concerned as I am about getting to dinner on time," Geoff commented to Kyle.

"Dinner, I don't think that is what they are worried about. I think we have a time limit that we can be away from the school grounds, and if we don't show up, they'll come searching for us, and we could get into trouble."

"Oh. I don't like getting into trouble. That sucks. Let's get going," replied Geoff as he adjusted his sunglasses and then his regular glasses.

"I still think you look silly wearing those glasses," said Kyle. "How do you manage to keep both sets of glasses on your nose?"

"Very carefully and with determination," replied the dark-haired, skinny boy.

Soon, the long, straight road loomed before them, and the trek down this road did not allow for any shore visits, so they made good progress. It was nice enough now for the boys to remove their jackets and wrap them around their waists or drape them over their shoulders. The goal was to reach the slight curve in the road by three o'clock.

"What are you doing for Thanksgiving?" Lothar asked René.

"My parents don't really celebrate the holiday, but they have some French-Canadian friends who do, so they are thinking about picking me up for the weekend," replied René.

"My parents always pick up my brother and me for Thanksgiving," Trevor added. "Which is next weekend, hmmm, so I had better find out if they will pick us up Friday evening or Saturday morning."

"Next weekend?!" exclaimed Kyle.

"Thanksgiving is in November. It's still October," added Geoff.

"It's Canadian Thanksgiving," said Tyrrel. "Most Americans do not realize that the Canadians also celebrate Thanksgiving, but it's on the second Monday of October. And if I recall correctly, they started the holiday first."

"Oh wow, I had no idea there was a Canadian Thanksgiving," replied Kyle. "In school back home, they always made it sound like something that only Americans celebrated…"

"So, what happens to those of us who don't go home?" asked Geoff.

"We stay at the school," said Tyrrel. "And have a day to do whatever we want."

"Or sometimes go home with other kids who have parents nearby that invite us to dinner," said René.

173

"Yes, that certainly would be nice," added Tyrrel as he and René both eyeballed Lothar.

"Okay, I see where this is going, but my parents have not said that they are going to be in town this year," replied Lothar.

René and Tyrrel showed visible signs of disappointment.

"What about Freya's family?" asked René as he brushed his long brown hair out of his face.

Lothar shook his head, "I can't invite you two to Freya's house. That's up to Freya, and she'll probably invite her girlfriends."

Tyrrel and René nodded appreciatively, knowing that certain boundaries of good manners could not be overstepped.

"But you would put a good word in for us, if the option came up, right?" asked René.

"You know I would. I can't make invites to places that are not my home," replied Lothar.

"Wow, two Thanksgiving days... which would mean turkey dinner twice during the fall," Geoff mumbled to himself.

Kyle felt his heart jump at the thought of being able to see Freya away from school, and then he realized that his grandparents lived just a short distance away. Would they have plans for the Canadian Thanksgiving, and would he be included, he wondered. He would have to ask them this evening when he returned to his laptop. He could also send them some of the pictures he took. The thought of asking if some of the guys could come as well was very appealing, but just like Lothar, it wasn't his house, and he was unsure whether he should extend the invitations.

When the boys reached the slight curve in the road, it was long past three o'clock.

"Okay, we need to make a decision here," said Lothar as he stood still and addressed the others. "It is three twenty now, and we are not far enough along to make it back in time by going around the island."

"What are you suggesting?" asked Trevor.

"That we go on the trail that goes through the forest and comes out along the airfield."

"I hate that route. It's never the same, and I usually get covered with dirt. I fell down last time I went on it," remarked Xavier, wrinkling his brow. "I got in a bit of trouble from my mom for tearing up a new pair of uniform pants, and I am now wearing uniform pants as usual."

"Hey, I understand your concern, but the other result is that we are late in returning to the Academy on time, and we lose our privilege of leaving the school grounds," remarked Tyrrel. "This means that I won't be able to collect all of my necessary data for the whole island, and if I lose the ability to go out, then I can't participate in the Academy Lake Awareness Project."

Xavier frowned and looked south down the road they were standing upon.

"I'm going on the trail. I can't afford to be late and screw up my science project," said the tall black boy with sincerity and conviction.

"I'm also going on the trail," said Lothar.

"I don't care. I have been around the island many times and through the trail, so going on the trail now seems most reasonable to me," said René as he started for the edge of the road.

Kyle couldn't see any trail and wasn't sure what to do. Geoff stood next to him, looking down the road south, then back to where René was heading into the vegetation.

"Is it that bad, the trail, I mean?" Geoff asked Trevor and Xavier.

"It sucks. It's muddy, rocky, and steep in some places, and branches are hitting you in the face," Xavier described with as much disdain as he could muster. "It's also creepy in some areas."

Trevor rolled his eyes at this comment.

"We don't need to bring that up again, do we?" sighed Trevor.

"I know what I saw, and it was real," responded the dark-haired boy.

"Xavier, it was the wind. It wasn't a chupa— whatsoever in the woods," replied Trevor.

"I'm not going in there," replied Xavier. "And that's chupacabra, Trevor."

Trevor rolled his eyes in uncomfortable disdain.

Geoff's eyes grew wider. "There are chupacabras on the island?!?"

"No, there are not," said Trevor firmly.

"There was something in that forest," said Xavier firmly. "I did not imagine it, and I am not a liar."

"Guys, René and Tyrrel have already disappeared into the forest, and I am going with them. Who's coming with me?" asked Lothar, not wanting to tarry any longer on this discussion.

Kyle turned to Lothar, "Have you seen anything scary on the trail?"

"No, but I also have never been on the trail at night like Xavier and Trevor during that one time, which is a secret. So maybe there is something out there, but I have never seen it during the daylight," replied Lothar.

Kyle looked down the road, then at the forested area, and then thought that he wanted to be able to go again and see more. "I'm going with you guys." Kyle turned to Geoff and asked, "Are you coming along or going with them?"

Geoff turned to Trevor and Xavier.

"Are you going on the road and risk being late?"

"I kind of have to, don't I?" replied Trevor, gesturing to Xavier, who stood with his arms folded across his chest, looking somewhat dour about the whole subject matter.

"You can come with us or go with them, but if you plan on going with them, you had better do it now."

Geoff turned to look at the forest area and saw Kyle and Lothar going toward some dense trees.

"Well, good luck getting back on time," said Geoff as he ran after Kyle and Lothar.

Kyle turned to see his awkward-looking friend scrambling to navigate through the underbrush to where he and Lothar stood momentarily. Lothar nodded and waved to Trevor, who waved back and then started southwards down the road with Xavier, who still looked quite upset.

"Are Xavier and Trevor going to be mad at us for not going with them?" asked Geoff to Lothar.

"No, well… not for long. Xavier will be pissed off for a bit, but then he'll be fine. Whatever happened on the trail really spooked him. Just act like nothing happened and don't bring up the subject unless he does, and you'll be fine," said Lothar.

"My mother's family is Mexican; do they all believe in chupacabra?" pondered Kyle aloud. "I have never heard them speak of it…but then again… they don't like me, so I guess they would not tell me if they did."

"Xavier's family is not Mexican but is Spanish. He can get pretty weird about that," said Lothar.

"Oh, I see," replied Kyle, not truly understanding what Lothar meant. Back home, anyone who spoke Spanish or had a Spanish last name was called Hispanic,

178

so Kyle was not sure what the difference was between being Mexican and being Spanish. He just hoped that the trail did not go anywhere near any chupacabra monsters and planned to ask his mom what the big difference was between being Spanish and Mexican. And perhaps ask her if chupacabras were real or not. He already knew what his dad would say.

Kyle followed Lothar into the forest on the rough dirt trail, which seemed to ebb and flow, with easy parts to walk on and more difficult areas. Some spots were hard and well-worn as if the trail had been there forever, while other areas seemed to be at the mercy of nature encroaching upon its boundaries. Looking ahead, Kyle could see the forest ground gently sloping upward, and the vast canopy of trees filled with orange, red, and yellow leaves. Lothar's red hair looked at home in this environment. Further up the trail, Kyle spotted René and Tyrrel ahead of them.

"So will this shorten the amount of time to get back to the school grounds?" Kyle asked Lothar.

"Yes, easily. And despite Xavier's feelings about it, there are some cool spots to check out along the way. There is a big circular rock formation in a clearing at the top of the hillside, and if you climb on top of the rocks, you can see the lake all around the island. The view is better in the winter when there are no leaves," replied Lothar.

"We gotta do this again," said Kyle.

"Oh, we will, if Tyrrel has any say about it."

"I like Tyrrel. He's incredibly smart," commented Geoff out of the blue. "And speaking of being smart, we still need to study for our French test."

"Oh, that's right! I forgot all about that," said Kyle glumly.

"Don't worry. I have the vocabulary sheet with me," Geoff replied with a smile. "We're getting out of that First-year class."

"Okay, start asking away," said Kyle as he hiked up the hillside following Lothar's lead with Geoff close behind.

"Une fille," said Geoff.

"A girl," replied Kyle.

"Un garçon," said Geoff.

"A waiter?" suggested Kyle.

"No, a boy," replied Geoff. "Un chien."

"A dog," replied Kyle.

"Un chat," said Geoff.

"A cat," replied Kyle.

Lothar looked back at them and wrinkled his brow.

"Un avion," said Geoff.

"A bird?" guessed Kyle.

"Oh geez!" Lothar stopped and turned around. "Your pronunciation is awful. If René hears you two, he's going to become unbearable. He'll turn into a French monster."

"You mean he's not already?" replied Geoff with a smirk.

Lothar laughed along with Kyle.

"No chupacabra could be worse than René when he is in full French mode. He gets so annoyed about stuff," said Lothar. He stared at Kyle and Geoff, who both looked a bit concerned. "He's standing behind me, isn't he?"

Kyle and Geoff nodded.

Lothar turned around to see René standing behind him with his hands on his hips.

"So, I am worse… than a goat sucking monster?!?" asked René with his full accent in flare and his hands reaching expressively for the sky.

"Yes."

Lothar and René stared at each other intensely for a few moments as Tyrrel came down the hillside to join everyone.

"Good. Then Xavier can no longer argue with me about stupid stuff. I am more fearsome," replied René finally with a look of smug satisfaction. "But seriously, why would I be such a monster?"

"Because you hate hearing people mispronounce the French language," said Lothar,

"And Geoff and I are trying to learn our French vocabulary for the test on Monday," replied Kyle.

"Oui, that is understandable. Give me the test sheet, and I will quiz you both," said René, who walked over to Geoff and took the list of vocabulary words out of his hand.

The boys hiked to the top of the hillside, practicing their French with René, who ensured they heard the correct pronunciation and understood the correct meaning of each word. The group reached the top to discover an open glade with large boulders arranged almost magically in a circular fashion, much like Stonehenge. The configuration of the boulders was not what surprised Kyle the most, but who was already perched upon them, looking out across the forest and the rest of the island.

Chapter 9: Monsters and Myths

As the boys came around the large fallen tree and shrubs that hid the downward-descending trail westwards, they emerged at the top of the hillside glade, where the enormous boulders stood, with seven girls already perched upon them.

"Hey, look! It's the Fabulous Five!" exclaimed Ivy, the ever-so-bold Fifth-year girl.

The five boys emerged from the forest trail to discover the seven girls staring at them.

"Well, that certainly is an interesting greeting," remarked Lothar. "I can live with being labeled as fabulous."

"I think it is a strange moniker," replied Tyrrel, looking at who was there. "I am not sure how they are making that quantitative judgment."

Kyle looked at Tyrrel, unsure he understood what the tall black boy had said.

"Sometimes he sounds like Mr. Spock from Star Trek," Kyle remarked to Geoff and Lothar.

"Thank you, but I bear a stronger resemblance to Mr. Tuvok on Voyager," replied Tyrrel with a slight smile.

"Either way, let's go see what the wildlife is up to," remarked René, who stepped forward to say hello to the girls.

Standing in the Boulder Glade was the dark curly-haired Ivy Rosenplat-Levi, along with Hanako Takahashi, Julia Westmoore, the winner of the archery tournament, Elsa and Sif, the two lovely Magnusdotter twins, the brilliant Lucy Robbinson, and Lothar's cousin Freya Wolff, who had stood atop one of the giant boulders with her red hair blowing in the breeze.

Kyle's heart jumped as he saw her standing up there.

All the girls seemed to stop what they were doing and gathered down to greet the newcomers to the Boulder Glade.

"Lothar, I thought you said that you were all going to walk around the island," said Freya as she managed to climb down from the tallest boulder.

"We were, but then we realized that we were not going to make it back in time. So, we took the trail," he replied to his cousin.

"Where are Trevor and Xavier? I thought they were with you," asked Julia Westmoore as she looked back at the area where the trail entrance to the Boulder Glade was located.

"It's a long story, but they decided not to take the trail," replied Lothar.

"Oh," nodded Julia, looking somewhat disappointed.

Kyle looked up at the huge boulder where Freya had been standing and turned to the slender, red-haired girl. "Is it hard to climb up there?"

"No, actually… it is quite easy. Want me to show you?"

"Yes, I'd love that. The guys were saying you could see all around the island and out to the lake from up there."

"Easily. Follow me," Freya instructed Kyle.

Kyle followed Freya and did what she did to climb up onto the large boulder, using the nearby smaller boulders as giant stepping stones. She climbed to the top with ease and held out her hand to help him up, which he gratefully accepted. Upon reaching the top, Kyle felt the afternoon breeze blow across his face unexpectedly. It made him feel a little unbalanced as he realized how high up he was from the ground. As he centered himself and tried to get comfortable with his footing, he looked around and could see so much in all directions. It was a great view.

Kyle smiled, turned to Freya, and said, "The guys were right. This is an awesome view. You really can see everything."

Freya smiled back at Kyle and then looked east across the island toward the Academy buildings, which stood tall in the near distance.

"I love how the school looks from here. It's such an unusual building," remarked Freya.

"Yes, I have noticed that, but I like it. I like being at the school," replied Kyle.

"Where were you before?"

"I attended several different schools since my parents got divorced. First up in Seattle with my dad, and then down in Reno, where my mom lives," said Kyle.

"Which one did you like better?" asked Freya as she continued to look somewhere in the distance, the wind blowing her hair back from her face.

"Well, I think the school in Seattle was better. I learned more, but I have a good friend, Dark Cloud, when I was in Reno, and I think he would have liked this place. It's so green. And there is so much water. Kinda like Seattle."

"Do you miss him?"

"Yeah, but he would have been gone anyway since he went to the new tribal school out at Pyramid Lake," he replied with a shrug. "So, whether I am here or there, I still would not have gotten to see him. And my mom didn't like him that much."

"Why? What did he do?" asked Freya.

"He had different ideas about stuff that she did not approve of. You know, religious stuff," replied Kyle.

"I see," Freya nodded appreciatively.

Continuing to look out toward the lake where Kyle saw the strange dark shape in the water, he ventured to ask, "Have you seen anything weird in the water? Lothar said your dad had."

"Oh, great, is Lothar gossiping about my family?" commented Freya.

"No, he wasn't saying anything bad. You see, I saw something out there that I can't explain, and he was telling me about the rumors of a lake monster," replied Kyle.

"Oh, you saw something?!"

"Yes, but I don't know what it was. It could have been a log or a boat. I don't know. I guess I am being silly, huh?"

"Well, my dad really believes that something is in the lake, and I don't think my dad is silly." Freya turned and smiled reassuringly at Kyle.

Kyle looked into Freya's blue-gray eyes and noticed how pale her skin was, with delicate freckles across her nose and around her eyes and cheeks. She had a wonderful, shy smile that was genuine.

"Well, as long as you don't think I am making fun of your dad. I did see something. I just don't know what," replied Kyle. Freya was the first girl who seemed to be beautiful and nice all at the same time. He liked that. Something about her made him feel good deep down inside.

"Hey up there!!" called a voice.

Freya and Kyle both looked down to see Geoff standing awkwardly, head and upper body tilted upward, to call out to them.

"Hey, are you two going to stay up there all day? Tyrrel and Lucy say we need to get going if we are to be back in time."

Kyle looked at Freya and then turned back to Geoff, who was adjusting his two pairs of glasses.

"Why is he wearing two pairs of glasses like that?" asked Freya.

"He's weird, but he's a nice guy," replied Kyle to Freya.

Freya eyed Kyle and then turned to look down at Geoff.

"We'll be right down!" Freya called.

"Okay," replied Geoff, still trying to adjust the sunglasses over his regular glasses.

"Those are ridiculous, you know," remarked René as he walked past Geoff with several of the girls around him.

Geoff wrinkled his brow and mouth in frustration but said nothing to the opinionated French boy.

Freya and Kyle joined Geoff, who waited for them to come down. The others had already started toward the east trail entrance to the Boulder Glade. The walk back to the school grounds took fifteen minutes, and they arrived just as large groups of students were collecting for the evening meal. Tyrrel excused himself from the others to go upstairs and put away his gear and science project samples.

"I see you all made it back in time," said Trevor with a triumphant smile.

"How did you manage to get here before us?" asked Lothar.

"I paid one of the local residents to drive Xavier and me to the school grounds," Trevor replied smugly.

"Why am I not surprised?" remarked Lothar with a laugh. "You always have a way of finding a solution that none of us would use. I'm glad you made it back in time."

"Where's Tyrrel? I have one of his soil samples still in my pocket," said Xavier, who was standing next to Trevor, also looking rather impressed with Trevor's solution to the problem.

"He went upstairs to put away his gear and samples before dinner," replied René with an arrogant hair flip. "You will have to hand it over to him at dinner or go upstairs now."

Xavier held aloft the sealed test tube, eyeing its strange contents, which was mostly lake water with small bits of organic plant material and some grains of sand swirling about. He shrugged his shoulders and said, "I'll give it to him after dinner."

Kyle eyed the sample and then Xavier. He then remembered he needed to ask his mother about the difference between being Mexican and Spanish.

After dinner, a movie was scheduled, and most of the Fifth-year boys planned to go, but Kyle wanted to call his mom and then his grandmother about Canadian

189

Thanksgiving. So, when the guys asked if he would join them, Kyle asked them to save him a spot and said that he needed to make a quick call to family.

"Kyle, will you take this upstairs and put it into my bedroom space?" Tyrrel asked, handing him the test tube sample that Xavier had shown the guys earlier.

"Sure, not a problem," said Kyle, taking the test tube and going upstairs.

Kyle entered the Fifth-year boys' room and walked over to Tyrrel's bedroom cubicle. He looked around the space, searching for the other samples, but not finding them, he then searched for an ideal place to put the sample on Tyrrel's desk. On the wall in the desk area was a picture of a black family together, looking happy, in a living room. Tyrrel was standing behind the couch with other children, and it appeared his parents and some other older relatives were sitting on the couch. Kyle stared at the photo for the longest time. He then realized there was no such picture at any of the places he called home. He pulled his thoughts away from the picture and found a safe place for the sample tube in a pencil holder.

Leaving Tyrrel's cubicle space, Kyle looked around to see if anyone else was in the room. It was all quiet, and he was very much alone. Kyle turned on the desk light, sat down at his desk, and picked up his cell phone, which had been charging during the day. He looked at the device and noticed that someone had tried calling him. It was his dad.

Kyle hit the return call button and listened to the simulated ring tone, then his dad answered.

"Hi, Dad! It's Kyle. You called," said Kyle.

"Yeah, how are you doing? How has school been?" asked his dad in a cheery voice.

"It's been great, Dad. I love it here. I have a group of friends to hang out with. What have you been doing? I'm so happy you called."

"I've been busy with work as usual, but I called because next week is the Canadian version of Thanksgiving, and since you are up there, I thought I would fly up to see you, Grandma, and Grandpa. What do you think of that idea?" he asked.

"That's awesome, Dad! I just found out about Canadian Thanksgiving. That's funny how you called today. Some of the guys are going off with family, while some of the others don't know what they are going to do," replied Kyle.

"Well, I could ask your grandmother if she would mind having a few extra guests," suggested Jon to his son.

"Dad, that would be great. You would do that?"

"Certainly. I will call her after I get off the phone with you. How many?"

"Well, there are Lothar, Geoff, Tyrrel, and René that I would like to invite."

"Four extras, I think that's possible. I will ask her, but wait until I email you back before making any invitations. She may want to ask Grandpa if he is up for a bunch of young boys running around the place."

191

"Okay, Dad. I'll wait. And thanks."

"So have you called your mom lately?" asked Jon Bergendahl.

"Actually, I was just going to call her to ask her something. You see, one of the guys thought there was a chupacabra on the island, and I wanted to know if those were real or not," said Kyle.

Kyle could hear his dad start to cough and then laugh on the other side. "You were going to call your mother about chupacabras! Oh, my goodness, I wish I could be a fly on the wall to see that reaction. Kyle, they are a mythical creature that is probably a wild or sick dog."

"Really? Xavier seemed to believe that he saw something in the forest. He is so scared that he will not walk on that trail anymore," replied Kyle. "He didn't seem like he was lying."

"You know, I am sure he saw something, son, but those creatures are often explainable by something rational. I would not bother your mother with such stories. It would only upset her."

"Okay, but I also needed to ask her some other stuff about why someone who is Spanish would not want to be called Mexican," said Kyle. "I thought everyone who was Hispanic was the same."

"Oh boy, okay... hold on... please don't ask her that. You like going to school up there, right? She's gonna go off the deep end if you ask her that. The chupacabra question was better." He heard a momentary silence from

192

his dad. Kyle could feel his own heart pounding in his chest, fearing that he had said something bad. Why didn't he keep his mouth shut and not say anything? Kyle agonized, and then his dad said, "What brought that question on?"

"I assumed that Xavier's family was Mexican, and one of the other boys said that Xavier was Spanish and not Mexican, and he tends to get upset about being called Mexican. I thought they were all the same since everyone who speaks Spanish or has a Spanish last name is called Hispanic," replied Kyle.

Kyle could hear his dad sigh in frustration over the phone.

"I wish you were here so we could have these conversations in person. People of Spanish ancestry come from Spain, a country in Europe, and individuals with Mexican ancestry, such as your mom, have their roots in Mexico. A long time ago, people from Spain invaded the areas of Central and South America in search of wealth, and some rather unpleasant things happened. As a result, the people of Spain colonized that part of the world and claimed it as their own. They passed their language on to the native people there, and some of the Spaniards married the native people and had families, so there's an ancestral relationship, but it's all very complicated. Mexico had a revolution from its European leaders, much like we did from England. So, in reality, the people who are labeled as Hispanic come from different countries with unique cultures and histories. So does any of this make sense?"

"Yes… I suppose. No, not really. Why would you call a group of people all the same if they are not or don't want to be grouped together?" Kyle asked, still thinking this all sounded quite odd.

"I have no idea. Laziness upon the part of the people here, maybe? But that is just my opinion. Somewhere, someone was too lazy to find out if someone was Brazilian or Cuban and decided to lump everyone together, even though they each have distinctive cultural backgrounds. Even the languages are not exactly the same. I know it doesn't make much sense. Sorry, Sport, the world is weird. I had a friend who got yelled at in the workplace for saying the word 'talk' instead of 'dialogue.' It makes no sense."

"So do you think Xavier will hate me because I am part Mexican?" asked Kyle.

Jon took a breath and sighed contemplatively.

"Kyle, I don't know this boy, but you have no reason to feel bad about your heritage. And the anger created long, long before you were born is no reason for you to hold any ill will toward Xavier. Treat everyone as an individual and evaluate them based on their own merit to determine whether you wish to call them friends or foes. That's what I do, and that method has served me well," replied Jon.

Kyle let his father's words sink in and settle into his inner self, and it felt right somehow.

"Thanks, Dad. I like that idea. I didn't want to dislike Xavier. He's just afraid of chupacabras," said Kyle.

Jon laughed.

"If they were real, I'd be afraid, too," said Jon.

Kyle was glad that his dad had called him and felt that a disaster with his mom had been avoided. He didn't want to upset her or have her want him to leave the Academy. On top of that, his dad would ask Grandma about the possibility of inviting his new friends to visit him in Caledon, which was exciting. By the time Kyle had walked downstairs to the movie hall and had joined the guys, the movie was halfway over, but he didn't care. He was happy. He felt resolved in how to approach things and decided not to worry.

The next morning, Kyle woke up to find a message on his phone from his dad, saying that his grandparents were happy to have four extra boys invited for Thanksgiving. Jasper would pick them up from the dock at ten o'clock in the morning on Sunday. The boys were to spend the night and return to school the next day in the evening.

Chapter 10: Canadian Thanksgiving

By the time Kyle was ready to ask the guys if they wanted to come to his grandparents' house for Thanksgiving, Freya had already extended the family invitation to Lothar. Lothar explained that he was expected to go since it was a family matter, and nothing had been said about anyone else being allowed to come along. But the others could accept the invitation.

"Kyle, you just made Tyrrel and René very happy. They did not want to stay here for the holiday, and I am sure that Freya invited all her friends who did not have a place to go," said Lothar as he took his seat in their Primary Languages class.

Tyrrel and René had just come into the room, arguing about something. Lothar looked at them and then turned back to Kyle.

"Of course, if they act like that, you may wish to reconsider inviting them to your grandparents' home," said Lothar.

Kyle just looked at Tyrrel and René, shook his head, and then finally asked, "So what are you two arguing about?"

"Nothing of any importance as usual," retorted Tyrrel.

"Music is not... unimportant," René replied.

"Oh, I see." Kyle nodded, not wanting to get involved. "So would either of you want to come over to my grandparents' house for Thanksgiving?"

René paused and looked at Lothar. Lothar shook his head and said, "I'll be with Freya's family, and I can't invite you two."

René turned back to Kyle and replied, "Well… since I will not be offending Lothar by accepting your offer, I would love to go."

"Yes, thank you, Kyle, for inviting us," replied Tyrrel as he took his seat. "You have brightened our holiday prospects immensely. How are we to get to your grandparents' house?"

"My grandparents are sending their driver to pick us up on Sunday, and he will bring us home on Monday evening. So, it will be overnight. Is that okay?"

"Sounds terrific to me. What about Geoff?" asked Tyrrel.

"I already asked him, and he is coming along too. He needs to get permission from his parents, though. Do you guys need to do that too?" asked Kyle.

"Not that I know of," replied René. "But of course, I usually go with Lothar when not with my own family, so I had better check to make sure it is all right."

"Me too," said Tyrrel. "But I think my parents will be fine as long as they know where I am. Can I get your grandparents' names and their phone numbers to give to my parents?"

"Sure," said Kyle as he opened a notebook, tore a piece of paper off, and wrote down his grandparents' names and phone number.

The week went by rather quickly without much excitement, and Geoff, René, and Tyrrel all secured permission from their parents to spend the night and have dinner with the Bergendahls at their home in Caledon. Plans were made to text message Lothar regularly to tease him about being stuck with Freya and all the girls. Kyle was very excited about seeing his father and sharing the wonders of Caledon House with his friends.

Sunday morning arrived quickly, and everyone wished each other a Happy Thanksgiving and safe travels as they made plans to depart or stay at the school. Students with parents waiting to pick them up at the island pier were instructed to be at the dock for the ferry by 9:00 a.m. In this case, Kyle, Geoff, René, and Tyrrel only needed a change of clothes and their necessary overnight gear. They boarded the ferry boat with Lothar and Freya, as Freya's parents lived in London, Ontario, and had taken the three-hour drive to pick her up, along with Lothar and her friends.

This was Kyle's second ferry boat ride. The first one happened when he was about six years old, and his parents had visited Victoria, Canada. He remembered a long, bumpy boat ride across choppy waters that seemed to last forever. He remembered feeling somewhat sick, and his parents took him out on deck to get fresh air, which soothed his uneasy feeling of motion sickness. This trip across the water would be much shorter and less choppy.

A cool breeze came across the lake, but nothing that would encourage rough waves. The skies were clear, and the day looked promising to be lovely and comfortable. The Fabulous Five hung out together on the boat with Freya's friends, who were also traveling.

Elsa and Sif, the Magnusdotter twins, were dressed in matching bright pink yoga pants and running jackets. They both had their blonde hair neatly tied back into ponytails and carried their matching bright blue overnight bags over their shoulders. Alongside them was Lucy Robbinson, still dressed in her school uniform, with a backpack on her shoulder. Lucy made an interesting contrast with the twins. The twins almost looked like Barbie dolls in comparison to Lucy. And Freya was somewhere in between. She was wearing dark gray yoga pants, a white T-shirt, and a bright green running jacket that complemented her hair color, but she was neither as shockingly bright as the twins nor as conservatively dressed as Lucy in her school uniform. Kyle had not had a chance to get to know any of them, only that they were Freya's closest friends.

Kyle leaned on the railing of the ferry boat as it pulled away from the shore of the island. He could feel the rush of the moist water-filled air come across his face. It was refreshing. Freya left her friends and stood beside Kyle at the railing.

"Is this your first Thanksgiving away from home?" she asked.

"Yes, and no. Ever since my parents got divorced, it has seemed like I was never home for Thanksgiving anymore. But this will be my first Thanksgiving in Canada with my grandparents." Kyle paused for a moment and turned to Freya. "I don't even know if Canadians eat turkey."

"Yes, we do, and a whole bunch of other things as well," replied Freya, smiling. "So, are you still enjoying being at the Academy?"

"Yup. It's a great place. The homework is pretty hard, but then again, I think homework has always seemed difficult," replied Kyle. "I have to work extra hard to concentrate for some reason."

"You'll get used to it. Look at Tyrrel. He got used to being here, away from his home in Las Vegas. That place seems so different from what it is here," remarked Freya.

"Yeah, it is. But he's super smart. At times, I barely understand him," replied Kyle as he turned to look back at Tyrrel, who was chatting with Lucy. "Looks like Lucy understands him."

"Well, of course she does. She has an IQ of 180 and gets high marks on all her tests. I wish I were as smart as Lucy," remarked Freya.

"Ah… I bet you get high marks on your tests and projects," said Kyle admiringly as he watched Freya's red hair flutter in the wind.

"Well, I do pretty well," she replied shyly. "But Lucy is the smartest girl I know. Elsa and Sif are also smart, but they sometimes like to pretend to be not as smart as they really are."

Before Kyle knew it, the ferry boat had reached the shore of Lake Simcoe, and it was time to disembark. He was disappointed that his conversation with Freya had to end, but he was excited to see his dad and grandparents and show his friends how amazing Caledon House was. His dad told him they could all go horseback riding if the weather was good.

After saying goodbye to Lothar, Freya, the twins, and Lucy, the remaining four boys trekked off the ferry to look for Jasper and the Bergendahls' metallic blue BMW sedan.

"Who and what are we looking for?" asked Tyrrel as he used his superior height to view the whole parking area.

"My grandparents' butler, Jasper, is an older guy, and he will be driving a metallic blue BMW," Kyle replied as he looked around.

"Does the man have style and look like he works for the royal family of England?" asked René.

"Well… yeah, that would be a good description of Jasper. He looks like a younger version of Bruce Wayne's butler, Alfred. Why do you ask?" asked Kyle, adjusting the weight of his overnight bag on his shoulder.

"I think that may be the man," said René, pointing out a man with arms folded leaning against a dark blue BMW sedan that was sparkling in the morning sunlight.

All the boys turned to look in the direction of where René was pointing, and then Jasper waved and smiled.

"That's him! Let's go," said Kyle, leading the way across the parking lot, making sure not to get lost or run over by the many people and vehicles arriving to pick up students from the school.

"Master Kyle! How are you? And are these our guests for the holiday?" asked Jasper cheerfully, but still retaining his usual sophisticated tone of voice.

"Yes, Jasper. These are Geoff, Tyrrel, and René. We had to leave Lothar to go off with his cousin Freya."

"Very well, Master Kyle. Shall we all get into the car now?" said Jasper as he opened the passenger side doors, walked to the back of the car, and popped open the trunk. "Give me your luggage, and I will put all the bags into the trunk."

Each of the boys handed their bag to Jasper. Tyrrel quickly opened his bag and pulled out the wireless keyboard and glasses, which somewhat resembled Google Glass. He then handed his bag to Jasper, who put it safely into the German-made automobile. Geoff called shotgun because he often got car sick, so he immediately made his way to the front seat.

"Wow, I have never seen a car with a white leather interior. This is cool. It looks like a space station inside!" exclaimed Geoff as he got in the front seat.

Jasper had to struggle to control himself from chuckling too loudly about Geoff's enthusiasm for the car's interior. After ensuring that all the doors were closed and the boys had their seatbelts latched, he began their journey down toward Caledon, where the Bergendahls waited for their arrival. Jasper informed Kyle that his father had arrived the night before but did not come along, as he wanted to make sure there was enough room for everyone in the car.

"So, is this your favorite car to drive? Do you feel like James Bond or a superhero driving it?" Geoff asked Jasper as they started to pull out of the parking lot.

Jasper smiled at Geoff and replied, "I do, indeed, like driving this car, and I only sometimes… feel like James Bond while driving it."

"Wow, this car is awesome," replied Geoff, making himself comfortable in the front seat. He then began examining all the controls on the dashboard, and then turned his focus on those on the passenger's front door.

Meanwhile, in the back seat, Tyrrel put on his odd-looking glasses and then placed the wireless keyboard on his lap. René was sitting in the middle and watching what Tyrrel was doing.

"What are you doing?" asked Kyle from the other side of the back seat area.

"I am testing to see if I can use this computer system successfully in a moving car," replied Tyrrel.

"That's a computer?" asked Kyle. "Some Google Glass-looking headgear and a wireless keyboard? How do you see what you are doing? There's no screen."

Tyrrel smiled.

"These are smart glasses. It's a prototype that I have been allowed to test."

"He was using it the other day when we went for a walk while he was collecting water samples," commented René as he tried to see if he could see what Tyrrel was seeing.

Tyrrel turned to René and laughed. "You can't get close enough to me to see what I am doing!"

"What are you doing?" asked Kyle, now completely mystified and eager to discover what the brilliant boy was doing.

"This is a prototype computer. It's like a laptop computer. This keyboard features solid-state memory, like a thumb drive, eliminating the need for spinning disks. And the keyboard is wireless, so no wires are required for the input device to function with the monitor device," explained Tyrrel.

"Cool! Where's the monitor?" asked Kyle.

"It's in the glasses headset," responded René. "It is très bien! I want one."

"So can I see?" asked Kyle.

"Sure, but be careful putting the glasses on. They are a prototype and are fragile," replied Tyrrel as he carefully took the glasses off and handed them to Kyle. "I still wish the system had some form of mouse or touch pad. The designers have not yet engineered that part of the system."

Kyle took the smart glasses, which looked awkward and delicate with exposed wires secured along the frames. They were not as fashionable as normal glasses, with wires and parts attached to the lenses. Putting on the lenses was an incredible surprise. He could still see the white interior of the car, with Jasper, Geoff, René, and Tyrrel inside, but he could also see what appeared to be a computer monitor screen displaying pictures and text. Kyle looked at what was being displayed, and it seemed to be Tyrrel's project for the Academy Lake Awareness Project. Kyle saw charts, photos, and a text report that Tyrrel was currently writing.

"I have never seen anything like this. Where did you get this?" exclaimed Kyle in awe.

"Technically, it does not belong to me. It's on loan to me to test. A group of Knights, who are also inventors and computer geniuses, create items that the kids at the Academy get to test. We tell them if the product is good or not. This item is similar to the Virtual Reality gear that has become so popular, but it does not require a smartphone to function. Everything is inside the glasses and the little keyboard. Last year they made a video game," replied Tyrrel.

"Oh yes, I think I played the game with Lothar just a couple of weeks ago," replied Kyle.

"Tyrrel gets to test all of the new technological stuff because he is a super brain," remarked René with a sense of pride for his friend.

"They trust me to give good feedback and not to break their prototypes," clarified Tyrrel.

Kyle carefully removed the special glasses and handed them to René, thinking that he would hate to be responsible for breaking such a device. René placed the glasses on.

"These are... très bien," commented René. "Each time I put these on, I am so amazed." René's face was beaming with enthusiasm as he returned the prototype glasses to his best friend.

"Tyrrel, can I try them on?" Geoff asked from the front of the car.

"Sorry, Geoff, but you would have to take off your glasses to put them on, and then you would not be able to see," replied Tyrrel as he carefully put them back on his head. "Perhaps the next version will work for people who wear glasses."

Geoff looked disappointed.

"I'm sorry, Geoff. There is nothing I can do about the device's limitations," Tyrrel apologized. He did not want anyone to feel left out.

"It's alright, I understand."

The awkward, pale-skinned boy pushed his thick glasses back up on his nose and tried not to make a face of disappointment. The feeling in the car was so tense that Jasper could not ignore the situation, and he knew the boys all wanted a fun adventure away from school.

"Master Kyle, I see a Tim Hortons up ahead, and they have iced mocha lattes. Does anyone want something to drink?" Jasper suggested, knowing he would regret getting coffee for a bunch of preteen boys, but he knew he had to do something to change the topic of conversation.

Everyone in the car loved the idea of getting iced chocolate coffee drinks, so Jasper pulled over to go into the coffee shop and procure five small, iced mocha lattes. This allowed the topic of trying the prototype device to disappear from the current conversation. They only had thirty more minutes till they arrived at the Bergendahls' lovely Caledon home. The remaining drive was a caffeine-filled, boisterous conversation about horseback riding.

"I am a great horseman and can ride any horse," bragged René with his usual French confidence.

"Well, I have not. I have never been to the stables on the Academy grounds or any ranch or farm. My family is from Las Vegas, where we see wildlife up on a stage with dancers," replied Tyrrel. "Will someone train me how to get on the horse properly?"

"Sure, not a problem. My grandpa has a professional horse guy, who can train…" Kyle started to explain, but René interrupted him.

"You mean a groom or a horse trainer, not a horse guy," remarked René.

Kyle wrinkled his brow momentarily and then replied, "Yeah, a groom and a horse trainer. One of each, and anyway, I already reassured Geoff that you all would be shown how to ride."

"I don't know how to ride either, so don't feel bad," said Geoff as he had remained somewhat turned around in the car to be a part of the conversation in the back seat of the sedan. "I can't wait to tell my mom that I got to ride a horse. It's better to tell her afterward because she will be all worried that I might fall off and hurt myself."

René looked at Geoff and said sarcastically, "I can't imagine how anyone would think that you should fall off a horse."

Geoff frowned. Tyrrel and Kyle looked at each other sideways.

"René, not everyone has the experiences and talents you have, so don't be a pompous goof," remarked Tyrrel, coming to Geoff's rescue. René was Tyrrel's best friend, and they seemed to have bonded since the first day they met. René appreciated Tyrrel's sharp mind and less emotional response, which was almost needed when René would get overly aggressive and arrogant. Tyrrel seemed to know just how to reel him back to civility.

"My Maman says that I have too old of a spirit for a child's body, and that I do not have the temperament to play well with other children," remarked René.

"You do seem… kind of mean at times," remarked Kyle. "But not all the time. I can't wait to see you ride. It's so much fun, and I am sure Geoff and Tyrrel will catch on really quickly."

"So how many times have you ridden a horse?" asked René.

"Probably not as much as you, but enough that I can make Pearl do what I need her to do. Pearl is the name of the horse that my grandpa likes to have me ride. She's supposed to be good with beginning riders. I like Pearl a lot. I've missed going on rides in the morning with her and Grandpa," replied Kyle.

"So, are there enough 'Pearls' for all of us to ride?" asked Tyrrel. "I am very much a city boy."

"Geez, I don't know. Jasper, do you know if there are more horses like Pearl at Grandma and Grandpa's house?" asked Kyle.

"The Bergendahls' own ten horses that are stabled at the property in the Caledon House, and five of them are suited well for beginning riders, one of which is Pearl," Jasper responded to Kyle's question. "There is no need to be concerned that anyone will end up with a horse that is difficult to handle."

"See, we should all have a great time," said Kyle, hoping that everyone would be happy and have fun.

This was his first time having friends for a holiday and a sleepover. And before he and the others knew it, Jasper was pulling into the driveway of the Caledon House. As Jasper exited the car to open the doors and pop open the trunk of the BMW, Lily Bergendahl, accompanied by her son, Jon, came outside to greet the boys. Kyle ran to his father and gave him a great big hug.

"Hey, Sport, how are you doing?" asked Dr. Bergendahl, hugging his son warmly.

"Doing just great, Dad!"

"Wow, you look great in the school uniform. So grown up," said Dr. Bergendahl as he stepped back a little to look at his son. "You might have even grown a little. Your mom will be surprised the next time she sees you."

Kyle nodded in agreement, not knowing how to respond to his dad's assessment of his appearance.

"So, who are these guys?" Kyle's dad turned to the three boys who stood a little way from Kyle, patiently waiting to be introduced.

"This is Geoff Powell from Vancouver, Washington," said Kyle, gesturing to the skinny, dark-haired boy with glasses.

"Hello, no relation to the bookstore," replied Geoff with a smile.

"And this is Tyrrel Washington from Las Vegas," said Kyle, gesturing to the tall black boy.

Tyrrel nodded and said, "Pleased to meet you."

"And this is René DuBois from… he's French," said Kyle.

"I was born in Paris, France. Pleased to meet you, sir," René responded.

"Well, I am thrilled to meet all of you. This is my mother, Lily Bergendahl. She's Kyle's grandmother and the lady of this fine household, so what she says is law here," said Jon, joking but somehow serious on another level.

"Oh, Jon, you make me sound like a tyrant to the boys," Lily gently scolded her son. "Come now, everyone, let's come inside so that you can get yourselves settled, and afterward we shall have lunch outside on the patio since it is such a lovely day out."

Lily ushered the four boys, plus her son, into the house to settle them with their overnight gear and arrange where they would sleep. Lily offered the boys a choice between private rooms or sharing a room with multiple beds. The boys all agreed that staying in the same room together would be the most fun.

"Now I could ask Jasper to put cots into Kyle's room or I could let all four of you sleep in the bunk bedroom downstairs?" said Lily, leading the way down the hallway that Kyle had explored previously and showed them a room that had three sets of bunk beds, a couch, a TV, a closet, and a bathroom directly off the bedroom. It was clearly a room designed for guests with children. The boys unanimously voted for the bunk bedroom, which would allow them the most time together and freedom to talk and have fun.

While Geoff, Tyrrel, and René decided which beds they would sleep on, Kyle turned to his grandmother and said, "Thanks, Grandma. This is terrific. I love you so much. You always make things so fun." Kyle hugged her as she appreciatively wrapped her arms around him.

"I am so glad we could have you here for the holiday," said Lily. "We all missed you."

"I missed you, too, Grandma," replied Kyle. "I told the guys about going horseback riding. Can we do that this afternoon?"

"Certainly, I have already let the grooms and the trainer know that today might be a horseback riding day. You and the boys can go after lunch," said Lily.

"I want to go too," said Jon. "I don't get much time with Kyle or much time for horseback riding like I used to."

Lily smiled. There were times when he seemed more like his old self. She felt bad about the situation between Jon and Marie. They used to be so happy. It was like they were the perfect couple.

Lily announced, "I'll let you boys settle in, and lunch will be served in about half an hour."

"Thanks, Mrs. Bergendahl," said several of the boys in unison as she stepped away from the bunk bedroom and started down the hallway.

After deciding which bed to sleep in, the boys had a few minutes before lunch was ready. Geoff looked around the room while Tyrrel and René text-messaged their parents that they had arrived safely at Kyle's grandparents' home. Geoff turned to Kyle after a few moments of looking out the window and then down the long hallway.

"Your grandparents have a nice house. I don't think I have ever been in such a fancy house before," remarked Geoff.

Kyle smiled a little and said, "Yeah, they do seem to have a nice place. They also have another home in Toronto, but I don't recall it. I was there once as a baby."

"Geez, what do they do to have so much money?" asked Geoff.

"You know, I really don't know. I think my grandma owns a big skyscraper building in Toronto, but other than that, I have no idea what they do," replied Kyle.

"Well, this is a nice place. I'd like to have a house like this someday when I get older."

"Wouldn't we all," remarked Tyrrel as he finished his message to his parents. "But my dad says that not everyone gets to have fancy stuff, and if you want stuff like that, you have to earn it."

"My mom says stuff like that as well," remarked Geoff. "She wants me to get good grades or else I will lose my scholarship to the Academy and have to come home."

"You have a scholarship, too," said Tyrrel, extending his hand out for a high five.

Geoff eagerly accepted this friendly gesture and gave Tyrrel a high five back and said, "Yup, it's a fifty percent scholarship where my parents pay half and the school gets the other fifty percent from a scholarship fund. I would not have been able to go if it weren't for this. What about you two?"

"My parents make enough money to pay for the tuition. My Maman is a film actor, and she does pretty well while my Père works for the Order. They travel a lot. My

Maman works in film in France, Canada, and the United Kingdom. She speaks three languages fluently, so it is easy for her to get parts," René answered.

"Your mom is a movie star?!?!" exclaimed Geoff. "What is her name? What has she been in?"

"I don't know if you would have ever heard of her since her work is mostly seen in Europe and Canada," René responded with little enthusiasm, as if he was very used to being asked these questions. "She does a lot of small parts but is very respected within the industry. I am pretty sure, as an American, you have never heard of her."

"Oh," said Geoff, somewhat disappointed. After a few minutes of silence, Geoff turned to Kyle, "So, do you have a scholarship?"

"I have no idea," replied Kyle. He had never thought about that. The discussion of money never came up, and he had always assumed that his parents paid for school. He paused, pondering the question, and then said, "I don't know who pays for it or how much it is."

"Really?" inquired Tyrrel.

"Really. I don't know."

"Well, are your parents super wealthy?" asked Geoff.

"No. My mom is a medical assistant, and my dad works for a university, I think, as a doctor of theoretical and applied physics."

"Your dad has a PhD in Physics!" exclaimed Tyrrel. "Now that is awesome. Do you think he would mind if I asked him questions about his work?"

"No, he loves his work and would probably love to share his thoughts on… stuff. I have no idea what he does," Kyle replied with a smile.

"So perhaps your grandparents paid for the Academy tuition," suggested René, back to the previous topic.

"I had not thought about it, but that would make sense," said Kyle, now realizing how much his grandparents cared about him. They must have had a great deal of faith in him and believed he would excel at the Academy.

It was lunchtime, and Jasper had prepared a delightful meal of homemade soup, sandwiches, and French fries, all made just the way Kyle liked them: hot and crispy, with minimal salt, and never soggy. The boys had their fill of Jasper's excellent cooking, and even René, who could be incredibly picky, loved everything and thanked Jasper for the superb lunch. The food at the Academy was considered quite good and was one of the school's major selling points; therefore, the boys were accustomed to good-quality, well-prepared, healthy food. However, Jasper was an excellent chef and rarely served a bad meal. After lunch, Jon Bergendahl escorted the boys to the stables, where they met up with the grooms, including a trainer who could assist the boys in learning how to ride.

"Dad, where is Grandpa? He always teaches me how to ride."

Jon turned to his son, "Your grandfather is on his way back home from a business trip. He'll be back tonight. He's not going to miss seeing us all."

"Okay," Kyle nodded appreciatively. He knew his grandpa was often busy with work and sometimes had to be away. "What exactly does Grandpa do for work?"

"Your grandfather," Jon explained as he watched the grooms bring out the horses. Then he observed Geoff put on a pair of strange-looking orange sunglasses over his regular glasses. He paused, watching the curiously awkward boy explain something with his skinny arms flailing about in a train wreck fashion. Dr. Bergendahl refocused his thoughts and returned to his son, "Your grandfather is basically retired, but he still sits on many directing boards and must make decisions and give valuable insight from his many years of experience. So, it is like he is still working, but only part-time."

"Oh, I see," Kyle replied, noticing Geoff and his strange sunglasses. "But what does he really do? Just sit in meetings and talk with people?"

"Essentially, yes," replied Jon.

Then, Kyle watched and listened to what was happening with the groom and his friends, and he felt the need to claim Pearl as his own quickly.

"This is Pearl, and she is my horse to ride," said Kyle, quickly walking toward the mostly creamy white mare that nuzzled him affectionately. "Isn't she pretty?"

A third groom walked up with Clyde.

"Who is going to ride on Clyde?" Kyle asked, looking around for his grandfather and then his dad.

"Oh, don't look at me," said his father, raising his arms. "I was not a great horseman, and I am a bit rusty. I want to ride on one of the easy-going horses."

"I am an experienced horse rider," said René confidently.

For some reason, this made Kyle nervous, and he turned to Tyrrel as the French boy walked toward the groom who was bringing Clyde over, "Tyrrel, are you sure he is an experienced rider?"

"Do not worry. René says a lot of things, but he does know how to ride a horse quite well," replied Tyrrel.

Kyle, Tyrrel, Geoff, and Jon Bergendahl all silently watched René greet the groom and Clyde. They talked for a moment, and then the groom handed the reins over to René, who easily mounted the horse, circled him around the grounds, and then rode over to where the rest of the guys were waiting with the other horses.

"Hey, you weren't exaggerating when you said you knew how to ride a horse well. I'm impressed," remarked Kyle as he sat atop Perl and waited for the others to get situated with their mounts.

Dr. Bergendahl was the last person to mount up after checking that Geoff and Tyrrel were comfortably situated with their mounts. While René performed several circle and figure eight maneuvers with Clyde, and Kyle attempted to copy him, Geoff and Tyrrel received their lessons on how to communicate with their horses. As soon as Jon felt sure that the two boys were comfortable receiving instructions from the grooms, he rode over to where René and Kyle were with their mounts. He also did a few maneuvers to make sure he knew how to communicate with the bay mare named Betty. Betty was one of the five horses that were well-suited for beginning riders. René had Kyle play follow the leader with him, as he had Clyde do something, then Kyle was to copy it with Pearl. Kyle did well, but not as quickly or as neatly as René did with Clyde. Jon watched the two boys having fun with the horses and waited for them to reach a stopping point.

"When Geoff and Tyrrel have the basics down, where do you guys want to go riding?" Jon asked René and Kyle.

"Where can we go? Are there difficult trails or simple ones for them to be able to handle?" asked René as he gestured back to Tyrrel and Geoff.

"Most of the trails just follow the rolling hills, a few streams, and some meadows, so Tyrrel and Geoff will be fine. I just hope you won't be bored," replied Dr. Bergendahl.

"No, Sir, I will not be bored. It is great to be back on a horse again. I have been banned from riding at the Academy since last year. I took a horse out for a ride around the island and then raced some upper-level squire students on horseback. The Academy administration was less than happy with me, so I must wait until January when the prohibition is removed," replied René.

"I see," said Jon, raising his eyebrows a bit.

"Don't worry, Dr. Bergendahl," said René, his French accent coming through a bit stronger. "I will not abuse this wonderful privilege of being able to ride such a magnificent animal as Clyde. I am so grateful to you and Kyle's Bonne-maman for giving me this opportunity." Then René turned to Kyle and said, "Thank you for inviting me."

This was a side of René that Kyle had not seen before. He was so sincere and repentant.

"Sure thing, René. I just wish Lothar could have joined us as well. I think he would have had fun too."

"Ah, he is fine in the company of his relatives and all those pretty girls. Don't feel sorry for poor Lothar," René said with a smile.

"Okay," said Kyle as he watched Geoff and Tyrrel slowly make their way on horseback by themselves to where he, René, and his father were waiting.

"Look who has made it!" exclaimed René to Tyrrel. "I knew someday that you would find yourself on a horse."

Tyrrel just laughed. "You know this isn't so bad. A little uncomfortable on the backside, though," said the black boy as he gestured to his seating arrangement.

All the guys laughed, and Jon warned them that they might be sore the next morning, so they should not ride too long. The afternoon was spent riding through several open meadows surrounded by thick, tall tree groves that were filled with brilliant yellow, orange, and red fall foliage, and across a few dry creeks. Geoff almost fell off his horse twice, and after the second time, Jon figured it was probably time to head back toward the house since the boys seemed to be growing a bit tired. By the time they arrived back at the Caledon House, the sun was starting to hang low in the sky, and the boys were famished. Jon instructed them all to go into the house and get washed up. Geoff had managed to step into a few large piles of horse manure and had to leave his shoes outside.

"I didn't see those there!"

"How could you miss two hot, steaming, smelly piles of poo?!" exclaimed Kyle, making a face. "Ugh."

"Yes, those were gross. I like horses, but their excrement has a less than pleasant fragrance," noted Tyrrel as he made his way first into the bathroom of their bunk bedroom. Tyrrel washed his hands and checked to make sure he wasn't dirty. "My trousers are a bit dusty. Should I change them for tonight?"

"Yeah, we had all better change since I bet we are sitting inside at the nice dining table instead of the outside table," replied Kyle, looking at his pants, which showed signs of dirt.

"I didn't bring an extra pair of pants," said Geoff.

"You can borrow a pair of mine," offered Kyle. "They will be street clothes, not uniforms."

"That would be great," said Geoff with a smile. "Boy, am I hungry! Are we having dinner soon?"

"I think so, but what I am looking forward to is tomorrow… and having turkey," said Kyle. "I love turkey."

"My father tried one of those deep-fried turkey fryers, and it turned out to be the best turkey ever," said Tyrrel with a big smile. "I do miss being home for our Thanksgiving."

"Aren't those fryers dangerous? I asked my mom if she would try that, and she went on about how dangerous they were and people getting hurt and houses burning down," remarked Kyle.

"Well, my father is no fool. And I helped him research the best and safest method. If you follow the rules for using the device, then you should be safe using the fryer method. My father always says that stupid people should stay out of the kitchen."

Tyrrel said this with great sincerity and poise, as if it were a great oration from days long past.

Geoff laughed and blurted out, "Someone should tell my mom that! She keeps trying to show my sister, Clara, how to cook, and all she does is burn stuff and set things on fire."

"Fire?" René responded with an incredulous expression. "My Maman is a fair cook, but we often eat out or have the housekeeper take care of the meals."

"Your parents have a housekeeper?" Tyrrel inquired.

"Yes, my parents are often too busy to tend to such household matters," replied René.

"All of this is so different from what I am used to," said Geoff earnestly. "There are times when all of this seems more like a movie than reality. I love hanging out with you guys. Back home, everyone thinks I'm some kind of geeky weirdo."

"That's because you wear those orange sunglasses," remarked René with a smile, and brushed his long brown hair out of his face.

The guys laughed and then realized that Geoff needed a fresh pair of trousers for dinner, so they headed upstairs to Kyle's bedroom to find an extra set. After a suitable pair was found, they all made their way down the elegant stairway to the marble foyer. Geoff made everyone stop at the bottom of the stairs.

"Now, doesn't this look like something out of a movie? Kyle, your grandparents' house is amazing."

"This is nothing. Wait till I show you the library with all the cool stuff in there," replied Kyle.

Jasper served another excellent meal, created with his usual flair. After the meal, Dr. Bergendahl had a new video game that he wanted to show the boys. The game console was set up in the room with the bunk beds, and the boys, along with Dr. Bergendahl, all sat together and played a few games. Then Tyrrel and Dr. Bergendahl started chatting about physics, leaving Kyle, René, and Geoff to play the video game. As the evening wore on, Dr. Bergendahl excused himself from the boys to retire for the night, leaving them to look after themselves. Kyle's dad urged that the boys get ready for bed soon and not stay up too late talking. Tyrrel watched Kyle win another game.

"You wanna play now?" asked Kyle.

"No, I'm fine, just watching. Your dad is brilliant. He's great to talk to," commented Tyrrel.

"I'm just amazed that you understood all that stuff you were talking about. I don't understand any of it. I will try to understand, but I lose focus. It sounds so complicated," replied Kyle.

"It is complicated because you have not been taught the basic foundations for understanding it. I bet you would understand if you had the basics down," replied Tyrrel.

"Perhaps," said Kyle as he tapped on the control button, repeatedly firing down one of Geoff's invading pterodactyls.

"Oh, that was my last one," complained Geoff. "René, you wanna play?"

"No, I think I have had enough video games for tonight," replied René as he lounged on his bunk with a book.

"Me too. Kyle, you're the champion," said Geoff, setting down the controls.

"Okay." Kyle turned to Tyrrel and asked, "Are you sure you don't want to play?"

"No, I'm fine. My mind is filled with all kinds of ideas. I should write them down," replied Tyrrel as he got up and pulled out the strange glasses and wireless keyboard.

Kyle turned off the gaming console and TV, then put away the controls.

"So why can't I use your prototype computer?" asked Geoff.

"Well, since you wear glasses, you would not be able to see clearly because the HUD does not compensate for your prescription. You can try them, but it will probably look blurry and might give you a headache," replied Tyrrel.

"I see. That sucks," remarked Geoff. "Do you think they will ever fix it and make it work for people like me?"

"They will have to in order to make them practical. Many people wear corrective eyewear, so having a product they can't use isn't very viable," replied Tyrrel. "Perhaps you should look into obtaining contact lenses."

Geoff nodded appreciatively.

"You can always read a book," suggested René as he continued to lie on his bunk and read.

"Speaking of books, did you say your grandparents have a library in the house with cool stuff?" asked Geoff.

"Oh, that's right. I forgot," said Kyle as he stretched a bit after sitting for so long on the floor playing Dinosaur

Tribe Wars. "I was going to show you the whole library. And it does look like something out of a movie. It makes you feel like you are at Hogwarts or some other amazing mystical place like that."

"Now that sounds intriguing," remarked René, looking up from his book.

"Can we see it?" asked Geoff.

Kyle looked up at the clock in the room, which displayed 9:35. His grandparents usually went to bed at nine o'clock, and he was normally expected to go to bed himself around this time. He could sometimes stay up till ten in the evening if there was a special reason. He looked at his three companions. This was a special occasion.

"We must be quiet because my grandparents go to bed at nine, and normally they want me to go to bed as well, or at least hang out in my room. So can you guys be super quiet?"

"Sure," said Geoff.

"Certainly," said Tyrrel.

"I'm up for a small adventure and can be very stealthy, if necessary," remarked René.

"Okay, then follow me. And we can't turn on any lights, I don't want to disturb Jasper either," said Kyle.

"I have a cell phone that works well as a flashlight," suggested René.

Kyle smiled.

"Then let's go. No shoes, so we don't make any unnecessary noise," said Kyle, removing his shoes.

The boys turned down the room lights to just one nightstand light and removed their shoes and anything else that might make noise. René made his cell phone flashlight ready. Kyle opened the door slowly and listened in the hallway to see if he could hear any noises. Hearing nothing and seeing that all the lights were either off or down for the evening, Kyle led the way down to the room at the end of the hallway, which was the library. Upon reaching the door, Kyle hoped that it would still be unlocked, just as he had found it last summer. He reached for the door handle and gently turned it to see if it would open. Much to his relief, the door opened.

"I saw a red light flicker. Did anyone else see a red light?" whispered Tyrrel.

"No, I just looked into René's cell phone and now I'm blind," said Geoff.

"Shhhh… Not so loud, guys," whispered Kyle. "Let's get inside the room and close the door."

René used his cell phone flashlight to show the way into the room, while Kyle carefully closed the door after everyone was inside.

"I saw a red light again," said Tyrrel in a low voice.

"I didn't see it," replied René. "Where was it?"

"Over there," Tyrrel pointed across the room.

The boys all looked in that direction and stood still for a moment, waiting to see if they would see the light. Nothing.

"Perhaps it is one of those flashing lights from a smoke detector or alarm system. You know, for the windows and outside doors," René suggested. "My parents have alarm systems like that, and they are always flashing when armed."

"It would make sense that the house is secured," Tyrrel responded to René's idea.

René then slowly used the cell phone flashlight to illuminate the entire room for everyone to see. Some light came from the sheer-draped windows, but only enough to give an idea of where the big furniture was in the room. When René's light descended upon the suit of armor, the boys all gasped in appreciation.

"Oh, let's go see that up close," urged Geoff, his eyes wide with enthusiasm.

The boys walked over to the suit of armor and the nearby glass display case that held swords and other items. René pointed the cell phone flashlight at the armor, and the boys admired it.

"Is it a real suit or just a display piece?" asked Tyrrel.

"I have no idea. It's made of metal and appears to be real," replied Kyle.

"What I mean… is this suit a real piece of armor worn by a knight or just a cool display piece?" Tyrrel clarified his question.

"I still don't know," replied Kyle.

René stepped forward and touched the suit. It appeared to be constructed of dark, silvery grey metal that had a few dents here and there. Despite the dents, it was smooth to the touch. It was a Maximillian-style suit of armor with ridges that gave strength to the design. There were no engravings or fancy heraldry anywhere on the suit. René stared at it for the longest time with the other boys.

"I have seen many suits of armor," René said finally. "In museums and castles back home and throughout Europe, and this one… looks like it could be real."

"Wow!" exclaimed Geoff. "That's awesome. Can you imagine wearing something like that? It must have been *really* heavy."

"Actually, the knights got used to wearing armor like wearing a jacket or a pair of trousers. It was normal. The smart knights with money to spend had their suits made especially for them, so that the fit would be comfortable all day long," replied René as he stood and admired the armor.

"René, put the light on the display case. There are a bunch of nice swords in here," suggested Kyle as he directed René where to shine the light.

The four boys stood around the long glass display case, which housed several swords placed upon velvet fabric and several sets of silver spurs.

"Do you see what I see?" Tyrrel asked René.

"I do," replied René.

"What do you see?" asked Kyle.

"These look like swords of the Order as well as spurs that would also have belonged to Knights of the Order long ago," replied René. "I know this because my father has a sword like the one in the back, and he also has his great-great-grandfather's spurs, which look a little like those ones down there."

"So, what does that mean?" asked Kyle.

"That someone in your family is a Knight of the Order," said Tyrrel.

"And that is the reason why you got to ride in the helicopter on the first day of school," said René.

Kyle stared at the display case filled with beautiful artifacts from the past, feeling both overwhelmed and a bit baffled. No one had ever mentioned anything about anyone being a knight in his family. Was it a secret, he wondered. And why would they keep that a secret?

"Guys, no one has ever mentioned anything about anyone being a knight," said Kyle. "Is being a knight some kind of secret?"

"It was in certain parts of the world," replied René. "Being a Knight of our Order meant death up until very recently, when countries finally realized how crazy those laws were."

"Why would being a knight be against the law?" asked Geoff and Kyle simultaneously.

"Because long ago, the Order that René's family belongs to was betrayed by the Roman Catholic Church and the French Monarchy," replied Tyrrel.

"So were *all* knights made illegal?" asked Kyle.

"No… just the… Templar," replied René with a thoughtful, faraway tone as he slowly looked upward. He then uttered something in French that no one understood and pointed his cell phone flashlight up at the wall where a large tapestry hung. The tapestry depicted an incredible scene of old, rickety sailing vessels leaving an embattled coastline of bright white, sandy beachside cliffs and then venturing out into rough, stormy seas. One of the sailing vessels was being torn apart by rough waves while Knights in other vessels looked helplessly on at the sight of the stricken vessel and its doomed passengers.

"That is the companion tapestry to the one Lothar's Grandpapa owns," said René in awe. "Someone in your family was a very important Knight. Not just any family would own that tapestry."

Kyle and the others felt the heaviness of the moment and remained silent. They could imagine the dreadful situation and the anguish felt by everyone present, and then Kyle asked, "So, there is another tapestry like this one? What is on it?"

"It is of the battle scene on the beach where the Knights and the Sergeants were trying to help their families, young pages, and squires flee from the murderous attacks and get to the ships. There is supposed to be a third tapestry that shows where the Knights and their families escaped to," replied René. "But I have never seen it, and neither has my own Papa nor Maman," René answered as he stared at the tapestry for the longest time in reverence with the other boys.

Kyle found himself sympathizing with the agonizing feeling it must have been to be on a nearby ship in the storm and not able to help those in the other vessel. He wondered who made the tapestry and marveled at how difficult it must have been to create something so intricate. He wondered why he had never paid much attention to the tapestry until now.

Suddenly, the boys were all startled by the loud beeping noise that René's cell phone made.

"Oh my gosh, that really scared me," commented Geoff as he instinctively clutched at his pounding chest.

"Yeah, that made me jump, too," commented Kyle, broken away from the spell of the tapestry's story.

"Your cell phone probably needs charging," said Tyrrel to René.

René clicked off the flashlight application and checked his phone.

"Oui, the battery is almost dead. We will not be able to use the flashlight app anymore tonight," replied René.

"We'll let's go to bed. We can always look at the tapestry tomorrow," said Kyle.

"It's pretty dark in here," remarked Geoff.

"I can find my way out. Follow me and keep close," said Kyle.

The boys made it quietly out of the library room and back into their bedroom. They all got ready for bed and crawled into their chosen bunks. Kyle lay awake in the darkness, his head swimming full of thoughts of knights fighting and sailing off on ships to escape, and then wondered who in his family could have owned such a special tapestry. Did he have any knights in his family? And what did that mean? Could he become a knight, too? And was his dad a knight? If so, why didn't he tell him? Luckily, Kyle fell asleep before René could start snoring. His head was filled with strange dreams that all vanished upon waking the next morning.

Early that morning, the boys feasted on freshly baked biscuits, sausage, and eggs. Kyle's grandparents and dad were already up and had gone off into another part of the house. Jasper tended to the boys' needs as he poured juice and hot tea for anyone who wished it.

"Jasper, I'm not sure I would like hot tea," Kyle said after Jasper offered to pour a cup for him.

"I just thought you and the other young masters would be quite tired after a late night of admiring armor and tapestries, and the tea would be beneficial," remarked Jasper with a completely stony-faced expression and tone of voice that alluded to no particular feeling concerning the matter.

Kyle and the boys stopped spreading jam and stuffing their mouths with eggs, looking up at the butler.

"Uh, how did you know that we were admiring armor and a tapestry?" asked Kyle, with the other three boys very still and listening.

"The Caledon House is fully alarmed and has a security system at the height of technology, Master Kyle. I could watch all four of you in high definition as you looked about in the library using Master René's cell phone as a flashlight."

"Oh, are we in trouble? We didn't touch anything or break anything. And I have been in there before with Grandma," said Kyle, feeling worried.

"No, you are not in trouble. The four of you triggered the alarm in that room. If you wish to visit the library in the late hours of the night, then I need to know so that I can deal with the alarm system."

"Oh, I'm sorry, Jasper. I didn't know that going in there would disturb anyone. As a matter of fact, we were trying to be quiet so we would not bother anyone," replied Kyle, feeling bad that he had caused Jasper to wake up.

Kyle looked up at the butler, who was holding a teapot full of steaming hot tea. Jasper eyed Kyle back and replied, "Next time, please let me know. Your grandparents own some very significant documents and artifacts that they have been entrusted with for safekeeping, and some of those items are in the library."

"Next time, I will make sure you know, or we will just go in there during the daytime," replied Kyle. "I'd like to try that hot tea, but I have never had hot tea before. Do you put anything special in it?"

"Certainly," said Jasper as he poured some tea into Kyle's cup. "Some people drink the tea plain, while others opt for sugar, honey, or cream, and some like a combination."

"Hey, Jasper, did you think we were burglars?" asked Geoff.

"I was not sure what to expect until I consulted the alarm system," replied Jasper. "It is unwise to assume anything."

"Jasper, can you tell us about the lovely, large tapestry that hangs in the library?" asked René as he resumed putting jelly on the biscuit he was preparing.

"Master René, I think the story that goes with that tapestry should be reserved for Mr. and Mrs. Bergendahl to tell. It is part of their family history, and therefore, they should have the privilege of telling the tale," replied Jasper with a smile.

234

After Jasper had tended to the boys' breakfast needs, he informed them that he was excusing himself to continue preparing for the family Thanksgiving dinner. Kyle quickly grabbed the butler's shirt cuff.

"Thanks for not getting mad or telling on us," said Kyle.

Jasper nodded and smiled and then left the room to continue his duties.

"Kyle, I guess you will have to ask your grandparents if they will tell us about the tapestry," said Tyrrel as he prepared to finish his last piece of sausage.

"I guess so. I hope they will tell us. Now I am very curious," said Kyle.

The Thanksgiving Day dinner would be served as a late lunch or very early dinner to accommodate the need to return the boys to the school that evening. Jasper hoped to have everything ready at two o'clock. Kyle was surprised to find his grandmother in the kitchen with Jasper, getting things ready. She always had this ability to look so classy and lovely, even when doing something as mundane as chopping up celery and wearing an apron.

"Hello, Grandma, I didn't know you were helping Jasper today," said Kyle as he walked into the kitchen with the guys.

"Kyle dear, I always help Jasper with big family or holiday meals. I used to love to cook when I was younger and learned how to cook from my grandmother," replied

Lily Bergendahl with a smile. "So, how are my young, handsome gentlemen doing today?"

Geoff awkwardly looked around and then looked at Lily, who looked back at him as if to say that he was included in that question. "Well… I'm just fine today. Jasper is a great cook. I love eating his food."

"He is an eating machine, Mrs. Bergendahl," responded René.

"He insists he has hollow limbs, but that is scientifically impossible. I suspect a high metabolism," said Tyrrel in one of his more Tuvok moments.

"Well, around two o'clock, we should have enough food to satisfy his great appetite," replied Lily as she placed the chopped celery into a glass bowl and then reached for a yellow onion.

"Grandma, do you know where Dad is?" asked Kyle.

"I think he might be in the front parlor checking his email. He wants to see what you boys want to do this morning," replied Lily.

"Thanks, Grandma," Kyle said as he led the way to the room his grandmother had described. There, he found his dad intensely focused on typing away on his laptop.

The boys stood quietly as the older version of Kyle typed furiously on the laptop, his complete attention seemingly focused on what he was writing. Kyle's father then slowed his typing pace and turned to the boys, who were waiting.

236

"Have a seat, guys, while I finish this last email," said Jon Bergendahl.

The boys took their seats in the room, which appeared to be used only for formal occasions, such as greeting special guests. It was the kind of room most American households no longer had. Dr. Bergendahl, with his laptop computer, looked out of place in the formal setting, which featured expensive-looking antique furniture and artwork. Everything was perfectly coordinated and was obviously selected just for this room. Kyle never knew what to do in this room, so he often stayed out of it. René looked comfortable, but Tyrrel and Geoff seemed a little ill at ease.

Finally, Jon looked up at the boys and asked them, "So what do you all want to do this morning? We should probably stay out of the way of the preparations for dinner. We could watch a movie in the movie room or do something outside." Jon looked over at René, whose expression told him precisely what René would have suggested, "Ah, but sadly enough, no horseback riding today. I am a bit sore from yesterday's ride."

René frowned slightly as he pushed his long hair out of his eyes.

The boys decided that watching a movie would be fun, which would allow Kyle to spend time with his dad and his grandfather, who also decided to join them. They all settled in the movie room, where Karl Bergendahl had installed a surround sound system some time ago. They turned up the volume and watched *Top Gun*, followed by the *Iron Man* movies. By the time they were ready to have

Thanksgiving dinner, the boys had visions of being either pilots or inventors of mechanical flying suits. Tyrrel was certain that someday such devices could be made, while René and Geoff argued whether American or French pilots were the best in the world. Kyle was pleased. Life was terrific with new friends, and he got to spend the holiday with his grandparents and dad. For the first time in a very long time, he had people to have fun with. And it felt like family and a home.

Jasper and Lily Bergendahl had set a lovely table for eleven people. An elderly couple from down the road, who were unable to join their children, came over to have dinner with the Bergendahls, but there was still an extra seat available. Jasper would join them at the table, but that left one empty seat. Kyle was seated between his father and Geoff, so he leaned over to his dad and asked, "Is someone else still coming?"

Jon looked at the table and the empty place and answered Kyle, "It's a family tradition to leave a seat empty on holiday feasts just in case a stranger comes in need."

Kyle thought that was nice. Everything was done beautifully, with the fancy candles lit on the table and all the fancy silverware and dishes. He watched as Jasper finished placing all the food on the table, which looked and smelled fantastic. All the guests were introduced to one another, and a friendly, polite conversation began as everyone took their seats. When Jasper was done bringing in all the necessary items and had taken his place at the table, Karl Bergendahl held up a glass filled with white wine.

"I would like to make a toast on this very fine day," said Karl Bergendahl with his Swedish accent still evident in his manner of speech. "I feel tremendously thankful to have my grandson Kyle and his young friends here, to have the Kleins here as our guests, to have my son Jon with us, to have Jasper as a part of our household, and to have the most charming, loving wife, my Lily, here with me. I never dreamed I would be so fortunate as a young man, and I just want to say I am so delighted. It is a family tradition on Thanksgiving Day for everyone at the table to say something they are thankful or happy about, and I would like it so much if everyone could say something."

Karl held his filled glass in his hand and then looked at Mr. Klein, seated directly to his left.

"Ah, well said, Karl," said Mr. Klein as he picked up his wine glass for the toast. "I am so thankful that while we miss our own loving family, we can enjoy the company of another loving family."

Mr. Klein held his glass in his hand and then looked at his wife, who sat to his left.

"I am happy that Jasper is cooking this year," she said with a laugh and held her wine glass.

Jasper smiled as he picked up his glass and said, "I am truly thankful to be included in such a loving manner with the Bergendahl family."

Lily Bergendahl picked up her wine glass and looked at everyone at the table warmly, and said, "Autumn is the season of great transition, which can be, in some cases, very scary. And I am truly thankful that so many of the transitions that have occurred lately have been happy ones."

Lily then looked at Tyrrel, who picked up his wine glass, which was more modestly filled than the adults' portions. He looked at the glass with some surprise and said, "I am thankful to be going to the Academy for another year, and… that my mother is not here to see me holding this glass of wine."

"Oh, my goodness," exclaimed René, who sat beside Tyrrel and picked up his glass. "I am happy that my family is French and is not so unsophisticated about drinking wine at the table." René looked at Tyrrel, who raised an eyebrow at his friend. "And… I am also thankful to have such a good friend as Tyrrel."

Geoff, who was sitting next to René, reached for his glass and nearly toppled it over.

"Uh, sorry about that. I guess I am happy that I didn't knock that over," Geoff said, laughing uneasily. "But what I would like to say is that I am thankful and happy to be invited along. This has been fun."

Geoff held up his wine glass aloft just like everyone else.

It was Kyle's turn. He had planned to say how great everything was, but then he remembered his mom, who would be without him this year for American Thanksgiving Day. The thought made him sad. He was so happy now, and he felt almost guilty that he had been so happy during these past few months.

Everyone was staring at him and waiting for him to say something.

"I'm happy and thankful that Mom and Dad allowed me to go to the Academy," Kyle finally said, pushing away his sad feelings for his mom. He picked up his wine glass and held it aloft.

Jon Bergendahl smiled at his son. He picked up his glass and said, "Here's to many more years of happy gathering." Jon was the last to make a toast, so he took a drink from his glass.

Everyone followed his example.

"Boys, if you don't want to drink the wine, you don't have to," said Lily, primarily directed at Tyrrel, who showed some concern about what his mother would think.

René had already taken his sip, along with Geoff, who was smacking his lips, trying to decide if he liked the taste or not. Kyle took a sip and then asked his dad not to tell his mom about it, because he didn't think she would approve.

Tyrrel smelled the clear liquid. It had an interesting odor that was unfamiliar to him. He wasn't sure if it was pleasant or unpleasant. He took a sip of the clear liquid. It had a strange fruitlike quality, yet it wasn't right. Tyrrel's expression said it all.

"You don't have to drink it, dear," said Lily, gazing at the perplexed black boy.

"It's really… odd. I don't think I like it," replied Tyrrel to Lily.

René rolled his eyes in disgust and took the glass out of Tyrrel's hand. He poured the wine into his glass and said something in French that either no one understood or no one wanted to acknowledge they understood.

"Well, that is now out of my hands," Tyrrel commented.

Jasper got up immediately, went into the kitchen, and came back with a bottle of apple juice and a can of soda. "Master Tyrrel, which would you prefer?"

"I would like the apple juice," replied Tyrrel.

Jasper opened one of the china cabinets, pulled out a crystal drinking glass, poured the apple juice into the glass, and then set it on the table for Tyrrel.

"Thank you," said Tyrrel, picking up the glass and taking a sip of apple juice. "Now that is a drink that I like."

Everyone busied themselves, loading their plates full of food and passing various dishes back and forth to each other. The satisfying quiet of people enjoying food fell upon the dining room. It wasn't until Geoff had piled his plate for a third helping that Kyle had recalled needing to ask his grandfather about the tapestry in the library.

"Grandpa, Jasper said that you were the person to ask about the big tapestry in the library," said Kyle.

Karl Bergendahl looked over at Kyle, then Lily, and then back at Jon and Kyle.

"It's been a while since I last told anyone about that tapestry," said Karl Bergendahl with a smile.

"It's an important story to our family, and it is important that Kyle knows it and that Jon hears it again for future generations," remarked Lily.

Karl smiled lovingly at his wife, who sat at the other end of the table.

"Then I will tell the story," said the senior Bergendahl as he sat back in his chair and smoothed his slowly turning white blonde hair.

"That tapestry is part of a set of three, which were created by several families long ago, back in the thirteen hundreds. They were created so that future generations would not forget what happened to those who were a part of the Templar Order when it was attacked. It is not a happy story… or a glorious one, but a tragic one of betrayal and greed," said Karl as he looked at his young audience and then at his older listeners.

"What most historians do not seem to recall is that the members of the Order did not just come from wealthy noble families, but all kinds of family backgrounds. If someone is truly worthy of being a Knight in our Order, then those with wealth would often sponsor the candidate, so that upon completion of training, they could obtain the necessary armor and equipment to serve with. The Order was strengthened by having good people, so assisting those who demonstrated exceptional qualities helped to reinforce the Order. It made achieving our goals more likely. Also, some Knights were married and had children. This is another fact that historians seemed to have forgotten or was lost to the ravages of time," Karl paused to look around to make sure his audience was still interested.

"So then, when the French Monarchy sent out the command under the strong encouragement of the Roman Catholic Church, it was not just single men who were warriors who suffered at the hands of these greedy, power-hungry villains. It was the wives, children, parents, grandparents, siblings, and even the animals that were associated with the Knight who were brutally slaughtered."

"Did these people do anything bad?" Geoff asked with an obvious expression of concern and distress.

"No, they were innocent folks," replied Karl Bergendahl.

"Geoff, it was somewhat like Anakin Skywalker going crazy after he joined up with the Emperor in Star Wars. Remember the scene when he kills all the Younglings," said Tyrrel.

"Yeah, that was awful," said Geoff, looking distressed.

"Indeed, it was," said Karl. "And that was a fictional tale. This one is real."

Kyle felt a deep sense of injustice well up in his heart and did his best not to interrupt his grandpa so that the story could be finished.

"The Knights, along with the Sergeants, Squires, and Pages, all worked together to get the word out that everyone must go into hiding, and some would have to flee for their lives. Those living in France had to flee, so it was decided to utilize their entire fleet of ships, including the ancient vessels from the long-forgotten Imperial Order, to save as many members and families as possible. The French warriors, who were attacking the Order, were specifically looking to kill the Knights, who were leaders and preservers of Templar knowledge. So, the Sergeants dressed as Knights to protect the Order and help preserve our way of life for future generations. Many Sergeants lost their lives to save the family members, pages, and squires from having to endure horrible deaths and torture-filled imprisonment. The three tapestries were created in honor of those who died to ensure that future generations would remember these gallant souls. And my family is one of the families that had the honor of keeping one of the three tapestries."

Karl Bergendahl concluded the story with a smile and a strong sense of pride. Everyone was quiet for a few moments.

"Dad, I always love hearing that story. Each time, you tell it a little differently but with the same message, and I seem to learn something each time," commented Jon.

"Dad, are you a knight?" asked Kyle.

"No, I am not," replied Jon.

"Why not?" asked Kyle.

"That is a topic of conversation for another time," replied Jon with a certain amount of weariness, as if this topic had come up many times before.

Karl and Lily looked at each other and then at Jon as if to acknowledge some secret topic. Jon looked at them, just shook his head, and said, "I don't want to discuss that right now. We just had a brilliant meal made by Jasper."

"Speaking of such things," said Jasper. "I have also brilliantly made some dessert as well. Is anyone ready for pie, or do you wish to wait until a little later?"

Jon looked at his watch and then replied, "I will have to take the boys up to Lake Simcoe in about two hours, so... could we have dessert in about an hour?"

Jon looked around at everyone else at the table, who were all looking rather full after the amazing turkey dinner and excellent side dishes. Jasper noticed the same response, which implied that dessert would be better appreciated in about an hour.

"Very well then," said Jasper. "I will serve dessert in an hour with coffee."

"That sounds perfect, Jasper," said Lily. "I suggest that the older folks retire to the living room, and our young companions should set about gathering up their gear for the trip back to school."

"Okay, Grandma. Can we be excused from the table?" asked Kyle, remembering his best manners for the occasion.

"Yes, you may be excused from the table," replied Lily with a smile. Lily then invited her elderly guests and her son to join her in the formal living room to chat and wait for Jasper to be ready with the dessert.

The Fabulous Five minus one went back to the bunk bedroom, packed up their belongings, and discussed the events of the weekend. They all felt sleepy from having stuffed themselves with so much food. René and Geoff looked as if they were going to fall asleep as they relaxed on their selected bunks. In what seemed like a short amount of time, Jasper came to their room and invited the boys to have pie and ice cream in the kitchen while the adults had dessert in the formal living room with coffee. Dr. Bergendahl finished his dessert rather quickly so that he could prepare to bring the boys back to school. He loaded their bags and had the BMW sedan parked out front and ready to go.

"So did everyone have a good time?" Jon asked the group of boys sitting around the kitchen breakfast table.

"I had an excellent time, Dr. Bergendahl. I enjoyed discussing physics with you," said Tyrrel with a big smile.

"Well, so did I. You are very knowledgeable for someone of your age," Jon replied with a smile.

Tyrrel grinned.

"That's what he does," said René. "I had a wonderful time as well. It was so nice to ride a horse again. Merci."

"I had a great time, too. Can't wait 'til I can tell my parents that there is a Canadian version of Thanksgiving. I had no idea," said Geoff. "I think we should celebrate both."

Jon laughed a bit.

"Good. Glad to hear that everyone had a good time. You too, Sport, right?" Jon asked Kyle.

247

Kyle nodded and smiled.

"Okay, is everyone ready for the trip back to Lake Simcoe?" asked Jon.

"I think so," replied Kyle.

Kyle said goodbye to his grandparents and then joined the others in the car for the trip back. Within about fifteen minutes of the drive, all four boys had fallen asleep, and Dr. Bergendahl had a peaceful drive up to the school. Upon arriving at the ferry platform, Kyle hugged his father and told him how much he had enjoyed seeing him and wished his mom could have been there too. It was the perfect holiday except for her not being there. There was nothing that Jon could say concerning this matter. It was what it was. He hugged his son warmly, thinking how nice it would have been if Marie had not changed so much in those years that seemed so long ago. One cannot control unfortunate events introduced by others with selfish motives. He knew it wasn't her fault.

Chapter 11: Preparations for Halloween

The next event that students of the Academy often looked forward to was Halloween, along with the activities associated with it. The older students had a costume dance, while the younger students participated in arts and crafts and a costume party. The event encouraged students to be creative and develop their social skills through interaction with one another. The Page Level students made masks, created simple costumes, learned the various histories behind the holiday, and participated in the pumpkin carving contest. On Halloween day, they would go trick-or-treating to the local houses on the island, and in the evening, they would play party games and watch movies. This was one of the few nights when the local inhabitants of the island could send their children to the Academy to attend the youth parties hosted by the school. Living on an island could make it a lonely place for the children of island residents, as the ferry boat was not running to take children ashore for trick-or-treat activities. The permanent residents were happy to participate in the door-to-door candy gathering in exchange for the safe evening party held by the school.

Kyle had no idea what he wanted to do for Halloween. He was expected to draw pictures of who or what he wanted to be in art class. Then his Primary Languages teacher, Sir Knight Mary, asked him to write a paragraph describing who or what he wanted to be and another paragraph explaining why he chose that particular identity. Halloween had never been so complicated. There were numerous choices, but each came at a cost. How would he ever make a costume for some of the characters that he wanted to select? The art instructor, Sir Knight Greta, had advised everyone to choose something that they were passionate about. It would make it easier to work on a project in which they were fully invested.

Kyle walked around the art room trying to get ideas. Some kids were going with a scary theme, while others, like a large group of little girls, all wanted to be fairy princesses. He wasn't interested in the idea of doing the scary stuff. It never appealed to him.

"Still no luck, Mr. Bergendahl?" asked Sir Knight Greta.

"No," he replied sullenly. "I just don't know what to do. And I think of something, but then it seems too complicated for me to be able to make the costume."

"Don't worry about it being beyond your ability to do. This is something we do every year, and very rarely does anyone have a perfect costume. It's about having fun and figuring out how to solve the various problems of the characters we select," replied Sir Knight Greta. "Go see what your friends are thinking about doing. Maybe they will inspire you?"

"Okay. I'll go do that," said Kyle as he realized that she was probably right. Perhaps he could work on a character who functioned well with his friends. Back home in Reno, he and Dark Cloud went as the Lone Ranger and Tonto. Dark Cloud went as the Lone Ranger, and he went as Tonto. It was good fun to see how people would react with their obvious roles reversed.

Kyle walked over to Tyrrel and looked at the drawing he was doing for his Halloween character. He had two drawings of men wearing lab coats.

"Who are these guys supposed to be? Are you going as a mad scientist?" asked Kyle.

"Oh goodness no. I am trying to decide between Enrico Fermi and George Washington Carver. Both are brilliant scientists and did so much for the scientific world."

"I would go with Nikola Tesla," said Lothar from across the table.

"Darn! That is a good choice," said Tyrrel, looking frustrated. "But I have already started collecting data and items for the costume."

Kyle then wandered over to see what Lothar was working on. Lothar also had two different drawings that he was doing. One picture showed a guy with his hair on fire, while the other looked like Han Solo.

"Okay, that one looks like Han Solo, right?" asked Kyle.

"Yes, that is correct."

"Who is the other guy?" asked Kyle. "Ghost Rider?"

"No. The Norse God Loki, powerful fire wight," said Lothar. "Not the Marvel comic book version."

"Hmmm," said Kyle, nodding. "Isn't Loki a bad guy?"

"It depends upon how much you know about Norse Mythology. He is a controversial person because he has been made into a villain by a conquering religion, not to mention that North American reconstructionism has misunderstood who he really is," replied Lothar. "Also, look at my hair. It's the perfect color, and my name has its origins in being based on Loki."

"Okay, I can understand that point of view. But I think Han Solo would be more fun to play," replied Kyle as he walked toward René, who was busy sketching a masterpiece with colored pencils.

"That is an awesome drawing of Iron Man, but I don't know who the other guy is," said Kyle, looking at René's drawings.

"This is Georges Guynemer. He was considered a top ace for the French forces during World War I," replied René.

Kyle thought both sketches looked great and would get René a high mark from the instructor, but he still did not know what to do about his costume idea. It seemed hopeless, and he lacked inspiration for the project. Kyle walked over to see what Geoff was sketching. He also had two ideas. One drawing resembled a Green Lantern character with a big red X slashed across it, while the uncensored version appeared to be a drawing of Yoda from Star Wars.

This additional Star Wars character prompted him to think about the Clone Wars series he had enjoyed watching. Being a Jedi would be awesome except that having a Padmé was not allowed, thought Kyle absently as he glanced at Freya sitting across the room with her girlfriends. But it would still be fun to be a Star Wars character, he thought. He wanted to be something honorable and also part of a team. Kyle looked up at the walls around the art room, looking for inspiration. Then he saw one of the drawings done by the older students. It was a picture of a knight in armor. It was at this point that Kyle got his inspiration and decided to be a Clone ARC Trooper. That would be his costume.

"I know what I want to do!" Kyle exclaimed. "I need to do some research. I need to find pictures of Clones."

"Clones?" said Tyrrel, wrinkling his forehead. "What kind of clones? Sheep?"

"No. Like Jango Fett-type clones," replied Kyle.

"Oh... cool idea," said Geoff. "That will go great with my Yoda."

"What made you think of that?" asked René.

"I was thinking about Star Wars characters and then noticed the drawing of the knight in armor up on the wall," replied Kyle. "I think I will look up Star Wars on the computer and search for pictures."

"If you find any good pictures of Yoda, get them for me," said Geoff.

"Sure," said Kyle.

Lothar looked away from his drawings and at Geoff and Kyle.

"If you and Geoff are going as Star Wars characters, then I shall go as Han Solo. His rebellious merc attitude seems like something I could deal with," said Lothar with a big grin, sitting up straighter. "Don't forget we must write papers and descriptions about the characters we choose."

"I thought you should have picked someone like Ron Weasley," remarked Trevor as he walked past the computer desks.

"Only if you dumped bleach on your head and went as Malfoy," retorted Lothar.

"Well, he was rich and came from an important family," replied Trevor, not feeling the least bit insulted.

Kyle ignored the friendly banter and pulled up a bunch of pictures of Clone Troopers on the Internet.

"I think this will give me some ideas about what I need to do to make a costume like this," said Kyle as he looked at it. Geoff and Lothar followed him to the computers and stood behind him, looking at the large flat screen.

"Remember, this project is about how you use your creativity and problem-solving skills. Not that you make a perfect movie-ready costume," said Sir Knight Greta, who seemed to have just walked up on them without a single sound.

The three boys jumped a little, not expecting the teacher to have been standing alongside them, looking at the computer screen with them.

254

"That's an excellent choice. And I look forward to seeing how you decide to deal with the complexities that arise from such a project," said Sir Knight Greta. "Collect more than one picture. Make sure they are from different angles so you can see the 360 degrees of information you will need."

The art instructor silently walked away to help other students.

"I told you she was stealthy," said Lothar to Geoff and Kyle, who both still had shocked expressions on their faces.

"She's kind of scary when she does that," said Geoff as he readjusted his thick glasses.

"Yes, and I'm glad she is on our side… She is on our side, right?" asked Kyle.

"Oh, yes. She does care about all of us. I think she is one of the better teachers here. Most of the instructors are great, but she truly feels that it is important that we understand and achieve our goals," said Lothar. "I like her even though I find her stealthiness a little disturbing."

"Send those images to your tablet so that you can join us at the drawing tables," said Geoff.

Kyle sent the images he had collected to be uploaded to his tablet, then rejoined the guys at the drawing tables.

The rest of the week went well, with progress made on each milestone of the assignment. Kyle was struggling with the new martial arts lessons involving the javelin. He was just not good at throwing the long spear-like object. It was horrible, but he was not the only one who found the javelin difficult to master or even throw at all. Tyrrel, René, Lothar, and Geoff also found the javelins to be unwieldy. And if the javelin lessons were not irritating enough, the best student in the javelin was a First-year student named Timothy. He was shy and quiet, but could easily hurl the long metal rod through the air like he was an Olympic athlete. It was bad enough to be awful at something, but to be outdone by a kid who was a First-year student was an ego-crushing blow to all the boys in the Fifth-year and Fourth-year. For Timothy, it was probably the first time in his life that he was the focus of so much attention, and hopefully it would draw him out of his intense shyness.

"How does he do that?" Geoff asked no one in particular as the Fabulous Five made their way back to their room to relax for a bit and then prepare for dinner.

"I don't know, but my shoulder hurts," said Kyle as he shrugged and moved his arm, hoping to make his shoulder feel less painful.

"If it doesn't feel better in the morning, you should go to the medical office and have it looked at," said René as he tossed back his hair out of his face.

"Yeah, I might do that," said Kyle as he tried to rub his aching right shoulder.

Freya walked up to the group as they were just about to enter the Fifth-year boys' room.

"Sif and Elsa want to know what you are going as for Halloween," Freya asked, directing her question to her cousin Lothar.

Lothar initially looked surprised and then appeared somewhat smugly pleased.

"I'm going as the ever-lovable... Han Solo," replied Lothar with a smile.

"Okay, then you'd better prepare yourself to have two Princess Leias hanging about," said Freya.

Lothar was quiet for a moment and then replied, "I think I can handle that."

Freya rolled her eyes at Lothar and then looked at Kyle, smiled, and then left for the Fifth-year girls' room.

"So, what was that all about?" asked Geoff.

"You don't know?" said Tyrrel, looking at Geoff with a certain amount of a Tuvok eyebrow rising. "Ivy will probably come looking for you soon."

"Why? Did I do something wrong?!" asked Geoff, not understanding the slowly changing complexities of childhood and preteen transitional phases.

"No, you haven't done anything wrong except make an impression upon her," said Tyrrel with a matter-of-fact tone of voice.

"Okay, well, I hope it was a good impression. She seemed very nice," Geoff responded.

"Don't worry, Geoff. It's nothing to worry about," said Kyle, watching Freya disappear into her room across the way.

"Since Freya brought this all up, are we going to try to enter the Academy costume contest this year? We could try for the group competition if we all wear stuff that goes together," suggested Lothar.

"I don't know, I was pretty much settled on going as Guynemer," replied René.

"What about you?" Lothar asked Tyrrel.

"I had pretty much decided upon Fermi since I admire the guy, and the costume isn't that hard at all. I am not much of a costume maker. I can write about Fermi for language class, and I should get a good grade," replied Tyrrel.

"Well, I am going as Yoda, and Kyle is going to be a Clone Trooper," said Geoff.

"That's an ARC Trooper, and hopefully Captain Rex," remarked Kyle.

"Okay, so that's enough people going as Star Wars characters that we could enter the multiple character contest," said Lothar. "Are you sure you two don't want to change your minds?"

"Yes, I am sure," said Tyrrel.

"Me too," said René. "My heart is set on being the famed French pilot of the Great War."

"Okay," said Lothar. "Then I guess the three of us are part of a Star Wars team, and they can enter as single characters."

"Truthfully, I am not interested in the contest. I want to get a good grade," said Tyrrel. "And Enrico Fermi is the perfect choice for me."

The boys got themselves ready to go downstairs to the dining room, full of energetic talk about the day's events. Even Trevor and Xavier expressed their frustration at being unable to excel at the javelin, while Timothy made them all look like clumsy fools. It was jointly decided amongst all the boys of the Fifth-year that they must have someone do better and save the honor of their year. Kyle was reasonably sure it wouldn't be him, as he felt his shoulder ache throughout dinner. As the boys finished a healthy meal of beef stew, French bread, and various vegetable and fruit side dishes, Kyle couldn't help but wonder why the costume contest was so important.

"Alright, what is the big deal about the costume contest? I thought we were just going to the Academy party dressed up to have fun."

"Well, that is a part of the festivities, but each year has winners for the single best costume and the group best costume, and then those compete against all the other age groups for Page Level, Squire Level, and Knight in Training Level, which I don't think we have many of those students here. The winners of the Page Level award get their photograph put into the school archives, and best of all, they get to go on a special field trip," explained Lothar.

"A special field trip? That sounds cool. What kind of field trip?" asked Kyle.

"Usually, it's an overnight trip to someplace that is educational as well as fun. Like going to museums, forts, musical performances, and stuff like that," said Lothar. "If you win as a group, the whole group gets to go, so it's like going on a trip with your best friends."

"Okay, I can see the appeal of this contest," said Kyle, smiling. "Dang, I had better get to work on figuring out how to make the best Captain Rex costume ever!"

"Now he gets it," commented Trevor, overhearing the conversation.

"This weekend, the craft room and the textiles rooms are going to be very busy," said Lothar with a smile.

Geoff was listening intently to this information as he shoved the last spoonful of stew into his mouth. His brow wrinkled a bit with concern.

"What if my Yoda costume isn't very good? How am I going to make the ears? And how am I going to make my skin green without being able to go to a store?" asked Geoff, looking rather worried.

"Don't panic. You can ask Sir Knight Greta for advice about the makeup concern. There are theater instructors for the Squire Level students who might be able to help with that. I know some of the older students are expected to assist younger students with projects, and they get extra credit for doing so," replied Lothar.

Kyle sat back in his chair for a moment, thinking. "Wow, I have never been to a school like this before. None of this stuff would have happened back home in my old school. It's like the teachers here trust the kids to think and do stuff."

"Well, it is a private school where one pays more," said Geoff. Lothar nodded in agreement.

After dinner, Lothar, Kyle, and Geoff sat down to plan how to help each other make their costumes the best. Lothar explained to Kyle and Geoff what they needed to do first and whom to ask for help, since neither had participated in the Academy Halloween contest before.

"Just remember, your assignments in the other classes have to be done, and no bad marks or else you may be disqualified from the contest," warned Lothar.

"That means I can't just focus on the art part of the month," remarked Kyle.

"Correct. One year, someone did that and got disqualified from the contest. The school does this to make sure students don't become too consumed by building costumes. Everyone must complete all the other required projects that go with it. That's why Tyrrel isn't interested in the contest. He wants to ensure his grades are good, which I can understand since he is so brilliant. He will probably be a Doctor of Science when he's grown up. You know, like engineering or mathematics. I bet he will go to an Ivy League school."

"Have you ever won?" asked Geoff.

Lothar laughed and turned slightly red in the face.

"Okay, tell us about it," said Geoff, sensing a good story.

"It was my first year at the Academy. Freya and I both started here at the same time as first-level students. She talked me into being Raggedy Andy, and she went as Raggedy Ann. You know, those dolls with the red yarn hair, except that Freya and I both have red hair..." Lothar replied, looking somewhat embarrassed.

Geoff laughed, and Kyle chuckled at the thought of trying to imagine Lothar dressed as Raggedy Andy.

"You can laugh at me all you want, but Freya and I got to go on the trip with all the other winners of the contest," replied Lothar.

"Where did you go?" asked Kyle as he sketched out his various drawings for Captain Rex. He was working on the sketch of the front, back, and side views of the proposed costume.

"We went to the Royal Ontario Museum and the Toronto Zoo. It was a lot of fun. We spent three nights in one of the fancy downtown hotels. I really want to go again," replied Lothar.

"Do you know where the winners will get to go this year?" asked Geoff.

"The rumor is that the locations might be the Ontario Science Centre and Fort York, but that's just a rumor. I'm not sure, but I think they decide after the winners are selected. Generally, they ask the older kids where they want to go. It was a lot of fun. Freya will tell you that. I think she wants to win again, too."

Lothar had completed two views of Han Solo, neatly done in colored pencil. He needed to draw two more for the assignment.

As Kyle worked on the leg armor of his Captain Rex drawing, he realized how much fun he was having, even though this was all part of a homework assignment. Back home, the teachers never did projects like this. He was informed that the school district had no funds for the teachers. Or somebody would complain about something, and then nobody would do anything fun. The grown-ups argued about the topic a lot. He remembered that with some of the holiday celebrations. It seemed like the adults made everything more complicated than it needed to be. Here at the Academy, the adults seemed to want to make learning more interesting on purpose, while back home, they just wanted to argue about stuff that didn't really matter. As Kyle erased a line that didn't look right, he wondered why not all teachers or schools were good places to learn or interesting. All he knew for sure was that he was happy to be at the Academy, where he was finally making friends and doing things together. The pain of missing his parents seemed less painful, especially when they took the time to respond to his emails or to do Google Hangouts with him. He also sent pictures to them, and even his mom started responding regularly. He now felt like he had a future to dream about.

"So why did Freya tell you that Sif and Elsa are going as Princess Leia? Do they want to be a part of our costume team?" asked Geoff.

Lothar paused, considering the situation, and then responded, "You know, I should probably ask them to join our team. What do you guys think?"

"Do they make good costumes?" asked Geoff. "Because we should not have anyone join us who will hurt our chances of winning."

Lothar frowned and then replied, "The twins rarely ever fail any project they set their minds to, but I don't think we should take the attitude that we only want teammates who are perfect."

"That's why you haven't won since Raggedy Ann and Andy," said Trevor as he walked by.

Lothar scowled at Trevor.

"Well, at least I don't use money to solve all of my problems," Lothar retorted to Trevor.

Trevor looked back and gave him a grumpy face, and then he strode off in his usual haughty fashion.

"Seriously, maybe we should ask the twins to join our group and anyone else who might want to be a part of our Star Wars team," said Kyle, thinking that having Freya as a teammate would be nice. "Is there a limit on how many of us can be part of a team?"

"No, there isn't. If we could get every kid in the Fifth-year to be a part of it, it would be no problem with the rules. The biggest problem would be that no one would agree to do the same theme. And coordinating the efforts to come off as being cohesive," replied Lothar.

"That would be a lot of fun, having a trip with our group of friends," commented Geoff as he imagined what it would be like.

"It would be great, but two of our best pals are doing their own thing with their hearts set upon doing those projects. They are already too far along now to be asking them to change their project choice," said Kyle, thinking about the whole idea. "We would have to make plans in advance to do this as a group, like for next year."

"That makes sense, so let's do the best we can this year, and I will talk with Sif and Elsa. Actually... I will go talk with them now," said Lothar, getting up.

"Do you want us to go with you?" asked Geoff.

"Sure, why not?" said Lothar with a smile. "Maybe we shall be very convincing as a group."

Kyle, Lothar, and Geoff left the Fifth-year boys' room and crossed the open area, which looked down into the indoor group play area for the Page Level students and toward where the girls' rooms were located. A few kids were sitting downstairs playing board games near the fireplace. It was still too early for a fire to be lit, but it was still a nice place to hang out. The center area was carpeted, while a tile floor surrounded the edges. There were plenty of tables with comfortable, cushiony chairs to sit and lounge in. Several bean bag chairs were down there, as well as an abundance of pillows. It was too dark to see out the huge glass windows now, but every morning the sunlight would bring in enormous amounts of cheery light to all the levels of the structure. The window sections went all the way up to the top floor.

When they reached the girls' section, Lothar went to the door labeled Fifth-Year Girls and knocked.

The boys could hear the room's occupants suddenly become quiet, and then someone answered the door. It was polite procedure to knock on the door and wait for the girls to respond. Boys were not allowed in the girls' rooms, and the girls were not allowed in the boys' rooms.

Kyle recognized the curly, dark-haired girl as she answered the door with an inquisitive expression.

"Hello, what do you guys want?" she asked in an almost enticing manner.

"I need to talk to Sif and Elsa. Are they in the room?" asked Lothar.

"Maybe. What are you going to talk to them about?"

"We want them to be a part of our costume team," blurted out Geoff in an enthusiastic manner, almost knocking his glasses off his nose.

"I see. That sounds like fun. So are all three of you on this team?" asked Ivy.

"So far," replied Lothar, starting to feel a bit anxious. "Are you going to let Sif and Elsa know that I want to talk to them?"

"Well… I suppose so," said Ivy, rolling her eyes as if she were contemplating the situation. "Okay, I'll go get them."

After a few minutes of waiting outside the door, Elsa and Sif appeared with Freya and Ivy as well. Lothar looked at them all and remarked, "I just wanted to talk to Sif and Elsa."

"Does that mean you don't want us?!" exclaimed Ivy as she put her hands upon her hips.

"Well, it wouldn't make any sense to ask you if you have already started a costume project that doesn't work with our theme," said Kyle.

"How do you know what we have selected?" retorted Ivy.

"Well, I don't. We know that Elsa and Sif were thinking about a project that went well with ours," replied Kyle. "And we thought we would ask them if they wanted to be a part of our team."

Freya watched as a couple of Fourth-year girls walked past, as if they were secretly interested in what their conversation was about.

"Let's go someplace else to have this conversation. We, girls, are a bit more competitive than you all may realize," said Freya as she encouraged everyone to follow her downstairs, where only a small group of First-year students were playing board games. It was almost their bedtime, so they would soon be leaving, which would give the Fifth-year students a chance to talk in private.

As the group found an oversized, soft couch to sit on, Geoff opted for a bean bag chair, which he dragged into the area and plopped himself into.

"I think this is becoming more intense than what I had originally planned," said Lothar. "Kyle, Geoff, and I just wanted to do something fun, and the prospect of possibly winning the contest appeals to us, so we thought if Sif and Elsa are also doing the Star Wars theme, then why not invite you two to join us?"

Elsa and Sif both smiled and replied simultaneously that they would like to join the guys' costume team.

"Terrific. Freya told me that you both were doing Princess Leia," said Lothar.

"We are, but we are doing different versions of her," said Sif. "I'm going as Princess Leia on Hoth, and Elsa is going as Princess Leia on Endor."

"That's awesome!" exclaimed Geoff.

Ivy looked at Geoff with a furrowed brow but said nothing.

"Do you think we could win the contest this year?" Lothar asked the twins.

The twins looked at each other as if they were sharing a secret. Then they looked at Freya and Ivy.

"Well," said Elsa. "You have to be very serious about doing a good job on your costumes."

"And no slacking off on your studies and getting disqualified," said Sif.

Then, both blonde-haired twins said in unison, "Freya and Ivy are also doing costumes that fit in with the Star Wars theme, so you would have to have them on the team as well."

Lothar looked at Freya, wrinkled his brow, and said, "Why didn't you tell me? Of course, you and Ivy are welcome to join us."

"I thought that you were so sick of being teased about Raggedy Andy that you never wanted to team up with me again," said Freya.

"That wasn't your fault. I know that, and we did win and had a great time. I want to win again," said Lothar.

"I really thought you were angry with me about that," said Freya, taking in a deep emotional breath and moving her long strands of red hair behind her ear.

"No. You're more like a sister to me than a cousin," replied Lothar. "And we are good friends, right?"

Freya shyly smiled. Kyle dreamily stared at her, thinking how wonderful she looked, and then caught himself before anyone noticed.

"So, all seven of us are a team then, right?" asked Kyle.

"Yes," said Freya, with the other girls chiming in excitedly. "We are a team."

"Terrific, then we all need to get to work so we can win that contest," said Geoff as he awkwardly struggled to get out of the beanbag chair.

269

"Nobody asked me what I am going as!" exclaimed Ivy.

"Oh, I'm sorry, Ivy. What are you going as?" Lothar asked in his most diplomatic voice.

"I'm going as a Twi'lek," she proclaimed proudly.

"Wow, that's going to be a tough one to do," remarked Geoff as he continued to struggle to get out of the beanbag chair. "Are you going to be a dancing girl or a mercenary?"

"Gee, I hadn't thought about that," pondered Ivy. "What are all of you doing?"

"I'm going as Han Solo," replied Lothar.

"I'm going as Captain Rex," said Kyle.

"And I'm going as Jedi Master, Yoda," Geoff replied with his bony arms extended out. "Will someone help me get out of this chair?!"

Ivy smiled at Geoff and reached for his hands to help him get out of the problematic, squishy chair.

"Going as Yoda, huh? That's an interesting choice," said Ivy, smiling.

Geoff nodded and smiled at Ivy, "Yeah, I like his character."

Everyone seemed happy with the arrangement of working as a team, and they quickly began discussing what kind of secrecy, if any, they should use regarding their efforts. Kyle looked at Freya and suddenly realized that he had no idea what character she had chosen to be.

"So… Freya, what are you going as?" asked Kyle.

"I'm going as a Jedi," said Freya. "I guess that means I'm in charge of you," she said with a smile.

Chapter 12: Costume Frenzy

The weekend was spent working furiously in the craft rooms, trying to figure out what was needed and how to create various parts. Tyrrel just laughed at the panic that was going on around him as he simply planned to wear his dress clothes with a lab coat for his costume. He devoted most of his time to focus on his required writing and research for the Halloween Project. Even though René was not working with the Star Wars group, he was intensely working on writing his research papers, including a description and personal reasons for selecting Georges Guynemer. He found constructing a reasonable facsimile of the famed aviation hero's uniform challenging.

The hallways and dorm rooms were buzzing with whispers of secret costume plans and excitement about the upcoming holiday fun. The intense frenzy of competition reminded Kyle of what his old school felt like back home, except that the feeling back there was more about the social cliques, with whispers and side glances across the room and hallways. Even arguments had erupted over the contest, with some teachers warning that students would be disqualified for unbecoming behavior. That was part of the challenge. Good behavior was a challenge in every aspect of life, and some circumstances were more tempting than others.

It was eight o'clock in the morning, with the sun happily coming through the windows of the Primary Languages classroom. The first assignment of the day was to take fifteen minutes to write in the journals. Kyle decided to write about his plans for the Captain Rex costume. This was one of the few times he had something he wanted to write about. It made writing easier when something interesting happened. Otherwise, he felt like he was participating in one of Tyrrel's experiments and was required to document each day's weather. That was starting to get boring. It was almost time to finish the journal entries when Sir Knight Mary came into the room looking somewhat stern and downright perturbed. Kyle peeked up at her as she looked up at the clock as if she were waiting for the fifteen minutes of journal writing to end. Usually, Sir Knight Mary was not so impatient about the writing time.

As soon as the clock showed that the time had passed, she said, "It has come to my attention that some students are taking this costume project and contest too seriously!"

Everyone stopped writing and looked up at Sir Knight Mary.

"This Halloween project was designed so students here at the Academy could experience the normal traditional fun that all North American children have at regular schools. We designed lessons to help you make informed decisions about planning your costumes and provided incentives, such as the contest. In the adult world, there are often rewards or incentives for dedicating special time and care to projects that require planning and team effort. But someone has gone too far..."

She stopped in mid-sentence. She sounded very upset. The students began looking back and forth at each other, then at Sir Knight Mary.

273

"Someone has destroyed a student's project," the elderly teacher finally said, straightening her wire-framed glasses, trying to compose herself. "I expect... along with all the other instructors here, better behavior than that from an Academy student. I am deeply distressed and saddened by this action."

Lucy Robbinson raised her hand. Sir Knight Mary acknowledged her.

"Whose project got ruined?" she asked.

"I do not currently know, but Sir Knight Greta was furious to find that someone had entered the art room and destroyed one student's project and possibly damaged several others nearby," replied Sir Knight Mary, shaking her head. "She and several other instructors are investigating. I find it inconceivable."

Everyone in the classroom sat in silence. Kyle looked around at the other students, who were all Fifth-year and Fourth-year students, and they all looked bewildered and shocked. During his time at the Academy, Kyle never had anything stolen from him or was threatened or treated poorly by anyone. He also wondered whose project had been destroyed and why. The thin, steely-haired woman finally composed herself and sat down at her desk, looking through her schedule of lessons.

"I would like everyone to prepare for the vocabulary quiz, and when you have finished the quiz, please take out your required reading and start on that quietly while others are finishing their quiz," said Sir Knight Mary.

She got up and wrote the module section on the board, making it easy for students to find on their tablets for the vocabulary quiz. Kyle found this to be an interesting way to take a test, as it eliminated the need to hand back all the papers and wait for the test results. Once the submit button was tapped, the test would be calculated, and the results would be available. He could also see what he answered incorrectly and what the correct answer should have been. The classroom was deathly silent during the test, more so than usual, and he found his mind wandering, hoping that his project had not been damaged. He hoped that none of his friends were victims of this awful deed.

He finished the vocabulary quiz with an accuracy of only eighty percent, which was lower than normal. He could tell his mind was not focused on the task. He quickly reviewed the words he had gotten wrong, feeling disappointed that he should have gotten most of those correct. However, he wasn't thinking about the test. Kyle set the tablet down and picked up the book he was supposed to read. It was *Call of the Wild* by Jack London. He liked the book and thought about how Rojo and Pickles would not have been ideal dogs for this adventure.

The day dragged on with no real word concerning what happened in the crafting room, but rumors circulated amongst the students. The martial arts class was cut short to give students free time to work on their projects. The Fabulous Five walked together from the outdoor grass field where the Javelin training was scheduled and toward the main complex to go to the crafting room.

"I hope my Yoda project wasn't destroyed," said Geoff for the twentieth time that day.

No one could get mad at him for being so one-track-minded since they were all thinking or saying the same thing.

"Your project wasn't destroyed," said Tyrrel with some authority.

"How do you know that?" asked René.

"When we were in the computer class, I had to step out into another room to get some upper-level software books, and I overheard some older students talking," replied Tyrrel.

"What did they say?" chorused the four other boys.

"They were saying that the costume project that was destroyed was a Second-year student's," replied Tyrrel.

"Really?" said Kyle.

"Wow, I can't imagine someone wanting to vent their frustrations on a little kid," remarked Lothar.

"Unless it was another Second-year student," speculated Geoff.

"I don't know, but the older students seemed to be freaked out about the whole thing as if something perplexingly odd was happening," replied Tyrrel.

The boys were almost at the main building when Tyrrel stopped them.

"Look, don't say anything about this while we are in the crafting area. The older kids shared these details with me, and I don't want to lose their trust. But the whole thing was apparently… caught on the crafting room surveillance cameras," said Tyrrel. "And these older students work on digital projects, so they were part of the team asked to help watch the files for anything."

"There are surveillance cameras?" remarked Geoff as he looked around the building's entrance hall.

"Yes. They are there for emergencies," replied Lothar. "If you look at the entrance to our room, there are cameras, but none in the actual dorm room. They are in all the group areas of the school."

"Hey, I never noticed that or even thought about it, but come to think about it, they are all over," remarked Geoff as he gestured with his skinny arms wildly. "I'm gonna have to start waving at those."

Rcnó rolled his eyes and shook his head. "You are so strange."

Geoff stopped waving his arms about, looked at René, and replied, "My mom says that my strangeness is part of my personal charm. Ivy seems to like it."

"Yes, she does," commented Lothar with a chuckle.

"So, zip your lips about this stuff while we are around other people?" Tyrrel asked before taking another step inside the building. The tall black boy had a most serious expression on his face.

"I think we can handle that, Tyrrel," replied Lothar, with the others nodding in agreement. "And if someone starts to slip up, the others will do something to help remedy the situation. Agreed?"

"Agreed," chorused Kyle, Geoff, and René.

With the assurance from his friends, Tyrrel felt better about going to the crafting room to work on projects. Upon their arrival, they found a hectic scene. At least half of the students of the Page Level population of the school were in the Page Level crafting room. Sir Knight Greta was busy helping students, as well as some of the older Squire Level students. They were getting training points to assist the younger students. Kyle needed help with making his armor. He had already cut out pieces of cardboard to test their size, ensuring they would look and fit correctly. The cardboard pieces served as effective pattern pieces for the sturdier material he intended to use for the armor. He could have just settled for the cardboard and painted it the appropriate color, but he really wanted to see if he could make something more advanced. He had to admit that he was somewhat inspired by René's effort on his WWI costume, and he did not want to let his group down by not working his best on his project.

He felt relieved that his project had been left alone and that none of his friends' projects had been damaged either. Kyle walked over to one of the Squire Level students, his thoughts centered upon what could make someone want to do such a rotten thing. The older student was tall and looked more like a grown-up than a student.

"So, what have we got here?" the Squire Level student asked Kyle, who seemed to stand in front of him with a glazed-over expression, holding his cardboard pattern pieces.

Kyle finally snapped out of the shock of looking at the older student. It was unheard of for the older kids to interact with elementary school-age kids back home. He remembered the teenagers in Virginia Foothills, where his mom lived, and how they barely acknowledged his presence when he was out riding his bike.

"Uh, I need help," Kyle said somewhat awkwardly. "I'd like to make the armor out of something better than cardboard."

"That makes sense. What kind of armor is it supposed to be?" asked the teenager.

"Clone Trooper. Specifically, Captain Rex," replied Kyle.

"I see, right on. This should be very cool. Have you decided what you are going to attach the armor to?"

"I was thinking about my old black sweatpants and sweatshirt. My grandma already said it was okay. Do you think I should tie it on or something else?" Kyle asked, having now overcome his initial discomfort about the other student's age.

"How do you feel about Velcro?" asked the older boy as he looked at the cardboard pieces. "Mind you, it would involve some sewing and some gluing."

"Oh, hey, that would be cool. It would just stick to me then," responded Kyle.

"Yes. I would recommend the lightweight Sintra plastic. You will probably want white if you are doing a Clone Trooper from Star Wars," said the older boy as he examined each of the pattern pieces. "I will pull out a sheet of white Sintra for you, and you will need to trace these out onto the plastic. Don't be sloppy about the lines. Make them nice and dark so we can see where to cut. I will assist you with the cutting, but you will need to handle all the sanding of any rough edges. Where are you working?"

Kyle pointed over to where Geoff, Lothar, Tyrrel, and René were sitting.

"Okay, I will bring a sheet over to where you are. Try to get the pieces close together and keep them at least half an inch apart. We want to have enough materials for everyone, so if you spread them all over the sheet, I will make you retrace them," said the older boy firmly but in a friendly manner.

Kyle nodded and waited for the Squire Level student to pick up the large sheet of white plastic and carry it to the area where he was working. The sheet was too big for the table, so the teenager placed it on the floor for Kyle. Kyle thanked the older student and started to figure out where he would trace the pieces onto the plastic sheet.

"Dang, this is… really hard to decide where to place all of these," commented Kyle to no one in particular.

"Be glad that we are not yet Squire Level; they have to follow a budget and document all the materials they use," said Tyrrel.

"What?! Are you kidding?" exclaimed Kyle.

"No. I am not," said Tyrrel.

"Why would the teachers make them do that?" asked Geoff as he carefully worked the modeling clay to shape a Yoda ear for his mask.

"Have you ever had your parents tell you that you can't have something because it is not in the budget?" Lothar asked.

"Yah," said Geoff.

"Well, the idea is for us to learn how to create budgets and be able to follow them," replied Lothar.

"Hmm. I'm glad that we are not yet in the Squire Level," replied Geoff as he rolled some more light green clay in his hands. "I just don't want to worry about stuff like that right now."

Kyle sighed and said, "I know what you mean. I'm having a hard enough time trying to figure out the best layout for these pieces, let alone worrying about budgets."

"So, has anyone heard or figured out whose costume project got destroyed?" René asked in a low voice.

"After Tyrrel told us it was a Second-year student's project that got destroyed, I started observing the younger kids, and from what I have observed," said Lothar, "I think it may have been a girl named Emerald Green whose project was destroyed."

"Emerald Green, isn't that name kind of redundant?" commented Geoff.

"Only if her middle name was verde," said Lothar with a smile.

"I think it is a pretty name for a girl," said Tyrrel as he stood up and stretched his long legs after sitting still for so long. "I have a cousin named Ruby."

"Is her last name red?" asked Geoff.

Tyrrel looked at Geoff briefly before answering, "No, it is Smith. Like my middle name."

Kyle had finally decided how he would place all the pieces on the white sheet of plastic and began tracing the shapes for cutting. He hoped this would work, as there were only a few days left until the project was due. It wasn't just that he wanted a neat costume to wear to the festivities; he also wanted a good grade for his efforts. Being with other kids who cared about their grades made him feel more inspired to try harder. He never felt so driven to succeed back home. He wasn't sure why. His mom kept trying to get him tested for something called attention deficit hyperactivity disorder, but Kyle didn't want to be tested. He didn't want the label. And he had been successful in thwarting her efforts, and now he was here, far away from her concerns. He wondered if she missed him.

"Kyle. Kyle!"

Kyle looked up from his project and deep thoughts to see Geoff standing next to him with his Yoda ears on a cookie sheet tray.

"I'm ready to put these in the oven and bake them. If they turn out, then I can glue them to my mask. What do you think?" asked Geoff.

"They look great," said Kyle.

Geoff went off with his clay Yoda ears. They would need about twenty minutes to bake on low heat. When they were finished, it would be time to get ready for dinner. Kyle meticulously traced all the cardboard pattern pieces onto the plastic and finished just before Geoff returned. Then the Fabulous Five packed up their craft projects for the evening. Geoff's Yoda ears had turned out fine and needed some time to cool, which was the reason why he was carrying them on a piece of cardboard. He seemed a bit excited and flustered when he arrived and nearly tripped, which would have had disastrous results for his newly made green earpieces.

"Guys, I have something to share with you the minute we get away from everyone," said Geoff in a hushed tone, which he managed even though he nearly tripped.

All the guys looked at him with some surprise, but nodded their heads and finished cleaning up their supplies quickly so that he could share whatever he found out. When they all exited the craft room and were alone for a moment, the guys turned to Geoff.

"What is the big hush-hush excitement?" asked Lothar.

"I found out who destroyed Emerald Green's project," said Geoff.

"Geez, shouldn't you be talking to one of the instructors about this?" commented Tyrrel.

"No, I overheard the instructors and some of the student aides talking while I was waiting for my Yoda ears to finish baking. Apparently, Emerald Green destroyed her own project. It was caught on film," replied Geoff.

The boys were shocked.

"What is going on with that? Did she blame someone else?" asked René.

"No. She didn't blame anyone or even complain about it," Geoff kept whispering.

"Why would she do that?" asked Kyle, frowning. "It doesn't make any sense."

"That's what the instructors and the Squire Level students discussed. They all wondered what had made her so upset that she would destroy her project. Some of them were speculating that she was being teased about her costume choice and perhaps that the stress of the project was too much for her, but that's not what is so weird about the whole thing," said Geoff as he looked around to make sure that no one was within hearing distance.

"Okay, so what is the strange thing about all of this? The fact that she busted up her project is crazy enough, don't you think?" commented Lothar as he rubbed his hand across his forehead and into his red hair.

"Get this, guys, she did this without touching anything! It's on film! One minute, she was looking at the project and seemed upset, and then, finally, it just exploded and broke into all kinds of pieces. That's how the other nearby projects got damaged. She didn't mean to mess up anyone else's stuff. They also don't think she meant to bust up her own either."

"Was there anything potentially explosive in her project, for example, the materials she used?" asked Tyrrel.

"No, nothing that could have exploded was used in the project. Not even a combination of items. Sir Knight Greta had that checked right away when she saw the film footage," replied Geoff. "At least that is what I overheard."

"Hmm. Come to think of it, I have not seen Emerald around all day. Have any of you?" said Tyrrel, trying to remember.

"No, I have not. And I usually notice her because she is a cute girl with remarkable green eyes," said René, trying to recall.

"Green eyes like Harry Potter? Maybe she was going as a Hogwarts student? And she blew up her project just like Harry blew up his mean aunt," asked Geoff with a lighthearted twist.

Kyle rubbed his hands over his face. This all sounded ridiculous.

"Why are we talking about her eye color, and what costume she was planning to wear?! She busted up her project. What happened? Did she rig the security footage or blow it up with her mind?! Aren't you guys freaked out just a bit?" asked Kyle, thinking this sounded very disturbing.

Lothar looked at Kyle with a raised eyebrow and replied, "There are people with special abilities, but of course, we have not seen the film footage, so it may not have been as exciting as Geoff is explaining it."

"Correct, this is hearsay evidence," said Tyrrel. "But there is a section of the school for gifted students with special abilities, but the Academy tends to keep that quiet. It's like having Jedi training under Emperor Palpatine's nose."

"My Papa says that his grand-père, who was a knight, could light a candle without matches. He would concentrate on the candle for about five minutes, and then it would light up," replied René.

"Couldn't your... grand... grandpa... be just playing a joke on him as a kid?" Kyle asked, still thinking this sounded like nonsense.

"No. It's a true story, and it was no joke," replied René, edging toward being offended.

Kyle decided not to say anything more. He did not want to call René's father a liar or any of his family members tricksters, but this sounded so much like something his dad would think was an illusion or a magic trick. His dad, being a scientist, taught him not to believe everything at face value and to question things that seemed unreal. He was surprised that Tyrrel was not

286

questioning the story as much as he thought he would. Tyrrel always seemed so logical and scientific.

The boys went to the dining hall, still chatting about what could have upset Emerald Green so much that she would even want to destroy her project. The consensus was that they were all relieved it wasn't someone being cruel and thoughtless who had damaged another person's project. When they reached the dining hall, they all kept an eye out for Emerald Green. If the story were true, she was likely being kept isolated from the other students until the Academy staff was certain she could control her abilities. Kyle just listened to the whole conversation, not wanting to believe that any of this was happening.

All he could think about during his meal of mashed potatoes, steamed carrots, and garlic herb chicken was that this whole thing was some joke being played on him. People simply do not blast stuff apart like superheroes. It could not be real. Kyle picked up his glass of milk and started sipping on it as the information concerning Emerald Green was shared with Lothar's cousin, Freya, who happened to sit down with them.

"So, have you heard anything new about the situation concerning the damaged Halloween project?" Lothar asked Freya.

"Actually, yes," replied Freya. "I heard the project belonged to a Second-year girl named Emerald Green. Apparently, some of the other Second-year girls were teasing her about the project she chose, which hurt her feelings. One of the girls close to her said she wanted her project to be perfect, so that the others would accept her, and well, the project wasn't perfect."

Freya finished and asked the guys, "Okay, you know something else. Spill it out."

Lothar smiled at his pretty red-haired cousin and replied, "Well, we didn't know that part, but yes, we do have other information."

"Okay, cousin, let's have it," said Freya with a smile.

"We also heard that Emerald Green was the victim, but we heard she did it herself. And she did it with… special skills," Lothar replied in a whisper.

Freya's eyes widened. She knew precisely what Lothar meant.

Kyle watched this with a certain amount of concern. Seeing Freya accept this news without any doubt made Kyle's stomach churn.

"How did you come about this information?" she asked sternly.

"Geoff and Tyrrel had two different sources. One of which said that this was caught on video by security cameras. But don't repeat that last one to any of your girlfriends," replied Lothar.

"Why?"

"Because Tyrrel learned it from the older kids, and he doesn't want to be known as a gossip," replied Lothar.

Freya looked over at Tyrrel, who nodded his head.

288

"Okay, I won't say anything about the videotape. I wish I could see that."

"Me too," said Kyle under his breath.

"So, have you seen Emerald Green anywhere in the girls' area?" asked Tyrrel.

"No, I have not. I saw her this morning, but I haven't seen her since then. I don't think anyone has seen her after lunch, including her closest friend, whom we were talking with," replied Freya.

"The school probably called her parents," speculated Lothar.

"That would make sense," commented Geoff as he eagerly listened to what was being said.

Kyle had had enough.

"This… is stupid nonsense. No one has superpowers and can blow stuff apart with their mind like… like… some Jedi Knight. It just doesn't happen," fumed Kyle as he stood up and left the table with his plate.

He placed his plate onto the return counter and left the dining hall without looking back. He felt so frustrated and wondered if they were all playing a joke on him. The anger and hurt welled up inside him, and he did not know what to do. He went up to the Fifth-year boys' room and stood in silence alone. He then realized he did not feel like being in there either, so he grabbed his jacket and decided to go for a walk. He ended up walking outside. It was 6:30 in the evening, and the light outside was somewhat dim, with a chill in the air. Perhaps being outside would clear his head. He wondered why the others would believe such a story. How could anyone blast stuff apart with their mind? And why would his friends, who seemed so rational, believe this stuff? Freya too.

He found himself walking out toward the circular rock formation known as Boulder Glade, where he and the guys had met up with the girls on that autumn day that seemed long ago for some odd reason. Freya looked so pretty standing on top of the highest rock, and she was so nice to him.

She said that when the leaves had fallen, one could see the lake easily from the top of the rock. Kyle decided to climb up to the rock and take a seat. He would enjoy the view if there were one to be had. About half of the leaves in the trees had fallen from the branches, so none of the trees were completely bare. He sat there for about fifteen minutes, the slight breeze from the lake coming across the island, blowing his hair, faintly from time to time, bringing a fresh cooling scent in the air. The sun was setting.

Then he heard rustling from somewhere below. He looked around and saw nothing. He was expecting to see a bird, but then he remembered Xavier's concerns. He hoped he would not see whatever creature that frightened Xavier so much. All was quiet again. And then he heard a noise again, sounding like something crushing dry leaves, as if someone or something were walking around below. Kyle could not see down below the boulder without risking a fall. He felt scared. What could be down there? Maybe it was just a deer or something. Did they have deer on this island, he wondered?

Another cooler breeze blew across the boulder top, making him feel chilled. Then a familiar face popped up from behind one of the other smaller boulders, which were needed for climbing to the top. It was Freya.

"Hi there. Can I come up?" she asked.

"Sure. It's a free country. Canada is… a free country, right? I can say that here too," said Kyle, feeling relieved that she wasn't Xavier's chupacabra monster but still somewhat perturbed about the dining hall conversation.

"Are you alright?" she asked as she climbed up to the top of the rock and sat beside him.

"I don't know," replied Kyle somewhat sullenly.

"Something is bothering you. And I am going to sit here with you watching that sunset until you tell me what's up," said Freya with a firm resolve. "The guys are concerned."

They sat silently for about ten minutes as the sun edged below the horizon line. Finally, Kyle had words that he could put together, and the intense silence seemed more comfortable as the beauty of the sunset came over him.

"The clouds look really pretty," remarked Kyle.

"Yes, they do. I like all the bright yellows mixed in with the soft pinks against the blue sky," replied Freya.

There was a pause of silence between them.

"Do you believe that Emerald destroyed her project using some kind of mental powers?" Kyle asked.

Freya could hear the edge in his voice.

"What exactly are you getting at? Is it that you don't believe she damaged her own project or that she has special abilities?"

"This whole special ability stuff. It seems like nonsense to me," said Kyle, shaking his head and furrowing his brow. "I mean, are the guys playing some kind of practical joke on me to see if I would believe it?"

The sun finally set, and the intense brightness faded into a more comfortable soft lighting.

"No, they are not playing a joke on you. Plus, it's only a rumor right now until we know for sure what happened. But they are your friends, and if they played a joke on you, it would not be about something like this," replied Freya.

Kyle nodded, and they were silent for another few minutes until it was Freya's turn to ask the uncomfortable question.

"Why do you think they were playing a joke on you?" she asked.

"It's the whole superpowers thing," replied Kyle with that edge in his voice again.

"So, you don't believe that people can have any abilities such as telekinesis or telepathy?" asked Freya.

"Yeah. It's made-up stuff, right? People don't move objects with their minds like a Jedi Knight. That's movie stuff and just make-believe," said Kyle, then paused. "Do you believe that people can do that stuff?"

"Well, actually, yes, I do believe they can," replied Freya calmly and kindly.

"Why?"

"Why don't you believe it is possible?" she asked.

"Well, my dad is a scientist. He says all that magic and superstitious stuff is nonsense. He seems to hate that stuff. My mom gets upset over strange things concerning religion. If she saw a film of a girl blowing something up with her mind, she would say it was demons or that the girl was in league with the devil. It makes me feel embarrassed that she says stuff like that. I don't want to be like that. I wish she were not like that," Kyle blurted out.

He stared at Freya for a few minutes in silence.

"I'm sorry. I should not have said all that stupid stuff," said Kyle.

"It's not stupid. You have a right to your own opinions," replied Freya.

Kyle eyed all the delicate freckles sprinkled about her face. She had to be one of the nicest people he had ever met. The light in the sky started to fade as every moment passed. Soon, they could see the first star twinkling in the sky.

"Well, uh... why do you believe that people can do superpower-type stuff?" Kyle finally asked.

"Because..." Freya took a deep breath. "I can do things that are out of the ordinary. I am just like Emerald Green."

Kyle stared at her for what seemed like a long time. So many thoughts were going through his mind. She seemed so sincere. She had never lied to him before. She never treated him poorly.

"Can you?" Kyle paused, wondering if he should even ask this. "Prove it to me?"

Freya smiled, yet looked a little nervous. She looked around and up at the twilight sky, which was gradually darkening.

"Yes, but I am not supposed to do tricks for people. I am not supposed to show off. You must promise that if I show you something, you will never tell anyone. People like me are in danger because of our abilities. It's just like the cartoons where governments will kidnap people and lock them away, or even worse. Religious fanatics will kidnap people and kill them because of their abilities. You must promise never to say anything."

Once again, Freya seemed very sincere. Now he had the chance to see what she could do. He wanted to see it to prove to himself that he was not wrong for liking her so much.

"I promise not to tell anyone," he said.

"Okay, I'm not sure if I will be able to do it, but I can do a form of healing energy, and sometimes, in the dark, you can see the energy flowing from my fingertips. It is dark enough that you should be able to see it, if it happens," replied Freya.

"Okay," said Kyle, somewhat skeptical.

"I need a few minutes to concentrate and clear my head," said Freya as she closed her eyes and sat up straighter, holding her hands in front of her like she was holding an invisible ball. "Some people do this for their Asian martial arts training. I am creating a ball of energy between my hands. And since you are familiar with Star Wars, you know what to expect. It looks a bit like the blue energy from the Jedi Masters and the Sith Master's hands when they fight using just the Force energy."

Kyle waited and saw nothing.

"What do you do with this energy?" asked Kyle.

"I can do some very basic healing techniques like help get rid of headaches and stuff like that," replied Freya.

She opened her eyes and started moving her hands like her fingertips were attached together by rubber bands. She was stretching and compressing something. Then Kyle saw something. He thought at first it was wishful thinking, and then he saw it again: small, delicate strands of pale blue-white light extending between her fingertips. Kyle just stared at it with amazement. It was nothing like Force lightning in the movies, but he could see it.

"How are you doing that?" he asked.

295

"I don't know," she responded. "I just do it."

"Is it dangerous?"

"It can be if not used correctly," she replied. "Put your hand in between my hands. Don't touch my hands and just see if you feel anything different about your hand while it's in there."

"Are you sure? You just said it could be dangerous."

"It's not right now," replied Freya. "And that requires an understanding that I don't know yet."

Kyle watched the faint pale blue-white light that seemed like delicate lightning between Freya's fingertips and put his hand into the area where it appeared. It felt colder than before, and the longer his hand remained in the area, the more it seemed to tingle, as if electricity was dancing on his skin. Not painfully, but different in a way he could not explain.

"It feels cold," replied Kyle.

"It's the energy. People who are well-trained and powerful can do hot and cold," replied Freya.

"It also tingles a little," said Kyle as he shyly pulled his hand out of the strange energy area between Freya's hands. "Can you do both?"

"Yes. The hot feeling is a more common skill. I had to learn how to adjust it to a warmer setting. Most energy healers can do warm right away. I am a little different," she said, shyly.

Kyle watched as Freya played with the strange energy emanating from her fingertips, which lit up the space between her palms. She could pull her hands apart and stretch them like taffy, then push them back together to form a small ball.

"How did you find out you could do this stuff?" asked Kyle.

"I was here at the Academy and was in the Tai Chi class, and the instructor was talking about energy, and then during the stances and practices for that, it showed up. I showed it to my instructor because I thought it was pretty," said Freya, reminiscing fondly. She smiled at Kyle and looked him directly in the eye. "And that's when I was enrolled in the special classes for students who have unusual gifts. It's to help us learn how to use these talents and keep them under control in situations like what happened with Emerald Green. I figure next week I will see her in my classes."

"What are you going to do with that skill?" Kyle asked, wondering if it had any practical value outside of school.

"I don't know yet," said Freya. "I know I want to become a knight, but I don't yet know what I want to do when I grow up. For some people, like Tyrrel, it's clear that he'll become an engineer or research scientist, but I'm not sure yet. Do you know?"

"No. I have no idea what I want to do."

"Are you going to become a knight?" asked Freya.

"I think I would like to, but I don't know how," replied Kyle.

"The Academy trains you as a squire, and you get assigned a mentor knight. You will have to make that decision this year. This is an important year at the Academy," replied Freya as she looked around and then at her watch. "We will lose the twilight and be up here in the dark."

"What time is it?"

"It is seven thirty."

"That's not too late, but I guess we should get back," said Kyle as he stood up on the rock and looked out toward the lake water, which he could still see faintly. He didn't want this moment to end. He liked being with Freya.

"It can be tricky to get down from here without a flashlight in the dark," responded Freya.

He didn't budge but continued to look out at the lake. Once again, he thought he saw something moving in the lake waters.

"Kyle, are you coming?" she asked, looking back at him as she searched for the best spot to go back down.

"Yes, but do you see that out there?" Kyle asked, pointing in the direction that he was viewing.

Freya moved closer to him and looked in the direction he was pointing.

"Where?" she asked.

298

"Just above the trees, and to the left of the lighted pole, and out in the water," Kyle instructed.

Freya looked to see something moving in the water. Her eyes widened.

"Oh, my goodness!" she gasped. "I see it too."

"What is that? Is it a log or a boat floating in the water?"

"I don't know," replied Freya, whispering.

Just then, a stout breeze blew across the rock tops with leaves and dust swirling through the air. It chilled them both, and they closed their eyes momentarily to protect themselves. When the wind had calmed down, they looked again and saw nothing, as the sky and ground grew darker.

"I don't see it anymore," said Kyle.

"Neither do I, and we had better get going. It takes fifteen minutes to get back to the school grounds. We are supposed to be inside by eight o'clock," replied Freya, who led the way off the boulders.

Kyle followed closely behind her, and then they rushed toward the trail that led back to the school.

"Do you think we saw the Lake Monster?" asked Kyle.

"I have no idea. My dad would probably say so, but I don't know what it was that I saw," replied Freya.

They walked quickly together along the trail and dodged the branches until they reached the Academy's groomed grounds. Kyle stopped Freya before they got any closer to the building entrance.

"Freya, I just want to say thanks for showing me what you can do," said Kyle, looking down at the ground and fidgeting a bit. "For some reason, I just didn't think that kind of stuff was even possible. I felt really upset, thinking maybe everyone was playing a joke on me. Now, I know I acted like a jerk."

"You weren't a jerk. You just didn't know," said Freya softly.

"I was a rude jerk, and now I gotta apologize to the guys for storming out like an idiot," said Kyle, struggling. "I feel so stupid. I always feel stupid."

"Just tell them that, and they will be fine. René and Tyrrel are always getting into arguments with each other, and they are still friends," said Freya.

Kyle looked at Freya's face, her blue-gray eyes looking kindly directly back at him, and he knew precisely why he liked her so much. She was a wonderful person. He nodded shyly in agreement with her, and together they went into the Academy building. They parted ways when they reached the dormitory level. Kyle took a deep breath and walked into the Fifth-year boys' room, apologizing for being a rude, stupid jerk. The guys responded well, as if nothing significant had happened. Lothar and René were playing the video game 88Day Race while Tyrrel and Geoff lounged on the sofa nearby and made commentary on the game.

"So, what changed your mind about stuff?" asked Lothar.

"Freya explained some stuff to me that made a lot of sense," replied Kyle without saying what she had shown him, although Kyle suspected that Lothar already knew about her abilities since she was family.

"Yes, I think she could explain it well," replied Lothar in his usual genial manner.

"Want to be a third driver on our team?" René invited.

"Yes, that would be awesome," said Kyle as he sat down and joined his friends

CHAPTER 13: HALLOWEEN AND LAKE MONSTERS

The few remaining days before the Halloween project presentation deadline went by very quickly. All written material and drawings had to be completed and submitted before the party day. There was a buzz of excitement in the air throughout the school about the party and contest, with an entire day dedicated to having fun. Even the instructors and staff members put on costumes for the day, and the students were to be the judges, voting for the best Academy staff costume.

On Halloween morning, everyone awoke knowing that all the papers had been turned in and the day would be nothing but a time of costume fun. Only some of the older students in the digital film and photography classes planned to do any work. The film group was wrapping up their documentary on the Halloween Projects and the subsequent contest. Students were asked to allow their older schoolmates to film them and interview them about the projects related to the Halloween festivities. These film projects would be edited for the upperclassmen to turn in for grades.

The day's schedule included breakfast, after which the students were allowed to put on their costumes and make any final touches they needed for the costume contest. The contest would take place at eleven o'clock in the morning to allow costumes to remain in their best condition before an active day of playing games, trick-or-treating, and later dancing and watching movies. All the winners would be announced that evening.

The Fifth-year boys' room was buzzing with excitement as everyone rushed around to get their costumes on.

Tyrrel was one of the first boys to finish dressing.

"That's not much of a costume," commented René as he struggled with pulling his long hair back into a ponytail. Guynemer did not have long hair.

"I'm a scientist," retorted Tyrrel as he smoothed his white lab coat that he wore over dress slacks, dress shirt, and tie.

"Yes, but you are always a scientist," commented René.

Tyrrel stood still and quiet as if contemplating what René said.

"Hmm. I speculate you are saying I am still me and not in a costume?"

"Precisely," said René as he struggled to put his horseback riding boots on as part of his military costume for Georges Guynemer.

Tyrrel stood silently for a moment, watching René put on his WWI French Aviation Military costume. His brow slowly wrinkled with thought.

"You know what, you are right. Next year, I will try to be something a bit more daring or further away from who I am every day," said Tyrrel. "I just love being a scientist so much."

Lothar smiled at Tyrrel, patted him on the shoulder, and said, "Next year, you go as Tuvok from Voyager. You'll still be you, but a bit more adventurous."

Tyrrel nodded in agreement.

"Or maybe Geordi La Forge," suggested Kyle as he pulled out his Captain Rex armor pieces. "He gets to do all the cool engineer stuff."

"No, Tuvok is more like Tyrrel's Vulcan personality," remarked René with a smirk.

"While I do appreciate the Geordi La Forge character on the Enterprise, I would have to avoid him and Captain Picard as potential characters just because they have French ancestry," Tyrrel said, looking at his best friend trying to put on his most serious Tuvok impression.

"Oui, and I would never let him forget that he chose to be a character with a grand French name," said René with a devilish grin.

Kyle finished attaching his Clone armor pieces over his black sweatpants. His gear looked pretty good except for his helmet. He was not happy with the way it looked. He hoped the group would not be marked down for its less-than-perfect construction. He shaped it out of poster board and covered it with white duct tape to keep the pieces in place. He didn't have the time or the skill to make it out of the plastic like the rest of his armor. He successfully replicated the blue accent marks on Captain Rex's armor and made sure his blaster gun looked correct for the part. He turned to see how Lothar looked in his Han Solo costume, and he looked great. He was a Han Solo with flaming red hair.

"Your costume turned out great!" said Kyle.

"Thanks, but it wasn't as hard to assemble as yours. You did a nice job," replied Lothar. "I wonder how Geoff made out with his Yoda costume. He will be the tallest and skinniest Yoda ever."

"No kidding. It'll be strange, but I don't think the judging will count that against us," said Kyle.

"I would hope not. I am not dying my hair brown," Lothar replied with a mirthless chuckle.

Then they both turned to see Geoff standing in his Master Yoda outfit with the mask he had handmade.

"Put the mask on," said Lothar.

Geoff carefully placed the greenish Yoda mask with pointy ears on his head. He was indeed the tallest Yoda ever. Geoff stood still for a few minutes before taking off the mask.

"You look great. Why did you take the mask off?" asked Kyle.

Geoff's expression was one of distress and pain. He replied, "I can't see out of the mask. I forgot to make eye holes."

"You're kidding, right?" said Kyle.

"Nope," said Geoff with a completely dejected look.

"We gotta fix this right away," said Lothar as he examined Geoff's mask. "You can't even walk around with this on."

"I know. I feel so stupid. I was just so caught up in trying to make it look right that I forgot all about the eyes," said Geoff.

"It looks excellent," said Tyrrel as he took the mask to examine it. "Maybe we could drill some holes for the eyes?"

"No, that might crack the clay," said René, who came over to examine the problem as he buttoned up the French military coat.

"But he needs to be able to see. This section here," Tyrrel pointed at the iris of the eye. "We pop this section of clay out and replace it with see-through plastic or glass. Sure, it won't be as nice as the original clay work, but he needs to be able to see where he is going, and this option should give him some limited vision."

"It is also cumbersome. You should have opted for a crafting foam solution," said René.

Geoff shrugged his shoulders and just made a worried face.

The boys sat down to work on the mask. Tyrrel and Lothar were already dressed, so they had the spare time to help Geoff fix it. René went back to putting on his costume, and so did Kyle. Kyle had to secure several straps and Velcro sections to ensure his Captain Rex Clone Trooper armor stayed in place. As soon as René and Kyle were dressed, the boys went downstairs to the art room to find something to replace the section of clay that Tyrrel and Lothar worked so carefully to remove.

"There should be something useful in the crafting area," said Lothar, striding about in his Han Solo costume with an extra sense of swagger.

They looked around the room, where other students were also trying to solve last-minute problems. Kyle looked at his helmet, focusing on the dark-tinted, see-through plastic.

"How about sunglass lenses?" suggested Kyle.

"I am not wrecking my orange sunglasses," replied Geoff.

"No, no. I meant the ones here for students to use for their costumes. We could pop the lenses out of the frames and glue them into the mask," said Kyle as he held up an inexpensive pair of sunglasses that were part of a drawer filled with stuff for costumes.

"Pure genius," said Lothar, taking the sunglasses out of Kyle's hands and giving them to Tyrrel, who immediately started to figure out how to pop the lenses out of the frames.

"Luckily, these are wire frames, so all I need is a tiny screwdriver to get this apart," said Tyrrel as he examined the glasses. "We also need glue. Lothar and Kyle, will you look for the right kind of glue for this material? We need a fast-acting glue that works on both plastic and clay. Geoff, stay here with me and help get the lenses out. You'll need to decide whether the lenses will be glued on the outside or inside of the mask."

"You were… fortunate that Kyle found those," remarked René as he adjusted the placement of his medals.

Geoff nodded in agreement as he took the first lens and tried to decide where to place it on the mask. In no time at all, the boys had made their repair to Geoff's costume, and they were on their way to the auditorium where the contest was to be held. The girls joined Kyle, Geoff, and Lothar as René and Tyrrel left to compete in the solo competition.

The First-year students presented first and were followed in ascending order until the Fifth-year students were called to go across the stage in front of the judges. The solo competitors went first, and then the groups were asked to present their teams.

Kyle looked at Freya's Jedi costume and marveled at how good she looked. She had her red hair pulled back, just like Qui-Gon Jinn, and had made a lovely textured brown wool, flowing Jedi robe that seemed to suit her perfectly. She smiled at Kyle and swished her lightsaber about with grace and flowing movements.

"Come on, Captain Rex, it's time for us to walk across the stage," said Jedi Freya.

Dressed as Han Solo, Lothar walked across with the Magnusdotter twins on each of his arms. One was dressed as Hoth Leia in white, and the other as Endor Leia with long flowing hair. Then Geoff came out as Yoda with Ivy dressed as a Jedi Twi'lek, and Freya also dressed as a Jedi, along with Kyle in his Captain Rex gear. They stood ready for the judges to look them over and stopped in an action pose for Tyrrel to take a group photo of them with Kyle's digital camera.

Tyrrel gave them the thumbs-up gesture after taking several pictures just to be sure. The group exited the stage to make way for the next group. All the students had their photos taken by older students working in the digital media class, who were tasked with getting everyone into good poses for the pictures. Their class assignment was to take cosplay action portraits of each costumed student as if each competitor needed it for a professional portfolio. This prepared the older students for potential work assignments in future positions, as well as for college submission requirements.

As Kyle exited the stage, he found a rather realistic-looking red-and-gold Iron Man standing there, nodding in appreciation. Kyle was impressed to see that the round arc reactor in the suit glowed bright blue, as it did in the movies.

"You all looked great. I'm impressed," said Iron Man in a somewhat familiar voice.

"Who is that under that mask?" Freya asked as she approached Iron Man and reached for his mask. But before she could open it, he lifted the faceplate of the mask to reveal that he was Trevor.

"You look lovely as a Jedi," said Trevor. "But I think, personally, I would have preferred it if you had dressed as Queen Amidala, and I could have gone as Anakin."

Kyle found himself glaring at Trevor under his Captain Rex helmet.

"You have a great costume, Trevor. Nicely done. But I like being a simple Jedi Knight with my lightsaber," replied Freya with a few elegant slashes and parries.

Trevor smiled at her and put down his Iron Man mask. "Hopefully, I'll be seeing you on the trip."

"We shall see, Trevor," replied Freya.

"You also would have made a brilliant Pepper Potts," remarked Trevor.

The rest of the day was spent having fun. The Fabulous Five hung out with Freya and her friends, planning their day of activities. They voted for the best staff costume. Kyle had a tough time deciding between Sir Knight Wolfram, dressed as a British redcoat, and Sir Knight Greta, dressed as the Marvel X-Men character Storm. She already had white hair and was wearing the strange contact lenses that made her eyes look spooky. She seemed even more spooky and less approachable. He decided to select Sir Knight Greta as Storm.

The students had lunch directly after the costume contest presentations, so the afternoon was completely free to visit the island residents for trick-or-treating, which most of the Page Level students participated in. Other onsite activities were also available. The staff and some older students volunteered to escort the younger students and utilize the school's faculty golf carts to transport them back to the Academy grounds when they became tired. Instead of a formal dinner, a buffet was set up with all kinds of food during the late afternoon and early evening, when the organized games were held. Then, after the games, the contest winners would be announced, and the dance for the older Squire Level students was to begin. An alternate activity of spooky movies was held in the auditorium.

The group stood staring at the day's schedule posted on the announcement board in the central area near the dining hall.

"What does everyone want to do now?" asked Lothar as he pulled his laser pistol out of his holster, spun it on his finger, and then re-holstered the toy gun again.

Freya watched her cousin with a critical eye. The Magnusdotter twins stood on either side of him, appearing to be enamored with his quick draw skills.

"I want to go trick-or-treating to a few houses," said Geoff. "I've never gone trick-or-treating in Canada. And well, most kids stop going when they reach Middle School or Junior High, so this may be my last time."

"I'm with that," agreed Tyrrel.

"Me too," said Kyle.

"I don't care. I just don't want to be standing around doing nothing," replied René as he straightened his medals and tucked his hair back into his hat.

311

"You know, you look cute with short hair," said Lucy Robbinson as she adjusted her cape to her Snow White costume.

"And you, with your very white skin and jet-black hair, are a perfect storybook version of Disney's Snow White," replied René with a smile.

Lucy giggled and managed to utter a thank you.

Tyrrel leaned into René and whispered, "She's too smart for you."

René wrinkled his brow. "You're not too smart to be my friend, so why can't I find Lucy attractive?"

Tyrrel just shook his head.

"Okay, so it is settled. We're all going trick-or-treating for a while, then coming back inside for games," said Lothar.

No one disagreed. With that settled, the little group, mainly in Star Wars costumes, set off with one Nobel Prize-winning scientist, one French Ace of the Great War, and a fairy tale princess.

They visited several houses along the island's west coast, the most populated area, and encountered Iron Man and Zorro along the way.

"Hello, Jedi Master Freya," said Iron Man to Freya.

Ivy tilted her head funny to Geoff and asked, "Who's that?"

Geoff leaned toward Ivy, held his Yoda mask in place, and said, "That's Trevor. Pretty cool costume, huh?"

"Yes, very nice. He tried to get Freya to dress as Pepper Potts," replied Ivy.

"Really? I think she would make a very pretty Pepper Potts," replied Geoff. "But I am glad she decided to do the Star Wars character."

Kyle listened and watched as Freya chatted with Trevor. He felt like his stomach had turned upside down. The odd feeling was unpleasant. He had never felt it before. He then realized that he was worried that Freya would like Trevor. The thought was confusing, and he did his best to push it aside and stay focused on having fun in his Captain Rex costume. He felt his jaw tighten, and he was relieved that his helmet covered his face.

"So, Freya, are you and the girls going to spend your whole day with the Fabulous Five?" asked Trevor with Zorro standing beside him.

"It was the plan. Are you and Xavier looking for a group to hang out with?" asked Freya.

Lothar noticed Kyle put his hand on his costume blaster pistol and grip it tightly. He leaned over to the silent-looking Captain Rex figure and said, "Only Han Solo shoots first."

Lothar watched as Captain Rex's helmet slowly turned toward him, then tilted in a questioning manner.

"You're gripping your laser blaster so tight that if it were not made of wood, it would crack," Lothar remarked to Kyle.

The Captain Rex figure stood still for a minute, then straightened up and let go of the toy pistol.

"Are you okay?" Lothar asked Kyle.

"Yes, I think so… maybe," Kyle replied quietly.

Trevor and Xavier joined the group during the trick-or-treat walk and then walked back to the school grounds with everyone.

"That elderly fellow knew that I was dressed as a World War One aviator!" exclaimed René with a certain amount of pride.

"Yes, and he knew who Zorro was, along with Snow White, but the rest of us were a complete mystery," laughed Tyrrel.

"Well, I don't think anyone knows who you are supposed to be," René remarked to Tyrrel.

"Yes, that may be true. But what is important is that I know who I am supposed to be," replied Tyrrel.

"Well, regardless of who we are all supposed to be, we have candy to last us a week," remarked Lucy Robbinson, looking into her basket and examining the different types of candy.

"I love candy," declared Geoff proudly.

"I don't think there are many kids who don't," replied Lucy.

"Hey, we should all have our pictures taken in fun poses with each other, just like those Cosplayers," suggested Sif Magnusdotter. "Who has a camera with them?"

"Kyle does," said Tyrrel.

"That would be so much fun. Kyle, can we take pictures with your camera?" asked Elsa as she twirled about in her Leia on Endor costume.

"Sure. That sounds like lots of fun, and then I can share them with everyone in digital format," replied Kyle.

"Oh, thank you," said Sif, hugging Kyle.

"Certainly," said Kyle, blushing under his helmet, momentarily forgetting his disapproval of Trevor's friendly demeanor toward Freya.

The discussion on the best spot to take pictures was almost unanimously decided to be Boulder Glade, but Xavier refused to go. Therefore, the group settled on another location on the Academy grounds, which was a manicured garden with a full hedge maze and stone blocks perfect for the students to pose upon in their costumes. The rest of the afternoon was spent having fun doing silly action shots, one of which Kyle insisted upon having several with Freya in a pose with him, like he was shooting at clanker droids, and she was fending off laser fire. Then the other Star Wars characters joined in for the photos until the camera's battery died.

"It's dead, alright. You'll have to put the battery on the charger," said Tyrrel, handing the small digital camera back to Kyle.

"Wow, that is the first time I have used up the battery charge," mused Kyle.

Kyle took the camera and put it into his belt pouch. He thought it was nice to have the camera his grandparents had thoughtfully given him. He loved the idea of having photos to share with his parents and them.

It was time for the indoor games to start. The buffet dinner had been set up, and soon, the announcements for the contest winners would start. This was the first time Kyle and the others had the opportunity to see the Squire Level students in a social setting. They all looked so big that Kyle was having a hard time distinguishing between Academy staff members and the oldest students. One of the older students was dressed as Superman and didn't need padded muscles to look like the Man of Steel.

"Wow, look at him!" exclaimed Sif and Elsa.

"He certainly is my idea of what Superman should look like," commented Ivy with stars in her eyes.

"Yes, he is rather perfect for the part, isn't he?" said Freya admiringly.

"Indeed, he has all the pretty girls admiring him," remarked René as he watched a couple of older girls dressed as Supergirl and Wonder Woman give the student dressed as Superman hugs and kisses.

"He's so handsome," Sif said to Elsa, who nodded in agreement.

"I guess we'll get to see him around next year," Ivy said breathlessly.

"No, you won't. He graduates this year," said Lucy. "He's the captain of the Academy soccer team." Several heads turned to Lucy with looks of inquiry. "Oh, I'm sorry. You call it football here in Canada, right?"

The Canadian-born students nodded, caught up in their thoughts concerning the new information.

"Huh, I am disappointed that Superman will be leaving," grumbled Sif to herself and Elsa.

"Well, his costume was nice. Shall we move on and get some food? I'm starving," said Geoff. The boys took this cue quickly and headed for the buffet while the girls lingered amongst themselves to contemplate the handsome Superman student.

The main event and buffet had been set up in the large entertainment and entrance hall, which featured high ceilings and was often used for fundraising parties and major school events. It was central to the whole school, with access to the main dining hall, movie theater, and ballroom, where the dance for the older students was to be held. Kyle had visited a few buffets in Reno while living with his mom, and this one certainly was impressive enough to compete with some of the better ones. The food was all fresh and presented in copious amounts with a wide variety. He wasn't sure where to begin. By the time Kyle picked up a plate and had a few ideas of what he wanted to eat, Geoff had already loaded his plate and was searching for a place to sit. Luckily, some of the girls had the forethought to grab a table space that was big enough for their group to sit at.

"Thanks for saving a table," said Kyle as he sat down and removed his helmet. "I'll save your seats while you get your food."

"Thanks, Kyle," said Sif and Elsa in unison as they energetically went off together to get their dinner. He watched the two Princess Leias disappear into the buffet area and then turned his attention back to the table to eat. The food was good.

Geoff was already seated and had started to dig into his meal with gusto.

"My, you have a grand appetite!" exclaimed Ivy as she sat down next to Geoff and watched him for a minute.

"I have to keep up my strength," Geoff said after swallowing a mouthful. "I have a very high metabolism and need to eat a lot… and often."

"I see," said Ivy, looking over at Kyle across the table. Kyle grinned at Ivy and raised his eyebrows while Geoff obliviously stuffed more food into his mouth.

It wasn't long before everyone else joined them at the table, ate their food, and watched what was going on around them. Some of the smaller kids were finishing up the planned indoor games and getting ready for their dinner. Announcements of the costume contest winners

318

were to be made soon, and the students were growing anxious.

"Who do you think will win?" Kyle asked no one in particular.

"I think your Star Wars group will win the Fifth-year student group, but I'm not sure about the single Fifth-year winner. There are several very good costumes," remarked Tyrrel with a dispassionate and somewhat clinical tone.

"But just because we win the Fifth-year group costume doesn't mean we win the field trip. We must beat out all the other Page Level winners for group costume," explained Lothar.

Kyle quickly scanned the room, looking for any other Page Level groups that might be strong competitors. He couldn't spot any others that appeared to be a group, except for a couple of Second-year students dressed as characters that looked like Dungeons and Dragons or Lord of the Rings type characters. He wasn't sure.

"I don't see that many groups," remarked Kyle.

"Neither have I, but I have seen plenty of single entrees that are quite good," said René.

Xavier placed his black Zorro hat back on and said, "Hideaki Takahashi has a cool costume of one of those big Japanese robot fighters, and I don't think my Zorro costume has a chance against that."

"You don't have a chance because you have been wearing the same costume for five years," said Trevor to his best friend.

"Well, that's because each year they say to pick someone or something that you'd like to be, and I'd like to be Zorro," replied Xavier with a certain amount of frustration. "My mind has not changed."

"You've worn the same costume every year?" said Kyle to Xavier.

"Not exactly," said Xavier. "I have made improvements and had to make new stuff because I got too big for the pants, shirt, and boots. And this year I made a brand-new hat."

"And it is a very nice hat too," said Freya.

Before the discussion could go any further, Sir Knight Wolfram, dressed in his 1700s British military coat and black tricorn hat, took the microphone in hand and started to get everyone's attention.

"It is that time of the year again," he said with a broad grin. "And I love this time of the year when the students of the Academy get to show off their creativity and ingenuity. I believe these projects reveal special parts of your personality that might not be seen under regular circumstances. They provide staff and instructors with the opportunity to get to know the real you, encourage you to pursue your dreams, and help expand your talents. This is what education is about. It's not just the vital facts of numbers, dates, and language rules, but about creating a foundation for a future life of professional excellence, success, and happiness. So right now, I am about to make some of you very happy."

The entire hall of students and educators had their focus upon the heavy-set man with the walrus-style mustache. Everyone was eager to hear the contest results, and some students poured out of other areas to listen to the results.

"I know that everyone is reeling from the suspense, so I am just going to read the winners of each Level, starting with the First-year students up to the Twelfth-year students. I will read the winners of the single entrant and then the group," said Sir Knight Wolfram. "And so on."

Everyone's attention was focused on the man in the red coat. Sir Knight Wolfram paused, gazing out at the students and staff members waiting. He smiled cheerily and then began.

"The First-year winners are Melinda Pattrick as a nature spirit and Timothy Mueller, Beth Davidson, Juan Carlos Castillo, and Cindy Johannson as Greek gods and goddesses," said Sir Knight Wolfram.

The room erupted in cheers and applause for the winning students before Sir Knight Wolfram could continue reading through the list. This happened as he read each set of winners. Kyle and the others sat anxiously waiting for their turn.

"And for the Fifth-year students, the winners are Trevor Allen Smith for his Iron Man costume, and wow, this is a big group... Freya Wolff, Lothar Wolff, Elsa Magnusdotter, Sif Magnusdotter, Geoff Powell, Kyle

Bergendahl, and Ivy Rosenplat-Levi for the Star Wars themed costumes."

The table erupted in excited shouts for joy. Tyrrel and René both congratulated their friends while Lucy hugged Sif and Elsa.

"Oh my gosh, I wasn't sure we'd get picked!" exclaimed Freya.

Kyle was extremely pleased but still held out hope that they would get selected for the big field trip. Their biggest competition would come from the First-year students, who all wore fantastic costumes of Greek gods and goddesses, and they would be hard to beat.

"It was an obvious choice that you would win," said René to Lothar, who looked pleased.

"Now the tough part comes to see if you can win the grand prize of going on the field trip," said Tyrrel.

"Yeah, the First-year students' group winners' costumes are pretty nice and clever," remarked Kyle, feeling concerned. "The way they used the materials to make their costumes… they will be tough to beat."

"Yeah, but there are more of us, and it is harder to get a big group like ours to all look good," said Geoff as he finished hugging Ivy. "I think we can win this. The materials we had to use were more complicated to manage."

"I am sorry you did not place," Lothar told René. "Your costume was done well. And it looked more like a film replica than just a costume."

"Yes, but it could not stand up to all the lights and wiring that Trevor put into his," said Xavier.

René nodded, smiled, and replied, "But I did get perfect marks for all my schoolwork regarding my costume. I might even get published in a WWI historical magazine."

"Oh, excellent!" exclaimed Lothar. "That's an amazing bonus for all your hard work! He'll be bragging about this for a while."

"I also got perfect marks for my work, but I knew my costume could not rival all the work that the rest of you put into all of yours. You all deserved to win," said Tyrrel.

Sir Knight Wolfram continued the announcements, and the cheers and applause followed each set. The tension in the room was building as the hopes and expectations of certain groups rose. Trevor looked confident while the Star Wars group seemed to be on edge, worrying about their younger competition. The next group of students to be announced was the youngest age level of the Squire Level students. Alistair Grennan won the single costume entrant for his Gandalf the Grey costume. Sir Knight Wolfram congratulated him on his excellent construction of a mustache and long white beard.

"You do realize that if we get to go on the field trip, it will be the first time we've done so since Raggedy Ann and Andy," Lothar remarked to Freya.

"Yes, I know. Perhaps we should be working together more often," replied Freya as she watched the older kids cheering and some expressing disappointment.

"Wow, some of the older kids take this very seriously," said Geoff to no one in particular.

"I noticed that, and they look like they put a lot more work into it, too," said Kyle, thinking back to the older student who had helped him with the plastic armor pieces.

"The older kids are doing projects that will help them get into college. They are building portfolios," explained Lucy.

"Portfolios?" asked Kyle.

"Yes. Some universities require a submission of a portfolio for entrance," said Lucy.

"I am already starting mine," said Tyrrel. Do you remember the water samples I collected? Well... those will help me with research projects later on. I have established that I am responsible and reliable, so I should have no trouble being allowed to do special projects with other scientific groups."

Kyle just stared at Lucy and Tyrrel. This was way beyond his thinking, and he felt somewhat out of place. He didn't even know what he wanted to do after he graduated from high school. He felt embarrassed and nodded in agreement as if what they said made perfect sense. He looked back at Sir Knight Wolfram, who had just finished announcing the winners for each year level, and now it was time to announce the big winner for the field trip.

"Alright, I want everyone to know this was a tough decision to make. The work this year was truly tremendous, and every one of you should be very proud of

324

yourselves and the Academy for having such great students who volunteer extra time to help their peers. The entire staff and I are very proud of the creative and academic work you have done so far this year. I feel very privileged to be here and be a part of your education," said Sir Knight Wolfram. "Sir Knight Mary, will you please bring up the sealed envelope containing the names of the Page Level student winners for the field trip?"

Sir Knight Mary, dressed as a very convincing Professor McGonagall from the Harry Potter series, strode toward Sir Knight Wolfram as she opened the envelope and pulled out the paper. Everyone seated at Kyle's table held their breath with anticipation while one of the Academy support staff members strode up with an armful of the classic purple ribbons that were meant for grand prize winners. Sir Knight Wolfram handed the microphone to Sir Knight Mary, who adjusted her wire-framed glasses.

"When your name is announced, please come up and accept your ribbon," she said, gesturing to the staff member holding the ribbons. "Our first recipient for the Halloween Costume Contest Grand Prize Field Trip Winner, Page Level for the best single entrant, is Trevor Allen Smith."

A fury of noise erupted from their table and around them as Trevor, looking so pleased with himself, stood up and strode toward Sir Knight Mary with his gold helmet face plate down to accept his ribbon and a bit of glory for winning. When he arrived at her location, he pressed a few buttons on his left-arm gauntlet, which illuminated various parts of his costume and made them move. He popped open the face plate on his helmet and thanked Sir Knight Mary as he accepted the big purple ribbon. This prompted the school to break out into loud applause. The costume was very well done.

"And now for the next set of winners, please know this was an extremely close competition between two of the five entrant groups. The winners for the Halloween Costume Contest Grand Prize Field Trip Winners Page Level for the best group costume are the Star Wars group of Kyle Bergendahl, Elsa Magnusdotter, Sif Magnusdotter, Geoff Powell, Ivy Rosenplat-Levi, Freya Wolff, and Lothar Wolff."

Another eruption of cheers exploded as Kyle and his friends jumped up from their table excitedly. They could barely contain themselves as they each walked up to the area where Sir Knight Mary stood waiting to congratulate them. Kyle gazed at the big purple ribbon, feeling excited about the prospect of going somewhere special with his new friends, especially Freya. Life had changed. The rest of the evening was spent talking and hanging out until the movies, the snacks, and the energy were gone. After Kyle had carefully removed his Captain Rex gear and put his helmet in a place of honor in his bedroom, he picked up the large purple ribbon and tacked it onto the wall right next to his archery ribbon. He had never won ribbons before, and he couldn't recall ever winning… anything before.

Kyle wanted to share this joy with his family. He wanted them to be proud of him, and he wanted to prove that his being at the Academy was truly worth the expense. The Fifth-year boys' room was finally quiet and dark. Everyone was already in bed and falling asleep. The urge to contact his family would have to wait until morning. Exhaustion came from the overwhelming elation of victory, and he had to succumb to the entreaty of sleep. It was not long before his head was filled with strange visions of himself, and his friends dressed in costumed adventures that made very little sense to the conscious mind.

Chapter 14: Homesickness and Finals

November came to Lake Simcoe like a winter warrior with a heart full of bluster and chill. It was no longer comfortable to step outside without wearing a warm coat. Wrestling had replaced javelin in martial arts class and was confined indoors. The students were required to wear athletic clothes for this activity. This would be taught for three weeks and would be replaced by Tai Chi, another indoor activity. Kyle had never done wrestling or Tai Chi, and soon found that he did not care for wrestling. However, Freya had expressed her enjoyment of Tai Chi, so he looked forward to trying it, reassured by her that he would enjoy it.

November also brought a significant push for new projects that needed to be completed before the winter break period. The Fifth-year students had finished reading *"Call of the Wild"* and had started *"The Hobbit"* by J.R.R. Tolkien. Kyle had never read a book of this size before and struggled to find time to read it. Sir Knight Mary had wanted the book to be read by November 15 so that she could have the class watch the movies and write a comparison and contrast paper concerning the differences between the books and the film versions.

Kyle sat in one of the soft chairs in the Fifth-year boys' room, reading, when several boys came in.

"Are you still reading that?" Trevor asked as he walked past Kyle, wearing a red poppy in his shirt buttonhole. He walked directly toward his bedroom cubicle without waiting to hear a reply to his comment.

"Yeah," grumbled Kyle as he tried to remain focused on the story.

"I'm not finished either. I really should get further along, or else I will fail the test on Monday morning," commented Geoff as he made a beeline straight toward his cubicle room.

"I'm done with *The Hobbit*, but I need a break from schoolwork. Anyone want to play a video game with me for about an hour?" asked Tyrrel, looking somewhat fatigued.

"Sure, I have just one more chapter to read, which I can do tonight. Everything else I am caught up on," said Lothar, who sat down on the couch in front of the TV where the game console was set up. He carefully pulled his red remembrance poppy from his shirt and removed his sweater, which he folded up. "I'm surprised that you want to play a game. I thought you were still working on that computer assignment," said Lothar as he handed a game controller to Tyrrel.

"I do need to finish it, but I just feel tired and unfocused," replied the tall black boy as he allowed his body to sink heavily into the couch.

Kyle heard every part of this conversation and noticed every noise that occurred in every part of the room, as if it begged to be listened to, so that it could distract him from reading. He tried to block out the sounds that beckoned him away from the words on the bright tablet pages in front of him.

"You don't look so good," said Lothar, taking a more serious assessment of his friend's current state of mind. "Are you getting René's cold?"

"I hope not. I hate being sick," replied Tyrrel grumpily.

"How did he get that in the first place? Hardly anyone ever gets sick here," commented Lothar as he selected a game for them to play.

"He was outside visiting the horses the other day when it was raining. Ever since he got to go riding at Kyle's grandparents' house, he's been doing the big countdown until he's allowed to ride again," replied Tyrrel.

"Oh, I see," replied Lothar.

Kyle finally had to get up. He could not focus. He went into his bedroom cubicle and turned on his computer. He hadn't checked if anyone had emailed him lately. Everyone was thrilled about the costume contest win, especially after seeing the pictures he sent of himself and his friends. His mom wanted to know who all the "little girls" were in the photos and seemed to be pleased for him about the field trip opportunity. Winter break was approaching, and Kyle was waiting to find out where he would spend Christmas this year. He had been with his father last year, but he had lived with his mom the year before, so he wasn't sure how this year would end up. He could already sense that the arguing had begun between his parents.

The next day was just as busy. Kyle walked across the dining hall, carrying his tray, and looked out the windows absentmindedly. It was stormy again outside, and even though he was wearing the white turtleneck sweater his grandmother had selected for him as part of his uniform and the hooded blue jacket, he still felt chilled.

It was now late November when Kyle started to feel a little strange about not being at a regular school. The American Thanksgiving holiday was just a few days away, and something didn't feel right. There was no planning for Thanksgiving dinner or chatter about going shopping the day after. He didn't miss the silly advertising or the fact that the Christmas displays were put up way too early, but he was missing something. He wondered if his mom would miss him and what she would do on Thanksgiving Day. It had always been fun to watch her carve the turkey, and she would give him small pieces from the bird that were too small for the serving platter. She made all kinds of other dishes, and sometimes he would help with them. There would always be a lot of tasty leftovers for about a week. After his parents separated, his mom invited her friends over for dinner. Everyone would stuff themselves and talk about their work, family, shopping for the next day's sales, and so forth. At the time, it was only mildly interesting, but Kyle found himself missing some of that. This year, there would be no turkey.

"You look miserable," commented Geoff, seated at the table beside him.

Kyle was surprised to find himself seated at the table. He did not even recall sitting down.

"Uh, I do?" he asked.

"Yeah, what's the matter?" asked Geoff as he picked up his ham and Swiss sandwich, preparing to take a bite.

Ivy sat down next to Geoff and frowned a little at his choice of lunch meat.

"I don't know," replied Kyle. "Do you ever miss home?"

"Yes," replied Geoff with a big mouthful of sandwich.

Tyrrel and René joined them at the table.

"What do you miss the most about home?" asked Kyle.

"Having one," said Ivy under her breath.

"I miss my parents, brothers, and sister," replied Tyrrel.

"I miss my Maman's voice. She likes to sing and hum tunes while she is cooking or doing other things in the house," said René.

"I thought you said your family has a housekeeper," said Geoff, his mouth still full of food.

René scowled at Geoff's lack of etiquette and replied, "We do, but my Maman likes to bake desserts."

"Geoff! Manners. Don't talk with your mouth full," remarked Freya as she sat down at the table, followed by the Magnusdotter twins.

Geoff chewed a bit more, then swallowed and said, "You sound just like my mother."

"Probably with good reason," remarked Lothar as he joined the table. "If you want to be a Knight someday, you'll have to curb that habit of talking with your mouth full. My father said in the old days, the Knights got into arguments about table etiquette, which caused a rule to be set that no one could talk while at the dinner table."

"That's a stupid rule. You mean everyone sits around in silence?" commented Kyle.

"Yes, pretty much. I guess it stopped the arguing that must have occurred," said Lothar, rolling his eyes slightly.

"The Knights argued a lot?" asked Kyle.

"No, not a lot, but they did not always agree," said René. "My family's history can be traced back long into the Order. We might even be related to Hugh de Payne."

"Who is that?" asked Kyle.

"You don't know?!" asked Lothar with some surprise.

"No."

"Well, neither do I, so let's hear about him. Who is he?" asked Geoff.

"He's the Order's founder along with several other Knights," replied Lothar.

"Oh, I see. That means he is pretty important," laughed Kyle, feeling somewhat embarrassed.

"What kind of school did you go to before coming here?" Trevor asked from another table, where he sat with Xavier and several other Fifth-year boys: Kevin, Wendell, and Pierre.

Kyle shook his head in irritation and replied, "Just a regular school. Nothing special. Not a private school like this one."

"Well, I can see why your parents decided to send you to a proper school. One of the American students said that *Call of the Wild* was on a banned book list," said Trevor. "Along with *Lord of the Rings*."

Kyle had nothing to say. He didn't know what to say. He had always been told that Americans had the right to free speech and a bunch of other stuff about respecting the diversity of others, so why would books like *Call of the Wild* or *Lord of the Rings* be banned, he wondered.

"Wow, that seems odd, Trevor, since there were the Lord of the Rings movies and all," said Geoff, making sure that his mouth was not full this time when he spoke. "Maybe you have your facts wrong. That doesn't make sense."

"We can always look it up on the Internet," said Tyrrel.

Everyone nodded in agreement that this was a good idea.

"So, what brought all this up in the first place?" asked Lothar.

"Kyle was feeling super homesick," replied Geoff.

"I'm not super homesick, but I miss having the Thanksgiving holiday in late November. It just feels like something… is missing," Kyle replied.

"Well, you are not the first American student to feel that way, and since the school has so many American students, they serve a Turkey dinner on our day for Thanksgiving," said Tyrrel.

"Really? Oh, cool!" said Geoff as Kyle's face broadened into a big grin.

"The school has a special menu for the year that takes into account holidays from other regions to assist in making the students feel less homesick. It may not replace family or traditions, but it does help," said Tyrrel. "My family makes great food, and they make a big production out of doing family stuff."

"I will never forget that awful Haggis they serve in late January for Burns' Night," remarked René.

"Haggis?" asked Kyle.

"Yes, it's a type of sausage stuffed into a sheep's stomach," replied Tyrrel. "We have a bunch of kids with Scottish heritage here, too, but they don't make all of us eat haggis. They do a variety of traditional foods from Scotland."

"For that I am thankful," said René as he prepared to dip his spoon into his bowl of soup.

"I like Walpurgis Nacht or Valborg, which is April thirtieth. It's like an odd version of Halloween and the celebration of spring's return. We have a bunch of cultural and historical research for that one," said Lucy.

"More costumes?" asked Geoff.

"No costumes for that one, but lots of other activities that revolve around culture and history," replied Lucy. "It's a celebration more centered around the northern European countries. They also add in some of the traditions adopted by Christianity and explain their origins."

"Hmm. It sounds... like... it will be a lot of work," replied Kyle. The other kids laughed at his assessment of the Spring Project.

"Yes, it can be a lot of work if you let it overwhelm you," said Tyrrel. "But I found it interesting since I had never heard of this holiday before. Back home, in Vegas, we just went to church, got candy, and collected Easter eggs during that time of the year."

"Well, I'm thrilled to have turkey dinner on Thanksgiving Day. It won't be the same as being with my mom or dad, but it sorta helps. I'll worry about this other weird stuff when it happens," said Kyle as he prepared to take the last bite of his sandwich.

"Which reminds me, are either of you returning to the U.S. for the Winter break?" Geoff asked Kyle and Tyrrel.

"My mother's heart would break if I didn't come home for Christmas," said Tyrrel. "Why do you ask?"

"My parents don't want me to travel alone, but money is tight, so they hoped I could coordinate with another student, and we could travel part of the way together."

"You know I live in Las Vegas," Tyrrel replied to Geoff.

"Yes, but there was a flight directly from the PDX Airport to Toronto, and if either of you were going that route..." replied Geoff.

"I came here on a flight directly from the Portland Airport," said Kyle. "So, I would guess it would probably be the same route going back."

"Why don't we figure this out when it comes time to fly home? We'll all sit down together and get our tickets," suggested Tyrrel.

"Okay, I'll let my parents know I am trying to work something out, but we gotta do it soon. My dad says the ticket prices will go up if I wait too long," said Geoff.

Tyrrel nodded appreciatively. "He has a good point. We should reach out to our parents tonight to find out what they'd like to do. Agreed."

"Agreed," said Kyle and Geoff in unison.

Kyle dreaded the idea of dredging up his plans for Christmas with his parents, but he knew he needed to do it. He would call them both after dinner time. In the meantime, Kyle was fortunate to have free time during his computer technology class, having already completed his assignment. Dr. William Bainbridge, the computer and technology instructor, also known as Sir Knight William, did not believe students needed to spend unnecessary time in class. He believed that if the student had completed the day's required task, they could use their time as they saw fit. Thanks to this novel approach, Kyle had extra time to visit the library.

The library was an impressive three-level structure with an open center where the staff waited on students. Large, dark antique wooden tables were set out, accompanied by old-fashioned card catalogue index cabinets and a few computer stations for searching books. Kyle had never seen a school library that looked like this, except perhaps the Getchell library at the University of Nevada, Reno. Although the design was different, the number of books to choose from was just as impressive. It also had an old card catalogue system as well as modern computers. He recalled going there with his mother, who needed to research something and could not find the right book at the local county libraries. He was just glad he did not have to find a parking space to get to this library. His mother had been so upset about the lack of available parking at the university that she vowed never to go there again. At the time, Kyle just thought it was a fun adventure to walk around the campus and stare at all the students. He later convinced her to grab a burger at one of the local student hangouts.

Kyle felt the peaceful hush of the library come over him as he entered. He needed to find a book about a place called Navy Island. Everyone in history class drew a topic from a jar, and based on their selection, they had to give a two-page report and presentation on it for class. He had never heard of the place, so he wasn't sure how to begin his search, and then he spotted Freya at the old-fashioned card catalogue cabinets. She had a drawer pulled open and was meticulously going through the cards.

Kyle walked over to her quietly and said, "Hi, Freya."

"Oh, hi, Kyle," she said, trying not to lose her place in the card drawer.

"What are you doing?"

"Looking for a book about Fort William," replied Freya.

"Never heard of it," said Kyle.

"Well, it's a place in Thunder Bay, which is on the coast of Lake Superior," replied Freya.

"Oh, I see," said Kyle. "I have to find information about Navy Island."

Freya smiled at Kyle and then wrote down the book number she wanted. She put the card back into the file and closed the drawer. She picked up her belongings and started to go.

"So where are you going?" asked Kyle.

"To find the book. Do you want to come with me?"

"Sure," said Kyle, forgetting why he came into the library in the first place.

He followed her up the stairs to the second floor, turned right, and then proceeded through a maze of shelves. They came across a shy, nervous-looking young girl with pale, white skin, short brown bobbed hair, and brilliant green eyes, carrying several books out of the stacks.

"Oh, hi, Emerald," said Freya.

"Hi, Freya," said the younger girl as she seemed to cheer up upon hearing Freya's greeting.

Freya continued down the stack toward the book she was searching for. The younger girl disappeared in another direction. Kyle stared for a moment in the direction where the younger girl had disappeared and then discovered that Freya had sat down in the stacks, some twenty feet away. Kyle joined Freya and sat down beside her.

"Was that Emerald Green? The girl who blew up her project?" whispered Kyle to Freya.

"Yes, and we should not be discussing this here," replied Freya.

"I had never seen her before. She looks so fragile and small. I didn't even know that she stayed at the school," said Kyle.

Freya continued to focus on finding a book that would give her the information she wanted about Fort William and replied, "Where else would she go? This is one of the few schools in the world that even offers her training on how to deal with her special abilities."

"I had not thought about that. I guess I thought she would leave because what happened was weird and embarrassing," said Kyle.

Freya stopped for a moment, frowned, and then looked at Kyle. Then she refocused on pulling out books and flipping through them. "It's only weird because people insist on making it so. She is very talented and needs to be trained, so she doesn't hurt anyone or herself."

"But I thought she was being teased by the other girls in her year," said Kyle. "What if they keep being mean? What will happen?"

"The Academy addresses situations like that. They don't ignore it as kids' stuff," replied Freya as she flipped through a book with a nice amount of text, photos, and maps. She closed the book with finality and got up.

"Well, I guess that is good," said Kyle, pondering. "Do you think the other girls will take this seriously and stop being mean?"

Kyle stood up and held Freya's gaze with seriousness. She stared back at him and paused for a moment as if thinking over what she was about to say.

"The Academy takes bullying very seriously. It is a breach of the code of conduct. It is conduct unbecoming of a Knight. If the behavior is not modified or stopped, the student will be banned from Knight Training and possibly expelled from the school entirely. The Order does not take that kind of behavior lightly. About twenty years ago, seven students were bullying another group of three students, and the Academy expelled the seven for breaking the code of conduct. I don't know exactly what they did, but it was bad enough that they were not even given the opportunity to change their behavior."

Kyle had never considered the possibility of being thrown out of the Academy. The idea was awful. It sounded like his worst nightmare, especially now that he had made so many new friends. This school experience seemed to change his life for the better.

"Dang, they must have been pretty mean," commented Kyle.

Freya nodded and looked at her watch.

"I have to go to Secondary Language class now," said Freya.

"Yes, I should go too," Kyle replied as he walked with Freya back the way they had come. "Will you promise me something?"

"Sure, but it depends upon what it is," said Freya.

"If I ever act like a jerk, will you tell me?" asked Kyle.

Freya laughed and reached out and squeezed Kyle's arm warmly and replied, "I doubt you'll ever need me to say that, but I promise I will tell you."

Kyle smiled and nodded as they continued their way out of the library.

He lamented not finding a book about Navy Island, but was glad he got to see Freya. Every time he thought about her squeezing his arm, he felt odd inside... but it was a strange and happy oddness.

That evening, he called his dad to find out what kind of plans had been made for him for the winter break period. He would be off from school for a whole month. After talking with his dad, Kyle discovered he would be going directly to his mother's home, and then, after Christmas, would spend time with his dad. Dr. Bergendahl liked the idea of having Kyle travel with some of the other students, so he asked Kyle to obtain Tyrrel's and Geoff's parents' contact information so that he could make arrangements with them directly.

A couple of days later, the parents made arrangements for the boys to travel from the Toronto Airport directly to Las Vegas, Nevada, where Tyrrel would disembark, leaving Kyle and Geoff to take the short forty-five-minute trip up to Reno, where Kyle would get off, leaving Geoff to finish the final part of the journey to Portland, Oregon. This made everyone happy.

It was the evening of the American Thanksgiving holiday, so the school served a turkey dinner that reflected the favorites of the United States. Kyle sat down with his friends, holding a huge plate filled with traditional meal goodies.

"You look pleased," Lothar commented to Kyle.

"Yup," said Kyle with a big grin. "I knew I liked turkey dinner, but I never realized how much."

"Well, we shall all be back home very soon. It's only three weeks until the break," commented Tyrrel.

"And I will be back in the sweet arms of Paris," said René. "I have missed hearing the French language spoken correctly, French food prepared correctly, and my Maman and Papa so much."

"How is it that you always manage to make something positive sound just a little insulting?" wondered Ivy as she rolled her eyes in disgust.

Tyrrel chuckled, knowing how René could be. René shrugged his shoulders and said nothing.

"I think it is part of being French, Ivy," remarked Lothar with a grin.

"Well, I am stressed out. I have so much homework to do and so many tests to study for," commented Freya as she placed her tray down, a frown of frustration taking over her normally serene-looking features.

"We have three more weeks," said Lothar.

"I don't," said Ivy.

"Why don't you have three weeks?" asked Kyle.

"Because she is leaving early to celebrate Hanukkah," said Geoff.

Ivy smiled, "You remembered me telling you about that."

"Of course, I did," replied Geoff. "You're my friend."

Ivy's dark brown eyes twinkled as she managed to smile just a little more.

"So, what are you two, a couple now?" asked René.

Ivy blushed, which was rare for the outspoken Jewish girl with a mysterious background, while Geoff just frowned.

"A couple of what?" asked Geoff.

Kyle shook his head, knowing that this was going nowhere, and Geoff wasn't ready to think about boyfriend/girlfriend relationships.

René raised an eyebrow at Geoff and said nothing.

"Our tickets are all ready," said Tyrrel, changing the subject to something less inconvenient.

"Yes, I have mine already printed out and put into my suitcase," said Kyle. "I think it will be fun to travel together."

"I would have to agree. This will be the first time that I get to fly with friends. It will make the trip more enjoyable," said Tyrrel.

"We should all keep in touch by exchanging phone numbers and email addresses," suggested Lothar.

"I think that's a wonderful idea," said Sif as her sister nodded in agreement.

"Let's do this before we forget," suggested Elsa as she pulled out her slim, Barbie-pink colored smartphone.

"I'd love to, but I don't carry my phone around with me," said Kyle.

"I don't have a cell phone, but I do have an email account," said Geoff.

"You don't have a cell phone?" exclaimed René as he pulled out his smartphone and turned it on.

"No, my parents don't have the money for it," replied Geoff, feeling a bit embarrassed.

"That's no problem since I am not sure my mom will let me talk that much on the cell phone. I guess it costs a lot every time I use it. But I can get on the computer as much as I want," said Kyle as he dipped his sliced turkey into the cranberries on his plate.

"And there is always Skype or Google," suggested Tyrrel.

"You all realize that Sir Knight Mary will assign us homework while we are away. She's warned us that we will be expected to read *The Secret Garden* and have it completed by our return," said Freya.

"I'm not going to spend all my time sending you text messages, cousin," said Lothar as he picked up his glass of milk. "I plan to be outside having fun in the snow."

Freya rolled her eyes and then replied to her cousin, "Lothar, I wasn't expecting you to spend all your time messaging me, but I don't know how much time I will have free for chatting online."

The two red-haired students stared at each other for a moment.

"Everyone, stand back, it is the battle of the gingers," remarked Pauline Windgate with a heavy British accent as she strode by with her dinner tray.

"Oh, shut up, Pauline," retorted Freya. "This is none of your concern."

Pauline flashed a haughty look at Freya. "A typical response from a hot-headed ginger," replied the Fourth-year girl with mousy brown hair as she strode away to a table with a bunch of Fourth-year girls.

"Want me to slap some sense into her?" asked Ivy. "I'll show her the meaning of hot-headed Jewish brunette."

"You'd only get into trouble," said Freya appreciatively.

"No, actually, I probably would not," smiled the brown-eyed girl with the olive complexion.

"She's just a stupid Fourth-year girl who doesn't know her place," remarked René, his accent flaring again.

"Well, I think she was rude. We were not even talking to her," commented Kyle, still eyeing the girl at the other table.

"Well, Pauline has been in trouble since she arrived. One of the Fourth-year girls told me that she was sent here in the middle of her second year because she got into trouble at her old private school back in England," said Sif.

"Her parents are not knights, are they?" said Lothar, still a bit steamed.

"No, they are not," said René.

"Well, that explains it," said Lothar.

"What's that supposed to mean?" asked Geoff. "Is there something wrong with students who do not have knights for parents?"

"No, that's not what I am saying," replied Lothar firmly. "It just seems like most of the children of the Knights were raised with the Order's code of honor, and it is usually students who are not children of Knights that act like jerks."

"Really," said Geoff with a frown and the appearance of being somewhat insulted.

"Sorry, Geoff. I noticed it myself as well. And I am not the son of a Knight. Don't take it personally. No one here thinks you act like a jerk," said Tyrrel with his usual air of intellectual confidence.

Ivy turned to Geoff, who was sitting next to her, "These are my friends, and the school would not have normally accepted my application because it is not geared to my culture and religion. Had life been more normal for me, I would be attending what you would call a top-notch Hebrew School, so I am even more of a stranger here than you are, and these guys have treated me well. They are my friends, so don't assume they will look down upon you because your parents are not knights of their order."

"So, what happened? Why can't you be where you want to be?" asked Kyle.

The table became instantly silent as all eyes turned to Kyle and Ivy. Some were shocked that Kyle asked the big question, while others wondered if she would answer it.

Ivy paused in contemplation, looked down at her food as if discerning what to do, and then looked up at Kyle. Her eyes were filled with tears that were in danger of spilling over. Kyle saw this and immediately felt bad for asking the question.

"I'm sorry, Ivy. I did not mean to upset you," said Kyle apologetically.

"It's not your fault," she replied. "I'm not allowed to answer your question. And I miss my parents and the rest of my family. I wish I could explain it all to you without having to keep such secrets. It would be so nice to pour my heart out about what has happened."

"You always seem so cheery and happy," remarked Geoff as he put an arm around the curly, dark-haired girl with his awkwardly long, skinny arm. "I had no idea."

"Perhaps it is just my people's nature to hide their sorrows with a smile," replied Ivy.

Kyle felt miserable for making Ivy cry. Sometimes he forgot that others may have worse family problems than he did. At least he had the freedom to talk about his family, where they lived, and what they did. It was a sobering thought as he realized that his worries about his parents arguing about his vacation time were nothing compared to the troubles that Ivy must have endured. One thing that attending the Academy had taught Kyle was that the world was a big place and that not everything centered around the United States. His view up until now had been so isolated.

Chapter 15: Winter Break

With only packing what he truly needed to take, Kyle was ready to go on the ferry boat out across the lake to the shore where his grandparents would be waiting to drive him, Geoff, and Tyrrel to Toronto Pearson International Airport. It was December, and the snowfall had been intense throughout the eastern region, especially in places like Boston. The ferry boat that morning had been dealing with ice buildup on the lake and would not be running, so the students departing that day would ride in the helicopter to the shore to successfully reach their travel destinations. The idea of an entire lake freezing up was very foreign to Kyle. He stood near the helicopter pad with Tyrrel and Geoff, who, despite the freezing temperature, were excited about having the opportunity to ride in the helicopter.

A cold wind blew across the aviation field of the school grounds, and Kyle felt the desire to sink his hands deeper into his pockets as the wind chill factor lowered the temperature even more. He was wearing his school turtleneck, school hoodie, and winter coat, but still felt cold. Tyrrel was wearing a brightly colored toque with his winter coat, while Geoff, in his jacket, added his green and yellow Timbers' scarf to help keep him warm. They stood there waiting with several other students who were also scheduled to leave at this hour. The helicopter returned from dropping off the first batch of students. The cold air hit Kyle's face with an incredible chilling force that left him wishing for the warmth of the indoors.

Once the blades had slowed to a safe rotation speed, the students, along with their luggage, were loaded onto the ride for their quick trip to the mainland. Geoff and Tyrrel were extra excited for the ride to begin. Kyle assured them the experience was just as incredible as everyone had told them.

"I can't wait to tell my sister that I got to ride in a helicopter," said Geoff, handing his bags off to the Academy staff member. The person wore a white winter parka with a red embroidered Templar insignia on the breast area, black trousers, and sturdy winter boots.

"This should be an interesting experience," Tyrrel agreed with a smile as he handed his bags off to be put into the helicopter.

Kyle followed Geoff and Tyrrel. Sitting down in the helicopter made him recall the very first day he arrived with his grandparents and the moment he first saw Freya. As he remembered this, he realized he would not see her or his new best friends for another month. The thought was a bit saddening, but seeing his mom and dad and sharing his school adventures with them would be great. He had emailed Dark Cloud, and they had planned to meet when the tribal school was out for the holiday season.

The helicopter ride was quick. Before they knew it, they had landed, and the Academy staff were already unloading their gear. The snow had been plowed, allowing the visitors to come and pick up their children. Kyle scanned the parking lot for the dark blue BMW sedan with no luck.

"I don't see them anywhere," Kyle said aloud with a certain amount of frustration as he felt another blast of cold wind blow across his face.

Geoff bobbed up and down, trying to keep warm while Tyrrel remained motionless and composed.

"Do either of you see the blue car?" asked Kyle.

"No," replied Geoff. "It's really bright out here, too. I should have worn my sunglasses. The glare from the snow is incredible."

"No, I don't. But I see a white SUV pulling over here with two men who look like your grandfather and Jasper in it," said Tyrrel.

"Where?"

"Over there," gestured Tyrrel.

Kyle looked to see his grandfather and Jasper pulling up close to the curb, where they all stood shivering in the cold. Karl Bergendahl smiled warmly at his grandson from inside the white Mazda CX-5 all-weather vehicle. It suddenly made perfect sense that they would not be in the sedan since the roads were probably icy. Jasper parked the vehicle, immediately exited, and opened the back storage to put the boy's luggage into the SUV. Karl stepped out and hugged his grandson warmly.

"You all look so cold out here," laughed the elderly man as he encouraged the boys to pile into the warmth of the waiting SUV.

The three boys got into the back seat. Karl asked them if they had their passports and plane tickets, and all the boys nodded in response. Jasper sped off down the road for the long drive in which everyone shared stories and well-wishes for the upcoming holiday season. In no time, Kyle hugged his grandfather goodbye and told him to send his love to Grandma. Karl oversaw the boys' successful passage through customs and to their destination concourse, where they would board the plane to the United States.

The plane ride was uneventful, with their first destination being Las Vegas, Nevada, where Kyle and Geoff said goodbye to Tyrrel.

Geoff and Kyle were transferred to another plane that would fly them up to Reno and then Portland.

"I hope they don't lose my luggage," said Geoff as they walked across the concourse to the gateway where their next plane would be waiting in about fifteen minutes.

"Me too," said Kyle as he carried his warm jacket and backpack. "Are you as warm as I am?"

"Yup," said Geoff, looking around at all the slot machines that were beeping and chirping with brightly colored displays. "What are those?"

"Slot machines," replied Kyle, without much thought after living off and on in Reno for several years.

"Oh. What are they for?"

"Gambling. You put quarters or even dollars into them, hoping you get more. Personally, I think it is a waste of time. You get more fun out of playing a video game," said Kyle.

"Have you played them?" asked Geoff.

"Heck no! Those are for grown-ups. You must be twenty-one years old to play them," replied Kyle as they walked along.

"Okay. Seems odd," commented Geoff as he started to smell the air. "Are you as hungry as I am?"

"No, probably not as hungry as you are, but I am hungry. I want a hamburger," Kyle said as he spotted a burger place he liked.

"Oh, that sounds good. I was looking at the pastry shop, but I think a burger would be better," agreed Geoff.

"Let's get them and then go to our gate," suggested Kyle.

The boys got their food and then waited for their plane to be ready for boarding.

When the boys boarded their plane, they looked out the window at the late afternoon skyline. The buildings were huge and extravagant.

"I like the bright lights and the cool shapes of the buildings, but it is bleak looking out there. The hills have no trees," commented Geoff.

"Yeah, the desert is like that," said Kyle.

"Is Reno like that?" asked Geoff.

"Yes, but we do have trees on one set of mountains to the west," replied Kyle.

"We have trees everywhere in Vancouver," said Geoff. "It's like Lake Simcoe. And then we have this zombie fog that shows up, and it's fun to pretend that zombies are coming, and you have to fight them off. My friends and I used to do that when we were younger. I miss playing that game. It was fun. So, do you miss the desert?"

"Not really," said Kyle, not having thought about it.

The plane hit turbulence just before it landed at Reno International Airport, which Geoff and Kyle did not enjoy. Geoff looked distressed as Kyle stood up and reached for his backpack and winter coat, which were stored in the upper compartment.

"Are you going to be okay?" asked Kyle.

"Yeah, I just didn't like that landing," replied Geoff.

"This area has problems with updrafts and downdrafts," said Kyle as he made gestures to go with what he was describing. "It doesn't always happen, though, so don't worry. And the flight isn't supposed to be that long."

"Yeah. Have a good Christmas," said Geoff, looking up at his departing friend.

"You too," said Kyle, turning and walking down the narrow aisle of the airplane.

Kyle trudged up the corridor from the plane door and into the gateway, where the sounds of slot machines beeping and singing assaulted his ears again. The airport looked pretty much as it used to be. It had an almost retro, nostalgic feel to it, he thought, as he recalled the layouts of the Portland PDX, Las Vegas, and Toronto Pearson airports. He was glad that the long trip was over, and soon he could sit and relax. It was early evening, and he was very hungry. When he finally got past security, he looked for his mother. He spotted her waving to him, looking very excited.

She embraced him with tears in her eyes.

"Oh, my darling, you have grown! Oh, my goodness," she exclaimed, hugging him tightly and then pushing him back to take a good look at him. "Your hair, it's gotten long. Don't they have a hair salon up there?! And you look so nice in your school uniform."

"Mom! You're making a scene," said Kyle, feeling a bit embarrassed.

"Oh, but you look so handsome in your school clothes. However, we must get your haircut. That will not do. And I think you must have grown about two inches while you were away!"

Kyle laughed at his mom's joyous response to him coming home, "I've only been gone for a couple of months. You never made this big of a deal when I was away at Dad's."

357

"It's just that I have missed you so much. Rojo will be excited to see you, too," she said as they rode down the escalator toward the baggage claim area.

After they picked up his luggage and walked to the car, they drove home.

"Are you hungry, Kyle?" his mom asked.

"Yes. I could eat a horse! Or at least eat as much as Geoff," replied Kyle.

"Well, I don't know how much Geoff eats. Is he one of your little friends?" she asked.

Kyle felt himself wince at the description *little* for some reason.

"Yes, Mom, he is one of my friends. He and Tyrrel flew with me on the plane. Tyrrel lives in Las Vegas, and Geoff lives in Vancouver, Washington."

"Well, it's very nice that you got to ride with your friends on the trip. I plan to visit your grandparents in Texas in a few months, so I will be flying to see them. I am still looking for work in a different location," she said as she slowly turned into their neighborhood on the southern end of town.

"Why do you want to leave Reno? I don't want you to go to Texas."

She sighed a little.

"Because the jobs here have no upward mobility for me," she replied. "We were supposed to have some big companies move into town, but nothing is happening. I applied to several of them and have heard nothing dear. Also, the rent on the house has become too expensive."

"I see," Kyle nodded.

"Having those big companies come here would make a big difference in making this a nice place to live again," his mom continued. "You remember Carol, don't you? She applied to one of those technology companies and heard nothing. Then she applied to that big car company and heard nothing. It's so disheartening. She's incredibly smart and talented, yet she struggles to get anyone to take her seriously. It's as if the HR department is discarding resumes without even opening them. It's as if she doesn't even exist."

Kyle nodded again, not really knowing what to say or fully understanding what his mom was talking about. He had never thought of jobs or careers as something to be obtained. It always seemed like people just went to them, so this was a new idea to him. Perhaps it was like when he was waiting to hear from the Academy to see if he would be accepted or not. It was a disturbing thought that one would have to be at someone else's whim to get a job and survive.

They pulled into the driveway of the modest single-story ranch-style house that his mother rented in the Virginia Foothills residential area. It was evening now, but Kyle could still see a bit around. No snow was on the ground, and he didn't need his heavy winter coat. They went inside, and the house had a familiar smell of home to it. Rojo went crazy seeing Kyle. Kyle knelt down to play with the very excited little Chihuahua, who was so pleased to see him.

"You remember me, boy," said Kyle to the happy little dog.

"Honey, put your things into your room, and I will start dinner. I bought everything to make your favorite tacos and beans dish," said Marie as she put her coat away and checked her jet-black hair in the hallway mirror.

"Okay, Mom. How long 'til dinner?" he asked.

"About thirty minutes or less. I have everything ready. Did you have any good Mexican food up in Canada?"

"No, we had no Mexican food at all. I have missed your cooking so much," said Kyle as he got up to take his things into his bedroom down the hall.

Kyle opened his bedroom door and turned on the light. The room looked so empty. It no longer felt like his space. So many of his things had been sent along with him to Canada, but not everything, so he wondered where it had all gone. He opened the small closet door and found it filled with neatly packed boxes, each labeled. Some boxes were labeled "Kyle's books," another "Kyle's toys," and another "Kyle's baby things." He stared at these boxes momentarily, wanting to open them, but they had all been neatly taped shut. He suddenly realized that she was very serious about moving away.

He stood in the center of the room, not knowing what to think or feel. The room no longer felt like it was his. The posters were gone, and his stuff was all packed away except for his regular sheets with Marvel superheroes on them. Thor, Spider-Man, Captain America, and the Hulk seemed to stare back at him in the colorless room. Kyle put his backpack on the bed and then put his suitcase on his old desk. She was serious about the idea of moving away. It hit him like a runaway truck.

"Kyle," called his mother cheerfully from the kitchen. "Will you please come?"

Kyle left his bedroom, walked down the hallway, and entered the house's main living space, cheerfully decorated for the Christmas season. He discovered that his mom had set the kitchen table with a bright-colored tablecloth, napkins, candles, and festive salt and pepper shakers that looked like fat mariachi players in fancy costumes. Kyle smiled as he picked up the funny shakers.

"Where did you get these?" asked Kyle as he picked up the funny figure of the player holding a trumpet and wearing a black sombrero. The crown of the hat was where the salt would come out.

Marie turned from the stove and walked over to the table.

"Your father and I bought them at a street fair somewhere in California. We were on a trip, and we stopped for lunch and came across this little street fair with all kinds of vendors selling stuff," she replied with a sad smile.

"Well, I like them. They are funny-looking," Kyle said with a smile to his mom.

361

"I am glad you like them. Sit down at the table. Everything is ready," she said, returning to the stove to retrieve the freshly browned meat for the tacos that Kyle liked so much.

The table was set like a great feast. Kyle reached for a flour tortilla and realized that these were the homemade kind that she rarely had time to make.

"You made tortillas like Great Grandma! I love these, but you always say they are too much work," exclaimed Kyle.

"Not for tonight, honey. I have missed you so much, and I wanted you to feel good after such a long day of traveling," said Marie, looking very pleased that her son had noticed her handmade tortillas.

Dinner was excellent, and after cleaning up the table and dishes, Kyle and his mom sat on the living room couch together and watched one of Kyle's favorite movies, *The Incredibles*.

With only about ten more minutes of the film to go, Kyle started yawning.

"Oh, sweetie, you must be exhausted from the trip. You should probably go to bed when the movie is done," said Marie as she gently stroked Kyle's hair away from his face.

"Yeah, I do feel tired," replied Kyle with another big yawn.

And before long, Kyle was saying goodnight to his mother, and he had crawled into his old bed. He felt his body sink into the familiar sheets, and the quiet darkness of the room fell upon him. Less than twenty-four hours ago, he was in Canada with all his friends. The room seemed very quiet. No snoring or talking in the distant corners of the room could be heard, and the window was now to his left as he slept, instead of above and behind him like in his cubicle. His bed was pushed up against the corner of the wall in the small bedroom. He finally fell asleep when exhaustion overcame him.

The next morning, he woke at eight o'clock when the sunlight started to pour through his bedroom window. It took him a few minutes to realize he was back in Reno. The walls were so bare and strange to him. He wanted to rectify the situation by putting his posters back up. The house was very quiet until he thought he heard the sound of little footsteps scampering down the hallway. It was Rojo. That was a joyous thought. Kyle had missed the strange little dog.

Getting up, he realized he was very hungry and had slept late. He was accustomed to eating breakfast at seven, waking up around six in the morning. And the time zone was different since he was now on the West Coast. He finally made his way down the hall into the kitchen with Rojo bouncing around excitedly. When he reached the kitchen counter, he found a note from his mom, written in her flowery handwriting, addressed to him.

Kyle,

I must be at work today. Since you were so tired last night, I thought I would let you sleep in a bit. Sorry that I can't make you breakfast. Milk and juice are in the fridge, and cereal is in the cabinet. Please don't leave the house, and I will be home in the evening around 5.

Love Mom

Kyle looked at the fridge, opened the door, and pulled out the orange juice. He stared mindlessly at the plastic container before going to the cabinet to get a glass. It felt like an eternity since he'd had to make his own breakfast and pour his own glass of juice. Jasper took care of everything at his grandparents' home, and at the Academy, everything was set up for them to get their food when they entered the dining hall. He poured the orange juice into his glass and stared at it for a minute. He used to do this all the time, but now it seemed so… strange. It reminded him of loneliness and boredom.

Kyle pulled a box of granola oat flake cereal down from the cabinet, filled a bowl, and then got out the milk. He set his orange juice and bowl on the kitchen table and sat down. Then he suddenly realized he needed a spoon. After getting a spoon, he sat down at the table with Rojo, looking eagerly up at him.

It was so quiet.

After a few mouthfuls of cereal and listening to the loud crunching in his head, he decided that turning on the

TV might solve the intense silence. There was nothing of interest on TV except for Big Bang Theory, which his mom did not want him to watch because she said they talked too much about grown-up subjects, but Kyle liked the characters. They liked comic books and action figures. What could be wrong with that, he wondered?

He finished his breakfast while watching Sheldon sit on his bed with a bunch of cats named after famous scientists. Kyle was sure Tyrrel would have known who all those people were. Then the show was over, and nothing else was on TV that he liked. He turned the TV off and noticed the missing video game console.

Kyle looked around the house, wondering what else to do. He decided that taking a shower might be the best thing, and then he would get on the computer later. The morning hours dragged on with an almost torturous effect as Kyle checked his email and phone for messages. Nothing. No messages from anyone. He decided to email Dark Cloud to see if their plans to hang out together next week would still happen. Dark Cloud's uncle would take the boys out for fun that day, and Kyle was looking forward to it. He had not seen the Native American boy for over half a year since he was last in school in Reno.

After the message was sent, there was nothing to do. The kitchen clock seemed to tick loudly in the silence as Rojo looked up at Kyle inquisitively. Rojo seemed to know that Kyle was feeling odd. There were additional clicking noises that did not match the uniform ticking of the clock as the hands geared forward ever so slowly. Kyle looked around. What could be making that noise? He walked over to the kitchen window, where the sound seemed to be coming from. Then he spotted the cheap solar daisy flowers bobbing happily in the sunlight as it came through the window.

"I am... really bored," Kyle said aloud to himself, staring at the happy flowers that swayed joyfully back and forth.

Back and forth they swayed until Kyle stuck his finger to stop the flower's movement. It gave him very little resistance. Then he let it go back to its happy dance in the sunlight.

"Oh. My. Gosh! I am soooo... bored," repeated Kyle.

This time, Rojo whimpered in sympathy.

"Is this what you do all day here alone?" Kyle asked the dog, whose ears perked up. "You must miss Pickles."

Kyle was desperate to find something interesting to do, so he went through his backpack and unpacked some of his belongings. He found his digital camera and then his school tablet. He looked at the tablet and then remembered the book that Sir Knight Mary had assigned for him to read. Freya had mentioned that she was worried about having enough time to read. Kyle looked at the tablet and realized he had plenty of time to read. He almost put the tablet away in his bag, but then decided that it would at least give him something to do. He made himself comfortable on the couch, wrapping up in a velvety soft blanket with a snowy Christmas tree scene on it. A nativity set sat on the fireplace mantle, looking lonely as well. Seasonal decorations were sparse.

The book's title was *The Secret Garden*. It did not sound very interesting to him. He doubted there would be any robots, wizards, or superheroes within the digital pages. He spent half an hour reading the book, finishing the first chapter just as he realized he was indeed very hungry. The book had a disturbingly familiar feeling to it. Mary Lennox, the main character, sounded like she was very lonely, which was exactly how Kyle felt. He realized that he already missed his new friends from the Academy. It was going to be a long vacation, and he hoped someone would find time to email or message him soon. Nothing had changed for his mother, but somehow, he had changed. Things were just not the same anymore, and it looked like the character in the story was about to have the same thing happen to her.

The next few days were pretty much the same until Dark Cloud and his uncle, John Greystorm, came to pick him up for a fun day. Marie Gomez held her tongue as she watched her son go off with the Indian boy, whom she did not approve of, but the boy had been Kyle's best friend for almost two years. As Kyle said goodbye to his mom and made the usual promises to behave himself and not cause Mr. Greystorm any grief, Kyle could sense her disapproval of him hanging out with the boy who was not a Christian. Kyle tried to push the thoughts of his mom's irrational disapproval out of his mind as he prepared for a fun day with his friend.

John Greystorm drove a large pickup with enough room for three to sit in the front cab. Kyle sat next to the door with Dark Cloud seated in the middle.

"I was going to take you boys out sledding today, but we don't have enough snow up in the mountains," said John Greystorm apologetically. "Unfortunately, I do have some errands that I have to run, and I thought I would take you to some places that you may not have seen. Does that sound good?"

"I don't care as long as I get to hang out with you," replied Dark Cloud, looking over at his uncle.

"And I'm fine with whatever we do as long as I get out of the house. I feel like I have been trapped for days like a prisoner," said Kyle, appreciating the chance to be with people. Rojo was fine, but not much of a conversationalist, and his mom was away at work most of the day.

It was just a little after eight in the morning when they pulled out of Kyle's mom's driveway. The day was clear and promised moderate temperatures, which was very unlike the typical weather for the area. Kyle wore his turtleneck with his hooded school jacket. His camera was tucked away in his hoodie, and his cell phone was inside one of the pockets of his cargo pants. His mom gave him a generous amount of money for lunch and any other activities he wanted to do. He suspected she felt guilty about not being able to spend time with him while he was home. He eyed the extra money and realized it offered him the opportunity to find something for his mom for Christmas.

"We are going up to Virginia City. I had some artwork for sale, and the storekeeper up there has a check ready for me. So, while I attend to that, I thought you boys might find it fun to walk around the town and look at the sights. The laser shooting gallery is also at the north end of town, which might be fun. Does that sound like a good way to start the day?" asked John Greystorm.

Both the boys agreed with the thirty-year-old single man's suggestion for the start of the day. When they reached Virginia City, they parked along the main street, where rows of 1800s-style buildings stood as a testament to the gold and later silver rush era that had established the wealth of the small mining mountain town, which was now primarily a living ghost town. Its fame increased even more when paranormal enthusiasts filmed investigations there. The sidewalks were not made of concrete, but of wooden boards, and they made a hollow sound as one walked. Kyle had never seen another town like Virginia City, Nevada. It was both beautiful and ugly at the same time. The shops had everything, from beautiful, authentic antiques to cheap, kitschy junk. It was still early for some shops to open, so Kyle and Dark Cloud strode leisurely down the rickety sidewalk. The town was decorated for the holiday season with cheerful lights and décor. The place had an odd pairing of past and present. They peered into the window of the chocolate store that was preparing to make the first batch of fudge for the day. The store displayed the giant mixing bowl and equipment near the front window for passersby to see. Dark Cloud and Kyle watched as the staff members added ingredients to the bowl and finally turned on the machine.

The girl inside the store smiled at the boys and then popped outside the front door to talk with them. She looked to be about eighteen years old.

"The fudge will be ready around ten o'clock or so," she said.

"Oh, great. Thanks for letting us know," said Kyle.

"We won't be open until nine, which is about fifteen minutes from now," she said.

"So do you make the fudge fresh every day?" asked Dark Cloud.

"Yes, every day we make a new batch. Sometimes, depending on how busy we are, we make up to three batches. We do have some fudge from yesterday that is already packaged," she replied.

The boys told her they would probably get some fresh fudge candy when they returned, and then they headed north to the laser shooting gallery. They passed another store that had a pair of silver earrings on display that caught Kyle's attention.

"I think my mom would like those for Christmas," Kyle commented to Dark Cloud.

"Which ones?" he asked.

"The ones with purple stones in them," replied Kyle as he gestured to the items in the storefront window.

"Those are amethysts," said Dark Cloud. "Uncle John has a good friend who makes a lot of pretty jewelry like that, but I think his friend's stuff is better."

"Really? So, you think these ones are not good?"

"They're okay, but I think they are overpriced," commented Dark Cloud, pausing momentarily. "And they are not as nice as my uncle's friend's jewelry."

"Hmm," Kyle thought about how much he had in his pocket and the price of the earrings. "If he bought the earrings, he would have no money for lunch or any fudge candy."

When they reached the old-time laser shooting gallery, it was nine o'clock. Kyle and Dark Cloud were the only patrons in the place. The clerk eyed them both as they came in, and when they walked up to the counter and requested change for the gallery, the man greeted them as he made the change.

"Wow, you boys are out early this morning. I rarely have anyone this early in the wintertime," said the clerk, who was dressed as a prospector and looked like he was about a hundred years old.

"I needed some time out of the house," replied Kyle as he eyed the old man with the white beard and greasy-looking hair. He wore a faded red long-johns shirt, dirty-looking pants, well-worn cowboy boots, and suspenders.

Dark Cloud turned aside to Kyle and mumbled into Kyle's ear, "And this is what we lost our land to?"

The clerk, who was hard of hearing and spoke very loudly, either did not hear Dark Cloud's comment or was ignoring the Native American boy. The old man laughed at Kyle's comment and nodded his head, "I remember

371

wanting to get out from underfoot when I was a young 'un, too. If you stayed around, the parents found chores for you to do."

Kyle and Dark Cloud focused their attention upon the gallery, which was like a stage, where hundreds of items had little round bullseye target sensors on them, and when they were hit with the laser, they would activate the piece that was hit. Some sent pieces spinning while others activated sounds and music. The rifles made a distinctive sound as they were fired. Each gun had one hundred shots, so one had plenty of chances to have fun with scoring a target hit. All scores over seventy-five received an additional ten rounds. Perfect and very high scores were rewarded with a prize. Each game was priced at $5.00, with no time limit.

Kyle didn't even care about getting a good score; he just loved hitting the different targets to see what they did. Dark Cloud, on the other hand, wanted a good score. By the time the boys had tired of the game, over an hour had passed, and it was time for them to meet Dark Cloud's uncle at the other end of town. The boys left the target shooting gallery and made their way back. They stopped at the chocolate store and each bought a chunk of fudge candy, then ate it even though it was still morning.

"I wish I could have bought the earrings," Kyle commented to Dark Cloud as they walked briskly up the wooden sidewalk, hearing their footsteps thump loudly with each step.

"Do you want me to ask Uncle John what he thinks?"

"Yes, that would be helpful. I feel bad that I have nothing for my mom. She made this awesome dinner for me when I got home. She made the homemade tortillas like her grandmother used to make," Kyle explained.

"I can ask Uncle John if his friend makes earrings with amethysts that cost less," said Dark Cloud.

Kyle pulled his hood up over his head as a chilling breeze rushed through the tiny historical town. It was a place well known for strong winds called the zephyr, which would surge through the high desert canyons with a lust for tearing off cowboy hats and the like. Kyle wondered if he was dressed warm enough for the day, but it was so much warmer in Reno than up at Lake Simcoe, where snow had already fallen.

John Greystorm was already waiting for the boys when they arrived at the truck. Dark Cloud explained that Kyle wanted silver earrings for his mom as a Christmas gift, but he had advised Kyle against the ones he saw in the shop down the road.

"Uncle John, do you think your friend has anything like what Kyle wanted that does not cost so much?"

John Greystorm contemplatively rubbed his cleanly shaved face and replied, "I think Ben Sparrow has some designs like that, and he lives in Carson City. I wanted to take you to WNC, which is in Carson City. My art show is still on display. Do you still want to see it?"

"Yes," said Dark Cloud with enthusiasm.

"Sounds great," said Kyle as he shut the pickup truck door, making the cold breeze go away.

"Then I will take you to see Ben Sparrow, my art show, and lunch. Think about what you want to eat," said John Greystorm as they headed to Carson City.

The silversmith, Ben Sparrow, offered Kyle exceptional silver jewelry he could afford, making his concerns about Christmas gifts vanish. After that, they all went to see John Greystorm's art exhibit at the student gallery at Western Nevada College. Kyle had no idea that Dark Cloud's uncle was an artist and had no expectations of what he might see. So often, Kyle had seen what people called art hanging on the walls, and most of it never caught his attention or imagination. It was either bland landscapes or some political or emotional statement that made no sense to him. The stuff referred to as modern art did not appeal to him either. Kyle believed art should be something you'd want to look at repeatedly. And John Greystorm's art was something that Kyle found himself looking at over and over. He wondered if René would have had an opinion about it.

It was brightly colored paintings of people who appeared to be Native Americans in modern times, with ghostly companions who seemed to be a part of their daily lives.

"Who or what are these beings that look like sparkly ghosts?" Kyle asked John.

John gazed at the painting of a Native American man dressed in a fancy suit, walking through what

374

appeared to be an Indian Casino, with a ghost-like wolf and a Native warrior following him. John smiled at Kyle and replied, "These beings that you refer to are our spirit guides, ancestors, and Gods of the people of the land here on this continent."

"I like the wolf," remarked Kyle, thinking of Lothar and Freya. "But the man in the suit doesn't seem to be noticing them. The people in some of the other pictures appear to be looking at them. What does that mean?"

"Not everyone is aware of their spirit guides, ancestors, or the gods of our lands," replied John. "Some choose to ignore them while others embrace the traditions of their heritage."

Kyle stared at the painting of a modern Native American man standing with one of the ghostly-looking figures wearing a strange headdress. Both were looking down into a valley that resembled Washoe Lake.

"This one is my favorite," said Dark Cloud, pointing at the ghostly, bluish man with white and purple accents. He wore an unusual headdress adorned with feathers that stood upright, and sparkling energy beamed upward and out. His clothes also appeared to resemble those of the local native Washoe or Shoshone tribe. "He shows up in other paintings. There is something about him that seems so familiar to me."

"You know, I like him too," said Kyle. "Who is he?"

John Greystorm answered, "His name is Washo. He is the guardian of this area and the people of the Wašiw Tribe."

Dark Cloud seemed to nod with appreciation as if a question had been answered for him.

Kyle turned to Dark Cloud's uncle and asked, "Am I ignoring my heritage?"

"What is your heritage? Where do your people come from?"

"My dad is Swedish and Canadian, my mom is Mexican, and the other half of her family is from Texas. I guess most of my family comes from Europe. But I don't understand what that means. It seems so obvious for Dark Cloud," said Kyle, struggling to express the feeling that he was having.

Dark Cloud frowned and then looked at his uncle. His uncle looked back at him and gave a serious expression as if he were thinking very seriously about what Kyle had said.

"It seems that it is not just my own people who are torn between cultures," remarked John Greystorm, looking at Kyle and then at his artwork hanging on the walls.

"Dark Cloud has told me that you have special abilities. Do I have someone or something with me that I am ignoring?" Kyle asked, looking over both shoulders, wondering if there could be a special companion for him, too. "Can you help me know if there is a ghost person for me?"

John Greystorm sighed and replied, "I don't think your mother would appreciate that. It would cause problems if I assisted you in finding your spirit guides and ancestral connections."

Kyle looked and felt disappointed, but he understood the reason.

Dark Cloud wrinkled his brow. There had been years of problems within his own family concerning religion and culture. His father was a devout Christian, while his mom was a somewhat passive follower of the old ways of her tribal ancestors. His father did not always welcome Uncle John since he brought the old traditions with him and did not want to adopt the white man's religion. Now, Kyle was asking for help, and his uncle felt uncomfortable offering his wisdom.

John Greystorm noticed that the boys seemed saddened by this turn of events.

"Let's go get lunch and talk about this matter afterward. With an empty stomach, one does not always make the best decisions," said John Greystorm.

The thought of lunch appealed to both boys. The three ended up at a pizza parlor, and John treated his young companions to two large pizzas, which were devoured in the space of an hour. It had been a long time since Kyle had pizza from one of his favorite restaurants, so this was a treat that he enjoyed immensely.

"I think I ate too much," said Kyle, rubbing his stomach as the three prepared to get into John's truck.

"I probably could have eaten more," said Dark Cloud.

Kyle looked at him sideways and said, "I have a friend from the Academy with whom you could have an eating contest."

"Bring it on. I will win," said Dark Cloud with a smile.

"I don't know, Geoff really likes to eat a lot," replied Kyle with a smile.

"We still have plenty of time, and the weather is good, and Kyle has important questions to ask. Our bellies are full, we should go someplace where we can talk of spiritual matters," said John Greystorm. "Are you both up for a bit of hiking?"

"Can I take pictures?" asked Kyle.

"Sure," said John Greystorm.

Dark Cloud nodded.

"Then I will take you to a place I like to hike once in a while when I need to be away from people and clear my head," he replied.

They drove south, past the large farming communities, until they reached the pine-forested hills on a dirt road. Dark Cloud's uncle explained that normally these roads would be dangerous at this time of the year because they would either be very muddy or covered in snow. Instead, the drought gave them the opportunity to be in this location during the winter without severe travel conditions. They reached a point where the truck could no longer safely go, and they had to hike up the road on foot. John Greystorm grabbed a small satchel, put it over his shoulder,

378

and handed both boys bottles of water to carry. Kyle was glad he was wearing his sturdy sneakers, but he still wished he had a scarf or gloves to ward off the cool wind that occasionally blew. They walked uphill until the boys were exhausted and had to stop.

"How much further, Uncle John?" asked Dark Cloud as he pulled his growing black hair back behind his ear.

"A little further. You could stop, but it will not be the right place to ask questions of the land spirits," replied John Greystorm, testing the boy's resolve.

Kyle, who had sat down on a rock feeling tired, got up and said, "No, I want to know."

"And I want to help Kyle," said Dark Cloud.

"Okay, then, further up the trail we must go," replied the apprentice shaman.

When they finally reached a spot where a small creek was barely flowing and the trees were tall and strong, John Greystorm had them stop hiking. Both boys were tired. They turned and looked back from where they had come, and the view out to the valley below was breathtaking. There was a feeling of peacefulness that held one's voice. The sound of the wind rushing through the tall pines and the ever-so-gentle trickle of the water moving through the nearly empty creek bed was the only sound they could hear. The sky was a bright blue, and the air was crisp and cold. Kyle felt chilled. He peeked at his watch. It was two in the afternoon.

"What do we do now?" asked Kyle.

"You both sit and relax and listen while I do what I must," replied John. "Normally, this is something that I would do with some preparation, but I know this may be the only day we can all be together."

Kyle and Dark Cloud sat down on small boulders near the edge of the mostly dry creek bed. They watched quietly as John Greystorm removed various items from his satchel and then walked around the area as if he were talking with some unseen person. Dark Cloud saw the questioning look on Kyle's face and made the gesture not to speak. When John Greystorm was done, he came back and sat down near where the boys were sitting.

"I have greeted the land spirits and other nature spirits in the area and asked them for peace and protection so that we may proceed with this task. I made an offering in appreciation of their assistance. Do not be disheartened if you do not get your answers right away. Many who seek spiritual answers often have a long path to travel and do not receive what they seek right away. This is often a lifelong journey of searching and contemplation. My nephew here may think me much wiser than him, but it is only that I have begun my journey long before he did, and I am further down the path," said John as he pushed his long black braid back over his shoulder.

"What do I need to do now?" asked Kyle.

"We have two options right now since we cannot do all the preparations… that are traditionally required by some of my teachers. I have studied with many different

380

people who have walked a spiritual path. I have some ability to sense if you have guiding spirits around you. Or I could try to have you learn how to sense them yourself. What do you want to do?"

"It would be easier if you did it…" said Kyle, pausing and staring out across the valley to the sage-covered mountains to the east. "But if I learn how to do it myself… then I could try again if it does not work the first time."

"Learn how to do it," encouraged Dark Cloud. "This is something I want to learn as well."

Kyle looked at his friend, whom he trusted so well, and then nodded to John Greystorm, "Okay, I'd like to try and do it myself. And then if I can't, can you help me?"

Greystorm replied, "I can already sense that someone here is connected to you. So, I will help you start this journey, but you may need to find other teachers as time goes on."

Kyle nodded.

"I want you to close your eyes and listen to the wind roaring through the pine boughs high above. Clear your mind of all worries and concerns," instructed Greystorm.

"Okay," said Kyle after a couple of minutes had passed.

"When I say ancestors, what is the first thought or image that comes to your mind?"

"My father and my Canadian grandparents," said Kyle.

"Why is that?"

"I feel drawn to them like I want to know more about them. I want to know more about the knights," Kyle said, opening his eyes suddenly. "I want to know more about the knights. I have knights in my family!"

"Good. Now close your eyes again," instructed Greystorm. "Knowing that your focus will be on your father's ancestors, I want you to think and feel the area surrounding you. More specifically, the space that surrounds you. We all carry ties to our loved ones, and these bonds appear as colorful ribbons emanating from our bodies. They connect you to others. They can be good or bad. You know I am sitting across from you, and my nephew, Dark Cloud, is sitting to your left..."

Kyle listened carefully to what Dark Cloud's uncle said, and each time, he focused on the person mentioned.

"Do you feel the trees, animals, the winds, or something else in the area?" he asked Kyle.

"I feel like the sky is huge and there is more. I can hear the water trickling in the creek bed. And... like... someone is standing beside me to my right," replied Kyle.

"What does this person look like?" asked Greystorm.

Kyle took a deep breath and focused.

"It's a man. He has blonde hair and wears a brown suit that looks old-fashioned. And he sometimes wears what looks like a Hogwarts robe over his suit," replied Kyle, feeling the chill in the air to the point of being an intense distraction. "I feel so cold."

Kyle opened his eyes as he shivered a bit and pulled his hood closer over his head. John Greystorm instructed him to close his eyes again and try to ignore the cold, but Kyle could not. Each time, he just felt like his feet and hands were icy. He opened his eyes again, realizing that the trees in the area were blocking the sunlight, and the sun would soon disappear from this part of the mountain.

"I just can't do it. I'm sorry. I guess I failed," said Kyle with a sense of disappointment.

"You didn't fail," laughed Greystorm. "You did better than most on their first try to sense the world that is unseen by human eyes." John got up and walked toward Kyle, who was now standing with his hands deeply sunk into his jacket pockets. He patted Kyle on the shoulder. "Listen carefully to me. You did not fail. This is just the beginning of your journey."

Kyle nodded shyly and turned to Dark Cloud, who looked proud of him.

"You did better than I did on my first try," said Dark Cloud. "I couldn't ignore all the outside stuff going on."

Kyle knew this was a good sign that his friend was pleased. He never knew Dark Cloud to lie or embellish the truth. John Greystorm looked up at the sky and his watch, deciding it was time to head back to the truck. It did not take them as long to get down the mountain, and it seemed to Kyle as if the trail had grown shorter. He was unsure if that had been his imagination or not, but he was glad to be inside the truck where the warm air poured out of the truck's heating vents. He couldn't stop thinking about the man's image and wanted to get home to draw a picture of him.

Later that evening, after he had said good night to his mom, he pulled out some paper and a pencil and started sketching what he saw in his mind. He wondered why he would see a man dressed like that and what it meant. He knew he had to keep this secret from his mom because she would disapprove of it. She would say it was the devil's work. He also figured that it was not something his dad would understand either, since he would think it was all mystical nonsense.

Chapter 16: Bored in Reno and Then Up to Seattle

Kyle spent a wonderful Christmas with his mom, despite her insistence that he attend church with her. She loved the earrings he had bought from John Greystorm's friend, Ben Sparrow, and wore them the next day. But the Christmas holiday was over, and Marie Gomez had to go back to work, and once again, Kyle felt terribly bored and lonely. Those old, lonely feelings wanted to haunt him like a bad video game cartridge. Luckily, Geoff, Lothar, and Tyrrel found time to send emails to him, which he looked for almost every two hours. Kyle's mom had not ignored the fact; her son had changed since he was last home. He was more social and grown-up than before, which made her proud of him, yet remorseful since her little boy was growing up.

Marie regretted that she could not take time away from work to spend with him, but she also realized that being bored and lonely was not good for him, so she made arrangements for Kyle to see his father sooner. Jon had a more flexible schedule, and at least Kyle would get to spend time with someone. Kyle hugged his tearful mother goodbye and boarded the Southwest plane for Seattle, Washington, where his father would meet him at the airport.

It had been about a year since Kyle had visited his father's Seattle home. The airport was still large with huge ceilings and giant glass windows that allowed a lot of natural light to pour in. Today was slightly cloudy with some rainfall, which was not uncommon for the Pacific Northwest. It was a dramatic change from the ultra-dry climate of Nevada, with the unusually dry winter. His dad had told him the weather had been cold and that he would need to wear his winter coat on the plane. On clear days, one could see the snowcapped Mt. Rainier in the distance, but today was cloudy. It almost looked like a few snowflakes were mixed in with the rain. He stared out the window for a moment with his backpack weighing heavily on his shoulder, and then he remembered that he should turn on his cell phone to let his dad know that he had arrived. His father told him to meet him by the baggage claim area.

Kyle looked around and suddenly felt unsure. He had no idea where the baggage claim was located, so he frowned as he walked about, looking for a sign.

"Do you need help?"

Kyle turned to see a tall elderly man dressed in black leather sneakers, black dress pants, a bright royal blue blazer, a white button-down shirt, and a wild tie in various shades of blue and green.

"Uh," Kyle said involuntarily, making him sound somewhat stupid. "I can't seem to find the directions to the baggage claim area, and I am supposed to meet my dad there."

The elderly man smiled at him and responded, "Well, I can help you out. My name is Chip, and I am a volunteer here at the airport. It's my job to help people just like you."

Kyle smiled and replied, "Great. That will make things a lot easier."

"Well, follow me and I will get you to your destination," said Chip, who appeared to be about six feet seven inches tall.

"You're really tall," commented Kyle as they walked.

"Yup, my wife used to say that to me all the time. She was very short and petite," said Chip as they strolled along.

"So, you volunteer to help people at the airport?"

"Yup, that's my job now. I used to be an airline pilot, but when I retired and my wife passed away, I just needed to feel the excitement of being near the airfield again."

"Wow, you used to be a pilot. That's so cool," replied Kyle. "What kind of planes did you use to fly?"

"These big ones like what you see out there, but they were not as fancy as they are now," replied Chip.

"Are they hard to fly?" asked Kyle.

"Not too bad as long as the weather is good," replied Chip. "Being a good pilot requires planning and focus."

"So why don't you fly anymore?"

"I got too old. There are health requirements, and well… as one ages, some things don't work as well as they used to. Well, here we are at the baggage claim."

Kyle looked around to see a large area where the baggage carousels were all set up. Some were working with luggage moving about on them, while others were silent.

"Do you see your father anywhere?" asked Chip.

Kyle looked down past several carousels and finally spotted his dad standing beside an active one.

"Yes, I see him down there," Kyle replied. "Thanks for walking with me."

"Not a problem, son. Take care," said Chip as he turned around and walked back the way they came.

Kyle adjusted his backpack and strode purposefully through the crowd of travelers to reach his dad. When Jon recognized him, he strode over with open arms to greet him with a big hug.

"I have missed you so much, Sport! How was your trip?" Jon inquired of his son.

"It was just fine, Dad. I'm so glad to see you. Did you have a merry Christmas?"

"Well, you know that I am not much one for Christmas, but if the question is… did everyone put on a cheery good mood for the winter season of celebrating, then yes, I did," replied Jon Bergendahl. "How was your mother? Is she well?"

"Yeah, she is fine. She's busy, though, and doesn't have much time for me. She made homemade tortillas and liked the earrings I got her for Christmas," replied Kyle with a smile.

"Good. I'm glad you're thoughtful. She lives in a location with a struggling economy, and I think she needs someone to be thoughtful of her. She seems to be trapped in that place, and since she didn't finish her degree, she's stuck in the work she does. Kyle, education is essential. Remember that."

"I will, Dad," replied Kyle, looking up at his father, who seemed sincerely concerned about his mom's well-being. It made him wonder if his dad still loved her.

"So do we need to find another bag?" asked Jon.

"Yes," said Kyle as he turned to the luggage carousel. "Is this the right one? I remember once looking for my bag on the wrong machine, and I was so frustrated and then super embarrassed when I figured it out."

"That's your flight number up on the board, so this is the correct one," said Jon, smiling at his son.

They found Kyle's bag and headed for Jon's SUV, which was parked in the airport's garage. It was late afternoon. Walking through the airport garage, Kyle could smell the moisture in the air. It was so different from the desert. Kyle liked the lush green of Seattle and wished his mom would move closer to his dad, so that he could see them both more often. If he didn't have to travel so far, it would be easier for him to go back and forth between their homes. Everything would have been easier had they not separated.

Once inside the car, Jon turned to his son and asked, "So are you hungry?"

"A little, but I'm okay," replied Kyle.

"You think you can wait 'til we get home?" asked Jon.

"Yes, I think I can."

"Great. I bought some fresh salmon this morning for dinner. Have you had any salmon lately?" Jon asked his son as he navigated through the busy streets of Seattle.

Kyle looked out the window, seeing a few raindrops misting the windshield. He was always amazed at how vast Seattle was and how congested the roads could be.

"No, I haven't had any salmon in a long time. I'd love some. I think it's my favorite type of fish," Kyle replied.

"It's one of my favorites as well, and that's why I learned how to make it. Do you still like sushi? I was thinking... I could take you to your favorite sushi place later in the week," said Jon.

"Yes, Dad. I will never stop liking sushi. Why would that happen?"

"Well, you have been away for so long, and I wasn't sure if your mom ever took you to get sushi."

"Naw, most of the sushi places in Reno are expensive, and only a few of them are okay. At least that is what I have been told. Most Reno sushi is smothered in a lot of gooey sauce. And the grocery store sushi is scary, if you know what I mean," replied Kyle. "Well... maybe the Sprouts kind are okay. I had some once. The lady there made the stuff every morning. She was nice and was willing to make what I wanted right then. It was good."

"I rarely like the grocery store stuff. It sits too long," Jon Bergendahl paused for a moment as if thinking. "You don't have to return to school until the fifteenth of January, but I don't have that much time away from work, so we will need to decide when you want to fly back to Grandma and Grandpa's house up in Canada."

"I am supposed to be there on the fifteenth. How long can I stay with you?" asked Kyle.

"We have a week where I don't need to be at work every day. Just a few hours here and there, so you won't be alone all day. Your mom said you were bored while she was away. I guess you have gotten used to having a lot of people around."

"I have. I like having friends to be with. And they are my friends and not just classmates. We have been emailing this past week. I miss them," said Kyle.

Jon glanced at his son momentarily as he drove. This was a good change.

The SUV paused at a stoplight as the rain intensified, with large white drops mixing in. Kyle's father turned on the wiper blades. It was starting to snow. They were almost home. Jon Bergendahl had a house in the area referred to as Queen Anne; it was one of the few modern houses there. Kyle always thought it looked like something out of a science fiction movie because everything was so clean and orderly. It was a three-story house with dramatic angles and huge picture windows. It was mainly solar-powered, despite the city's typically cloudy weather. The yard, in contrast, was lush, green, and full of flowers and vegetation. It was like walking into a jungle. Kyle used to enjoy the summers there, often playing under the tall trees in the backyard. He liked this house. It was a stark contrast to the modest ranch-style home that his mother rented back in Reno.

Once the garage door opener had stopped closing, Kyle could hear Pickles baying from within the house. The minute the door opened, the happy white and tan-spotted basset hound cheerfully barked and wagged her tail at Kyle and Jon.

"Oh, Pickles!" exclaimed Kyle. "It's been so long, my pretty long-eared girl."

Kyle reached down and affectionately rubbed the ears of the loose-skinned, long-eared hound dog he had not seen for over a year.

"I'm glad she still seems to know me," remarked Kyle as he followed his dad upstairs into the central part of the house.

"Bassets have long memories, Kyle. She would not forget you," replied Jon as he switched the lights on since it had already become dark.

Once Kyle was settled in the room that he usually claimed while staying with his father, he came downstairs to the second level, where the broad open kitchen was located. His dad was busy getting everything out to make dinner.

"Asparagus?" his dad said, holding up the package of spear-shaped vegetables.

"Sure," said Kyle as he took in the vast, vaulted ceiling with the shiny, polished metal lamps hanging down from above the kitchen. Directly opposite the kitchen was the combined living room and family room, where a large flat-screen TV hung on the wall above the fireplace. It was the perfect house for entertaining and hosting parties.

"Then wash your hands and you get to clean the asparagus, snap off the ends, and put them into the asparagus steamer," replied Jon with a smile. "I don't want you to get soft and lazy by having Jasper and that fancy school prepare all your meals. It's important that we, guys, are capable of being self-sufficient."

Kyle smiled and then went to the sink to wash his hands. It wasn't too often that he got an invitation to help prepare the food. His mother did all the cooking, and he usually got stuck doing table setting or cleanup. After enjoying a great dinner of broiled salmon and freshly steamed asparagus, Kyle and his dad sat in the living room, watching the snow fall while they watched TV.

"Did you have snow in Reno?"

"No. It was weird. The drought is really bad there," remarked Kyle with a frown. "And Mom packed up all my stuff from my room. I think she is *very* serious about moving."

"That's interesting. Didn't you say she was thinking about going back to Texas?" asked Jon.

"Yup, that's what she said. She seems… stressed about work. She spends a lot of time working," replied Kyle, suddenly feeling somber. Kyle looked around the room and up at the high ceilings of the modern-looking house. "Dad, you aren't going to move, are you?"

"Not that I have any plans, no. I mean, there is currently no reason for me to want to leave Seattle or this house," replied Jon, trying to reassure his son.

"Good. I like this house, and I don't like the idea of losing my home. With Mom wanting to move, it's like I will lose my home with her."

"Oh, Kyle, she loves you very much and will always make a place for you in her home. I can't imagine that she wouldn't. I do wish that I could have you here more often. I miss the time when you lived with me and attended school here. You did like the school here, didn't you?"

"Yes, I liked it. It was nice… that seems so long ago. I don't have any friends here anymore. I have friends at the Academy and Dark Cloud in Nevada, although he isn't going to the regular school anymore," replied Kyle. "I still wish you and Mom were together or at least lived in the same city."

"I know. We have had this conversation many times. It's just not the way things have happened. Your mother and I don't seem to agree on anything anymore," said Jon.

"Why?"

Jon looked at Kyle and replied, "I don't know. We used to get along so well."

"How did you and Mom meet?"

"I was attending the University of New Mexico, doing my undergraduate studies in Physics, and that's where we used to live in Albuquerque. Do you remember that?"

"Sorta, it was very desert-like and warm," replied Kyle slowly, then he yawned.

"Yes, that's correct. Your mother was attending a community college there, and we crossed paths at a bookstore where we both worked part-time while going to school. We were so happy then and so full of joy," Jon replied with a sigh of resignation.

Kyle looked at his dad as he felt another impending yawn. His father looked sad.

"You must be exhausted," said Jon, watching his son's repeated yawns. "You should probably get to bed now. I don't have to work tomorrow, so we can do something fun together. Think about what you might like to do."

"Okay, Dad. Do I need to be quiet for Chris?"

"Oh. No, Chris graduated this fall semester and has moved out. So, the downstairs is no longer a 'no-go zone' until I get another grad student that needs housing," replied Jon with a smile. "I already miss him, and so does Pickles, but he's got a great future ahead of him. He's going to get his PhD from Harvard."

"Harvard. Sounds so fancy," commented Kyle as he sleepily trudged up the stairs. "Goodnight, Dad."

"Goodnight, Sport," replied Jon.

The next morning, a light dusting of snow had fallen on the ground, which would eventually disappear when the next batch of midday rain fell. Storms were predicted for the next couple of days. This put a wrinkle in Jon's plans to take Kyle hiking. It would be too unpredictable due to the stormy weather. Kyle suggested visiting Pike Place Market, the Space Needle, and a few other spots where he could take pictures to share with his friends. The others had already shared pictures of ski trips and other fun activities with their family. Kyle did not want to appear to be slack on this aspect of keeping up with his friends.

Freya had emailed some pictures of her and Lothar at a large group gathering, where it looked like people were having a lot of fun. Lothar was saluting the photographer with a drinking horn, and Freya just looked like her usual pretty self. Kyle saved the picture to his tablet, wishing he had a smartphone to download it and carry with him. Kyle had shown his father the picture at breakfast while answering a late-night message.

"Wow, both redheads. Are they brother and sister?" asked Dr. Bergendahl.

"No, they are cousins, though," replied Kyle.

"And they are good friends of yours?" asked Jon.

"Yah, I think so," replied Kyle as he put some butter on his toast and then picked up the almost empty jelly jar. "Do we have any more quince jelly?"

"Doubtful. I will have to go to one of the farmers' markets for that. Perhaps someone at Pike Place will have some."

"I like this stuff, but I hardly ever see it anywhere," remarked Kyle.

"It's been replaced by other jams and jellies that marketing people think consumers ought to buy," replied Jon as he carefully cracked open his soft-boiled egg.

"So, if you are in marketing, you get to control what people want to buy?"

"It seems so, although they only control stupid people who don't know their own minds," replied Jon as he carefully scooped the hot egg contents out of the shell with a spoon.

"So, it's like a Jedi mind trick?" asked Kyle.

"Not as elegant or as straightforward as that. They try to convince people that their product is what they want and will use whatever means to make the consumer feel that way, such as using images to create emotional reactions. Sometimes they just plain lie and then have lawyers write up purchase agreements that are too difficult for the average person to understand, that remove the consumer's right to complain or get their money back," Jon said, and suddenly stopped and looked at his son, who was staring at him. "Sorry about that... I just switched cell phone services because the provider was a nightmare. I am feeling a bit bitter."

Kyle raised eyebrows at his father. "Dad, you were starting to rant."

"I know. I feel that the quality of life has changed significantly since I was your age, and I am concerned. The general population seems so stupid," Dr. Bergendahl wrinkled his brow in frustration as he scooped the contents out of the second half of his soft-boiled egg. "We have so many new, wonderful technologies, but humanity hasn't improved. People often think they are improving, but politics and marketing work to make it appear that way, and the public tends to believe it. They exchange one prejudice for another, acting as if it is justified. That won't be fixed until people get outraged, and they will probably do the same stupid thing again, just with different definitions. I think Humanity needs an evolutionary improvement step."

"Dad, maybe people seem stupid because you are really smart?" suggested Kyle.

Jon looked at his son and smiled, "You are such a kind soul. I hope you know how proud I am of you."

Kyle just nodded and smiled shyly, "Thanks, Dad, I love you too."

"Speaking of difficult topics, how are you doing in school? And are you getting along with that Xavier boy?"

"Aw, he's fine. I think I overreacted about all of that," replied Kyle.

"Good. I'm glad to hear that. What do you think of the Academy? Are they teaching you things that you find worthwhile or interesting?"

"I hate French class, but I don't think it is bad to learn French. I feel stupid being with the little kids. At least I have Geoff with me," said Kyle, getting up to put his dishes away.

"You seemed to have enjoyed the costume project and reading The Hobbit," said Jon as he got up.

"I didn't think I could read a book that big," said Kyle. "We never read anything like that back in my old school. And the costume contest was fun. It was a lot of hard work."

"Do you think you could build another costume if you had to?"

Kyle thought for a moment and then turned to his dad, "Yes. I think I could. And perhaps an even better one. I know what mistakes I made on the one I have. I wish you could have been there to see it in person. It was so much fun to wear."

"So have they told you where you get to go on the special trip?" asked Jon.

"Not yet, but I have been told it will be someplace interesting. And we may get to stay overnight a day or two, which is also exciting."

Jon finished putting away the dishes from breakfast, picked up his keys and cell phone from the charger, and headed toward the coat closet.

"Go get your coat," Jon instructed Kyle. "We need to get going."

The rest of the day was spent wandering around Pike Place Market and then visiting the Space Needle when there was a break in the storm, allowing for a good view of Mt. Rainier and downtown Seattle. Kyle took plenty of pictures to share with his friends. Jon bought Kyle some clothes and a few other items for Christmas, as they hadn't spent the holiday season together. After lunch at a trendy café Jon liked to frequent, they walked down the city sidewalk to where the car was parked. There were many shops along the way with unique and interesting stores, some of which Kyle wondered why anyone would go inside them. As they passed a mom-and-pop bookstore, Kyle studied the window display, which featured a variety of steampunk books, comics, toys, videos, and assorted steampunk cosplay accessories, such as goggles and hats. A picture caught Kyle's attention. It depicted a male steampunk character, dressed in a Victorian-era brown suit with a white, stiff tab collar. It reminded Kyle of the image he had seen in his mind back in the Sierra Nevada Mountains with Dark Cloud and his uncle, John Greystorm. It had slipped his mind, but now it was firmly back in the forefront of his thoughts.

Kyle knew his dad wouldn't take this kind of thing seriously. He would consider it to be superstitious nonsense, or primitive tribal hallucinations, or at least something along those lines. It just was not a topic he felt comfortable discussing with his dad, let alone someone like his mom. Kyle honestly wanted to know if the image was real or just his imagination conjuring something he wanted

400

to be true. The world seemed to offer no answers concerning such matters.

The rest of Kyle's stay with his father was spent making the most of the afternoons when his dad was not working. During those morning hours when Kyle found himself alone, he sat with Pickles reading *The Secret Garden* or sending messages back and forth between the other members of the Fabulous Five and Freya. René sent pictures of himself with his parents in France, Tyrrel sent photos of him doing activities in Las Vegas with his brothers and sister, and Lothar sent pictures of him skiing and then building a snow fort. In contrast, Geoff sent a more eclectic series of photos of things in Vancouver, WA, and Portland, OR. He also sent a picture of himself standing in front of Powell's bookstore, with some added text on the photo stating that he was not affiliated with the bookstore owners. Kyle chuckled a little at Geoff's quirky images. His friend was wonderfully weird.

Kyle was glad to see these messages come in. Earlier during his vacation, he had not heard from anyone and started worrying. He also made sure to share some of his pictures with his grandparents. He missed them, too. However, that would not be for long, as his time with his father passed quickly, and the day had come for him to travel back to Canada.

Jon was dismayed to discover that the direct flight routes to the Toronto Airport were no longer available, and Kyle would be waiting in the Vancouver location for hours. This thought made Jon Bergendahl uncomfortable. The loss of Chris as a house sitter and dog sitter made his ability to plan for such events troublesome.

"So, Dad, what are we going to do?" asked Kyle.

"I am leaving Pickles here in the house, and that lady friend I introduced to you the other day, Teresa, will pick her up if I get delayed. She has a key to the house, and Pickles likes her," explained Jon as he turned off his computer and started to get ready to leave for work. "I am driving you up to Vancouver, B.C., tomorrow morning, where you will take a flight directly to Toronto Pearson Airport, where your grandparents will pick you up."

"So, I can't just take a flight from here?" asked Kyle.

"No, something has changed when it comes to flying directly to Toronto," Jon said with a scowl. "And I don't want you to sit in an airport for hours waiting to make your connection. I'm sorry. I miscalculated. I really should have checked this all out better."

"It's okay, Dad. I could do it," said Kyle, trying to make things easier.

"No, it's not okay. It's my job as your father to protect you, and I don't feel that it is safe to let you go on your own for that long," replied Jon. "You are not old enough."

Kyle could tell his dad was deeply concerned about these changes in available flights. He put his arms around his dad and hugged him. Jon responded with a smile and hugged Kyle back.

"The world is becoming a strange place that I don't understand. And I should have planned better. I should have made sure I could travel with you," said Jon, rubbing his forehead in frustration.

"Dad, I am not angry with you," said Kyle.

"I appreciate that, but I am angry with myself. I should not have assumed that things would remain the same in this ever-changing world. I know better than that because of my work," said Jon, looking at his son, who now had worry marks in his expression. Jon suddenly felt even more guilty. "Everything will be fine. I will be back this afternoon, and maybe we can watch a movie together."

"Sure, Dad, that sounds good," replied Kyle, feeling a bit less worried. His dad seemed to recover, refocus, and act like his usual self.

The rest of Kyle's stay with his dad was enjoyable, and the two-and-a-half-hour drive up to Vancouver, B.C. was also interesting. Kyle had never been to this large west coast Canadian city. They crossed over many large bridges that allowed travel over huge waterways. The city also had many tall buildings, like those in Seattle. This was nothing like Reno, and he wondered what Dark Cloud would think of the densely populated region. Soon, he found himself saying goodbye to his dad and promising to call him as soon as he landed in Toronto. Kyle had his tablet with him, along with some snacks, and was prepared for the over four-hour flight. He would immerse himself in the world of Miss Contrary Mary Lennox and her discoveries about the moor and the hundred-room mansion of her uncle.

Chapter 17: René's Battle

When Kyle was settled back at the Caledon House, he had a week before returning to the Academy location up at Lake Simcoe. This, of course, would give him more than enough time to finish reading *The Secret Garden* and just get used to being back in a different time zone. This seemed to be a new aspect of his life of traveling. He was grateful that both of his parents lived in the same time zone, so he didn't have to adjust to different time zones when visiting them.

Kyle tossed and turned in his bed, which was unusual since he generally slept very well at the Caledon House. He wondered if a visit to the bathroom or a drink of water would affect his ability to sleep. He got up and looked out the bedroom window that faced the driveway section of the house. Looking out and expecting to see nothing but a snow-covered yard, he was surprised to see several cars parked outside that had not been there when he went to bed. Kyle thought this was curious and decided to slip out of his bedroom quietly to see if he could figure out what was happening.

He walked silently down the hallway toward the stairway landing and saw a dim light in the fancy foyer. Typically, there was no light on. Kyle looked about, remembering what happened in the library and the silent alarm system. He cautiously walked down the stairs barefoot, making no noise. He strained his ears to listen for a sound. When he reached the bottom step and touched the cold marble floor, he thought he could hear something coming from the direction of the library hallway. He turned

404

toward the mostly dark section and noticed a light coming from underneath the always locked door.

Walking slowly toward the door, he looked around for any red blinking lights that might be part of an alarm system. He could hear muffled voices talking. It sounded like several different people. As he drew closer to the door, he could hear the conversation more clearly and could tell that his grandparents were in the room, speaking with at least five other people. Kyle felt his mouth go dry and wondered if this was something he really should be doing. Then he heard a woman's voice that sounded familiar.

"The Dubois boy had to be sent to the Wolff residence for his own safety," said the familiar female voice that was not Lily Bergendahl.

"Do you believe that this kind of violence could follow to places such as the school here?" asked a male voice that was not Karl Bergendahl nor Jasper.

"We can't assume that it won't. We must be aware of some historical prejudices that have been held against us. Some of which are quite inaccurate, but nonetheless, we have many generations that are ignorant of the truth and will believe all kinds of… propaganda," replied the familiar female voice.

"There have even been TV shows claiming to be historical in nature that state the Order's members ate babies. And because it was still illegal for us to be out in public at the time, we had to endure their lies and fabrications. Heck, there was even a drug group somewhere using our name!" said a voice that sounded a lot like Karl Bergendahl.

"So, what should the Order do? We are not ready to be a military force. When we reasserted our right to be part of an open society in 2007, we gathered and decided that some of our old goals, such as being guardians of truth and knowledge, should be our top priority. That's why we built schools and developed the oldest location in Canada to be an openly Templar school. Are we to arm engineers and musicians?" asked a voice that Kyle was sure was Lily Bergendahl, his grandma.

"We have to do something," said one of the male voices. "We can't be naive and just assume that because this location is in a relatively peaceful part of the world… nothing could happen."

"Firstly, we must make sure all our security measures are up to date and in order, and that means the computer systems as well. We strategically installed more security cameras, and we should always have at least a few personnel on site who have received combat or security training. We can't afford to have something like what happened in Norway, so yes, we will need to arm a few engineers and musicians," replied the familiar female voice. "North America is a relatively peaceful section of the world, but that could easily change."

"Everyone involved in security would have to be trained, of course, according to each country's legal requirements," said another younger-sounding male voice. "This may take time and should start right away."

"So, then back to the DuBois situation," the other male voice said.

"Hold on," said the familiar, unknown female voice. "I have this odd feeling like we are being watched. Will you please go check the door and windows?"

This made Kyle's heart jump as he scrambled down the hallway to get out of sight with no time to get upstairs unseen or unheard. He hurried into the formal living room and hid behind one of the large sofas. He heard someone open the door to the mysteriously locked room and then walk down the hallway. The lights in the foyer came on, and a man dressed in a dark suit stood quietly, looking about. He stood still as if he were listening for any movement. Kyle ducked further behind the sofa and tried to control his breathing as he felt his heart pounding away in his chest. It was so intense that he almost wondered if it could be heard. After about three minutes, the man in the dark suit turned the lights off and silently strode down the hallway. Kyle heard the door close. He let out a gentle sigh of relief and sat behind the fancy sofa until he felt like his heart had stopped pounding so intensely.

Kyle had never been so scared in his life. He sat behind the sofa, trying to relax. The image of the man in the brown Victorian suit came to mind again, and he suddenly felt a sense of calm. He told himself that even if he got caught, no one would hurt him. His grandparents loved him. He began to get up to return to his bedroom, but the image of the man in the brown suit grew stronger, and he felt compelled to sit down again. Then he heard the door down the library hallway open, and light poured out of

407

it again, and he could hear the voices of the people within the room.

"Was anything out there?" asked the female voice.

"No. I waited for a few minutes in the dark just in case, but I saw nothing," replied the man in the dark suit, who then closed the door, and the light disappeared.

Kyle swallowed hard. His mouth was dry. He had a strange inclination to believe that the image of the man in the brown suit had warned him. The idea sat curiously with him. It was comforting and a little spooky.

When Kyle had safely reached his bedroom again, he lay awake wondering what was going on. He wondered if the DuBois boy was a reference to René, and if the reference to the Wolff residence was Lothar or Freya. Something strange was going on, and he would have to contact Lothar in the morning to see if anything unusual had happened. Kyle finally fell asleep to a night of fitful dreams. The next morning, he woke up early and got onto his computer to send a message to Lothar. The strange cars were all gone from the driveway as if there had never been visitors to the house. By the time he had breakfast and dressed for the day, Lothar had already messaged him back.

Lothar suggested they talk in person rather than over the Internet. This somewhat surprised Kyle, but he agreed. Lothar said that since he lived in Cambridge, which was not that far from Caledon, he would invite Kyle to come over to play in the snow, and then they could talk privately about what was happening. Kyle agreed to ask his grandparents if he could visit Lothar at his home in Cambridge the next day.

Kyle went downstairs to find his grandma sitting at the kitchen table, engrossed in her Android tablet, while his grandpa sat at the table, sipping coffee and reading a newspaper. Lily Bergendahl looked up from her tablet and smiled at her grandson, who appeared apprehensive.

"Is there something on your mind, Kyle?" she asked.

"Well," Kyle hesitated. He had never asked his grandparents to take him anywhere before and was unsure if he would be overstepping polite boundaries. "Lothar Wolff, one of my friends at school whom you did not get to meet last Thanksgiving, has invited me to come over to his house tomorrow and hang out for the day and play in the snow. Is that possible? He lives in Cambridge."

Lily flashed a quick look at Karl, who peeked over his newspaper to look at Lily upon hearing this request.

"I think that can be arranged," said Lily with a smile. "Cambridge is reasonably close, so I don't think that should be a problem."

Kyle had a strange feeling about their reaction to his request and did his best to act as if he suspected nothing and knew nothing about last night's visitors.

"Lothar is the kid with the red hair dressed as Han Solo in the photos I sent," said Kyle.

Karl Bergendahl looked at Lily and responded, "Oh yes, I remember seeing that photo. We wondered if he might be the son of someone we know, and the fact that he lives in Cambridge might mean he is related to our friend. Can you get his address for us so that Jasper and I can take you over there?"

"Sure, that's not a problem. I'll go message him now," said Kyle, wanting to leave the room before he revealed something he should not have.

After Kyle showed the address to his grandpa, it was confirmed that Karl Bergendahl knew Lothar Wolff's parents. It was decided that Kyle would visit Lothar in the morning and stay for the afternoon. Karl Bergendahl stated that he had some business to attend to in London, Ontario, so letting Kyle hang out with Lothar for the day would be fine. Kyle's sense of curiosity made him feel restless to the point that he worried it would tip his grandparents off that he knew something odd had occurred. He decided to shut himself away for the rest of the day to finish reading *The Secret Garden*. He needed to complete the book before returning to school, which was in less than a week.

It was hard waiting until the next morning, and it was difficult not to discuss anything online, as Lothar had requested. Kyle felt a pang of guilt about not sharing his new mystery with Geoff and Tyrrel, who had emailed him that day. Kyle told them he was back at his grandparents' home until school started. Both Geoff and Tyrrel said they would travel a day early, arriving at the Academy ahead of schedule so they could recover from the fatigue of travel and adjust to the East Coast time change.

The next morning, Kyle got up early and dressed warmly for a fun day of being outside in the snow. He was ready to leave when his grandfather said it was time to go to Cambridge. Karl Bergendahl took the white Mazda SUV. This was one of the few times that Kyle saw either of his grandparents actually drive a vehicle. Jasper stayed with Lily since she needed to go to Toronto for business purposes. She told Kyle that she had a meeting about one of the fancy buildings she owned in the business district. Kyle wished it had fallen on another day. He would have liked the opportunity to see the building she owned and explore more of the big Canadian city.

The drive to Cambridge was uneventful, despite the region's substantial snowfall, and it was a lucky day with clear weather and fair roads that allowed the elderly man to navigate safely to the Wolff family home. Kyle was greeted by Lothar, followed by René, who was mysteriously staying with Lothar. The boys let the adults talk to each other, and then the boys disappeared into the mostly wood-paneled house. The interior of the home had a warm, cozy ambiance. Kyle was not surprised to see that Lothar's dad had the same shade of brilliant red hair that was cut neat and short, with a reddish beard that somewhat resembled Commander Riker's on Star Trek. Lothar's mother was a pretty, slender woman with bright, golden blonde hair and delicate, narrow features.

Once the three boys were safely tucked away in Lothar's bedroom with the door securely closed and the radio on just enough to be heard, Kyle's suspicions that the "DuBois boy" referred to the other night was indeed René.

"What is going on? Does René normally stay with you?" asked Kyle.

"No, he doesn't. And what did you hear?" asked Lothar and René at the same time.

Kyle sat back against the wooden frame of the double split-level bunk beds that were in Lothar's room. René and Lothar looked eager to hear what Kyle had to say.

"Well... I woke up the other night and happened to look out the bedroom window; the driveway was filled with a bunch of strange cars. But when I went to bed, no one had come to visit my grandparents. I thought this was *really* odd. I crept out of my room to see who was visiting and if anything was wrong. People don't normally visit in the middle of the night... unless that is a Canadian thing?"

"No. People go to bed and generally don't have parties in the middle of the night after everyone goes to sleep," replied Lothar, making a slight face at Kyle.

"So, what happened next?" asked René.

"I crept down the stairs quietly because the house was mostly dark. It was not like when my grandparents had guests. Jasper is usually making things in the kitchen, ensuring everyone is well-fed and comfortable, and this... was... weird. Remember where the library was?" Kyle asked.

"Yes," replied René with a nod.

"Well, down that hallway is a door that is always locked. I have no idea what is in there, and I just figured it was none of my business. On this night, light was coming from under the door, and the voices of people talking could be heard. I could hear my grandparents speaking with other adults," said Kyle.

"What did they say that made you want to contact me about René?" asked Lothar.

"Well, they mentioned something about the DuBois boy staying at the Wolff residence. And well, I think that made me think of you two, and well, here you both are," said Kyle.

René and Lothar exchanged a glance, then turned to Kyle.

"Did something happen to you?!" exclaimed Kyle as René pulled back his long brown hair away from his face to reveal what appeared to be a large bruise and serious scuff marks across the side of his face.

"It will get out sooner or later," said René, looking sideways at Lothar. "I got into a fight back home in Paris. We have a lot of immigrants living in Paris now, and they do not understand our culture or the way we do things. They don't respect our way of thinking."

"You did hear about the horrible shootings in Paris, right?" Lothar asked Kyle.

"Vaguely. There was something on the news about some terrorist type guys that shot some people who ran a magazine," said Kyle, meekly trying to recall what he heard. The news broke on the day he was traveling by plane.

"Well, my parents knew one of the people who had been murdered. Everyone was deeply distraught. There has been a great deal of tension over the recent years in

Paris with so many people who come to live in France but do not appreciate our rich heritage and highly intellectual way of viewing life," replied René with a certain amount of pride for his country. "My Maman said that normally Parisians embrace a certain amount of cultural variety, but some groups just do not understand our way. And some of these pigs roam the streets making disturbing and ugly comments about the lovely French girls, and there was a group of them saying terrible things about my Maman when we were out shopping, so… I took them on."

"The nut took on three older boys and got his butt kicked," said Lothar.

"You should have heard what they were saying about her!" retorted René. "I was not going to stand for that."

"You took on teenagers?!" Kyle exclaimed.

"Yes, but those boys were nothing but…" René's insults were interrupted by a knock on the door. All three boys became instantly quiet.

"Lothar, can I open the door?" said a female voice.

"Sure, Mom," said Lothar with a quick sunny disposition.

"I am planning on making homemade soup today and wondered if you all would like that for lunch?" the slender blonde woman with the same green eyes as Lothar said.

"That would be super," said Lothar while Kyle and René nodded in agreement with him.

Shortly after Lothar's mom closed the door, the boys decided to have their conversation somewhere else where they could not be overheard. They put on warm coats and went outside to inspect Lothar's snow fort and the view of the nearby small lake. The three boys added more snow to the fort walls and searched for fallen branches they could use as support for the top of the window frame. The walls were about a foot deep and seemed sturdy.

"So, what happened to your face?" Kyle asked René.

"They slammed me into the stone wall of a nearby building after I called them a few appropriate names, the rude troglodytes," said René.

Lothar shook his head in amusement and said, "You have been hanging out with Tyrrel too much."

"What did they say?! And… what's a troglodyte?" asked Kyle.

"Primitive cave dwellers, I think," replied Lothar.

"They implied some nasty sexual things and said they were going to do them to her," René replied, gritting his teeth. Kyle looked shocked. "My Maman is a beautiful woman. She is often in the public eye, doing charity work when she is not pursuing acting roles. They should have more respect for her, and every French woman! They acted like they had a right to be so foul and vulgar."

"Didn't your mom hear these guys?" asked Kyle.

"No, they were speaking Arabic. She doesn't know that language," replied René.

Lothar patted another handful of snow onto the snow fort and asked, "Do you think they would have attacked your mom? Or was it just guys blustering?"

René paused from digging out the snow. The expression on his face shifted from one of indignation and outrage to something more complex. It was as if he was trying to fight off something more, and then he appeared to be fighting back tears.

"I'm not sure. They did not know I was there at first, and they sounded as if they were seriously planning to hurt her. It scared me," replied René. "The whole thing scared my parents, too. These felons got away, and since people know who my Maman is, my parents decided to go to their home in Switzerland for a while, and they sent me to Canada early. The shootings made everyone very upset."

"What a minute, you understand Arabic?!" exclaimed Kyle.

"Yes, I hear it all the time back home, along with some German and Turkish. I also understand the Swiss language of Romansh. Not many people know that one," said René with a certain air of superiority.

"And you can speak all these languages?" asked Kyle.

"No, not all," replied René. "But I can understand what is being said most often."

"René is what some would call a language savant. I don't think anyone in the Page Level students is as good as he is with languages," remarked Lothar. "He makes the best study mate for language tests."

René smiled and replied, "Well, some of us just have a talented ear."

"What do you two think of the fact that there was a secret meeting in my grandparents' house, and you were mentioned?" Kyle asked.

The other two boys were silent for a moment, and then Lothar replied, "It's obvious that your grandparents are Knights. You get to ride in the helicopter; they have special historical artifacts from the Order, and now they are holding secret meetings in their home. You are the grandson of high-level Knights."

"The big question is… why isn't your dad a Knight?" commented René.

Kyle stopped putting snow on top of the branches to build the upper window frame and looked at both of his friends.

"I guess that is an important and curious question. And why hasn't anyone ever talked to me about being a knight?" he responded to his friends. Kyle pondered the thought some more and said, "Maybe they don't think I am worthy of being a knight."

Lothar wrinkled his brow and looked at René. René shook his head in disagreement and said, "No, that cannot be possible. You are probably one of the kindest and most trustworthy kids I know. I don't see how that could be possible."

"Maybe I am not smart enough," suggested Kyle.

"Okay… you are certainly not a Tyrrel Washington or a Lucy Robbinson, but you are no idiot either. Being a Knight is a combination of the right attributes, some of which are honesty, courage, and loyalty, and these are things you seem to have at the core of your personality. If you don't have those, then you can't be a Knight. It doesn't matter how strong, brilliant, creative, talented, or wealthy you are; you can't be a Knight if you can't pass those three basic core attributes," said Lothar. "There are more qualities necessary to being a successful Knight or one that is capable of holding a high rank, but if you can't pass those three basic ones, then you're out the door."

The three boys stood quietly in the cold, silent outdoor air for a moment. The clear January air seemed to hold the three of them within the moment. The snow sparkled brilliantly; there was no wind, and the only sound that could be heard was a distant vehicle driving down the semi-rural country road, some distance from where the middle-class housing development was located. There were farms and natural areas all around the neighborhood in which Lothar lived. Kyle looked about. It was a nice place to live. René started rubbing his hands together as he puffed out steam from his mouth to watch it dissipate. Kyle cocked his head to the side and looked at René.

"What?" he said, his accent sounding particularly strong again.

418

"What are you doing?" asked Kyle.

"I am pretending to be a dragon. I am imagining what it would be like to have fire coming out of my mouth and warming my cold hands," René replied with a smile.

"I thought knights were supposed to kill dragons," Kyle remarked.

"Only stupid ones do," Lothar remarked as he stooped to pick up more snow for the fortress.

"But what if the dragon eats people?" asked Kyle to see where this line of thought would go.

"Why would a dragon eat a human?" asked René, still rubbing his gloved hands together and making small steam clouds in the air. "I think eating a cow, sheep, deer, or perhaps a giant tuna fish would be much better. I doubt dragons would want to eat people."

Kyle watched Lothar take the lump of snow and start to form it into a round shape about the size of a softball. Lothar had a strange look on his face as René continued to talk as if he were a dragon and speculated how big and wonderful he would be. René appeared to be completely self-absorbed in his oration about how magnificent he would be and did not notice the perfect throwing size of the wad of snow that Lothar held. Kyle picked up on this and walked casually to the other side of the snow fort, acting as if he were continuing to collect snow for the fort. Instead, he started making several snowballs for himself, just in case he needed to be ready.

In a matter of minutes, Kyle had managed to make himself a small arsenal with the snow that compacted together so well. Then Lothar let loose his surprise and hit René in the chest with the snowball he was making. René was shocked and bent down to make a snowball while both were surprised by Kyle's barrage of snowballs from behind the fort. This erupted into a massive snowball battle between the three boys, none of whom gave up until they were all thoroughly soaked and cold. By the time they were done, it was close to noon, so they were all very hungry after spending the morning outside.

The rest of the day was spent playing outside, then getting warm inside, watching videos. By the time Karl Bergendahl arrived to pick up Kyle, he was exhausted and ready for the peaceful car ride home. Kyle slept well that night. The next morning brought forth new ideas that Kyle thought he should focus on before going back to school. He had finished reading *The Secret Garden* and wondered if he could find the journal that he had seen months earlier in the library. He had hoped the book would shed more light on his family's heritage, particularly why his dad never spoke of the Knights and didn't seem to be one. He wondered if he should ask his grandparents or even his dad, but sometimes adults didn't like being asked specific questions. Kyle did not want to be in a situation where he was told to drop the subject.

After breakfast, while his grandparents were busy with other things, he made his way down the hall to the library. He paused for a moment next to the door, which was always locked, and where he had heard the voices. He stared at the doorknob and noticed that no light came from under the door. He looked back down the hallway to make sure no one was approaching and reached for the doorknob to see if it would open. The door was still locked. Kyle wasn't surprised since it had always been locked. He continued to the end of the hallway, where the library door was, which opened as usual. The room was always impressive, with its high ceilings, walls of books, artwork, and other fabulous items that never failed to impress or capture his imagination. The room had a special feeling to it, not to mention it had a distinct scent, unlike the rest of the house.

He glanced over at the huge tapestry of the sailing vessels in stormy distress and then made his way to the bookshelf where he recalled finding the handwritten journal. He pulled out the book, which appeared to be the journal he had read from before. It was sticking out about a quarter of an inch more than the other books, which, now upon more serious examination, all appeared to be journals of the same kind. Kyle looked at the front of the leather-bound book and opened the front section, which was entirely handwritten. The first page read:

If found, please return to

Lily Clara Hanni

Journal 1963 – 1964

Kyle flipped through a couple of pages. It was a daily journal written by a girl, which surprised Kyle, and he wondered if the name Lily could be that of his grandma. He flipped through the book to find the entry about the archery competition. He found the entry and read more, finally realizing that when she wrote in the journal, she was the same age as he was now. It felt odd as he read another section.

...the Archery Master wants me to spend all my martial arts training time to become a great archer. He says that I have the potential to become very good. He said that if I improved enough, I could participate in other competitions outside of school. This is all so exciting. I can't wait to tell my big brothers about this. My mother will think this is not what a 'proper young lady' should do, but I don't care about that. I want to be like my brothers.

Kyle paused for a moment, trying to recall if he had ever heard his grandma mention older brothers. He could not recall. It seemed that each time he sat down and read through these journals, he ended up with more questions than answers. He debated whether he should read anymore. It was his grandmother's journal, which he normally thought was something private. He looked at the shelf on which it was and saw that there were many more journals. Then he realized that it was not confined to just one shelf, but many shelves had books that could be journals. Kyle flipped forward to take just one more peek at the journal.

...and ever since Chris died, my parents have been so worried about Thor and Ru and their duties as Knights. I know I want to be a Knight, and so does Kyle. Kyle and I

can take on the responsibilities of running the school when Mom and Dad are gone. I know we can do it. That will leave Thor and Ru to do the things they want to do. I know I'm just a kid now, but I think the family tradition of running the school is essential, especially since we cannot be Templar Knights in the open public. I can't imagine going anywhere else. I hope Mom and Dad will let us be the ones to take care of it. Since Chris is gone and Thor and Ru want to do other things, they have mentioned passing the school on to other Knights. I think I can do this.

Kyle sat back, letting what he read sink into his mind. He wondered if he was named after the Kyle that she mentioned. He also wondered what had happened to Chris and where Thor, Ru, and Kyle were. And the school. Did her family run the Academy? Why was this never told to him, he wondered. Once again, more questions than answers. Looking up at the rows of books that could be journals, he got up and pulled one off the upper shelf. This one had a leather cover, and the paper, slightly yellow, felt different; the smell was unique and rich, like that of antique books. This time, the handwriting was more challenging to read and appeared to be in ink that reminded Kyle of the pictures he had seen of the U.S. Constitution. The lines were delicate and thin in some parts and heavy in other sections of the letters. There were even droplets of dried ink and smudges here and there. The book's entries were not everyday, although they appeared to be fairly frequent. The date for the entry was surprisingly old, Kyle thought, and marveled at the idea that something like this could exist that long. He thought of his journal and wondered if someone would read it someday. He laughed at the thought and felt sorry for the poor soul who should read his. It was so dull.

The entry appeared to be dated '*23 September 1730*' and Kyle recognized the name Hudson's Bay Company within the paragraph. Still, the handwriting was so difficult to read that he wondered if it was even written in English. He did not recognize any of the words. Kyle put the journal back where he had found it and decided to read more of his grandmother's journal. He could read her handwriting, and it was written in English. He wanted to know what happened to the brothers and had hoped she would mention them again in her journal entries.

Chapter 18: The Fabulous Five Reunited

Kyle walked through the doorway of the Fifth-year boys' room to see that most of his roommates were already making themselves comfortable back in their bedroom cubicles. Xavier was already following Trevor around while Oliver Cortez, Wendell Schultz, Kevin O'Dell, and Pierre Levesque were busy sitting around the video game console, engaged in a rather loud and boisterous video battle. Then Kyle spotted Geoff coming over to him while Tyrrel, René, and Lothar were all in René's cubicle, chatting.

"I see you decided to come a day early as well," said Geoff with a big smile. "How have you been doing?"

"Pretty good. I finished the required reading and then started visiting my grandparents' library to look at the journal I found, and discovered there is a whole bunch of them," replied Kyle with a smile. "I think that my grandma's family may have started the school here in Canada."

"Oh wow, you're kidding me, right?" said Geoff.

"No, it really looks that way," replied Kyle as he made his way to his cubicle room with his bags. Geoff followed.

"Hey, did you hear what happened to René?" Geoff asked in a lower voice, so that only Kyle could hear him.

Kyle nodded and looked up at Geoff after he opened his bag and started to remove his belongings.

"Yes, I found out about it a couple of days ago by accident. He certainly has a lot of courage to stand up to guys bigger and older than him," replied Kyle.

"Oh, no kidding. I'm not sure if I could do that. Three older kids," said Geoff, shaking his head. "He's lucky they didn't hurt him worse."

Kyle looked over at René.

"He looked worse a couple of days ago. It doesn't look as bad. I imagine it must have hurt when it happened," Kyle said to Geoff.

"So, when did you see him?" asked Geoff.

"He was staying at Lothar's house, and my grandparents live only about an hour or so away from them. Lothar invited me over to visit. We all had a blast playing in the snow. It was a nice change to get to play in the snow. We didn't have any in Reno, and we don't get much in Seattle. It usually melts fast," replied Kyle as he continued to unpack his two bags.

"We get snow in Vancouver. Sometimes we get ice storms, too, and the streets are like a giant ice arena. My mom hates that. One year, we had a massive storm with snow that was a foot deep, with a layer of hard ice about an inch thick on top. That was awful to shovel off the sidewalk," Geoff started to ramble on. "My mom was really stressed about traveling to work and that people may slip and fall."

Kyle looked up at his awkward, skinny friend and mused to himself that he missed this strange guy. There wasn't anyone like him. He was the first person Kyle made friends with at the Academy. Kyle finished putting away his things as he listened to Geoff go on about the weather in Vancouver and how the Columbia River affected the region's climate.

"Hey, I'm done unpacking. Let's go join the others," suggested Kyle.

The rest of the day was spent either relaxing or organizing for tomorrow's classes. Friends reunited and caught up on events of the past month-long holiday season. Kyle kept an eye out for Freya. He wanted to ask her about his experience with the man in the brown suit. She seemed like the one who would not laugh at him for being strange. Much to his disappointment, he didn't get a chance to talk with her since she was busy with the girls, so he figured he would find some time to speak with her alone in the upcoming week.

That night, before going to bed, Kyle checked his email and sent messages to all his parents and grandparents to let them know he was alright and settled in at school. Kyle found an email from Dark Cloud.

Hello Kyle!

I have exciting news. I have a special connection with the spiritual protector and father of our tribe, Washo. And yes, I know it sounds like the county and the tribe's name, but those names came from him. My uncle says this is very special, and I have an important role to play in the future. He feels it is essential for me to learn our tribe's language

427

and history, as well as many other things. He is going to talk with my parents about me living with him down in Walker River, where he plans to move. Uncle John says there is a bad influence on Reno, and he wants me to study away from there. I guess the best way to describe it is that the dark side of the Force is clouding things there. Lol

I will let you know what my parents say. I am excited about this. I want so much to understand and be close to my ancestors. You should do the same. Please let me know if you discover anything more about the man in the brown suit.

Dark Cloud

Kyle let the words sink in. Dark Cloud had a special connection to someone significant to his people. A strong connection to his ancestors was meaningful. Important enough for him to leave his parents' home and study elsewhere. Kyle noticed the parallel. Dark Cloud understood the importance of his culture and the need to protect it from vanishing due to modern ideas. Kyle had never given much thought to his ancestors before, until the past few months. He had knights in his family. He had never felt a sense of pride or even interest in his family heritage until recently. He had always thought that he was somehow not good enough and that his heritage was bad in some way. These feelings were not something he shared with anyone. It was one of the reasons why he felt so drawn to Dark Cloud as a friend. Dark Cloud loved his heritage and the history that came with it. The tribes on the east side of the Sierra Nevada Range held events centered on their heritage and culture, and would also attend other Native American events in various areas. Historically, the tribes did not always get along, but then again, no groups existed without some conflict arising once in a while. Kyle never saw anything about celebrating being Swedish or Canadian. He wondered why. There was a holiday called Cinco de Mayo, which commemorated the Mexican defeat of a French army, but Kyle always felt that it was an odd thing to celebrate. It was not an American victory. He liked the food and music, but it was like going to a wedding and not knowing the bride or groom. Kyle sat and sighed, his muscles in his face twisting into a scowl.

"If you keep that expression on your face, Freya will not be interested in you," said Lothar, who was outside his bedroom cubicle, looking over at him.

Kyle jumped. And Lothar laughed.

"Sorry, I didn't mean to surprise you, but you looked pretty unhappy," remarked Lothar while Kyle caught his breath and felt his heart rate start to slow down again.

"I was reading something and then… thinking about it," replied Kyle.

"Geez, it must have been important," said Lothar, walking into Kyle's cubicle.

"Sorta," replied Kyle. "Do you know much about your family heritage?"

"Yes, we have a lot of German and Irish ancestors and relatives, but nothing to make me scowl like that. What's the deal?"

"I don't know. Do you feel ashamed of your heritage?" asked Kyle.

"No," responded Lothar with a bit of emotion.

This caught Geoff, René, and Tyrrel's attention, and they decided to come over to see what was going on.

"Why would you ask me something like that?" asked Lothar.

"Like what?" asked Geoff.

"He asked me if I was ashamed of my heritage!" said Lothar.

"I ask because it seems like I should be ashamed of my heritage, and I don't know why," said Kyle.

"Are your parents old hippies?" asked Geoff. "My parents have some friends who are old hippies, and they say all kinds of negative things about white people and how oppressive we are. They say we are destroying the world and ruining the environment."

The boys looked at Geoff with raised eyebrows.

"Well, they do. They are nice people, but they have some unusual ideas about certain things. I think they smoke pot. At least that is what my sister and I suspect. They smell odd at times. They have a cool farm outside of Portland, Oregon, where they grow awesome vegetables and do as many things as possible to be self-sustaining.

My parents hang out with them and have them over for dinner from time to time. And at the dinner table, they sometimes talk about how white people are bad," Geoff responded to the other boy's looks of inquiry.

"So why do you think they hate people of European ancestry?" asked René, taking it a little personally.

"I don't know," answered Geoff. He frowned a little and looked down at the ground.

"Oh, I have seen people like this," said Tyrrel. "There are white people who hate themselves because of the slavery that happened in the United States. They seem odd to me, if you ask me. They stick their noses into other people's business, act important, and tell people of minority ancestry how they should be. I think they have a mental illness, personally."

"They sound like idiots," said René. "Why should I feel bad about my family? I didn't do anything bad in your country."

"Look, guys, I don't want everyone to get upset about all of this," said Kyle, rubbing his hands across his face. "I just feel confused. We have black history month in America, and we are supposed to celebrate diversity, which seems to be all about everyone except my dad and his parents. What's wrong with them?"

"Nothing. Nothing is wrong with them," replied Tyrrel. "My grandparents often talk about the times when they were young, and they couldn't use the same bathroom as white people, and a whole bunch of other illogical requirements. People were just plain mean at times, but it's not just white people who were mean, though. If you read the history of places like New York City during the 1800s, it was violent, dirty, and just plain criminal. People with Irish heritage were treated just as badly as black people. So… no ethnic group is perfect, and no ethnic group is all bad. People should be evaluated on an individual basis and not put into irrationally constructed conceptual boxes."

"I thought we were supposed to call you African Americans," said Geoff to Tyrrel.

Tyrrel looked at Geoff with a raised eyebrow and responded, "My grandparents feel that we are Black Americans. We are a part of the making of the United States, and while we have African ancestry, we are Americans first and foremost."

"Oh," said Geoff as he took in a breath to say something else, but was cut off by Tyrrel.

"But some black people like having a different image of themselves, so they prefer African American," replied Tyrrel, trying to relieve Geoff's evident confusion and discomfort. "It depends upon the individual and how they wish to see themselves."

"It is all about language and semantics. Obviously, there is a part of your country that is trying to control you through the use of words and culture," said René with his arms folded across his chest.

"Well, I am not ashamed of my ancestry. And I am tired of always seeing the bad guys in TV shows being Nazi Germans. You know, not all Germans were Nazis, and I am tired of Irish people always being drunk or fighting," said Lothar.

Kyle was now starting to feel tension in his neck and jaw. He wondered if he would get a headache.

"I'm sorry, guys. I didn't mean to make everyone upset," Kyle said apologetically.

"Who's upset?" said René. "This is the fine tradition of impassioned discussion, which we, the French, are magnificent at. And I am proud of my heritage. You should be proud of yours as well. All of it."

Kyle managed to smile at the cocky French boy's stance on the topic. René even stood proudly and puffed his chest out a bit. And he realized that just because other people may not think his Canadian and Swedish heritage was important or good, he did. He loved both of his parents and realized that he needed to find a way to make the Mexican part of his family like him as well. The things he saw back home in school and on TV were biased against part of his family, which he found unfair. He was not going to allow that attitude to be a part of his life. He would take Dark Cloud's advice and be proud of his ancestry, embracing his newfound love of things Canadian and Swedish. And somehow, he would find a way to incorporate his Mexican heritage as well.

"Hey, guys!" said Trevor, coming over. "It is bedtime, and the lights are supposed to be out. The nighttime 'nursemaid' that trolls the hallways wants us to go to bed."

The boys all looked at their watches or the clock on the wall and immediately responded to Trevor's announcement. They said their good nights and turned out the lights, leaving further discussion for another day. Kyle lay awake in bed, trying to relax so he could drift off to sleep. As he turned onto his side, he realized that someone was standing next to his bed. The thought made his heart jump, and he froze in place as he slowly opened his eyes and peeked at the see-through person who stood near his bed. It was a man dressed in a brown suit, with blonde hair, a mustache, and round wire-framed glasses. The ghostly figure seemed to know that Kyle could see him. The man smiled and nodded at Kyle and then disappeared.

The next morning, Kyle decided to find time to chat with Freya. She was the only one he thought could offer any insight into this situation, besides Dark Cloud, but he was over two thousand miles away, and Kyle wanted to talk in person. He didn't think the man in the brown suit was scary, just surprising, and he wondered if he could communicate with him somehow. Kyle had seen TV shows where people talked with ghosts, but his dad always said those shows were entirely made up, and his mom said they were all devil worshippers. So that left Kyle wondering what was real. He saw the man in a Victorian-era brown suit. He was real. But the question of whether others would believe him or think him crazy bothered him. He liked going to the Academy so much, and he did not want to jeopardize what he had grown to love. He remembered back to third grade in Seattle, where one of the kids claimed to have seen a UFO, which resulted in a lot of teasing and silly nicknames. Kyle didn't want that. He

434

hated the idea of fear holding him back from sharing what he saw.

Breakfast on the first morning back was hectic, with all the students excited about the day ahead. Between the girls taking up every moment of Freya's time and everyone wanting to hear about what happened to René, Kyle could not find any time to speak with her privately.

"The rumor is that you got your arrogant, sorry butt kicked while back in Paris," said Pauline Windgate, unexpectedly to René.

René frowned and straightened up in his seat at the dining table.

"You are misinformed," René said calmly with a steady gaze. "I got my wonderful arrogant *face* bashed while back in Paris."

Pauline pursed her lips slightly.

"I stand corrected. Too bad it did not improve you," she replied and walked off with some of the other Fourth-year girl students, who all seemed very impressed that she should speak to an older student in such a fashion.

The Fabulous Five all looked at each other.

"What the heck was that about?" asked Geoff.

"She's a rude cow," remarked Lothar.

"Certainly not a candidate for Miss Congeniality," said Tyrrel as his eyebrow was still somewhat raised in a Tuvok manner of expression.

"I don't like her," remarked Kyle as he finished drinking his orange juice. "I wish she would go back to where she came from."

"Agreed," said Tyrrel.

"She sounds like a rude BBC correspondent," remarked René.

"And it's not like any of us can hit her. She's a girl," said Lothar.

"Yeah, and fighting is already frowned upon," said Geoff, looking over where Pauline went with her friends. "Why do you think those students like her?"

"I have no idea. She's a female bully," remarked Kyle.

"Maybe she'll learn that she doesn't have to act that way. Maybe her old school was like that," speculated Geoff.

"Well, she will have to change a great deal before I will want her to even stand in my shadow," said Lothar.

"It's almost time for class," said Tyrrel, looking at his watch. "Let's get going. We have more important things to do."

The Fabulous Five made their way to Primary Languages class, where Sir Knight Mary had already prepared the day's lesson well in advance. She and her teacher's assistant were a well-oiled machine that managed the large classroom that was divided into two age groups. The boys would not escape Pauline, but in this classroom, nothing but the best behavior was expected. Sir Knight Mary, like all the instructors, expected good manners and students to follow the code of conduct.

The first part of the Fifth-year students' lesson was to take a test regarding the reading content of *The Secret Garden* by Frances Hodgson Burnett. Kyle was relieved that he had finished the reading and should be able to do well on the test. The test consisted of two parts: a multiple-choice section and a short essay section, which Kyle was not accustomed to. As each student completed the test, Sir Knight Mary accepted their test and ensured they each received the new book that was the required reading. Sometimes these books were in tablet form, while others were loaned out copies. This time, it was a paperback of *Treasure Island* by Robert Louis Stevenson. Kyle smiled and thought it would be more fun to read about pirates than a sad, orphaned girl in England. He was free to find some place to sit and read, which meant he could leave the classroom. He looked for Freya. She was already gone. And so were most of his friends, except Geoff. He was engaged in a battle with his pencil, paper, and eraser.

Kyle decided to find Freya if possible. He quickly walked about and glanced at his watch. The new martial arts class was to begin in fifteen minutes. He decided to head over there in hopes of finding the others hanging about. It was then that he spotted Freya sitting by herself, reading in the Page Level hangout space. She was lounging on the large sofa with a paperback book in her hands.

"Hello, Freya. Do you mind if I bother you?" he asked.

She looked up from her copy of *Treasure Island*. She was already halfway through the book.

"No, I don't mind. How was your winter vacation?" she asked.

"Eventful," he replied. "And that is why I was hoping to talk with you. I think you are the only one who would understand. Since you have special abilities."

Freya made a face and put her fingers over her mouth in a gesture that told him not to talk so loudly.

"We are not supposed to talk about that stuff outside of the special class," replied Freya.

"I'm not in your class. I... uh... had something weird happen. Actually... I had two weird things happen," he replied in more of a whisper.

"Okay," she nodded and said quietly. "We need to make plans to discuss this later and in a safer location."

"Alright," Kyle replied, having a hard time not simply staring at her. "I see you have read far already. Is the story any good?"

"Sure, it's fine if you like pirate stories," replied Freya. "We had better head to the martial arts class." She put her book into a small, colorful satchel and got up.

Kyle got up as well and asked, "Do you know what we will be doing now? I was happy to see the Javelin stuff go away."

Freya laughed as they headed toward the classroom. The Magnusdotter twins joined them.

"What are you two doing?" asked Elsa.

"Heading to class," replied Freya.

"She means... why are you two hanging out together?" clarified Sif.

"We were talking about the new book assignment," replied Kyle. "Freya is already halfway through it."

"She always reads fast," commented Elsa.

The group entered the training area in the gym, where indoor activities were held. There was a cart filled with wire mesh helmets and another with swords. Some of the other students were already waiting there, even though it was still early. The Fabulous Five members finally arrived and joined Kyle.

"What are we doing?!?" asked Geoff, wide-eyed.

"It's fencing! The sport of the gentleman warrior," said René with a flourish as if he already had a blade in his hand.

"I take it that René likes fencing," Kyle said to Lothar, who was smirking.

"Which one of us doesn't? It is one of my favorites," said Lothar.

"So, we fence with the girls? Isn't that unfair?" asked Kyle.

The Magnusdotter twins, who were still in earshot, turned and gave him a stony gaze in stereo.

"As a beginner, I would advise you to hold your tongue when it comes to expressing certain assumptions. Currently, our age group does not have an advantage or disadvantage. That is considered to happen after or during the puberty stage of Human development," said Tyrrel.

"Oh. Okay. I have stepped in dog poop again, haven't I?" replied Kyle.

"You certainly have," said Lothar as he watched the Magnusdotter twins join their friend group, and then the girls would turn and look their way. Then the girls would go and talk to other girls.

"And there you are. You now have a giant bullseye on your chest, my friend," said René, tapping Kyle on the chest several times.

"Terrific," said Kyle, knowing that every girl in the class would be gunning for him.

Once fencing was over for the day and everyone had been assigned their equipment, Kyle could still feel the ire from some of the girls, but it was starting to simmer down. However, for the next week or two, the girls made an extra effort to ensure he knew they were his equal. In most cases, they were his superiors, as he had never done fencing before.

The weekend had arrived, and the snow was starting to melt. The chance to build snowmen or have snowball fights was dissipating rapidly, so the guys decided

440

they wanted to plan one last snowball battle up in Boulder Glade. They had already invited the Fifth-year girls and boys, but they had a holdout.

"He is refusing to go," said Trevor with a frown.

"Come on, Xavier," said Lothar. "We will all be there, including the girls. You will not be alone."

A bunch of the boys had gathered around the couch, hoping to get Xavier to change his mind.

"No. You guys do not understand," said Xavier firmly. "And you will just think I am crazy."

"Well… I sincerely doubt there is a chupacabra on the island, but I do not doubt that you saw something that gave you great concern," remarked Tyrrel. "This happened … how long ago? Your third year here?"

"Yes, it was during the fall of the third year," replied Trevor.

"I bet that creature has long moved on. No one here has seen anything scary on the island, right?" asked Tyrrel, looking around at everyone in the room. He was tall enough to make a quick survey of those standing in the room, who were all shaking their heads in a negative response.

"Xavier, Tyrrel has a point. That was two years ago," added Trevor.

Xavier appeared to be considering what the others were saying. It all made logical sense. But what he saw was not rational. He started to shake his head.

"Guys, what was out there was not normal," he said.

"Well, can you tell us about it?" asked Kyle, now knowing what it was like to see a ghost in his cubicle room, which was not normal.

Xavier sighed.

"How do I know you won't just tease me about what I saw and call me a liar?" retorted Xavier. "I might be better off just staying here and missing the snowball fight."

"What if we all promised… swore an oath like a Knight to not tease you about what you saw?" suggested René.

"I'd be willing to do that," said Kyle.

"So would I," said Geoff as he slowly opened a snack bag of trail mix. "I live near Portland. We see a lot of strange stuff. Saw a naked guy riding his bike on the bridge over the river once during rush hour traffic."

Several of the boys turned to look at him. Geoff nodded to them as he chewed a mouthful of trail mix.

"Alright, but I will only tell those that solemnly promise not to tease me or… share with anyone else what I am about to tell you," said Xavier. "And… I want this promise on paper."

"You want us to sign a contract?!" exclaimed Oliver Cortez. "This is crazy."

"Come on, Oli. We can keep our mouths shut like real Knights," said Kevin O'Dell.

"Pretty sure, the Fabulous Five are willing to sign your knightly gentlemen's agreement. Tyrrel can write something up," said René.

"Oh, thanks for volunteering me," said Tyrrel, rolling his eyes, going off to his room cubicle to get something written up.

Within five minutes, Tyrrel printed out a basic promise not to tease or share what Xavier was going to tell them about on that day. Each boy who was present had to sign his name, which also included Pierre Levesque and Wendell Schultz, who had just walked back into the room after brushing their teeth in the boys' bathroom. They had no real idea what was going on except that they could not tell anyone or tease Xavier about what he was going to share. Trevor made sure the door to the Fifth-year boys' room was closed.

"Alright, I only know part of this story," said Trevor, sitting down next to Xavier.

Xavier looked around to see if everything was secure and that everyone present had signed their name on the piece of paper. He took a deep breath.

"During our third year, there was a photo contest that I wanted to win. The picture could not be Photoshopped. It had to be completely natural, and I wanted to win. My Grandpapa is a professional photographer, and I wanted to impress him. I want to be a photographer like him. He travels all over the world for companies like National Geographic," Xavier began. "And I wanted a picture of the lake with a full moon reflecting upon the water. Trevor agreed to come with me."

"I had nothing better to do. Besides, if I got into trouble, I was pretty sure my parents could buy me out of it," said Trevor.

A couple of the boys rolled their eyes but said nothing, waiting for Xavier to continue his story.

"We slipped out of the room and headed for the outside shoreline area of the island," said Xavier.

"Oh, I remember that," said Kevin O'Dell. "You guys asked me to be the lookout for you."

Trevor and Xavier both nodded.

"I tried taking pictures closer to the school ground, but I could not get a shot with the moon reflecting correctly in the water, so we had to walk up the road farther away. It was very dark except for the fact that we had a full moon to help us walk down the road," said Xavier.

"It was pretty fun to be walking around at that time," remarked Trevor.

"Hey, is he telling the story or you?" asked Lothar, giving Trevor a look.

"Alright. Alright. I will shut up," said Trevor.

"I took some good pictures by the lake's shoreline, but I thought I should try to get some from higher up. The idea of going to the Boulder Glade came to mind, so we found the trail. And it was awful in the dark. The trees blocked the light from the moon. It was really bad, and I ended up falling down several times. Luckily, Trevor brought his flashlight, so we made it up to the Boulder Glade. I managed to take photos from up there. It wasn't easy to climb back then, since I was shorter. We kept hearing strange noises coming from the bushes and tall grasses. You remember that, right?" asked Xavier, turning to Trevor.

"Yes, I remember that. It was rather spooky, as we heard things moving about but never saw anything... until we saw those deer. It was deer foraging out in the glade," replied Trevor.

"Yes, but what I saw was *not* a deer," Xavier slipped back into his defensive mode.

"We understand. Keep telling the story," said Lothar.

"Well, I finished taking the pictures. And Trevor was searching along the edge of the glade with his flashlight for the trail directly back to the school grounds. It was faster. We were also a bit concerned about getting caught. He was starting to get annoyed with me for taking so long, and I was having trouble making my way off the boulders," replied Xavier.

"Oh, I get that. They are easier to climb up on and harder to get off," said Kyle. "Especially when it gets dark."

"When were you out at Boulder Glade in the dark?" asked Geoff.

Kyle just shook his head, not wanting to explain, and gestured to Xavier. Geoff got the idea and shut up.

"At first, I thought it was a deer. It was a dark shadow that emerged from the trees, but it somehow seemed even darker, and it had glowing eyes, which were super creepy. I didn't think deer's eyes glowed like that. And there was something else... It moved strangely, and all the hair on my arms stood up; I felt a chill run up my spine. I wanted to call out to Trevor, but I couldn't say anything. I just watched this thing from behind one of the smaller boulders. I was hiding behind it. And it was coming closer toward the boulders very slowly, like it was stalking. The moonlight did not seem to make it any brighter."

Xavier paused for a moment, rubbing his arms and licking his lips.

"What do you mean, not brighter?" asked Tyrrel.

"I mean... the deer in the open area where the moonlight touched the ground... they looked lighter in color. This thing... did not. It still looked black. And... it looked like a greenish fog was around it," added Xavier.

"A greenish fog? Like smoke?" asked René, who was now completely captivated by Xavier's story.

"Uh, maybe. I was terrified. I felt like my heart was going to pop out of my chest. And there was this awful, heavy smell that made me want to cough, but if I coughed, then it would know I was there. Just like in scary movies, you know. I pulled my shirt over my mouth and nose," Xavier explained.

"How did you get out of there?" asked Kyle.

446

"Luckily, it went after one of the deer," said Xavier. "That's when I was able to catch up to Trevor. I ran as fast as I could."

"Too bad you did not take a picture of it," said René.

"If I did, it would have heard the noise of the camera clicking," said Xavier.

René nodded appreciatively.

"So, what did it look like? Did it look like a weird deer?" asked Geoff.

"It was not a deer, and I am not even sure it walked on four legs like a dog. Um… it seemed to walk… hunched over, and I was not sure… what it was doing. I told a friend from back home in LA, and they said it was a chupacabra," said Xavier.

"So that is where that came from," said Trevor, nodding his head, finally understanding why Xavier would come to that conclusion.

"I don't think anyone has ever seen a chupacabra here," remarked Kevin, making a face. "Maybe we could look up some of the local First Nation stories. Maybe they will have something that matches that description."

"Guys… I never want to see that thing again. I still have nightmares about it," said Xavier.

CHAPTER 19: SNOWBALLS, GHOSTS, AND LAKE MONSTERS

The next morning, everyone in the Fifth-year of the Page Level students had a hearty breakfast, dressed in layers, and tucked snacks into their pockets for a fun snowball battle. Not everyone wanted to get hit with snowballs, so the group was divided into two groups: one building forts and sculptures, and the other engaging in battles. René found it difficult to decide which group he wanted to be a part of, as he liked both activities equally. But his sense of warrior pride drew him toward the conflicts with most of the other boys. Ivy convinced Geoff that he needed to assist them in building the forts, but everyone knew it was to keep him out of harm's way. Believing that the girls sincerely required his help, he cheerfully agreed to build forts and snow sculptures, a few of which he accidentally knocked over.

The morning's fun went well, and Freya found herself wanting to join the boys for a short while in the battle. Hanako was having fun, and she was a good snowball thrower. Freya offered to help her build snowballs and perhaps learn how she managed to be such a good shot. The Japanese girl told her that she simply focused on the task and did it. Freya nodded her head and decided to make snowballs and watch what Hanako was doing. There had to be something that the dark-haired girl was doing that made her so good. Freya watched as Hanako's latest snowball hit Lothar squarely in the back as he tried to duck for cover behind a boulder.

"Do not pack them too tight or too loose… or too big. My hands are small," instructed Hanako.

448

"Why not tight?" asked Freya.

Hanako turned to Freya and replied, "It was agreed before the game started to avoid others getting hurt. I am also told not to aim for the head. Only below the head is a target."

"I see," said Freya as she took more care in how she made the snowballs.

"I have hit Xavier five times now. He is distracted. Kyle is hard to hit. I have not hit him yet," said Hanako. "Watch. It is like he has the senses of a Jedi Master."

Freya watched as Hanako prepared to throw a snowball at Kyle. Kyle was looking around. He tossed his ball and grabbed another. Hanako threw her ball at Kyle, and suddenly, a man in Victorian clothing made Kyle duck. Freya was shocked.

"Did you see that?" she asked Hanako.

"Yes, he ducked just in time," said Hanako. She did not mention the man in the brown suit.

Freya could see the man in the brown suit, who appeared to be from another century. He had a neatly trimmed mustache, wore wire-framed glasses, and was dressed in a bowler hat. He was rather dapper, she thought. She continued to stare, and then he turned and looked right at her. He knew she could see him. Freya quickly ducked down.

"Hey! I am out of snowballs," complained Hanako.

"Oh, sorry," said Freya as she started to make more quickly.

Hanako took one of the balls that had just fallen apart. She looked at Freya and said, "Are you alright? You don't look well."

"Uh… yeah… my stomach feels funny. I might go back to the fort building group," said Freya.

"Okay. Thanks for helping me," Hanako said with a nod and slight body gesture.

"You're welcome," replied Freya as she slipped away from where Hanako was doing her snow battling.

Freya felt her heart pounding as she quickly stole a glance back over to where Kyle was located. She didn't see the man in the brown suit. She looked about and decided to head off into the trees to gather her thoughts. She turned, and there he was, just two meters away. Freya turned away and ran toward where Kyle was hiding in the snowball battle.

"Kyle!" she called out to him, exasperated.

Kyle turned to respond to her and got hit by René, who let out whoops of joy.

"Ow!" exclaimed Kyle as he ducked behind the rock. "Freya, what's up?!"

"There is a strange man in a brown suit hanging around!" she exclaimed.

Kyle's eyes widened.

450

"When you say brown suit… do you mean dress suit like from the old west cowboy times?" asked Kyle.

"Yes!"

"Oh. That is what I wanted to talk to you about. I think he is my spirit guide," replied Kyle. "And he is standing right behind you."

"What?!" Freya exclaimed, turning around to see the rather friendly-looking apparition of a well-dressed gentleman. She grabbed hold of Kyle.

Kyle laughed, feeling both thrilled and amused at the same time.

"I don't think he will hurt you. At least as long as you do nothing bad to me. I think that's how it works. I am not sure. I was hoping to get some advice from you," said Kyle.

"Oh. I see," said Freya with wide eyes, still staring at the ghost. "Uh, how long has he been around?"

"Since I asked Dark Cloud's uncle for some help," replied Kyle. "I had better remove myself from the playing field. Let's go sit somewhere safe and private."

"Good idea. Will he follow us?" asked Freya.

"Probably. He has been keeping an eye on me in the dorm room when I sleep."

"That's kind of creepy," replied Freya.

"Huh. I thought he was being nice and protecting me," replied Kyle.

The ghost nodded his head in agreement. Freya took a deep breath and turned to Kyle.

"Kyle, I am sorry that I did not make time for you. This is extremely important. I will speak with the Special group teacher when we return. Can you communicate with him?"

"I can talk to him, and he seems to understand, but I cannot hear him," replied Kyle.

"Well, the fact that we can both see him is amazing," said Freya.

The ghost pulled out his pocket watch and tapped on it.

"Oh, he needs to rest," said Kyle. "I will see you later, man in the brown suit."

The man seemed to smile and then dissipated. Kyle was about to say something to Freya when they suddenly heard Hanako yelling something in Japanese. They both turned to see Hanako standing on top of one of the boulders that allowed for a view of the lake waters, pointing out to the lake. Several others scrambled atop boulders that still had snow on them to see what she was pointing at. She was still speaking in Japanese quite adamantly. And no one understood her.

"What is going on?" Freya asked Sif and Elsa.

"Hanako... we think she is seeing something important out there?" replied Sif.

"What is she saying?" asked Kyle, following some of the others to get atop the boulders.

"She is repeating the word…saw…chee ho…ko… whatever that means!?" said Lothar from above, looking out at the lake. "Oh! I see it!!!"

"Where?!? What do you see?!" asked Trevor.

"It looks like the lake monster… You know, like Loch Ness," replied Lothar.

"Shachihoko!" exclaimed Hanako, pleased that someone else saw what she was pointing at.

Lothar nodded to her and smiled and repeated, "Saw-chi-ho-ko!"

Now, everyone was trying to scramble up the boulders, even the icy ones, with several students slipping down before they could make it to the top.

"Guys! It looks like it is gone. I don't see it anymore. It's not worth getting hurt for," said Lothar, watching Tyrrel and René trying to navigate to a viewing place.

Tyrrel halted his efforts to climb the smaller boulder in front of him. He frowned and then looked up at Lothar.

"I see. Did anyone manage to take empirical data of the sighting?" asked Tyrrel.

"Uh," Lothar looked at Hanako and everyone else who managed to get on top of the boulders and asked, "Did anyone take a picture?"

Kevin, Sif, and Lucy all turned to Lothar with expressions of remorse, their palms to their foreheads in frustration.

"Nope. None of us thought to take a picture," replied Lothar, feeling a bit stupid. He finally saw something that could have been the creature known as the lake monster. "Sorry, Uncle Kurt... I could have gotten proof for you." Lothar turned to his cousin, who stood below on the ground.

"Hey, Freya, I guess your dad was right," he yelled down.

"I know," she replied.

A couple of days after the big lake monster sighting, everyone was still chatting about what they thought the creature truly was and where it came from. Hanako and Lothar were pressed into drawing pictures of what they thought they saw, which had mixed results.

"That is a terrible picture. And that is what you saw. That could be anything," remarked Trevor to Lothar. "At least Hanako's picture is more interesting."

"Yes, but she got to see it more than I did," retorted Lothar, feeling frustrated. "And I am trying to document what I saw... not embellish it."

"Well, at least you got to see it. That is cool," said Geoff.

"Yeah... it looks sorta like what I thought I saw earlier in the year," said Kyle, looking at the drawing. "It's hard to tell if it is a log in the water or an upside-down boat."

"I would suspect a boat would have sunk by now," added Tyrrel.

Freya came over to where the boys were relaxing and asked Kyle to speak with her. Kyle was always eager to spend time with Freya.

"What's up?" asked Kyle.

"It's time that I introduce you to the Special Abilities teachers," said Freya. "Come with me."

"Okay," said Kyle.

"Hey, Kyle, where are you going?" asked Geoff.

Kyle froze, unsure of what to say to Geoff, as he knew it was an invitation-only meeting.

"Uh," said Kyle.

"Kyle agreed to help me with something. He'll be gone for only a few minutes," replied Freya firmly. She then took Kyle by the arm and led him away, and he did not resist.

Geoff watched them go with a slight frown and then headed back to sit with the guys.

Kyle followed Freya to a different part of the school where the older students were located. They wove through a series of hallways with many closed doors. Many of the doors had labels, such as "Clean Room" and "Cybernetics

Lab." The door they stopped at was labeled "Special." Kyle thought that was curious.

"Strange name," commented Kyle.

"Well, they are not going to call it *Paraphysical Training*, are they? It is currently kept somewhat secret since they are unsure how regular people will react to us," replied Freya, tapping in a key code and unlocking the door.

It was at that point that Kyle realized most of the doors in this hallway had high-tech locking systems, just like those found in a James Bond film. Images of sterile high-tech scientific equipment and gleaming white walls came to mind, with chrome-coated devices. He was impressed and a little nervous about what he would find on the other side of the door. It was nothing like he expected.

The room had a large, cozy stone fireplace, a large picture window with a view of the gardens, a skylight above, numerous pictures and paintings of beautiful places, soft, comfortable furniture to sit upon, a stereo system, drawing tablets, candles, blankets, and a small kitchenette. It looked like a great place to hang out. Waiting for them inside were Sir Knight Greta, Sir Knight Anthony, and Sir Knight Wolfram. Kyle recognized them all, but was less familiar with Sir Knight Anthony, who oversaw the senior Squire Level students.

"Come in and take a seat, Kyle," said Sir Knight Wolfram cheerfully as he invited him in.

Kyle liked Sir Knight Wolfram. The slightly balding, heavy-set man with the big mustache was easy to talk with, and Kyle always felt as if he could go to him for help if he ever needed anything. Sir Knight Greta made him nervous, and he was unfamiliar with Sir Knight Anthony. Kyle took a seat as instructed near the instructors while Freya politely sat off to the side.

"So, what has Freya told you about this group?" asked Sir Knight Wolfram.

"Uh… very little because she said it was secret. And that it was to help students with unusual abilities," replied Kyle, worrying that he would get Freya in trouble. "I told no one."

Sir Knight Wolfram smiled.

"Freya is not going to get into trouble," he assured Kyle.

"Yeah, I would not want that. She was trying to help me," said Kyle.

"We understand that," said Sir Knight Greta.

"Please tell us about what brought you here," said Sir Knight Anthony.

"You mean the ghost… or spirit guide?" asked Kyle.

"Exactly. How did you realize this… spirit guide was around?" asked Sir Knight Wolfram.

"Well, he seemed to turn up after I went with my friend Dark Cloud to meditate on ancestors with his uncle, who is training to become a shaman," Kyle answered.

The three Knights looked at each other without saying anything, and then Sir Knight Greta concluded, "He opened himself up to the unseen world by participating in a ritual. Luckily, it was done by a reputable person."

"And this must have attracted the attention of the ghost," said Sir Knight Wolfram.

"The next question would be, is this just some random ghost that has latched onto Kyle, or does he have a purpose?" said Sir Knight Anthony.

"Oh, I think he has a purpose. I drew a picture of him. Freya saw him too," said Kyle.

"Well, that is helpful," said Wolfram. "Can you talk to this ghost?"

"I cannot talk with the man in the brown suit, but I think he understands me. When he needs to rest, he gestures to his pocket watch," said Kyle.

"Extraordinary," said Sir Knight Greta. "You have already developed a strong connection with this entity. What is his demeanor?"

"His what?" asked Kyle.

"He seems friendly," replied Freya.

"Yes, I would agree with that. Sometimes he watches over me at night," said Kyle. "He doesn't make me feel afraid."

"Like a guardian angel type," said Sir Knight Anthony.

"He doesn't have wings or a halo. He wears a brown suit, hat, wire-framed glasses, carries a pocket watch in his vest pocket, and a mustache a little like Sir Knight Wolfram's... except much smaller," said Kyle.

Sir Knight Anthony looked amused by Kyle's observation.

"Sounds like a stylish individual," said Anthony.

"Indeed," said Greta. "I wonder if there is a purpose to such detail."

"How often do you see this man in the brown suit?" asked Wolfram.

"Almost every day," said Kyle. "Sometimes I get busy with the guys, and I forget about him, but he doesn't seem to mind."

At this point, Sir Knight Wolfram seemed to be preoccupied by something and was nodding to Kyle. The man closed his eyes for a few moments and then said, "I am getting the impression of something here... that is benign." Sir Wolfram looked up at Kyle and then said, "We'd like to work with you in perfecting your skills. Would you be interested in that?"

"My skills?" asked Kyle.

"Yes. You possess the paraphysical skill of being able to perceive ghosts, and perhaps we can help you learn how to communicate with them more effectively. At least that way, it won't become a problem. Sometimes, when ghosts discover that someone has the ability to communicate with them, they become excited and start bothering the living person. They do not necessarily mean to be obnoxious, but sometimes they lack patience. Training helps one function better with paraphysical skills," explained Wolfram.

"Oh. Yeah, I guess. That sounds like a good idea," said Kyle. "We are not going to tell my mom, right? Because she would disapprove of that."

The three Knights looked at each other with some concern.

"We usually do not keep secrets from students' parents," said Sir Knight Greta.

"She might take me out of the school, and I do not want to leave. I love going to school here," said Kyle.

"Perhaps your father?" suggested Sir Knight Anthony.

"He does not believe in that kind of stuff," said Kyle.

"Alright. I think the three of us need to discuss some options, and we will get back to this later," said Sir Knight Greta. "In the meantime, I want you to be able to work with Sir Knight Wolfram if something becomes upsetting."

"Yes, ma'am," said Kyle. "I understand."

"We cannot include you in the class without a guardian's approval, but you can come to me anytime if you have a problem. We need to keep things quiet for the reasons that young Freya here has already told you. And I am granting Freya the freedom to discuss such things with you. But no one else… understand?" said Sir Knight Wolfram, looking at Freya and Kyle.

"Yes, sir," said Freya.

Kyle nodded, feeling glad that at least he could talk to someone if he needed help. He wondered if he could find a way to get his dad to understand. He seemed the most likely to give his consent.

Chapter 20: The Costume Prize Trip

All the winners of the costume event were excited to learn that they would be treated to five days in downtown Toronto, seeing three live performances in the theaters, plus a tour of a historical theater building. Kyle had never attended a live theater performance and was unsure what to expect.

"Your parents never brought you to a live performance?! That is outrageous! What kind of parents do you have?" exclaimed René, getting up from the soft couch in the common area of the dorm room.

"René, not everyone comes from a family that appreciates the arts as much as yours does," Tyrrel tried to smooth over any hurt feelings.

"They never had any time," explained Kyle.

"Live theater is also expensive," added Geoff. "And... I am looking forward to this. My parents didn't take us to many things either, because it usually meant going into Portland. My parents always said that Portland was a crazy place where radical cyclists would terrorize the car drivers, and the city was organized poorly. It's a bit unfortunate, since there are many cool places to visit in Portland. My favorite was Voodoo Doughnut, but my sister prefers the Japanese Gardens and the Pittock Mansion. She keeps thinking there should be ghosts there. The road there is scary narrow, winding, and it nearly made me barf. Good thing I was sitting in the front seat."

462

Geoff stopped and realized the others were staring at him. "What?!"

"You are rambling," retorted René.

Geoff made a face and scrunched up his eyebrows. He then adjusted his glasses.

"How did you survive your previous school?" asked Lothar.

"I went to a private charter school in Vancouver," replied Geoff, not entirely realizing what Lothar was asking.

"Guys… this should be a lot of fun. Do I need to be prepared for anything?" asked Kyle.

"No. Just go and have fun… and don't let the older kids kill Geoff for rambling," René said the last part privately to Kyle.

Kyle nodded. He knew Geoff could get overly excited about stuff and talk too much.

"Hey, don't forget I will be there too. I have been to quite a few shows myself over the years," added Lothar, feeling a little ignored.

"They did have movie theaters where you come from, right?" René asked Kyle.

Kyle rolled his eyes in exasperation, "Yes, of course we have movie places where I come from, and yes, I have seen movies in the theater."

"When are you leaving?" asked Tyrrel.

"We are departing this Friday," replied Trevor as he walked across the common area of the Fifth-year boys' room.

"That is tomorrow. Better make sure you have enough clean clothes to take with you," suggested Tyrrel.

"Oh, good idea," said Kyle, turning to go into his bedroom cubicle.

"I had not thought of that," said Geoff glumly. "I also need to make sure I have a few provisions just in case."

The guys watched them go, then turned to Lothar.

"I'm already packed. With everything I need," he replied with a confident grin, a touch of sarcasm, and a sense that no one seemed to be concerned about him.

The next morning could not come quickly enough for the eager field trip winners. Everyone had their bags ready and boarded the big ferry boat to go ashore. Two large passenger vans were waiting to transport the seventeen travelers to Toronto. The two drivers would also be treated to rooms and show tickets as part of the fee arranged by the school. All the Page Level students would ride together with Sir Knight Lesley Alborough, and both Squire Levels would ride with Sir Knight Anthony. Geoff tried to persuade Sir Knight Lesley to let him sit up front because of his car sickness, but she convinced him he would be happier in the first row, where he could chat with his classmates. This, he finally agreed to. Kyle had hoped to sit next to Freya, but Trevor managed to sit next to her and Elsa. Ivy sat in the first row to visit with Geoff, so Sif sat with Lothar and Kyle. The hour-and-a-half trip went smoothly with lots of chatter in the Page Level van. It got so loud a couple of times that Sir Knight Lesley had to ask the kids to lower the volume of their chatter. She had a reputation for being kind but could also be stern when necessary. She was not the kind of person to be messed with. If you treat her well, she will treat you well.

Once they arrived at the Holiday Express hotel in downtown Toronto, the students waited in the lobby, chatting while the adults dealt with reservations and check-in procedures. This was the first time, besides the Halloween costume contest, that Kyle found himself in the company of the older students. Akira Nakamura, Bradley Livingston, and Alistair Grennan were busy eyeing some pretty girls who were part of another tour group of students their age. Kyle listened to their comments and realized they were just as nervous as he was about the fairer sex. Apparently, reaching the sixth and seventh years did not make one instantly confident around girls. The older boys always seemed to know what they were doing, but that was an illusion. Kyle's unplanned education about girls came to an end when the Fifth-year boys headed up with their bags to their assigned room. When they were settled in, they were to gather downstairs for lunch and be ready for the tour of the Elgin & Winter Garden Theatre.

"Neat room," commented Geoff, dropping his bag on one of the beds.

"It's alright. I have seen better," remarked Trevor appraisingly. "There are only two beds. I suppose we'll

465

have to share. I am taking this one. Kyle, you and Geoff take that one, and Lothar will share with me."

"Who died and made him boss?" murmured Geoff, picking up the side of the bed with the nightstand. "Kyle, I need this side for my glasses to be within arm's reach. I hope that is okay with you."

"I am fine with that," shrugged Kyle as he walked over to the window to look out at the view. The room was on the twelfth floor. He could see a park not far away and the tall spire of a church, which looked like one of the ornate churches with elegant architecture. He felt that this trip should be fun, with so many new and exciting things to see. And he was with friends.

"Hey, Kyle, are you gonna unpack?" asked Geoff.

"Not really. I'll just put my stuff on the desk and leave it in my suitcase," replied Kyle, still thinking about the view.

Trevor already had his items stowed away along with Lothar and Geoff. They headed downstairs after deciding who would hold onto the keys. Trevor insisted that he have one of the cards, and Lothar agreed to be the caretaker of the second keycard. Having Trevor in the mix was a different experience. It was as if he were accustomed to having everything his way. Kyle wondered if Xavier agreed to that. Downstairs in the lobby, the entire group from the Academy gathered with Sir Knight Anthony and Sir Knight Lesley. First, the group would have a quick lunch at a local burger shop and then head over to the Elgin & Winter Garden Theatres for the arranged tour. The unique and historical theaters were a special kind, where one theater was constructed on top of another. Kyle had his camera with him to take photos and share with his family. He also took pictures of himself and the guys having a great time, making sure a few of them included Freya.

The theaters were lovely, and Kyle marveled at their grandeur and the intricate decorations inside. It felt like a cathedral. One of the older students, Gaston Cochrane, was especially excited about the theater. When they walked upon the stage, he ventured to sing a few lyrics of some song he knew, and his voice rang out beautifully. The tall, lean male from Antigua had a clear, sonorous voice. His skin was dark brown, and he had dark curly black hair trimmed short, much in the fashion of Tyrrel's. But they were nothing alike. Kyle had learned from the others that Gaston planned to become a teacher of the fine arts. He spoke with a strong accent, which Kyle found hard to understand at times.

"Which costume was his?" asked Geoff.

"He was dressed as the original version of the Cylon from Battlestar Galactica. I wish I could have made my Iron Man as good as his Cylon," replied Trevor.

"Oh yes, I remember that one. Pretty cool," said Kyle as he took a couple of pictures from the stage.

"Gaston, you should be on the stage as a performer and not as a guest," commented Vikki Carter. She was one of the Tenth-year students who won with the ghost costumes. "I love how your voice sounds from this stage."

A couple of the other students nodded in agreement. Gaston bashfully smiled and shook his head in appreciation of their kind words.

"Can you sing something else?" asked Marie Brendelhower, who was standing next to her friend, Vikki.

"Uh, sure. What would you like?" replied Gaston.

"How about something from *Cats*?" suggested Vikki.

"Oh yes," agreed Marie.

"Alright. I know some of the lyrics to *'Memory.'* Give me a moment to collect myself," said Gaston, and then he began to sing. *"Memory... Turn your face to the moonlight... Let your memory lead you..."*

"Wow, that sounds amazing," said Ivy. "He should be on the stage."

Geoff nodded in agreement.

Several of the older students applauded him, and Gaston seemed both embarrassed and appreciative of the accolades.

The tour also took them up to the Winter Garden Theater, which was decorated to resemble a giant tree canopy. The walls were also painted to create the illusion of a lovely forest.

"Kyle, take a picture of me with Lothar so that I can send it back to our families," requested Freya as she marveled at how pretty the upstairs theater was. "Too bad we don't get to see anything here."

"Yeah, why is that?" asked Sif, looking at Elsa, who was thinking the same thing.

Sir Knight Lesley overheard and replied, "Because we were too late to get the tickets for a show here, so we opted for the tour, which they were nice enough to schedule for us."

"Oh," said the twins in unison.

"This place is magical," said Ivy, smiling and spinning like a dancer. "It must be wonderful to see a show here. It must be incredible to perform here."

"Probably," replied Geoff. "But I think they need more concession stands or at least vending machines. What if someone were to need a snack?"

"Here," said Kyle, offering Geoff a candy bar that he had in his jacket pocket.

"Oh, sweet! Thank you," said Geoff, opening the wrapper immediately.

It was time to move on to the next room, and then the two-hour-long tour was over. The theater's technicians needed to prepare for the upcoming show that evening, so all guests were asked to leave the premises. Everyone piled into their assigned vans and was driven to an upscale restaurant in the downtown section, where one of the former students had become the head chef of his own restaurant. He wanted to treat the students to a special meal, demonstrating that with hard work toward a goal, they could achieve their dreams. The students were thrilled to be treated to a Gordon Ramsay-style meal.

Geoff was in heaven. When the group arrived back at the hotel for the evening, everyone was very full.

"Oh... my... god... I think I am actually full!" exclaimed Geoff.

"That was excellent food. I don't think I have ever eaten a six-course meal before," remarked Kyle, and he flopped down on the bed. "I just might die."

"This trip has started better than the last one that Freya and I went on," commented Lothar.

Trevor sighed as he stood next to his side of the bed.

"I have had many meals like that before. My parents like fine dining and entertain many important people," said Trevor. "I will have to tell them about Lazy Dog Bistro. I think they would be impressed. And it would be nice to support a fellow Academy graduate," added Trevor as he removed his sweater and placed it upon his suitcase.

"Your parents have a lot of money," commented Geoff.

"Yes. But it's not as fun as it may sound at times. Sure, I have whatever I want, but I'm expected to look and act in a certain way. And... well... family outside of my parents also expect certain things. Most of them are not Knights and... they can be... very money-oriented," said Trevor.

Kyle and Lothar exchanged glances. This was a side of Trevor that none of them had seen before.

"I get that. I have some weird relatives, too. Some of them think my family is odd, but I try not to let it bother me. I mean… what can you do about strange relatives?" said Geoff.

"Not a whole lot," replied Lothar to Geoff as he watched Trevor continue to fold all his clothes neatly in silence.

"So, what are we doing tomorrow?" asked Kyle.

"I think we are going to the… Princess Alexandra Theater to see *RAIN: A tribute to the Beatles*," answered Lothar.

"That should be fun and uplifting," said Trevor.

"The Beatles… I think my dad liked them, but he used to say he preferred the early music to the later stuff. Something about them being happier when they first started," said Kyle, trying to recall.

"They wrote good music, too bad that they can no longer perform together," commented Trevor.

"Why is that?" asked Geoff.

"Because two of them are dead," replied Lothar.

"Oh," said Geoff. "That *is* too bad. So… how are we hearing their music?"

"There is a group called Rain that works to perform Beatles' music like the original band members. My dad said he saw them some time ago and said he enjoyed the concert," replied Trevor.

"Neat," said Geoff. "Is anyone else feeling tired?"

Just then, there was a loud knock on the door. Lothar got up to see who it was. It was Sir Knight Lesley, so he opened the door.

"Hi, guys. Just checking up on you all," she said, entering the room, making sure all four boys were present. "Breakfast is served downstairs in the lobby with a variety of items. Be sure to get going early. We are scheduled to attend the matinee show. I want everyone to be showered and neatly dressed. Remember, we represent the Academy while on this trip. So... don't stay up too late. Okay?"

A chorus of yes could be heard from the boys.

"Sleep well, and if you have any problems, I am in the room across the hallway from yours," she said with a smile. "Goodnight."

"Goodnight," several of the boys replied to her.

Lothar locked the door.

The next morning, Lothar, Geoff, and Kyle all woke up to the sound of Trevor already in the shower.

"Damn! Does he always get up that early?" asked Kyle, scratching his head.

Lothar yawned loudly and finally replied, "Yup. He has always been that way."

The next three days flew by with three shows in two different fantastic theaters. After watching The Heart of Robin Hood, the group engaged in lots of pretend sword and archery play, with all the girls eager to be the new version of Maid Marion. The final performance they saw was at the Prince of Wales Theatre, where they watched *The Lion King*, which also inspired the Fifth-year group, all of whom mimicked parts of the performance. The trip went very well, and it was their last night in the Holiday Inn room with a view of the city. Kyle was having trouble falling asleep. So many thoughts were going through his head. Geoff was already fast asleep next to him, and it appeared that Lothar and Trevor had also fallen asleep. Lying in bed, he could faintly hear an emergency vehicle siren going off somewhere down below. Other than that, it was quiet. His thoughts strayed to Freya. She was so lovely. He loved her red hair and freckles. Did freckles go away, he wondered. He could not recall seeing any pictures of older women with freckles. He liked her freckles. She was perfect. And she seemed to like him, too. Life was so different, he thought. He was so happy. Then a stray thought hit him. He was happy, but his parents did not seem to be. The feeling was perplexing and sad. The joy seemed to ebb away from him as he thought about life with them.

It was then that the man in the brown suit appeared and seemed to sit down on the side of the bed next to him. Kyle was surprised to see him. The air was a little colder now. The man in the brown suit looked concerned and shook his head.

"I was happy until I thought about how sad my parents are," Kyle whispered to the man in the brown suit.

The ghost nodded and adjusted his glasses in contemplation. He then looked at Kyle and mouthed the

473

inaudible words, "Not your fault." He then pulled out his pocket watch from his fancy vest pocket, tapped it, made a sleepy gesture with his hands and head, and finally pointed to Kyle. Kyle understood that the ghost wanted him to go to sleep.

Kyle nodded, suddenly feeling more tired, and drifted off to blissful unconsciousness.

The trip back to Lake Simcoe was spent reliving the enjoyable moments and experiences from the journey. They laughed at some of the goofy photos taken by Kyle. This also included the older students, with whom the younger group had now formed a bond. It now felt like they had a deeper connection with Alistair Grennan, Akira Nakamura, Brad Livingston, Aeneas Georgiou, Marie Brendelhower, Vikki Carter, Anthony Accardo, and Gaston Cochrane. They now shared something special with these older students, and when they saw each other in the hallways or at mealtimes, they acknowledged one another.

CHAPTER 21: LEAVING EARLY FOR SPRING BREAK IN TEXAS

Time passed quickly, and much to Kyle's sorrow, the fencing class was over. He loved learning how to parry, riposte, and lunge. The challenge of the sport was inspiring. He hoped that next year he would prove himself good enough to be invited to the school tournament. He still had a lot to learn. And now it was time to learn the basics of Kung Fu. He started to enjoy fencing after the girls finally understood that he didn't mean anything bad by the comments he had made on the first day of class. Afterwards, they seemed to be joking with him rather than being angry. It had become a game. But learning the basics of Kung Fu was not as fun, in his opinion, even though he agreed it would be more useful than fencing in everyday life. Everything had returned to normal after a couple of weeks had passed since the trip to Toronto, with the freshness of the excitement over. It was now a fond memory. New reading assignments had started, along with more language tests. Geoff and Kyle had hoped to be allowed to learn French with the Third-year students. Preparations for spring had begun.

It was just after the day's classes were over that Sir Knight Wolfram asked Kyle to speak with him privately in his office. The rest of the Fabulous Five gestured to him that they were heading to their dorm room and would be down for dinner afterwards. Kyle nodded and then followed Sir Knight Wolfram.

"So, I hear you had a splendid trip to Toronto," said the man, making small talk.

"It was a lot of fun. I got to see a bunch of new places I had never seen before. Live theater is great," remarked Kyle. "I had a great time."

"Good, good. That's the point of these trips: to help broaden the horizons of our students and reward them for a job well done. I am glad that you enjoyed it," said the Knight as he ushered Kyle into his office and closed the door. After the door was shut, the man turned to Kyle. "But I did not bring you here to chat about theater. This concerns the Special Class for which you should be enrolled. I looked through your records."

Kyle nodded and listened, wondering where this was going.

"According to the documents, your grandparents also have the right to make decisions for you as well as your parents. And since you were uncomfortable about addressing the topic to your parents, what about Karl and Lily Bergendahl?" asked Wolfram. "Your grandmother was a student of the Academy, so she knows what education here is like."

Kyle thought about this for a moment. His grandparents took an active interest in what he was doing. He trusted them. If they made a decision, it would not be based on an angry, religious attitude that didn't make sense to him, nor would it be due to being closed-minded about unusual things. And they truly seemed to be concerned about his well-being. He knew he was being unfair to his parents. They were both busy, but... he felt like he should matter more. Perhaps they didn't have time for him. He turned and looked up at Sir Knight Wolfram, who was waiting patiently for his response.

"Sir Wolfram, I think I would be fine if you told my grandparents and let them decide," Kyle finally answered.

Sir Knight Wolfram nodded and gave Kyle a reassuring smile.

"Okay. I will do that. I also need a bit more information on this man in the brown suit. It is essential for us to have an understanding of where he may have come from and why he wants to be around you. Can you give me a description of him?" asked Sir Knight Wolfram as he sat down at his computer.

"Sure," said Kyle. "What do you want me to tell you?"

"Everything. When did he show up? Where were you? How does he make you feel? Is it always the same? What does he look like? Does he do anything special?" asked Sir Knight Wolfram.

Kyle took a deep breath and started to think about where to begin.

"I can explain or describe all of that," said Kyle, starting to think. "He first showed up in Nevada. I was in the mountains with my friend Dark Cloud and his uncle. We were talking about being more connected with our ancestors." Kyle paused, trying to recall things. "He usually wears a brown suit like you see in old pictures of the West, but not the gunslinger style. He seems… respectable and proper, if that makes any sense. He wears

477

wire-framed glasses and a mustache, somewhat like yours, but smaller and less bushy. His hair is a light color. He often wears a bowler hat, and he carries a pocket watch in his vest pocket. He uses it to communicate with me. Like… to tell me that he needs rest or that it's late, and I should go to sleep. I have even seen him in one of those university professor-type robes. You know the long ones."

Wolfram nodded to Kyle as he took notes and typed them on the computer.

Kyle proceeded to retell all the times he had seen the man in the brown suit and how it made him feel. When he was done, Sir Knight Wolfram asked Kyle if he would sit down with one of the older students who was studying drawing and anatomy. The student was considering a career as a police sketch artist. He wanted Kyle to work with the student to help get a picture drawn of the man in the brown suit. Kyle thought this would be interesting and agreed to meet with the older student to do the drawing.

In the springtime, another break was scheduled for students to spend time with their families for the various religious observances held during this time of year. Most students seemed excited about visiting their families. Kyle was scheduled to stay at his grandparents' house, and his father promised to come and visit for a whole week. He was also assured that he could have Lothar come over and go horseback riding at least one day. René was going to stay with his parents in Montreal since his mother was making a film in the area. Geoff and Tyrrel both headed back home to see their families and planned another flight together. It was a week before everyone was to head off

478

for break, and projects were due, while others were being scheduled for completion over the break. Sir Knight Mary had issued everyone a new book to read during their vacation. Some students were surprised to see *Harry Potter and the Sorcerer's Stone* by J.K. Rowling being assigned as reading material.

"Well, I have seen the movies; this should be easy," commented Oliver Cortez a little too loudly. "Why are we reading this?"

Sir Knight Mary adjusted her glasses and eyed him.

"Stupid move, big mouth," commented Trevor, with Xavier snickering.

Sir Knight Mary stood up and addressed the class while they were still busy writing in their journals.

"Often movies are inspired by books, but seldom do they follow exactly the details within the text. Since Mr. Cortez had brought up the fact that *The Sorcerer's Stone* was turned into a movie," she paused and eyed all the students in the class who were now looking up at her. "How many of you have seen the movie *Harry Potter and the Sorcerer's Stone*?"

All the students raised their hands.

"Good. One of the first tasks that you will be required to note is the differences between the movie and the book. I expect these observations written up and handed to me upon your arrival after the spring break period has concluded," said Sir Knight Mary.

Kyle could sense the collective tension and annoyance that filled the classroom. He turned and looked at Geoff, who was looking frustrated, and Freya, who just rolled her eyes in disgust. René looked like he was holding back French swear words. Only Tyrrel looked as if it did not bother him in the slightest. All Kyle could think about was that the book was huge. He wondered if he would be able to read it all and make notes at the same time.

When class was over, several people made disparaging remarks to Oliver, who just shrugged his shoulders.

"How was I supposed to know that she would hear me?" said Oliver.

"She has always had good hearing," remarked Lothar.

"And I thought I was going to be able to enjoy my holiday with my family," chided Ivy as she walked by, looking very annoyed.

"I guess we all make mistakes," said Kevin O'Dell.

"Just usually not that bad," remarked René.

"Hey, you get into hot water all the time, René," retorted Oliver. "Remember the horse thing."

"Yes, but my mistakes are more interesting and grander. Yours are... just mundane stupidity," René replied, swishing his long hair back with a toss of his head.

Kyle rubbed his face in exasperation and murmured, "How am I going to get through all this? I had

480

to work really hard at getting *The Secret Garden* read over winter break."

"Don't worry," said Freya, overhearing. "I can help you with the notes if you don't get through it all."

Kyle looked over to see her kind and hopeful face.

"Thanks, Freya," he replied. "You are a lifesaver."

"I'm looking for Kyle Bergendahl!" said a loud adult voice in the hallway.

Kyle's eyes widened. For a moment, he wondered if he was in trouble for cheating by getting help from Freya. However, that had not yet transpired. He wondered why an adult was asking for him.

"He's just behind me," said Tyrrel.

Sir Knight Wolfram made his way through the students, leaving the language classroom. The normally jovial instructor looked concerned. His mustache twitched a little in agitation. When he found Kyle, he seemed a little out of breath.

"Kyle, I need you to come with me right away. There is a family emergency," said Sir Knight Wolfram, leading Kyle down a different direction toward where the main offices of the school were located. The remaining Fabulous Five, along with Freya and several other Fifth-year girls, paused to watch them leave. They all heard the words… *'family emergency*.'

"That is never a good thing to hear," said Ivy, making a face.

481

The others nodded in agreement with concern.

"I hope he will be okay," said Geoff, watching Sir Knight Wolfram and Kyle disappear around a corner.

Kyle could feel his heart pounding in his chest as he kept pace with the round yet robust Knight that led him into the main offices, where Lily Bergendahl was standing. She looked stately, dressed in a pale pink skirted suit. Kyle was relieved to see her, yet she looked concerned.

"Grandma... what's wrong?" asked Kyle.

Lily Bergendahl took a deep breath and then calmly replied, "Your... other grandmother has passed away. And your mother needs you. I am taking you to meet her in Texas."

Kyle was hit with the enormity of the situation. He was silent for a few moments. It was like his brain could not believe what he was being told. A strange sensation coursed through his body, making his tear ducts well with fluid.

He looked up at her and said, "Grandma Sarah is... gone?"

Lily nodded her head solemnly.

Thousands of images and thoughts assailed him. She was nice to him. She was the one who tried to make him feel okay when he had visited the Texas portion of the family. Why did she have to go away? The idea almost seemed unreal, as if people dying only happened in movies and books. He felt odd as he tried to understand the reality of the situation.

"What… happened?" asked Kyle. "I didn't think she was sick… or even old enough to die. You are supposed to be very old… before you die," he said. Tears started welling up in his eyes and cascading down his cheeks.

Lily wrapped her arms around him. Her perfume smelled soft and soothing to him as she held him. Time seemed to flow strangely, and it had been long enough that his four friends discovered what had happened. They helped one of the school assistants get his coat, pack his backpack, and a small suitcase for the trip. Lily handed him a handkerchief to wipe his eyes and blow his nose with. His head hurt, and his ears were ringing. Before he knew it, he was sitting in the backseat of the BMW, and Jasper was driving them somewhere. He didn't recall getting into the car. At some point, he fell asleep. When they arrived at the airport, everything seemed to blur, and he mindlessly followed his grandmother, doing as she told him. The plane ride was supposed to be three and a half hours, and Kyle found himself wide awake, unsure what to do with himself. His bag had been checked, but he still had access to his backpack and coat. He opened the zipper to the main compartment of his backpack. Inside, he found a copy of the first Harry Potter novel. He did not remember putting it in there. He didn't remember anything at all. He couldn't even remember where his grandparents lived. It was just somewhere between Houston and Austin. When they arrived, it was raining in Houston. They had to go through customs to get his bag. It was on the other side of customs that Lily spotted Marie waiting for them. Marie was noticeably upset, but she was pleased to see Kyle and

Lily making their way toward her. Kyle ran up and gave his mother a big, long hug.

"Oh, Marie, I am so sorry," said his grandmother's voice. "Please call me if there is anything that I can do to help you."

Once again, time seemed to be disjointed, and before Kyle knew it, he was in a car with his mom, driving away from the airport. He could barely remember saying goodbye to his grandma. His living grandma… The rain was coming down, and his mom seemed odd. He did not know what to say to her.

"Mom, I am so sorry that Grandma Sarah died. What happened? No one told me what happened to her," said Kyle, frowning and trying to recall if they had, but he did not remember. "I did not know she was even sick."

"Sweetheart, your grandma died in a car accident. Something happened with the tires on her car, and she crashed," replied his mom with tears rolling down her cheeks as she tried to stay focused on the road. "So, she was not sick. It was an accident."

"Oh," replied Kyle.

"Are you hungry?" she asked.

"A little… yeah," he replied.

"We have a long drive ahead of us, so we will stop at the first place that looks good. Do you want something like a burger?" she asked.

"Sure. How long is the drive?" asked Kyle as the wiper blades flipped back and forth almost hypnotically.

"Two hours. Maybe you can find some nice music on the radio," said Marie.

"Okay," replied Kyle as he searched through the different radio stations, trying to find something he liked and something he could understand. Several stations were all in Spanish.

The rain continued to fall during the entire car trip, and the sound of the wiper blades made Kyle feel sleepy. They found a burger shop and a gas station in a small town and then headed off again into the strange landscape, which was remarkably flat. When they arrived at the family ranch property, it was evening, and there wasn't much to see. They were greeted warmly by Juan Gomez, Kyle's grandfather. He looked very sad but tried to be cheerful for them. He looked exhausted.

Grandpa Juan, or Abuelo Juan, hugged his daughter warmly and looked as if he was doing everything he could to fight the grief from overwhelming him.

"The rest of the familia will join us tomorrow," he said with his very thick accent. "Mi querida hija… you can have your old room, and Kyle can sleep in Alvaro's room. Antonio is coming with his wife and children. We may need to move everyone around again tomorrow night. The others have not said if they are staying in the house. I still have the motor home that a few could sleep in," said Abuelo Juan, trying to stay focused on taking care of his family.

"Oh, Papa, I am so sorry. This seems so wrong," said Marie, hugging her father.

"I know, I know. I can barely believe that she won't come through that door smiling, with bags full of flowers and groceries to make a big meal. She loved cooking and baking. She... was my everything," he replied sadly.

Kyle found it difficult to hold back tears.

"Everyone comes tomorrow. The phone has been ringing. So many kind people who loved your madre so much have called me or come over. They give me warm hugs. Many are bringing food and flowers tomorrow for her life celebration. And Father Andrew was so kind as to help with arrangements for the mass. Alvaro has been working with the father to make sure it will be something your madre would like," said Juan Gomez, shaking his head with emotions pulling him in several directions. He was so proud of his youngest son for stepping in and taking charge of the difficult decisions. "Do you and Kyle need anything to eat?"

"No, Papa. We already ate and are just fine. Do you want me to make you some hot tea?" asked Marie.

"No... well... that might be nice," he finally said.

Marie hugged her father again, took off her jacket, and handed it to Kyle.

"Please put my coat in the bedroom on the left, and could you bring in the rest of the bags for me?" she asked Kyle, offering him the car keys.

486

"Sure, Mom. I can do that," he replied, feeling that at least he could do something to help. It was strange to see his Abuelo Juan so upset. The man was usually so very quiet. At least that was what Kyle recalled from two years ago.

He stepped out into the rain and quickly retrieved the bags from the hatchback. They were awkward and heavy, and it was dark out, but he was determined to get this done for his mom. She needed his help. Kyle made a conscious effort to be a helpful son. He came back into the house with soaking wet hair, and his mom didn't notice. Usually, she would complain, but her mind was elsewhere.

The next morning, the sky had cleared, and the air was fresh. His mom, his grandfather, and Uncle Alvaro, who occupied the small ranch foreman's house, all had breakfast together and were dressed and ready to go to the morning mass that would be held in Grandma Sarah's honor. They all got into his mom's rental car, since Alvaro's truck wouldn't comfortably seat everyone, and it seemed like they drove endlessly across flat land sparsely decorated with a building or a tree. It was nothing like Nevada, where the landscape was dominated by tall mountain ranges and broad valleys filled with sagebrush and isolated ranches. It was so flat. While Kyle sat quietly in the back seat, he listened to the adults discussing the plans for the day. When mass was over, they would head back to the family homestead and greet those who came to honor Sarah Gomez's life. Kyle overheard that one of Grandma Sarah's older friends had access to the house and would make sure everything was ready for the reception. Several of her friends wanted to help, so they planned to work together to make everything just right. He also heard that his Uncle Antonio would meet them at the church with his entire family. He and his wife, Renata, had six children. Kyle recalled some of these children. They were the ones who would not speak to him in English. He was not too excited about seeing them. Cousins from other areas were to arrive, including the Buckner side of the family. Both of Grandma Sarah's parents were still alive, and they also wished to attend their daughter's memorial services.

Kyle had never attended a funeral, mass service, or any other type of memorial service. He was unsure of what to expect. He was wearing his school dress uniform, which consisted of slacks, a white button-up shirt, a tie, dress shoes, and a pullover sweater with the Academy crest upon it. It was the nicest clothing that he had. His grandfather and uncle were both dressed in dark colored suits, while his mother wore a simple black pantsuit and had her hair neatly braided up. She always looked nice, Kyle thought to himself. When they arrived at the church, it was a modest church, unlike the one he had seen in Toronto. There were no flying buttresses or gargoyles. No giant saint statues lined up along the outside, or enormous stained-glass windows heralding a beautiful interior, echoing hours of work by craftsmen. It was nice and peaceful inside, with tasteful décor featuring many nicely carved wooden pews, a few stained windows depicting angelic scenes, and some statues.

"You need to stay close to me, Kyle," his mother instructed as they respectfully entered the main room, where a giant cross was displayed with Christ on it.

The church was filling up. People would pause near a bowl containing water, dip their fingertips into it, and then apply some to their foreheads. Kyle also noticed others taking special short bows as they reached the center aisle between the pews. These were people who cared about Sarah Buckner Gomez, the daughter of the great cattle rancher James William Buckner. Kyle had never met any of the Buckners. The service seemed nice, but somewhat confusing, as he had to kneel, stop kneeling, get up, kneel again, and stay seated while others went to receive the Eucharist. Kyle wondered what that was all about and why his mother hadn't gone up with the others.

"Mom, why are you not going?" Kyle whispered to his mother.

"Because I am no longer allowed to. This is not my church," she replied, looking around as if expecting to see someone.

"Oh," said Kyle, acting like he understood, even though he did not. It seemed... confusing. She was a Christian, and this was a Christian church. Why did she not count? He understood why he did not, because he was not part of any religion, but it seemed odd to him that she would be excluded. The adult world was often very curious. His thoughts turned to his four new friends and then to Freya. He missed them.

He spotted his cousins sitting with Uncle Antonio and Aunt Renata. One of the older kids looked over at him as they got up to take communion and then sneered at him. Kyle sighed. This was not going to be a pleasant experience. He hoped he could avoid them. At the very

489

end of the mass, everyone turned around to the people around them and wished each other, "Peace be with you." He liked that part. It was like a Jedi saying to another, *"May the Force be with you"*. It was a kind and gentle sentiment that everyone could share, agree upon, whether you were one of them or not.

When they finally returned to the family ranch, several cars were already parked on the property, and buckets of brightly colored flowers were placed everywhere. A large portrait of Grandma Sarah sat in the living room, surrounded by lots of flowers. Kyle could see Abuelo Juan tear up a little as he gazed upon her picture and the flowers surrounding her.

"She loved flowers. We have one field set aside to grow flowers for the flower markets," he said to no one in particular.

Kyle was standing next to him and said, "I did not know that Abuelo Juan. Did she have a favorite one?"

Juan turned to the grandson whom he had spoken to very little and smiled. There was nothing wrong with this boy. Why did he treat him so strangely, the aging man wondered. He finally responded to Kyle's question, "She did not have one favorite but many. What she liked best were flowers… that were brightly colored. Lots of daisies, crisantemos… mums, irises… so many that I can't recall right now."

Kyle smiled and replied, "Then I bet she would have liked all these buckets of flowers around."

"She would," Juan Gomez nodded. "She also loved baking and throwing parties, so I bet she would want you to find something good to eat before too many people show up. The best goodies may disappear fast."

"Okay, abuelo," said Kyle, following his grandfather's advice.

Within fifteen minutes, the large ranch house was filled with people, from family to friends. Kyle did his best to stay out of the way while he watched people come and go. Being a child, he was overlooked, and people spoke in front of him about all kinds of matters. It was as if he were not there or invisible. He began to recognize who the Buckners were and was eventually introduced to his great-grandparents, James and Julia Buckner. They seemed very nice, but were very old. Not all of Grandma Sarah's siblings attended since two of them had died while serving in the military. There were so many names and relations told to him that he started to lose track. It seemed like a blur. He decided to get some dessert and sit down on the stairs out of the way of everyone. He casually worked on the piece of cherry pie with vanilla ice cream and just let his thoughts wander off. Then, a well-dressed woman about his mother's age stood several feet away from him and gazed up in his direction. Her clothing looked expensive, as if she were one of the Buckners, but her hair was jet-black and her skin was tan, like one of the Gomez. She had smoldering brown eyes and wore makeup that made her look like one of the Kardashians. She also had expensive-looking jewelry, similar to what Grandma Lily had.

Kyle looked up at her and then back at his pie. He could feel her staring at him. He started to wonder if he was doing something wrong. He looked up, and she was still looking at him. She walked toward him.

"You even look like Jon," she said with a slight edge to her voice.

Kyle wasn't sure how to respond.

"Uh, yeah. My dad is Jon Bergendahl," replied Kyle.

She brushed her perfectly cut hair back with a handful of long, painted fingernails and said, "Yes, I know."

Kyle felt uncomfortable. He struggled to think of how to handle the situation. Geoff came to mind.

"The pie is delicious. You should try some," said Kyle.

She gave an unfathomable expression, and then his mother came over.

"Olivia! What are you doing here?" asked Marie.

"She was my mother, too. I have a right to be here… just as much as all these other people," she replied with a slight sneer.

Marie turned to her son.

"Kyle, you should go outside and hang out with your cousins," she said. It was not a suggestion but an order.

Kyle was surprised. His mother's demeanor had dramatically changed. He finished his last mouthful of pie

492

and stood up to do as she asked. He was suddenly forgotten as the two women spoke to each other.

"Where are you staying?" asked Marie in an accusatory tone of voice.

"I thought I would stay here. It was… my home, too," replied Olivia.

"Our room is occupied," said Marie.

"There are two beds in that room," countered Olivia.

Marie paused. She then turned to Kyle.

"Kyle, you will remove all your things from Alvaro's room, and you will put them in my room. Your Aunt Olivia requires a place to stay," said Marie with that same crazy edge in her voice that made Kyle feel uncomfortable. She always spoke that way when something really upset her.

"Yes, Mom," replied Kyle, carrying his plate off to the kitchen.

He headed toward the kitchen, weaving between tearful mourners and people sharing thoughts and memories about his Grandma Sarah. The Gomez kitchen was one of the largest rooms in the house and had been remodeled within the past few years. The house, built in the 1950s, had a classic ranch house feel, complete with a broad veranda that wrapped around the building. It was two stories tall and had a tornado basement. It was nice, but it was starting to age. The kitchen was a terrific upgrade, featuring bright colors that made it feel inviting, along with fancy, high-polished appliances and colorful lighting. As he headed for the sink, he overheard more conversations.

"Did you see? Olivia is here," said an unknown female to his Aunt Renata.

"Oh," Aunt Renata's face turned to disgust. "Why is she here? She has already caused so much grief to this family. I had better tell Antonio."

"So… what exactly is the problem?" asked the older woman who appeared to be about Grandma Sarah's age. "Sarah never spoke of her much. She looks like she is doing very well for herself."

"Well, her job is not the problem. She works as a buyer for a major retail chain. You know, one of those people who selects the items that get put into the stores," replied Aunt Renata.

"Wow, that sounds like it would be a fun job," replied the older woman.

"Well… she has probably sold her soul to get that position. She causes nothing but trouble. I need to tell Antonio," replied Aunt Renata, rushing past Kyle without even recognizing him.

The unknown woman raised an eyebrow and watched as Renata made her way through the crowded kitchen.

Kyle looked over at the older woman. She smiled warmly at him as he held his plate and fork.

494

"Oh, aren't you a sweetheart for bringing your plate. Who are you?" she asked kindly.

"Grandma Sarah was… my grandma. I am Kyle. Kyle Bergendahl. Marie is my mom," he replied.

"Aw, I've heard so many good things about you from Sarah," said the woman, giving him a side hug and taking the plate. "I was one of your grandma's friends at the church. We did a lot of baking fundraisers together. She was an exceptional baker and incredibly kind. I wish I knew her better. She was best friends with Alberta."

Kyle nodded, not knowing what to say except, "I miss her."

"We all do, sweetie," said the woman as she rinsed the plate and placed it into the dishwasher.

The dishwasher was starting to look full, and the woman appeared to be wondering if she should turn it on. Kyle wandered on, hearing snippets of conversation. He didn't want to go outside and be with the other children. He had successfully avoided them. It was easier to hide amongst the adults. He then remembered he was supposed to move his belongings into the room that his mom was using. As he made his way through the house, he heard adults discussing a car accident that seemed unusual. There was considerable speculation that something was wrong with the car, despite its relatively new condition. Kyle realized that Grandma Sarah's death was unexpected to everyone present, and they were trying to make sense of the car accident. He heard that she was a good driver. He heard various discussions concerning

495

maintenance and quality as he passed through the crowded house. He made his way upstairs and found what used to be Alvaro's room. He packed up his things and paused to look at his backpack, which he had not opened. Then he noticed, in the corner of the room, a desk and chair with unfamiliar items piled on and around them. He did not recall those things being there before. He walked over to the desk and saw a woman's purse, fancy-looking luggage, and a matching makeup box with a fancy gold antique-looking hairbrush and mirror set sitting next to it. The mirror seemed to emit a green light. He walked over to investigate the face-down mirror and started to reach out to touch it when the man in the brown suit suddenly appeared.

Kyle was a bit surprised. The man looked extremely worried, shaking his head and mouthing the word, 'No!' Kyle stopped reaching for the mirror, which seemed to give off a strange green glow that made no sense to him because it did not look modern or high-tech at all. Why would it have lights, he wondered. The man in the brown suit pointed to Kyle's things. He understood the suggestion. Kyle grabbed his stuff and headed to leave the bedroom, which made the man in the brown suit look relieved.

Then she appeared in the doorway.

Olivia was standing in the doorway and said to him, "Find anything interesting?"

"No. I just got my stuff... like my mom told me to," replied Kyle, feeling very unsure.

She smiled at him. She was very attractive. But she was also somehow… creepy was the word that came to Kyle's mind. He didn't know why.

"Ah, you poor thing. I must have surprised you, and… the loss of your grandma has been very shocking. She wasn't very old… and to die in a freak car accident. She was always a good driver. I never felt afraid to ride with her as a kid," said Olivia, who seemed to be blocking his ability to leave the room.

Kyle just nodded solemnly while holding his bag with his backpack slung over his shoulder.

"Well, I have all my stuff out of the room. Not sure what you want to do about the sheets, but I guess you can decide that with Abuelo Juan," said Kyle, hinting that he wanted to get past her. "I need to put this stuff in Mom's room."

"It used to be her room and mine," said Olivia, placing a hand on Kyle's shoulder. She slowly moved out of the way while still having her hand on his shoulder. As he moved through the threshold of the doorway, she removed her hand and watched him march down the hallway to the other bedroom.

Kyle closed the door behind him and suddenly felt the urge to lock it. The man in the brown suit was nowhere to be seen. Kyle found the other bed and sat down upon it, feeling very strange. He was suddenly fatigued. He decided to lie down and then fell asleep.

Suddenly, he heard a loud banging noise. Someone was banging on a door. Kyle roused himself from his deep slumber and could hear his mother banging on the door, calling for him. He got up, realizing the door was locked.

When he opened the door, his mother was both angry and happy at the same time.

"Kyle! Why was the door locked?! Are you okay, sweetie? You look so tired," she said.

"I fell asleep, Mom. I'm sorry," he replied, not fully awake.

Grandpa Juan was also outside the door, along with Uncle Alvaro. They both looked concerned. Kyle felt bad. He glanced about the room. The sunlight was gone. It had to be late afternoon or early evening. He had not planned to sleep that long. He had not planned to sleep. He just wanted to lie down for a bit.

"As long as he is okay. There is no need to get upset," said Grandpa Juan with his Mexican accent coming through heavy.

"We were so worried. We did not know where you went," replied his mom. "The other children had not seen you at all."

"I just felt *really*... tired. I brought my stuff into the room to make space for Aunt Olivia," said Kyle.

The adults fell silent for a moment. It was odd.

"Well, it is time for supper. Come down and have some food. Alberta is still here, and she would love to meet you," said Grandpa Juan.

Kyle nodded as he tried to brush away the sleepy feeling and followed the three adults back downstairs. They passed the bedroom that Olivia was now using. The mirror and suitcases were still sitting where Kyle had last seen them.

Alberta Johnson spoke with a very Texas accent and seemed delighted to meet one of her best friend's grandchildren. Most of the mourners and well-wishers had tapered off and gone home. Uncle Antonio and Aunt Renata went off with the Buckner part of the family to give Juan some time to rest. He was starting to look overwhelmed. He was glad to see that so many people cared for his beloved Sarah, but his heart was breaking inside. The very thought that she would not be next to him when he went to sleep at night or would laugh at him when he stuffed too many handkerchiefs in his pockets felt painful. He was always misplacing his cell phone, but she always knew where to find it. And her cooking felt like love. She took great care in what she did and treated everyone with kindness, regardless of their social status, whether rich or poor. She was a wonderful person, and the world lost one of its best people.

Olivia entered the large kitchen to grab something to eat.

"Well," said Alberta, sounding very tired. "I am mighty tired, and I think I need to get some rest. Juan, if you need anything, please don't hesitate to call me. I can help." Alberta walked over to where Juan was sitting and gave him a hug, clutching her purse in her hand.

"Thank you so much, Alberta. You have been a blessing. My Sarah would be so happy that you helped me with such... an undertaking," Juan gestured to the large kitchen and the house as a whole. "The Holy Spirit walks with you."

Alberta nodded kindly and glanced momentarily in Olivia's direction and then back at Juan, "I hope so. God bless you, Juan."

Alberta then saw herself out the front door.

The room became somewhat quiet and still. The only sound was from Olivia finding something to eat from the items that had been packed away into the large refrigerator. She put the food on a plate and heated it in the microwave. When that was done, she stood by the counter and just eyed everyone who was now silent.

"So, is that the last person to go? I was outside on the porch chatting with the neighbors, and they finally went home. They said they would stop by in a couple of days to check on you," said Olivia.

"Why are you here?" asked Marie.

"Because Mom died," answered Olivia. "Why are you?"

"Because I actually care," retorted Marie with a bit of an edge in her voice.

"Oh, I care. But none of you like me because I am no longer Christian," retorted Olivia.

"That's not the reason," murmured Alvaro.

500

"Alright, alright… children… this is not the time to have these arguments," said Juan, looking very tired. "Everyone is welcome. Your madre would not want you to fight."

"I'm not the one starting it," remarked Olivia, slamming her fork down on the plate.

Kyle caught Uncle Alvaro making a face, and his mother looked very irritated, her arms folded across her chest. He was starting to wish desperately that he was back at school with his friends. He wondered if he could retreat upstairs and start on his required reading homework. This felt bad.

"Mom? Can I go upstairs and do my homework?" Kyle asked, breaking some of the tension.

"Yes. That is a good idea. Don't forget to brush your teeth," she said as he immediately started to make his way out of the kitchen and toward the front room where the stairway was located. As he moved further from the kitchen, he could hear the conversation continue.

"None of you wants me here! You are all jealous that I am successful," said Olivia.

"No, we are not," said Alvaro. "It just feels weird you being here after you upset Mama so much."

"What do you mean?! I… upset her?" said Olivia in a harsh voice.

"Yes, Mama was worried about you, and you got mad at her for being concerned," said Alvaro. "And then… she… just dies suddenly."

"I want you to stay away from me… and my son," added Marie. "I know you are up to no good with… that stuff you have been doing."

"I see. Mama was the only one who loved me," Olivia sounded like she was starting to cry. "None of you cares about me. You are jealous! I am not staying here."

Kyle heard high-heeled shoes walking quickly, so he scampered up the stairs to get out of the way. He knew Olivia would go upstairs for her belongings. She sounded distraught and was crying. He started to feel bad for her. He was surprised that no one tried to stop her from leaving. He was almost at the bedroom door, where his things were now stored, and looked down the hallway to see Olivia reach the top of the stairs. She noticed him and turned in his direction. She had this calm and somewhat smug look on her face. The expression, for some reason, scared the heck out of Kyle, and he immediately went into the bedroom and closed the door. He started pacing the bedroom, feeling uneasy.

"I wish Dad were here," he whispered to himself.

The man in the brown suit appeared, nodded sympathetically to Kyle, and then gave him a cold pat on the shoulder. Then the man suddenly pulled back his ghostly hand, as if something had shocked or hurt him. His face twisted into a worried expression before he disappeared, leaving Kyle feeling even worse.

There was a loud slam of the front door. Kyle went to the bedroom window and looked out to the front yard, where all the cars had been parked earlier. He saw Olivia put her bags into a black Mercedes-Benz sports model. She closed the trunk and then looked up at Kyle as if she knew he was watching her from the bedroom window. Kyle felt scared and stepped away from the window, hoping she would just go away. He heard the car motor start up, followed by the sound of the vehicle driving away.

He thought about going back downstairs, but changed his mind. He wanted to call his dad, but he figured that would upset his mom, so he called Lothar instead. He did not answer. So, then he called Freya.

"Hello?" said Freya. Her voice was like heaven.

"Uh, hi, Freya. This is Kyle. Can I talk to you?" he asked.

"Sure. What's wrong? You sound strange," she said.

"I feel strange. We had the funeral mass and the memorial gathering today for my Grandma Sarah, but... that wasn't what was strange. My mom and uncle got into a fight with my Aunt Olivia. And to be honest... she seems ... creepy," replied Kyle.

"How so?" asked Freya.

"I can't explain. It doesn't make sense to me. Everyone is acting weird," replied Kyle. He was shivering.

"I think that is normal when loved ones die. When my grandpa died of cancer, everyone acted strange for a... like a month after he passed away," she replied.

"Oh. Well... I don't like it. What should I do?" said Kyle.

"Keep busy. That's what I did," answered Freya.

"Alright. Thanks, Freya," said Kyle. He wasn't sure her advice would help. Images of Aunt Olivia kept going through his mind.

"It's bedtime, and I am not supposed to be talking on the phone. But I heard it ring and thought maybe it was my parents. They are the only ones who call me at school," she said.

"Oh yeah, right. I am sorry. I don't want to get you in trouble. Thanks for talking with me," said Kyle.

"Sure thing," said Freya before she hung up.

He felt a little better. She was right. He could try to stay occupied and let the grown-ups handle their own affairs. He got ready for bed and pulled out his copy of *Harry Potter and the Sorcerer's Stone*. Reading the book should help him get his mind off his troubles. After an hour of reading, he felt better and decided to go to sleep. He placed the book on the nightstand and fell fast asleep.

Chapter 22: Mom Doesn't Approve of Witchcraft

When Kyle woke up the next morning, he felt rested, and the strange feeling seemed to have gone away. His mother's bed appeared to have been slept in, but she was nowhere in sight. He decided to get up and see what was happening. He could hear voices downstairs. He found his family in the kitchen. His mom was making breakfast for Alvaro and Abuelo Juan.

"Good morning, Kyle," said Uncle Alvaro with a big smile and a slight Texas accent. "You are just in time for breakfast. Papa and I were thinking about eating your share."

"I would not let that happen," said Marie, suppressing a laugh.

Grandpa Juan just smiled and took a bite out of a homemade biscuit with marmalade. Marie had made biscuits, sausage, and eggs for breakfast. She handed Kyle a plate along with a glass of orange juice.

"Thanks, Mom," said Kyle as he took a seat at the large family dining table.

"Did you sleep well?" she asked him.

"I guess so," said Kyle. "I still feel sorta tired."

"Did we keep you up last night with our long night of talking?" asked Grandpa Juan.

Kyle shook his head and said, "No. I did not hear you."

"Papa, I had better get going. That field in the north corner needs to be plowed over again before we can plant, and it is not going to do it by itself," said Alvaro, getting up and bringing his plate to the sink. He finished his coffee and then set that down, too.

"Alright. Are you sure you do not want me to get the other tractor out and help you?" asked Grandpa Juan.

"No. You need to take a break, and that other tractor needs to be inspected. It was making some odd noises, and, well, after mom's accident, I'm uncomfortable with anybody driving something that hasn't been thoroughly checked. Bob Kenny is coming over today to take a look at it. Perhaps you could keep an eye out for him?" said Alvaro.

"I can do that," said Juan, feeling a little better that his staying at the house would serve some useful purpose, such as getting the second tractor ready. After Alvaro left, he turned back to Marie and Kyle. "A ranch cannot wait for a broken heart to mend. Work must be done. I am sorry that we cannot be better company."

"It's okay, Papa. I understand, and I am serious about what we discussed last night," she said firmly.

"But you have a life in Reno. A good-paying job, a home, friends?" said Juan.

"I can get another job," replied Marie. "I don't own the house."

Kyle's eyes widened.

"See. You have surprised the boy. He was not expecting to leave his home," said Juan to his daughter.

"You and Alvaro need help. You are all alone here," she countered.

"There is Antonio," said Juan.

"But he lives all the way in Elgin, and he doesn't have time to stop by that often. He's very busy with his veterinary practice," replied Marie. "And Renata has all those babies to look after. The youngest one doesn't even walk yet."

"That is southeast Elgin, so it is a little closer. They have a very fine house with a nice swimming pool and lots of space for the children to play," said Grandpa Juan, thinking about Antonio's home.

"I know, Papa. Antonio has a very nice house, but he must work hard for it. He does not have time to look after you. If I were to find a job close by, then I could stay with you. Alvaro is using the other house to live in, and before you know it, he will find a girl, get married, and have less time to spend with you. I should come," said Marie. "I don't have much furniture or many belongings. It's mostly me, Kyle, and Rojo."

"Mom, who is watching Rojo?" Kyle asked, feeling suddenly worried about the little dog.

"Carol has him. He is fine," replied Marie. She then turned her attention back to her father. "I should get ready to move right away, before the bad weather comes. We have only a short time."

"Alright. I can see your heart is set upon it. But what about Olivia? She does not have a husband or any children. What if she wants to come here?" wondered Juan. "She travels a lot. Perhaps she would be happy coming and going?"

"No. You cannot have her stay on this property. You know what she is doing. It's bad. You will get hurt. Alvaro and I think she is up to no good. And if you ask Antonio, he will say the same thing," replied Marie, who then noticed Kyle listening wide-eyed. "Kyle, go get dressed. We need to get some errands taken care of before you go back to the Bergendahls."

"Yes, Mom," replied Kyle, suddenly feeling like he was delegated to being a baby again. That tone of voice, which she used when irritated and when his aunt was mentioned, reappeared instantly. He started to feel tired. Perhaps taking a shower would wake him up.

As soon as Kyle was dressed, he and his mom went to run errands while Grandpa Juan met with the man about the tractor. He was a well-known mechanic in the area who traveled to different farms and ranches to do basic maintenance and repairs. He pulled in with his big truck, which had numerous special compartments for tools, as they were preparing to leave. Soon, their rental car was out of the driveway and on the long, open flat road with not much to entertain Kyle. He brought his book along because he knew she would be in long meetings about jobs and moving. The story was interesting and rather amusing, and he had gotten to the part where Harry had discovered that he was a wizard. The Dursley family was annoyingly awful. Kyle had realized that the book was even better than the movies. And he liked the movies.

His mom parked the car in a lot for a tall, well-built-looking structure that appeared to contain numerous professional offices. The parking lot was neatly paved and organized, with perfectly trimmed shrubs and trees. Manicured sections of lawn had small sprinkler heads placed evenly about. It was a place where people who wore dressy clothing worked, carrying briefcases and sipping fancy coffee. Kyle closed the book to look around.

"Where did you get that trash?" she demanded.

"What?" Kyle asked, looking around for candy wrappers.

"That satanic book," she clarified. "It's about turning children into witches! I will not have you reading such sinful garbage."

Her demeanor was filled with deep-seated anger, making Kyle feel very uncomfortable.

"But Mom! It's my schoolbook. I need to read it," Kyle explained as she held her hand out to take the book from him. "And so far, I have read nothing that seems… sinful."

She looked shocked as she took the book.

"They asked you to read this for school?!?" she exclaimed.

"Yes. We are supposed to read it and compare it to the movie version," explained Kyle.

509

"And you have seen that movie?!" demanded Marie.

"Well, yeah. What kid hasn't? It was a fun film to watch. They get to fly around on brooms, catching gold balls with wings and outsmarting bad guys. It's like weird soccer in the sky," said Kyle.

His mom looked like she was gonna explode.

"I knew I should have insisted that you go to All Christ Saves Private School. You are on the path to ruin. I will talk to your father later. You stay right here in this car until I come back."

Kyle said nothing but watched her walk into the office building after putting his book into the waste bin located just outside the structure. Kyle was breathing hard. The book did not belong to him, and she had no right to throw it away. It was his duty to return that book to school. The waste bin was not far away. Kyle took a deep breath. He got out of the car, leaving the door open, and dashed over to the waste bin, where he fished the book out. Luckily, there wasn't much in the bin. He raced back to the car, hoping she hadn't seen him. He hid the book under the seat and then pulled out the cell phone, wanting to call his dad or Grandma Lily.

The original plan was for him to have a fun vacation with his dad. Instead, his Grandma Sarah died, and he got stuck with his upset mom, meeting a bunch of strangers, and then... that creepy woman, his aunt. It had been a horrible couple of days. This was not a vacation, and he was going to be in trouble with Sir Knight Mary for not completing his homework. He wanted to excel in school and prove that he was worth the money his family spent on him. What would Freya and the guys think when he came back and wasn't even able to finish reading half of the book? He would look like a giant loser.

Kyle found his digital camera in his jacket pocket. He flipped through the photos on it. Pictures of Geoff eating a big sandwich, Tyrrel taking water samples from the lake, René and Lothar acting silly on the boulders, and Freya... just being her beautiful self. He studied the freckles on her face and how her eyelashes looked. He managed to zoom the camera in on her eyes. They were an interesting gray-blue color. He missed them all. He did not want to leave the Academy. It was the first time since his parents' divorce that he felt consistently happy. He loved his mom and dad... Rojo and Pickles... both sets of grandparents... Uncle Alvaro seemed nicer than before... he missed Dark Cloud, but he was happier with his uncle... and there was Jasper, but his new friends made him happy. He felt like he belonged with them. He hoped they felt the same way. He thought back to the five candy bars he had found stashed in various locations throughout his luggage. He knew Geoff put them there. There was a copy of the drawing of the man in the brown suit; Freya had made sure that it was placed in his backpack. His study notes for French and the required Harry Potter book were carefully placed in his backpack, which was Tyrrel. René made sure he had all his best clothes and all the parts to look proper for the funeral. And Lothar made sure the cell phone, camera, and archery ribbon were packed along too. They knew what was important and cared about him.

Kyle decided to show Grandpa Juan and Uncle Alvaro his archery ribbon. He needed to make the effort to show them that he cared about them, too.

After a long day of Kyle's mother investigating storage units and places to find employment, she seemed even more determined to move back to her family home in Texas and look after her father and youngest brother. It sounded like she already had leads on several jobs. Kyle knew not to say anything. It would not help, and… maybe she did need to move back to Texas. Perhaps she would be happier here, he wondered, looking out at the bleak landscape. He had noticed that she was trying to hide the fact that she had been crying. During their errands, as they drove about and stopped for lunch, she seemed to be a mix of sadness, worry, and anger. That evening, they gathered around the large dining table for a nice dinner before Kyle and his mom left the next morning. She had arrangements for Lily Bergendahl to take Kyle back to Canada. Lily had stayed in Houston for a couple of days to attend to some family business, and neither of them thought Kyle should travel alone after such an experience.

"This looks like a feast, Marie," said Grandpa Juan, smiling. "Your madre would be so proud of you. You could be a baker like her."

"No, I will never be as good as she was. But I have her recipes, and I can try," replied Marie.

"Well," Alvaro paused with a big mouthful of homemade Tex-Mex cheese enchiladas. "These are just as good as Mama's. She would say you followed the recipe just right."

Marie seemed to blush a little.

"These are good, Mom," said Kyle, enjoying the rare family time. "Mom? Can I bring something to the table to show Abuelo Juan and Uncle Alvaro?"

Marie looked up at Kyle and said, "Yes, you may… as long as it does not make a big mess."

Kyle got up and went to a side table, where he had set the red second-place ribbon. He held up the ribbon and said, "I got second place in the Archery contest at school."

"Oh, hey, that is fantastic!" exclaimed Uncle Alvaro, looking at the brilliant red ribbon.

"Bring it over here so your old abuelo can see it," said Grandpa Juan with a big smile on his face.

Grandpa Juan carefully wiped his hands with a napkin and then reached out to hold the brilliant red ribbon in his hands. The ribbon said, "Second Place Archery Competition Academy Fall 2013." His eyes sparkled as he marveled at the boy's prize.

"This is wonderful, Kyle. You should be very proud of yourself. I did not know you were an archer," he said to Kyle.

"I didn't know either. I love archery. Next year… if I get to attend again, I can select certain athletic classes to focus upon, and I want archery to be one of them."

"Well, this is quite the accomplishment. Marie, your little boy is growing into a man," commented Grandpa Juan. "That must be an excellent school."

Marie just nodded.

"Let me see the ribbon," requested Alvaro.

"Are your hands clean? This is a special trophy," said Grandpa Juan.

Alvaro rolled his eyes and stopped what he was doing to make sure his hands were free of any food particles. He then took the ribbon from his father and looked at it.

"This is a nice ribbon. It's almost as big and fancy as some of those horse show ribbons," laughed Alvaro as he handed it back to Kyle, who placed it back on the side table so he would not forget to pack it away in the morning. He wanted to show it to his dad, Grandma, and Grandpa Bergendahl when he got back to Canada.

The rest of the evening went very well, and Kyle found himself hanging out with Uncle Alvaro playing a video game. His mom was upstairs getting her things ready for the next day, and Grandpa Juan had decided to turn in early. He had an appointment with some lawyers in the morning concerning Sarah's passing.

Kyle just finished playing and handed the controller to Alvaro, and then suddenly asked, "Why is Aunt Olivia so weird?"

Alvaro's eyebrows raised, and he forgot what he was doing with the video game. He looked at Kyle and took

514

a deep breath. He quickly glanced around as if to make sure no one was listening and then turned to his nephew.

"She's a witch," he replied.

"A what?!?" exclaimed Kyle. "You mean like in the Harry Potter movies?"

"No. That's just fun stuff. She's the old-world bad kind. She's a witch," replied Alvaro.

"But I didn't think that stuff was real. If you ask my dad, he will say that stuff is nonsense. Right?" replied Kyle, feeling perplexed.

"I wish your dad were right, but one cannot ignore one's senses," replied Alvaro.

"So, is that why she and my mom do not get along? Did Mom mistreat her with her ultra-religious attitude?" asked Kyle.

"Actually, it is the other way around. Marie, your mom, saw Olivia do something that terrified her, which is partially why she left the Roman Catholic Church. She prayed for help and… nothing happened… and then she must have talked with one of those ultra fundamentalist types that convinced her that our church was not good enough to keep away the bad stuff. She switched churches, and then she and your dad started having trouble…" Alvaro paused for a moment as if in thought, "…I do not know all the details… but Mama was deeply concerned about both of them. She was distraught that her daughters no longer got along with each other. They used to do everything together and were always so happy."

515

Kyle sat quietly for a moment. This shed a new light on everything. It even changed the way he saw his mom. She wasn't being mean and weird to him. She was scared. He thought about the odd green light he had seen coming from the mirror. It was spooky.

"Uncle Alvaro... I saw something odd when Aunt Olivia was here. Do old-fashioned handheld lady's mirrors have green lights attached to them?"

Alvaro shook his head, making a face.

"Not that I know of. You mean like those silver antique ones that they used to use in the old days?" asked Alvaro, watching Kyle nod his head. "No, those do not have lights attached. What did you see?"

"I saw a green glowing light coming from the mirror," said Kyle. "It was Aunt Olvia's stuff."

"Did you touch it?" he asked.

"Well, I was going to... and then I thought I might get into trouble," replied Kyle, leaving the ghost out of the story. He did not want to freak out Uncle Alvaro.

Alvaro took a deep breath. He looked nervous now. He grasped the video game controller tightly, and his hand shook slightly.

"Probably a good idea. Uh... I don't think you should tell your mom about this conversation," said Alvaro, looking toward the hallway where the stairs were located.

"Yeah. I think you are right," said Kyle. "Thanks for telling me all this stuff. I didn't know."

516

"Sure thing. You had better get to bed. You have a long day of travel ahead of you," said Uncle Alvaro, turning off the game system.

Kyle stood up and watched his uncle turn off the equipment. And then the man turned to him.

"It's very hard. I feel like she has done bad things, but I have no proof. There is no one to turn to for help. And I don't know why she went that way. I loved my sister, but she no longer feels like a sister to me. My heart is broken. I wish Olivia would return to being the sweet girl she used to be. My beloved sister… Your mom feels the same way," said Alvaro.

Chapter 23: Back to the Caledon House

Kyle found himself in a hallway with many doors. It seemed like his Grandpa Juan's home, but it felt strange. It felt darker and longer than normal. He was trying to find his bedroom. It was time to rest since he felt so tired. His mom would be upset that he hadn't gone to bed like he was told to. For some reason, he was angry at his mom, but he couldn't remember why. He had to find his bedroom. All the doors were closed, and the hallway was dark. So very dark. He reached for the various doorknobs to open the doors, and they were all locked. On the right side and the left side of the hallway... All the doors were locked. Then he spotted a door ahead that seemed to have some light coming from the other side underneath the door. It was a yellow glow at first as he strode up to it to reach for the doorknob. He looked down at the light pouring from underneath, and it seemed to transform from a regular light into a green fog that was flowing from beneath the open section between the door and the floor. It swirled and billowed like smoke, but it was green. This confused him. What was this?

He was told somewhere not to open the door in case of a fire. Was this a fire? Why was the smoke green? The green smoke seemed to curl around his bare feet and ankles. He tried to step back, but his feet would not lift off the floor. It was climbing up his legs. Kyle wanted to scream as he struggled to move and couldn't. His heart felt like it was racing as he tried to call for help. A feeling of panic and fear overwhelmed him.

His mom woke him up, telling him he was having a bad dream. She brought him a glass of water, handed him one of her childhood stuffed toys, and suggested that he go back to sleep since they had a long day ahead of them.

Kyle tossed and turned in his sleep that night. He did not sleep well and woke up feeling tired. He managed to push himself forward and was ready to leave when his mom wanted to go. They said many tearful goodbyes with promises from his mom to return soon. She already had several companies interested in interviewing her for job positions, which seemed to please her. Kyle chose not to express his mixed feelings about her move to Texas and the decision to give up their home in Reno. He knew he would probably never see Dark Cloud again. They could exchange emails, but he noticed that Dark Cloud spent less time on the computer now. He was probably making new friends and learning new things from his uncle. On the other hand, he thought to himself, his Uncle Alvaro and Grandpa Juan seemed nicer than he recalled. His cousins were still jerks, but they did not live on the family ranch. He hoped he would not see Aunt Olivia ever again. She was... creepy.

Before he knew it, he was waving goodbye to his mom as he and his grandma headed toward the international flight section after checking their bags. He was on his way back to the Caledon House.

"Kyle, are you alright?" Lily Bergendahl looked at her grandson, appraising him.

"I guess so. I feel… exhausted. And I don't know why," replied Kyle as they walked together up the concourse.

"You have had a hectic couple of days. Not to mention the loss of your grandmother. How is Juan Gomez doing? Is he alright?" she asked.

"He seems okay, but very sad. It was like he was trying to appear to be okay," said Kyle. "Does that make sense?"

"Yes. Many people who experience the loss of a dear loved one will try to be strong for the other people around them. He also had to consider all his children. They just lost their mother," explained Lily.

"Yeah. I miss her too, but… the idea of my mom dying… is too horrible to imagine," replied Kyle. "I don't want that to happen."

He looked up at her as they paused to find the gate for their plane.

"Unfortunately, dying is a fact of life. We all must go at some point," said Lily philosophically. "But… many believe that death is not the end of our existence and that we go on to do other things in another form."

"So… ghosts are people without bodies?" asked Kyle.

"That is the idea that many people assume to be true," said Lily, not sure where all this was going. She had been briefed about the special class to which Kyle had been invited at the Academy.

They boarded the plane and took their assigned seats in the business class section. They were both very comfortable, and Kyle sat next to the window, looking out at Houston's Bush Intercontinental Airport. It was raining again, but he could still see nothing but flat land. He wanted to read his book, but was unsure if he was allowed to. He reached into his backpack and pulled out the Harry Potter book.

"Grandma, am I allowed to read this?" he asked her.

Lily Bergendahl looked at the book and gave Kyle a quizzical expression.

"Why wouldn't that be allowed?" she asked.

"Mom said it was evil… or bad… or something… because it has witches in it," replied Kyle.

Lily raised her eyebrow and made a face. Kyle could tell that she knew something was up. She paused for a moment as if pondering what to say.

"You may read that book around me. I know it is nothing but fiction and fantasy about a young boy figuring out who he is," replied Lily.

"So, witches aren't evil?" asked Kyle.

Lily made a face and replied, "Those witches in the story are not real. The word *witch* is just a name given to someone who uses magic in those tales. In real life, not everyone who practices magic is a witch. That idea came from ignorant, frightened people who didn't understand what magic was. The term witch was never meant as a compliment. It was an old label for a female magic user seen as selfish or harmful. Long ago, people who were afraid would call anyone practicing magic a witch, without understanding what they were actually doing. Many women who worked as herbalists or midwives were branded witches simply to stop them from practicing the healing arts, much like pharmacists do today."

"Why would someone do that?!" exclaimed Kyle quietly.

"Money. Power. People who did not want someone else to have a business practice that they could not control. The Knights Templar suffered from this very same attitude. The Knights were powerful and wealthy, but the King of France refused to repay the money he owed them, and the Pope resented the fact that the Knights understood the spiritual world as well as, if not better than, he did. That frightened him and men like him. Men who were afraid of losing power. The common people often sought the Knights' advice. They were trusted. The selfish people started making up stories to frighten the general population, so that they could get their way and remove the Knights allowing them to forfeit the money they owed, steal the land belonging to the Order, and ruin the trust that the Knights earned with the people of Europe," said Lily feeling a bit more comfortable talking about the Knights to her grandson.

"So are witches bad or just people mislabeled?" asked Kyle.

"Real witches… are bad," she finally replied, not liking the topic. "Why is this so important? I did not think the Harry Potter series focused on such things."

"Hmmm, as far as I know from the movies… they don't," Kyle paused and took in a breath. "I met Aunt Olivia."

Lily Bergendahl's eyes widened.

"Oh, I see. Now I understand," replied his grandmother.

"She's a real witch, isn't she? Uncle Alvaro said so," said Kyle, backing up his assertion with an adult's opinion.

"Yes," replied Lily sadly.

"I also got the idea… that maybe she caused problems between Mom and Dad," said Kyle.

"Yes, she did. Your father never told you what happened? And I suppose, your mother never said anything either," sighed Lily.

"No. They won't tell me anything. Dad freezes up and Mom gets mad," replied Kyle.

"Your mother and father used to love each other very much. And when your father had been injured badly in a car accident, she stuck by him through all the surgeries and the loss of his friends, Sir Knight Thomas and Sir Knight Robert. They were killed in the accident. They all went to college together after being at the

Academy," she started to explain. "Thomas and Robert were both Americans."

"Dad was at the Academy?" asked Kyle, feeling very surprised.

"Yes, he was. He doesn't like to talk about it because he feels the Order betrayed him and the others. He felt the Order would only take European Knights seriously and ignored those in the U.S. who wanted to be Knights. He stepped away from the Order. This broke his heart, and all he had left to love was your mother, Marie. He focused on his studies and his relationship with your mother. They were very happy together. Your grandfather, Karl, and I focused on repairing the Order's attitude toward Knights outside of Europe. In the old days, it was illegal to be a Templar Knight by law, so the Knights had to hide. Luckily, many noble families in Europe secretly maintained their traditions as Knights, keeping the Templar legacy alive. As a result, an attitude developed that only nobility would be considered for the role of Templar Knights, a secret arrangement. In 2007, the laws were changed. Our families had already long ago moved to the Americas and brought our family traditions with us," said Lily.

"So... Dad is not a Knight?" Kyle asked.

"He is not a Knight," replied Lily sadly. "He opted for a different group of people to put his intellect and efforts toward. He believes technology and science are the way forward for humanity. He works on projects that are... amazing. He develops incredible concepts from storybooks that are now coming to life. I look forward to the day when his work, along with the work of the people he collaborates with, will be accessible to the general public. It will bring hope of a better life to many people."

"What exactly does he do?" asked Kyle, hoping to get an answer to an old question.

Lily smiled at Kyle and replied, "I cannot tell you. Besides, I have only a very vague idea, but it is top secret. And I am not allowed to share with anyone the little tidbits that I know."

"Because you made a promise," said Kyle, looking at her. She nodded her head. "I get that. I had to retrieve my book from the garbage can after my mom threw it away. It's not my book, and it was loaned to me with the expectation that I would return it so others could read it. I didn't want to be the loser who lost the book. It was like I had promised to return it."

Lily smiled.

"I would have replaced it for you, but I congratulate you on your courage and fortitude in retrieving it from the garbage can," Lily said with a smile.

"So...how did Aunt Olivia make trouble for Mom and Dad?" he asked, hoping to understand more.

Lily frowned as if she did not want to discuss the matter. She took a deep, calming breath in and then out.

"Marie and Olivia were very close as children," Lily paused. "And mind you that I do not know all the details, or if what I know is the exact truth. However, your father sometimes felt that Olivia was unhappy with the relationship between him and your mother. At first, he thought she had a crush on him since she made overly friendly advances toward him. She acted as if she wanted to be more than friends. Do you understand that?"

Kyle nodded.

"But later, he started to suspect that she wanted to get rid of him, so that Marie would spend all her free time with Olivia. She was jealous of Jon taking Marie away from her," Lily explained. "Jon thought Olivia wanted to control Marie. Then they got married, and then you came along, and the problem just got worse and worse," said Lily. "The fact that they had a child together meant that they were forever linked. A thought that Olivia... possibly could not bear."

Just then, the steward came by asking if they wanted anything to drink. Lily opted for a cup of coffee while Kyle wanted a soda pop. The steward also told them that their lunch would be served in about an hour, which made Kyle happy. He was still feeling tired, so he thought some food would make him feel better. He rummaged through his backpack, finding his French notes and the drawing of the man in the brown suit. The copy of the drawing caught Lily's attention.

She picked up the picture and asked with a smile, "Where did you get this? I didn't know there were any drawings of Alvar Bergendahl."

Kyle's eyes widened.

"You know him?!" exclaimed Kyle.

"Well, I never met him, but I knew who he was. He was one of the two brothers who immigrated to Canada to start a new life. He was your grandfather's great-uncle. He was also one of the instructors at the early version of the Academy school. He taught mathematics. We have portraits of him back at the house. He never married, so all his personal belongings were given to his brother's family. We have his wire-framed glasses and a beautiful pocket watch that was given to him by the faculty," she replied, not knowing how significant this was to Kyle.

Kyle felt his jaw drop open. He never dreamed that the man in the brown suit was someone from his family.

"Grandma, he is the reason why I was asked to be a part of the special class," said Kyle. "That drawing was made by one of the older students studying to be a forensic artist. And he drew that from the description I gave him! Freya saw him too."

Lily Bergendahl put a hand to her throat and absently touched the pearls she was wearing as this information sank in. She was not sure what to say.

"My goodness, Karl would be excited to hear about this. I was told you saw something or someone, but the details weren't explained. They said you needed training, so I agreed that would be a wise course of action," replied Lily.

"Wow, Grandma, this is so exciting," said Kyle, feeling both exhilarated and tired at the same time. "I can't wait to talk to Grandpa and Freya about this. She saw him too. Everyone seemed worried about this ghost guy who

527

was appearing. And he is… an ancestor… just like what Dark Cloud and his uncle were talking about. I made a connection!"

Lily wrapped an arm around Kyle warmly and said, "Yes, you did."

The rest of the flight was spent reading, followed by a break for lunch, and then a nap. When Kyle fell asleep after lunch, Lily picked up the book and began reading it herself. She figured she should know precisely what was in the book since Marie had been so concerned. Time passed by quickly, and before Kyle knew it, he was in the BMW with Jasper, driving them back home from the Toronto Airport. He felt so exhausted and just slept all the way home to the Caledon House. He hardly recalled getting back to his grandparents' home, where he overheard vague conversations about his pale and tired state. The idea of grief causing him stress and making him so tired was discussed, but he seemed unwell, according to Grandma. She sounded worried.

The next morning, Kyle woke up to the sunlight pouring through the sheers of his Caledon bedroom window. The light was pleasant and cheerful. Everything felt unreal. His Grandma Sarah was gone, his mother was moving to Texas, his aunt was a witch, and the man in the brown suit was… Alvar Bergendahl. He opened his eyes and saw a man standing nearby. He thought it was Jasper at first, but it was Alvar Bergendahl, the man in the brown suit. He looked down at Kyle and smiled. He looked concerned, even though he gave him a friendly smile.

"Are you Alvar Bergendahl… my… great great… great uncle?" Kyle asked the ghost.

The man in the brown suit nodded. Kyle was pleased to have a proper name for the ghost.

"It's time to get up, huh?" said Kyle.

The ghost nodded and then slowly dissipated.

Kyle yawned and got up. It was later than he usually got up. He decided to head to the bathroom and wash up first. He was not especially hungry. After he was dressed, he went downstairs, hearing a familiar voice. It was his dad.

Kyle rushed downstairs and called out, "Dad!"

His dad came to the stairway landing and gave him a big hug.

"How are you doing, Sport?! So glad to see you. It has been a while. How are you doing with the funeral and all?" Jon asked his son.

"Oh, Dad, it is so good to see you," said Kyle, hugging his father tightly. "Everything has been so crazy. I am happy you are here."

"You must be hungry. You missed breakfast," commented Jon.

"I… just feel tired. Not really hungry," replied Kyle.

This reply made Jon frown a little.

"Yes, your grandmother said that you seemed awfully tired. Was anyone sick back in Texas?" Jon asked as he led Kyle into the kitchen and fetched him a glass of orange juice.

"Uh," Kyle paused to think. "No. No one was sick. They were just sad."

Jon Bergendahl nodded in agreement with his son's assessment of the situation.

"How is your mom?"

"She is upset, but she is trying to hide it. She is moving to Texas to take care of Grandpa Juan," answered Kyle. "She already has job interviews set up."

His father looked surprised.

"Oh, so she is planning to move out of Reno. That will make things more complicated," commented Jon.

"You mean with me?" asked Kyle.

"Yes. Texas is further away. It is in a different time zone from the Pacific Northwest. It is a longer flight for you to travel," his dad paused for a moment. "How did things go with your mom's relatives? I know you had some trouble the last couple of times when you visited with them."

"My cousins are still jerks, but Uncle Alvaro seemed nicer this time. I like him. He seems like a good guy. And Grandpa Juan seemed super sad, but... I think he likes me. I will miss Grandma Sarah. And... I... met Aunt Olivia."

His dad's face dropped, and his expression changed dramatically.

"I didn't know she would be there. I should have gone with you. I should have been there for Marie," his dad said more to himself than to Kyle.

Just then, Lily and Karl came into the room. Jon turned to his parents.

"Did you know that Olivia was going to be there?" he asked them.

"We had no idea, son," replied Karl Bergendahl.

The mood in the house changed. Kyle could feel it. Everyone looked very serious and stressed.

"We've got to get one of the experts here right away," said Jon. "My technology friends cannot help with this paraphysical stuff. We need someone to examine Kyle. And me now. I hugged him. Mom? Did you hug Kyle?"

"Of course I did, dear," replied Lily.

"Me too," said Karl. "How would I know not to hug my own grandson?"

Jon just shook his head in frustration.

"I know, Dad. I'm sorry," replied Jon, trying to dial back his anger level.

"What's going on?" asked Kyle.

Jon turned to his son and said, "Your Aunt Olivia… is not a very nice person, and she does stuff that hurts people."

"Yes, I know. She's a… real witch. Not like a Harry Potter kind of witch," replied Kyle. "But a bad kind like from a creepy horror movie."

"That is correct, and you are showing symptoms of something she likes to do to people," replied Jon.

"What? I didn't touch the mirror! The man in the brown… Alvar… told me not to touch it," said Kyle. "So, I did not touch the mirror with the green light coming from it."

"What do you mean by mirror? What mirror did you see?" asked Lily.

Kyle sighed, not realizing any of this was even important. He felt so sluggish, too.

"I had to move out of Uncle Alvaro's old bedroom, so that Aunt Olivia could stay. She put her stuff in there, and there was a mirror that was face down with glowing green light coming from underneath. I was going to look at it… until… Alvar gestured to me not to do that," said Kyle. "I didn't know she did bad stuff."

"Who is Alvar?" his dad asked.

Karl and Lily both had surprised looks on their faces.

"He's the ghost I can see. Grandma said the picture of the ghost looked great… great? Uncle Alvar," replied Kyle. "But I wasn't going to tell you about that because I thought you would think I was being silly."

Jon was struggling to focus between the ghost, Olivia, and the creepy mirror. Too many weird things were being thrown at him all at once. He normally dealt with people who were purely scientific in nature. Hard, cold facts that could be measured and defined clearly.

"Alright... obviously the ghost does not seem to be a threat, so let's stay on the mirror topic. Explain," asked Jon.

Grandma and Grandpa remained quiet as they stood and listened. Both had concerned looks on their faces.

Kyle struggled to concentrate. His mind was foggy, and he felt drowsy. He took a deep breath, hoping it would help him focus.

"Aunt Olivia had a pile of her belongings in the corner of the room, and on the desk was an old-fashioned fancy mirror and brush set. Like the silver types you see in old movies. It was glowing green from the mirror side. I was going to look at it, thinking it had lights or something special. But Alvar told me not to touch it, so I got my stuff and left the room... but Aunt Olivia showed up before I could get out and blocked the doorway. I don't recall what she was saying anymore. But... she did put her hand on my shoulder for a long time, which made me feel kind of... uncomfortable. You know, like when you are asked to shake hands with someone you don't like," Kyle attempted to explain.

"Yes. I understand that," said his father. He looked over at his parents.

"Jon, I will call one of the experts right away and explain the situation," said Lily, leaving the room.

Kyle scrunched up his face into a scowl and asked, "What do you think she did to me? She didn't slap, pinch... or punch me. There was no cackling or wand waving. No magic potions. She was just... bitchy." Kyle was a little nervous about using that word, as his mother considered it an inappropriate word for a kid to use.

"We understand that Kyle," said Karl Bergendahl. "Witchcraft is a complicated matter that has methods that are often hidden and done in a manner that appears to be something harmless."

Jon temporarily had his hand over his mouth as if in contemplation as to what to say to his son. He did not want to frighten him, yet he wanted to explain things.

"We think... or I should say speculate... that she attached a... cable, a strand, a thread, a data stream... it is hard to explain because you cannot see it and there is no way currently to use scientific methods to search for it. But we suspect that she may have attached one of these to you, and that is why you feel exhausted," said Jon, looking at his son. "Of course, we could take him to the doctor to run some tests. Maybe he has an infection?"

Karl Bergendahl eyed his son and replied, "That is exactly what she would want. We could do both if you feel like he is not showing any signs of recovery after the expert looks him over."

"How do you know so much about this stuff?" asked Kyle, looking at his father and then his grandfather.

"Knights are often trained concerning matters such as these, and if they have the right gifts, can skillfully assist people who are victims of such dealings. However, unfortunately, most of our training recently has been driven by the necessity of dealing with non-paranormal events that have occurred. We have been forced to focus on the mundane matters of the world," replied his grandfather sadly. "We suspect that your Aunt Olivia did something to break apart your mother and father."

"They can do stuff like that?!" exclaimed Kyle with feelings of outrage.

"Yes," his grandfather answered, because the topic was too painful for Jon.

Jon had sat down to be at eye level with Kyle. He looked like he was going to say something, but Kyle could see the pain in his father's eyes. He could not talk about it. It hurt too much.

The four of them waited out on the patio. Lily thought fresh air would assist everyone in clearing their heads from what they were all concerned about. It was surprisingly pleasant and sunny that early spring day by the winterized pool. Jasper made sure everyone was comfortable, and before long, three people arrived at the Caledon House to examine Kyle. Much to Kyle's surprise, it was Sir Knight Wolfram, Sir Knight Greta Tyrson, and another Knight he did not recognize, Sir Knight Andreas Kurt Wolff. The name sounded familiar, and he did have red hair. He wondered if he was Freya's father. They all came out onto the patio to stand around and talk with his grandparents and father. But then Kyle realized they were doing something else. Kyle was sitting on one of the flowery lounge chairs in the middle of everyone, answering some of the same questions that his dad and grandparents had already asked. He began to feel uneasy. Somewhat dizzy. Then he saw Alvar, the man in the brown suit, who was trying to communicate something to him. Kyle attempted to focus on what Alvar was trying to say, but then Alvar made a face as he was almost hit by something greenish-black that was thrashing through the air. Alvar looked mildly injured and surprised.

"Alvar!" exclaimed Kyle.

Everyone stopped and turned to Kyle.

"Something hurt Alvar!!" Kyle cried out.

"He will be fine. We are trying to deal with one of those negative strands of energy, and it must have hit the ghost," said Sir Knight Wolfram. "Can you still see him?"

"Yeah," said Kyle, trying to focus on Alvar. "He's holding his arm... like he got hit with something. He doesn't look pleased. I can see... other... then..."

Kyle suddenly passed out.

Kyle woke up in his bedroom at the Caledon House. Everything was quiet. For a brief moment, Kyle wondered if it was all a dream, but usually, dream details disappear after you wake up. He felt okay, but his Grandma Sarah was dead. His mom was moving to Texas, and so many weird things had happened. It felt like a movie rather than real life. He sat up on the edge of the bed. Someone had removed his shoes. He looked around and saw them nowhere to be found. He felt okay. The room felt super quiet and still. Kyle stood up, went to the closet, and opened the door. His shoes were there. He slipped his shoes back on and decided to find everyone. He felt different. It was not bad, just different. It seemed like he felt more like he did before going down to Texas.

Downstairs, he found them standing around in the kitchen. It was late afternoon, and Jasper had started making dinner. They were all helping him. When he came into the room, everyone stopped and looked at him.

"Kyle, how are you feeling?" his father asked.

"I'm okay. A little confused. I was asleep?" said Kyle. "What happened? How did I get into my bedroom?"

"Yes," his dad said. "You were asleep."

"You passed out, and we had to move you to a more secure location to remove those magical energy cables that had been locked onto you by your aunt," said Sir Knight Andreas.

"If you start feeling strangely tired again, tell us right away. If you feel like you are having thoughts that are... not normal for you, tell us," instructed Sir Knight Greta.

Kyle nodded.

"Am I going to be okay?" asked Kyle.

"We believe so," said Sir Knight Wolfram. "You must understand that you have now started down a path that you cannot return from. You know things. Things that regular people do not understand. Things that regular people may find scary, frightening, …and may cause them to react negatively. Many will think you are lying or simply crazy. You must take the lessons in the Special Training class seriously. We have your grandparents' approval, and now… we have your father's approval. Your father has also informed us about the situation concerning your mother. You should not talk to her about these matters."

Kyle wanted to comment, but changed his mind.

"I know you may feel that it is wrong to keep secrets from your mother, but she is not ready to handle these matters. She is too frightened, so we need to prepare you to protect yourself and possibly her if necessary. This takes training and dedication. Are you willing to be serious about this?" asked Sir Knight Wolfram.

The kindly overweight Knight wanted to make sure Kyle understood.

"Yes. I understand, but… don't you think we ought to help her?" asked Kyle. "And what about Uncle Alvaro and Grandpa Juan? Why are people like Aunt Olivia allowed to be that way? Why is she doing this?!"

"We don't know why people make bad choices in life," replied the red-haired Knight, who was probably Freya's dad. "If we understood… that level of complexity of human behavior, we would be a lot wiser individuals and could probably solve most of the wars that happen before they become significant conflicts."

The three expert Knights stood close and had their full attention on Kyle.

"All we can do is train our Knights to be prepared and give them the best possible tools to be able to assist others who do not have this level of skill or perception. You must realize that this is a gift with responsibility. Talents must run throughout both sides of your family, or else your aunt would not be able to do these harmful things," added Sir Knight Greta.

"So, we can't help Mom?" he asked.

"Not now, but hopefully later. We need to make sure you are protected first, and then able to defend yourself. Part of that is learning how to understand when you have been attacked in a paraphysical manner, as opposed to… having an upset stomach from bad food. Some novices will think that everything bad that happens to them is an attack from an enemy of some sort. It's natural to be spooked by this new understanding of our environment," said Sir Knight Wolfram. His mustache twitched a little as he smiled and said, "You and the Fabulous Five like Sci Fi action stories, don't you?"

"Yes," replied Kyle, wondering where this was going.

"Well, the characters in Star Trek and Star Wars have shields around their ships to protect them from space debris, radiation, cosmic storms, blasts from unfriendly vessels, and even space-dwelling monsters. I want you to imagine that you are a ship traveling through space, and you need to put your shields up in case you encounter something out there. That is part of the training you will need to complete. It's not all blasters and swords.

Sometimes, basic shields are the best defense against bad guys," said Sir Knight Wolfram, hoping to reassure Kyle.

"This is a lot to deal with so suddenly. Do you think you are ready?" asked Sir Knight Greta.

"Freya is more than willing to be supportive in this matter," added Sir Knight Andreas.

Kyle looked at everyone contemplatively and finally answered, "Alright. I can do this. I want to learn."

All the adults looked relieved, and the rest of the evening was spent sharing good food and stories about various events and experiences. They all wanted to hear more about Sir Knight Alvar Bergendahl. Karl and Lily brought out the pocket watch and glasses that had belonged to him, and later showed everyone the portrait that hung in the library. It was explained to Kyle that Alvar was likely serving as a guide to help him become a Knight. This was not unheard of in the Order's long history. Becoming a Knight of the Order was a forever thing. He also learned that not all cables or connection threads were bad. Many were good connections, so one had to be careful when dealing with such paraphysical realities.

After spring break, Kyle returned to school feeling well-rested and prepared to work on the additional studies required in the Special Abilities class. He loved the idea of seeing Freya more often. His classmates had all sent him email messages of condolence for the loss of his Grandma Sarah. And when his birthday came in early May, the Fabulous Five, along with Freya and some of the girls, planned a birthday celebration with cupcakes, cards, and a few gifts. They all knew his father was busy with work, and his mother was moving from Nevada to Texas and would not have a chance to visit him.

The group had gathered in the Page Level common area, where they enjoyed birthday cupcakes, including a special one with candles.

After Kyle blew out the candles, Geoff asked, "Did you remember to make a wish?"

"Yeah," nodded Kyle, thinking about what he wished.

"Don't tell anyone. It won't come true if you say it out loud," said Elsa.

Tyrrel made a face and said, "Superstitious nonsense. But… I hope your wish comes true."

"Me too," said Kyle. His wish had been for these kids to remain his friends for the rest of his life.

Lothar and Freya brought him his birthday gift as the group sat around stuffing themselves with frosted cupcakes. Freya just smiled while Lothar explained about the gift.

"This is from all of us. We all pitched in to get this for you," said Lothar.

Kyle was surprised and honored. He opened the card that had all their names on it, including a few unexpected others from the upper grade levels.

"Thank you so much. This is really nice!" said Kyle.

"Oh, hey, aren't we supposed to sing the birthday song?" asked René.

"Of course we are," said Trevor, with Xavier standing next to him nodding in agreement.

"I know this one!" exclaimed Ivy as she pulled Lucy and Sif close to her to start the happy birthday song, which the rest of the group joined in with mixed degrees of harmony and key variations.

Kyle started to laugh as he held onto the package that Freya had placed into his lap. When the questionable singing had ended with joyous laughter, Kyle began to open what he considered a large package. He had no idea what it could be. The outside of the plain box had a brand name on it that he had seen before, but he could not recall where. And then he opened it. He was shocked. And pleased.

A brand-new archery quiver with twelve arrows, a sturdy leather arm guard, and a fancy four-finger trigger release. Kyle was awestruck. His friends were pleased with his reaction.

"Oh... my god! This is awesome!! Thank you so much. I can't wait 'til archery class comes back," said Kyle with a big smile. He ran fingers over the quiver and gently touched the feather-like ends of the arrows. "You all are so terrific for getting this for me. Thank you."

"And we expect you to do great things on the archery field again," said Lothar.

542

"Oh yes, we want a first place next time," suggested René.

"But no, pressure," laughed Geoff.

"I will do my best," replied Kyle.

At the end of the school year, Kyle decided that he wanted to become a Knight just like the others in the Fabulous Five. He hoped he would have a lifetime of friendship with these boys. And now that he shared a special gift like Freya's, he knew she would also be an important part of his life.

He decided to stop complaining to his mom about her moving. He realized that he needed to be supportive of her. What she was doing was hard. And he would try to be helpful. He now understood why his parents had left each other, and he did not want to make their situation any worse.

It was a couple of days until everyone would leave the school for the summer and return home. Kyle sat on one of the large boulders in the Boulder Glade, feeling the warm late-spring sunshine on his face. The island flora and fauna had come back to life from the cold winter and had started to embrace the warmth of summer. The air was fresh, and he had finished his tests for the day. The others were still working on their final projects. He sat with his eyes closed when he heard someone approaching. He turned around and saw nothing. Then, he turned the other way and could see Freya climbing the boulders to reach the top.

"So, this is where you disappeared to," she said.

"It's nice up here," he replied.

"This is one of my favorite spots to go when I just need some time alone," she replied.

"I'm sorry. But I got here first, although I could use company," he said.

Freya smiled.

"I didn't mean that I needed to be alone now, silly. I just wanted to relax in the sunshine," she replied softly.

"Oh."

"Do you know if you are coming back to the Lake Simcoe location?" Freya asked.

Kyle nodded and said, "Yes. They believe I need a stable location to support my studies. I am not going to transfer to one of the other locations."

"Good. I am glad to hear that. I would miss you," she replied.

"I'd miss you, too. And the guys," he answered. "Everyone is coming back except a few people in the Fifth-year boys' group. I guess some students move around to get a broader education by living in different parts of the world," he said.

"That's correct. There is a school in Las Vegas, but Tyrrel's parents wanted to make sure he was away from home. Something about gang activity being a distraction," she replied, pausing for a moment. "So, how are you doing? I have not had a chance to speak with you much about what happened in Texas."

Kyle sighed.

"I am still having nightmares about Aunt Olivia," he paused to clear his throat. "I think I may have... picked up on something darker than what I explained to everyone. Alvar is around and wakes me up from these dreams when he can. But I still feel this... terror. The way she looked at me. I keep wondering what she did to scare my mom. It must have been terrible. Something so scary."

Freya put an arm around Kyle and said, "I will always be willing to listen to you and give you a hug when this stuff happens. I understand."

"Thanks, Freya," he replied. "I love having you as my friend. You and the guys are the best."

www.ingramcontent.com/pod-product-compliance
Lightning Source LLC
Chambersburg PA
CBHW051055030726
47504CB00006B/1633